Life (AUTOSAVED)

THE THREE INITIATES

W.E. BROWN

CONTENTS

CONTENT WARNING

This book contains language and situations that are **not** suitable for those under the age of 18. Readers take caution as the material presented involves sexual misconduct.

You have been warned.

This book is dedicated to the voices in my head,

"You create your own reality," they always said,

Moment to moment the spirits led,

To create a story, my mind to spread.

Daimon (Greek)

i) *A divinity or supernatural being of a nature between gods and humans.*

ii) *An inner attendant spirit or inspiring force.*

Daemon (Latin)

i) *An attendant power or spirit; genius.*

ii) *A supernatural being whose nature is intermediate between that of a god and that of a human being.*

Demon (English)

i) *An evil spirit; devil or fiend.*

ii) *An evil passion or influence.*

iii) *A person considered extremely wicked, evil, or cruel...*

PRELUDE

The creature sharpened the blades of his dozen knives and hung them around his quarters, ten-thousand blades of all sorts and sizes suspended in the dense, murky air of the Uver. A rapid knock on the chamber door brought him to full attention, granting permission for the guest to enter. A smirk played on the creature's face foreshadowing the upcoming news he knew to be in his favor.

"Master," the messenger bowed deeply on the obsidian floor, "Please honor me the permission to speak."

The creature's chuckle boomed, echoing to infinity in the endless realm. "Go on, Baal." He rested his chin on his taloned, leather palm, awaiting what he already expected. Everything was going according to plan.

The Lord of Knowledge, Baal, proceeded with his news. "We have received signs of the Young Ruler's return."

Again, the amplified laughter escaped the master's lips maniacally modulating in its tone, layered voices belonging only to one gargantuan beast; its vibration shook the soft sway of knives into a clanking mess of metallic chimes. In his enormity, he splayed his arms away from his center, cackled once more, and then descended to where Baal was, embracing Baal in what could be likened to an amiable hug with a form that encased the lord, mere rubble to a boulder.

"Go, Baal! No one must know. Preparations must be made. Go at once, time is of the essence."

At that, Baal hastened out of the realm. The master smiled in conceit tinged with the slightest percentage of uncertainty. Things could turn out the way they did centuries ago for his assembly of lords, doomed to repeat his conquest throughout the ages. Master carefully calculated his moves in order to guide the sought power to his station. The Young Ruler's return meant that dominion rested as pure potential in the hands of the demons, something the trinity of masters fought to obtain for themselves.

With the Young Ruler's return, either peace or destruction could be brought; it would be the decision of the subject—the truth of its nature dwelled in the beating heart of its vessel. Of course, nothing was finite. The legends of the Young

Ruler were ancient; many of demonkind disregarded this as myth, only used to strike fear into the hearts of the weak and greed into the hearts of the mighty. As for humanity, this would begin a paradigm shift akin to divinity or impiety, the making of the world's end and by that same standard, a new beginning. Whether or not one chose to believe in this prophecy did not do away with its legitimacy, and as foretold, a web was spun to encase those in its proximity to become believers against their wills. The return of the Young Ruler would herald in a world unseen like ever before when realms once thought myth blend, bend, and shape the mundane into either the miraculous or the monstrous.

1

THE BOY WITH RED EYES

With only one class left in the day, Ian felt irritable to a point beyond touchy—the overwhelming pack of books weighed him down on his journey up the staircase, rushed by the flow of students behind him. This daily routine of his had him fatigued beyond all measure. He was expected to get up at six in the morning to embark on the bright yellow prison vehicle to a building that determined his future: Willard High School. In a mindless haze, he enacted this repetitive flow—the predictability of his school days became his comfort zone. He had only one job and that was to keep his grades up, but was that all he was good for?

He felt as if his ability was beyond any of the dull-personality drones that glided past him and for a second, he felt an urge of motivation, of power. Yet, as fast as it came, it disappeared. Ian was a strange kid, known by those around him in this sleepy, average sized Virginia town as Red Eyes. Although a two worded allegory of the red-tinted sclera of the cliché potheads, when it came to Ian Frances, it had a different definition. Red Eyes was, in fact, rather straightforward, calling it like it was—Ian Frances had bright, blood red irises. Many believed it to be a gimmick, many of whom have not known him for the five years of his residency and continued to call him Red Eyes: The Adopted Son of the Frances Family.

And as for Ian, this was his revelation; he did not see Red Eyes as an insult or slander as he, too, wondered how or why this came to be. This question to himself replayed frequently until it became redundant, almost like pondering the origin of flattened gum on a sidewalk. He contemplated about the strange course his life had taken—adopted four times without prior knowledge of what he'd done to end up in a different home, each with faces that claimed they loved him—he pushed the thought away in order to bask in the now.

He was seventeen. Dark, moppy shoulder-length hair and a soft face just recently touching the edge of masculinity, evident in his cheekbones and budding jawline. Although a walking enigma, he did not hesitate when striking conversations with others. He was such an outgoing person that often others felt as if they were the recluse. His generosity was something taken for granted; the people he displayed it towards were usually the ones to gossip about him as strange ol' Red Eyes, discretely keeping their distance however best they could. Of course, Ian noticed. But he never made it known—he was used to it.

Who could blame a boy his age to want to know his origin, so badly it hurt? Physically and mentally. Deep down he knew he was an abomination, yet he forced himself to feel like a divine personification of the person he wished to be. He promised he would never think of himself differently, a promise broken ever so often. He did not know who he was but knew who he could be.

The class worked as silently as they could manage. The Friday spirit was heightened with less than two hours of school; chatter was a sure thing while confined in the arid classroom.

"Quiet, please," the sleepy-eyed English teacher called out, known as Willard High's pushover, Mr. Willis. The man was too nice for his own good and the advantages taken by the student body and fellow teachers were plenty. Mr. Willis, while interrupted, did his sweep upon the students to see their work ethic. It came as no surprise that he would stop at the kid in the black t-shirt with his head on the desk.

"Mr. Frances," Willis called in a sing-song voice. Ian did not stir. The teacher adjusted his tie, placing his favorite ball-point pen in his shirt pocket, briskly readying the pursuit of his target. "Ahem," he voiced, "Mr. Frances, I believe we are still in the middle of class."

Ian was well awake, no doubt about that. Answering back to Willis' demands would be too much of an effort for a day well over. For Ian, displaying bouts of rebellious behavior was common this year. He was an average student at best and as of late, all of that had been on a dawdling decline. Sure, he still made decent grades and barely challenged the law, yet his attitude towards adults had taken on the tone of peer familiarity.

Ian remained, head tucked into arms with a habitual façade of fatigue. "For two consecutive days you've slept in the middle of a lesson." The class looked onto the welcoming opportunity to instigate the rising conflict, a ritual that was well-overdue this school year. "Up. Now." Pushover Willis was... well, not his usual pushover self today. Perhaps life's gimmicks had finally dawned on him in this instant, realizing the many times he had been duped; a possible midlife crisis was at play.

"Alright. Two-day's detention."

"What?!" Ian snapped up at the unfair play. "You can't do that!"

"And the dead rises."

"Mr. Willis, how can you do this? There are less than thirty minutes of school left. Hell, it's Friday, too."

"Well, then you can spend the remaining thirty minutes in the office. You have been warned multiple times. Now get a move on." Willis was now seated, clicking through his email at the back desk. From his periphery, he could see a gobsmacked Ian, not sure whether to stay or go.

"Well?"

Ian's rebellious stage was still burgeoning; he caved, grabbing his things and headed to the office. "Have a good weekend," Willis called out before the final click of the door.

The decision of whether Ian cared or not was definite: he didn't. Any excuse to stretch his legs was a good one. The route to the office was a long one considering their polar locations, extended by two separate stories. This did, however, influence Ian's value of life. He forced himself to think positively, attempting to push down what he really felt. Being optimistic for what he got back in return seemed like a wasted effort.

For why he went to the office instead of loitering elsewhere was obvious: he sucked at this bad boy business. And when Principal Cane looked Ian up and down with a dissatisfied sneer, Ian instantly wanted to turn back around. Ian just knew that the look of contempt was not for his lack of respect, but rather for the strangeness of his appearance.

"Ivan Frances. What can I assist you with?" Mr. Cane asked, studying the face of the delinquent student.

Ian began to feel a bit nervous knowing he was being silently judged, yet he took a confident step forward and voiced in an earnest tone, "It's Ian. Apparently, I have detention now. On a Friday."

"Yes, on a Friday. I just received a call from Mr. Willis telling me you'd be on your way. Please, have a seat in one of those chairs. But don't get too comfortable," he huffed a breathy chuckle.

Ian, with an indirect roll of his eyes, invested a sarcastic laugh and claimed the chair furthest away from Mr. Cane's desk, on which sat a computer with an outdated monitor, a phone, other principalesque trappings, and a "Number One Dad" coffee mug. Ian snorted silently, which Mr. Cane picked up as an invitation.

"So, Ian. How are your parents?" Cane asked.

"Uh, good?" Ian replied to the generic question. His parents and the assistant principal hardly ever met.

"Keeping the grades up?"

"Yep."

"Ah."

If someone could own the reward for awkwardness, it would be given to these two, who both silently expressed some sort of abhorrence for each other. Ian could not stand feeling the prying distaste Cane held for him having shared such a proximity only a single time during his freshman year, and numerous times in passing—each time he could feel Cane's stare crawling on his skin. Ian couldn't help but prepare himself for *the question.*

"So Ian, your contacts..." Mr. Cane started with a pointed finger and a questioning gaze.

Ian prepared his script and finished with, "... are not contacts."

"Then what is it? Some kind of surgery or whatever the kids are doing these days?"

"Who knows. My first parents must have been drug addicts. That may be it." Mr. Cane pretty much sucked in his words, more embarrassed than apologetic. The words were strange—*first parents.* Cane cleared his throat. "Don't feel bad. You're not the first to ask. Or the second. Or third, fourth... you get it," which, coincidently, did the exact opposite.

"I apologize, Ian. I was not informed that—"

Ian smiled largely, "Don't *feel sorry* for me. Weird ol' Red Eyes isn't a direct result from a dysfunctional family." He began to ramble, "Actually, three prior dysfunctional families, but who's counting? I'm a mess!" And with that Ian concluded with an honest, overdue laugh. Cane's skin turned to a shade of beet-red. He was unsure whether to express sympathy or laugh at this kid with such a life that anyone would predict to be delinquency in the making. Instead, he faced the exact opposite.

"I uh, oh. Uh..." There had not been a time in Cane's employment that he encountered a kid such as Ian. He dealt with many adopted teenagers, yet while facing Ian, that was the least of Cane's concerns.

Ian continued to smile with the hue of pink hinting at his cheeks from the uncomfortable air presenting itself once more. A sudden phone call saved both of them. "Mr. Cane," he answered. "Uh huh... I'll be right there." Secretly relieved, Mr. Cane withdrew from his desk. "I have to go run an errand. You seem like a well-behaved kid so I trust that you can keep yourself out of trouble. Obviously, there's no detention today since it's Friday. You can leave when the bell rings. Enjoy your weekend."

Ian's shoulders drooped in relief. "Wow. Thanks, you too."

The principal flashed a smile and closed the door behind him.

Soon enough, Ian was walking towards his bus amongst the rowdy rush this frigid February evening. His lips tugged at the corners, barely able to contain his excitement once he spotted the subject of his affection. The fog of his breath escaped through his smile when watching the mess of blonde hair bob towards him.

Of course, it would be the one and only Spencer Holland. Willard's faculty and staff regarded Spencer to be the boy genius of their graduating class not only by having the highest GPA but by also displaying knowledge beyond the curriculum taught in public school. Spencer stood at 5'5", six inches short of his significant other. He wore a pair of slim, rectangle-framed glasses that always seemed to slide down the bridge of his nose, something Ian regarded as signature to Spencer. As far as appearance, Spencer would fit in with the remaining population of suburban kids, his blonde hair slightly curling outward towards its edges, and a pair of blue eyes that always seemed to captivate its onlookers.

Ian proved to be the primary one to gaze into these eyes, just as Spencer was to Ian's, and this moment was exemplary of such. Ian couldn't help but to wear a goofy smile, rushing by

Spencer's side to close the distance between the bus together. "Hi, you," Spencer nudged at Ian with an elbow, returning a smile almost identical. "You seem really happy today." The two walked with just enough space between each other. They did not hold hands. Did not show any signs of affection. As much as Ian yearned to, Spencer would ultimately be the one who took most of the naysayers' say. Spencer was not ready to express his orientation publicly. Ian, a little discouraged at first, understood Spencer's decision as he had a city-wide rep as large as it was fragile. Spencer's life depended on this reputation, a choice made for him, not by him. There was more to Spencer than people knew, yet no one seemed to want to.

Ian replied, "It's because you're here, Spence." Spencer snorted and climbed the steps of the bus in a dignified manner.

Ian boarded carefully behind Spencer who responded with, "Like this is the first time I've heard that. You have to be more original to impress me."

They sat together at the seat marked as the emergency exit, a tradition set since middle school. The bus began to fill with students. "Please stop acting like you're not impressed," Ian brushed his shoulder against Spencer's.

"Who said it was an act?" smarted Spencer.

"Touché." The bus lurched to a start after the last of the students boarded.

They were dropped at their neighborhood stop sign, left in the exhaust of the bus to walk the rest of the way into the neighborhood. Ian proceeded towards his home, followed by an exerted Spencer. Their homes were only a block apart—the two never saw each other often enough in school. To live in the same neighborhood proved to be a blessing to their barriers. Ian interlocked arms with Spencer when the bus was safely out of view to head up the steps to his house. Spencer lagged behind as Ian trekked upstairs to his room.

Typically familiar with his boyfriend's conduct, Ian noted how quiet Spencer was being. The uncomfortable kind of quiet, as if something was being repressed. Ian decided not to pry at the moment; he would ask if it persisted. The journey to Ian's room was completed with a toss of his backpack and a silent crash onto the bed. He looked at Spencer standing at a distance with a flighty look about him.

"What?" Spencer asked, attempting to redirect Ian's line of sight.

"What do you mean, 'what'? Have a seat. You practically live here." And obediently, Spencer followed Ian's command without question. Without commentary or mouthing off, nor the intellectual quips he would add to dull banter. Yep, something was wrong, Ian concluded.

"Spence, you've been quiet the whole way here. What's up?" Ian said, curling a ringlet of Spencer's flaxen hair between his fingers.

"Nothing. Just tired s'all."

"Then here," Ian stood, adjusting the pillows on his bed and smoothing the crumpled sheets. "Bed is all yours."

Spencer resisted, "That's okay."

"You act as if this is new. You've known me for five years, yet you still act like a stranger to my house." Ian playfully smiled hoping to get one back. Instead he received a weary sigh. "Are you going to tell me what's really wrong or not?"

Spencer shook his head slowly, saying, "I told you, I'm tired."

Ian pushed Spencer onto the bed, bracing himself above him. "I call bullshit."

"Ian, you're crushing me," Spencer complained with a half-smile.

"I don't care. Tell me what happened."

"Get off of me."

Ian teased, "Not until you tell me what happened." Spencer fell silent. Ian looked into Spencer's shifty eyes and his gradually reddening cheeks. "Let it out, babe."

Spencer sniffed and then blurted, "It was Michael."

Ian felt his anger spiral up from the predictability of this conversation. He sighed, "That asshole again? What did he do this time?"

Now that he was cracked, Spencer engaged in a mopey rant; his slight feminine drawl was consistent. "For starters, I saw him at lunch pointing me out like some orangutan in a fucking exhibit to his cronies. It didn't get to me then—I couldn't have cared less. Then, in seventh block, he started calling me out because, as usual, I scored the highest on the test. He was jealous, I guess, so he started rattling off every name out of the 'Insulting Diminutives for the Incognito Queer' book. But really, Ian, it doesn't bother me."

"Again?" Ian stood defiantly, "Bullshit. Spencer, I've had enough. This guy needs to either learn some goddamn respect or just fucking kill himself. I'm not putting up with his shit anymore."

Spencer held onto Ian's arm to imbue calmness. "Honestly, I'm alright. They're just words."

"Whatever. I'm kicking his ass tomorrow."

"No, don't," begged Spencer. "I can handle myself and there's no need for you to get in trouble. That's overreacting."

"I don't care if it was underreacting. I'm still saying something to him. You're not going to take his shit anymore."

"And you're not going to settle all of my problems, Ian! Just let me handle myself for once!"

Ian was amused at Spencer's backlash, and oddly, so was Spencer. Ian was accustomed to Spencer's lack of interest to most all of Ian's decisions, usually supporting Ian in its execution.

At a composed, lowered voice, Spencer continued. "I may not be strong like you, but I don't need you always coming to the rescue every time I cry."

The room existed in silence for two minutes. The intense atmosphere left Ian at a loss for words. He realized his boyfriend's incredible smarts, but he could not accredit Spencer as someone able to defend himself. *Give him a little space,* Ian pondered, yet he could not help but to feel like he *needed* to protect Spencer. Or perhaps Ian was being clingy, something a lifetime of adoption ensued upon him. Ian needed at least one thing in his life to feel solid and controlled. His best friends seemed the closest to permanence.

"Alright. I'll give you your space," Ian said, but of course it was a lie, to Spencer and himself. There was no way Ian was letting him confront a guy twice his weight backed by a posse of neanderthals all by himself. Fact was, Ian hated space. He wanted to be reassured that something always remained by him, that even one person cared for an odd boy such as himself. Spencer seemed relieved at Ian's reply. "But as soon as Michael lays a hand on you, all rules aside, I'm going for his throat. Got it?"

"I suppose that's better than nothing." Spencer looked down at his feet. "Thanks, I guess."

Ian crashed onto him once more, capturing Spencer in a headlock. "You guess? Bitch, I'm sacrificing an arm and a leg for you and all I get is, 'I guess'?" They both laughed, this time it was genuine. A laugh like this was the type shared every day between the two. Ian was sure that he and Spencer were guaranteed a future together although they were only juniors in high school, barely touching the footholds of life. Whatever it was they had, Ian thought quite frequently, it better be present for the rest of his life. He could not take another betrayal. As the enigmatic numbers counted backwards each day, Ian knew he had to do everything in his power to ensure that the ones he loved would remain.

2

VISITORS

His arrival through the inexplicable apertures that inhabited Earth provoked the familiarity experienced around a century ago. Baal took a moment to feel the brittleness of the dead leaves underneath his palms, holding one up to the sunlight he just so recently flinched away from. Archives of information—experiences, sensations, sounds, smells, sights—crashed into him as they once had during his preceding visitations to this corporeal realm.

He trekked on cloven-clawed tarsals, normal for the indigenous beings of the Uver. What he was had many names throughout each earthly culture, dating back to the origins of every human civilization. No matter what name Baal's race was given, they always enacted the same quality of indescribable fear into the minds of humanity: demons, they were, in every sense of the word.

Behind Baal, the once Messenger, now Ambassador, was another of his kind, yet hundreds of times weaker and insignificant: an intermediate Servant by the name of Travius. Travius was assigned to Baal after his Lordship two centuries ago. Unspeakably fond of one another, Travius was no stranger to stepping outside of the caste system when commenting towards Baal's decisions. He waited impatiently by the Sentinel's side, another being vowed to Baal's allegiance. Hazth, the Sentinel, was ways more obedient toward his Lord, something Travius regarded as weak. Hazth was rather new to Baal's control, less than two decade's familiarity. He was reserved, quiet, respectful, and willing towards a being capable of ending his existence within a second. In other words, fearful.

With claws digging into the damp ground, Lord Baal gazed upon the dim horizon. "Let us be on our way. Our mission should be rather quick."

"Are you finally done bathing in recollections?" Travius remarked, walking a steady two feet behind Lord Baal.

"Remind me why I have not killed you yet, servant?" Baal spoke. His voice was filled with an authority that would easily make his servants cower. Either brave or moronic, Travius always seemed to challenge his Lord in one way or another, something seen as the greatest mistake any of the lower classes would pay with by certain death.

"I believe we have a remarkable relationship, would you not?" Travius' response eased a smile from Baal.

Baal was well aware that he let his personnel break the social barriers that no other imp or intermediate would dare to fathom. For a Lord, Baal was considered soft as well as the youngest of the Third Gate's legion. Many have attempted his murder in order to assume his position of power, yet in every instant, they were all reminded of the unimaginable strength Baal composed, repenting at their target's very feet, all too late of course. Baal spared no sympathy for traitors.

"No. You disgust me. Hazth! Walk to the left of me," Baal commanded.

"Yes, Lord Baal." In a rush, Hazth stumbled into position in a mess he knew he would undoubtedly be punished for later.

Travius the intermediate servant sneered at the Sentinel. "What a clumsy fuck. I don't understand how you even made it this far, Sentinel. Hasn't some demon attempted to rip your foreign heart out yet? Hey Baal, how is something like that supposed to be your guard?"

In a quick, swift motion, Baal had Travius by the neck, legs dangling, and lungs struggling for air. "Know your place, servant! Have you grown so comfortable as to address me as your familiar? I am your Lord, address me as such." When thrown down, gasping for his breath, Travius made an effort to stay in position. "How is something as pitiful as you a servant, let alone alive? You will lose an eye next time since I feel rather generous lately."

Baal looked at his Sentinel—Hazth could not decide whether to return the look or for his eyes to remain posed at the ground. Frankly, Lord Baal frightened him to the core.

"Hazth?"

"Yes, my Lord?"

"Are not you glad to be back amongst humanity?" Baal asked this in such a way, there seemed to be only one acceptable answer. Sporadic, at that. Should there be a riddle behind this, Hazth would be too fearful to contemplate; he could never come close to figuring out Baal.

Hazth hesitated, eyes shifting left and right. "Yes, my Lord." He made sure to learn from Travius' mistake.

Baal studied his face—one with such smoothness and evident humanity—a bit more before turning away. "They are a stunning species. How long has it been since you were last here? Ten, twelve years?"

"Fourteen years, my Lord."

"And you are—what—thirty-two years of age?"

"Yes, my Lord."

"Ah. If you are lucky, your family may still be alive if merchants have not taken an interest yet." Hazth sucked in a sharp air ever so slightly. He would not show his vivant emotions to the beasts so void of such to even find commonplace. "Travius, check our location," Baal commanded.

Contemplation against Baal's order remained only in thought this time as Travius posed his hands upward, projecting a black, ghostly film forming topography above the ground. "We are here, Ba—my Lord." Travius pointed along the east coast, "In this general area. It seems it would be days, a month before we are even close to the target. How will we know?"

Baal squatted, resizing and arranging the ghostly map. "Let us head west," Baal said, ignoring Travius. "We need vessels to tether ourselves." Although they were presently on mortal Earth, the three remained on an adjacent plane. Physical interaction was possible, yet it would take a considerable amount of effort to interact with the indigenous beings, let alone be seen by them. Once he established his target, he would need to acquire a vessel worth its weight—he would possess as many times as it took to find the perfect one.

Master chose Baal out of thousands of lords to carry out this mission—to fail would only beget irredeemable humiliation. He was the one selected to bring their prophecy into fruition; it was a privilege and an honor to walk within this realm. Baal refused to let this opportunity fall from his grasp.

3

LOST CAUSE

"U no!"

"That is so not fair, Ian. You just had three cards in your hands," complained Stephanie.

Spencer joined in, "Yeah, Ian, what happened to that other card?"

"You guys should pay attention. Your go," Ian said. Spencer placed a yellow *draw +2* card on Ian's.

"You can't get me with that," boasted Stephanie, who laid down a card of the same. Ian looked at the two with playful disgust as he reached for the draw pile.

"I'm sick of this game," he said.

"Why? Because you're losing?" Spencer stuck out his tongue, promptly pounced on by Ian, crashing into the pile of cards neatly stacked on the floor.

"Aaaand there goes our game. Nice," sighed Stephanie. She was one of Ian's first friends since his sporadic move here to his current residence. At first, she and Spencer were attached by the hip, a solid duo with an inseparable friendship. Stephanie and Spencer were alike in such a way that they considered one another their twin in every aspect besides the obvious gender and race. She was black with fair, dark mahogany skin. As the youngest in the group, she stood at 5'6", both her and Ian leaving Spencer in terms of height. Her proclivity towards dreaming, day or night, made her a bit spacey from time to time, however she trailed Spencer with ease in the field of education, although somewhat ambivalent towards it. She was far more content in her imagination than to make practical decisions about her inevitable adulthood, often feeling isolated from others as a result, a self-inflicted battle.

It was Friday evening, and after a day of doing slim to nothing, the three grew restless, resorting to the revival of old fashion fun. Although old fashion fun was perhaps outdated, they still enjoyed the company of one another. And as always, Mrs. Frances arrived home after a busy day at the office. It was routine to catch the three together, Mrs. Frances realized, to a point where it felt necessary. Sincerely, she was proud that Ian found a family outside of her own, presently still in disbelief of his previous family records. The trip to the foster home a little over five years ago was clearly an act of God; He presented Jennifer Frances and her husband, Greg, a remarkable oddity as a son. Ian's poor soul had not been broken, a resilient spirit that never ceased to inspire.

Jennifer made her presence known when placing her purse and keys down on the end table at the entrance. In the adjacent room, she saw the kids carry on with their antics. "Hi, Steph. Spence." The nicknames Ian frequently used became a household habit. The two turned around with the cheeky smiles they always seemed to wear, greeting Mrs. Frances home, asking how her day went, how she was feeling. Spencer and Stephanie were regular weekly visitors (in Spencer's case, daily) and were merely an extension to her adopted family. She loved them as her own.

Ian raced to his mom in a blur, followed by his bickering friends in heated discussion. "Mom, tell these two that I am totally right in placing a *draw +4* directly on a *draw +2*."

"That is so wrong—"

"Who would even—"

"—just mad because he doesn't know—"

"—make sense!"

The twins bickered in unison against Ian in hopes that his mom would agree. She just smiled to herself. It was moments like this that blocked any doubt or insecurity she felt when faced with her adopted son's peculiar eyes. She couldn't help it. And she hated herself for it. She hated herself for having remotely an inkling of fear, an inkling of distrust. Jennifer and her husband shared the sparsely mentioned feeling, containing it only between themselves, brought up at moments of pure intensity. These moments were when Ian's irises would appear to glow at times of excitement, and when his pupils would slim into a thin ellipse in a bright room. The intensity would again ensue when scolding Ian, needed discipline for house and family life. Without a doubt, there would be the predicted teenage backlash that seemed to always be a part of the whole adolescence transformation, yet with Ian, there was more. The way he spoke would lead one to think an ancient force was being suffused into his being—not with his grammar or syntax, but with only the air rushing upwards and out of his throat. It could not be detected through sound; it was something instinct brought to attention.

And Jennifer, as a mother, usually forced herself from abandoning the situation, feeling as if she were the one being disciplined. Yet Ian was the sweetest child Jennifer, and she was sure anyone for that matter, laid eyes upon. Although blunt when asked for his own opinion, he conveyed it with sincerity, reassuring himself as a source who could always remain honest. She was positive that there was more to Ian than what she saw.

"I'm sure rules came with the game. Use the Goggle you kids are always on," said Jennifer, referring to the popular search engine.

"Actually, Mrs. Frances, Goggle is a proper noun, and therefore needn't the 'the' in front of it," Spencer remarked.

Jennifer snorted at Spencer's automatic, elevated diction when in his explicatory mode. She found it cute. "Thank you, Spencer. I'll remember that next time." Spencer blushed, feeling a bit abashed. "Are the twins staying for dinner?"

"My mom is on her way to pick me up in an hour or less. It's a little too late for me," Stephanie said while cleaning up the presumed-complete game.

"Again? We miss having you as a dinner guest. What about you, Spence?"

Spencer replied, "Considering I've eaten here the past couple nights, I don't want mom upset that I've missed another family meal. I'll go home today. Thanks though."

Refined dismay crossed Ian's face. It was a Friday and he was going to spend the remainder of the night without his friends at his side. It was always hard to part with these two internally, even if it was for an hour.

Scratch that, the remainder of the weekend.

Monday was there in a flash. Ian was climbing the steps towards honors chemistry in a borderline-ratty pair of Vanz (Jennifer's nemesis; Ian's comfort). And frankly, although the start of the day, he was feeling uneasy by those around him. Even five months into the school year, everyone found his presence to be amusing. Their gazes crawled across his skin—he could feel the prickles of their judgment seeping in.

Ian walked with a slightly arched, backpack-weighed spine, keeping his eyes on the ground. Soon he was in class sitting beside Stephanie, who always calmed Ian by presence alone. The tardy bell brought the remainder of the class together and signaled the start.

"You almost arrived late today," said Stephanie, stuffing a mini donut into her mouth.

"Yeah, I walked Spence to class."

"Really? I know how anal he is about you making it to class on time. He let you? Why?"

"Hell no, he didn't let me. It was more like following behind him. I wanted to make sure Michael wasn't there being a turd and all."

"Oh, that's right. You told me about Spencer's little rant on wanting to protect himself."

Ian readied pencil and paper for the class, copying the warmup assignment. "Yeah, well, he means it. Cussed at me the entire time."

Stephanie passed Ian a donut. "I can't say I blame him. You are always there to jump to his defense at all times. It can get annoying."

"Annoying? You know how he was in middle school. If you ask me, he hasn't changed much."

"You never really gave him a chance to defend himself, though."

Ian dropped his pencil, "C'mon, Steph. You're guilty of this, too. You want to defend him as much as I do."

Stephanie looked away to hide her discomfort, "Okay, yes, I do, but I give him his space. He's a skinny, short nerd. People always wanna pick at those things, especially a combination. Plus, his incognito gayness that everyone with a gaydar can see through."

"See? Exactly why I have to be there."

"No. He has to know what he's capable of. What do you expect him to do when you're not there?" Ian was silent. "It's bound to be uglier than you intended when push comes to shove. The guy's not useless," she concluded with a sip of coffee. Ian knew he could not win against Stephanie when it came to reason. She always seemed to know what to say, even if Ian didn't want to hear it.

For most, if not all, of first block, the class was made to take notes that a majority would never study. Stephanie stopped without realizing, her eyes wandering the room. She looked at Ian gripping his pencil; the familiarity of it initiated a flashback. She thought back to the third month of sixth grade when Ian entered their class as a new student. It all seemed so recent—how scared he looked, how fragile his gaze was. She knew as soon as he was presented to the class that the kid had no confidence in new surroundings. He was wearing hand-me-down clothing a size too big for his frame and had a round face that instantly deemed Ian as her newest crush. Their teacher at the time asked Ian to introduce himself, and it was then that Stephanie noticed Ian visibly shaking. No one seemed to care about his presence as the teacher urged him on. *"Tell us your name,"* she said. Ian remained frozen in place. He finally spoke with the softest voice, facing the floor ever since he entered.

"My name is Ian Montgomery, I mean, Ian uh... Ian Frances." The class mumbled—it was strange how anyone could mess up their last name. The teacher smiled, urging forth another

question, *"Where did you move from, Ian?"* He was silent for at least five minutes, as Stephanie recalled; she could only feel humiliated for him. He wrapped himself in the oversized sleeves. *"I was adopted,"* he said. The class broke all etiquette, blurting, screaming, pointing, laughing. It wasn't because of Ian's statement—the class, she was sure, heard no part of that. It was because, at that moment, Ian lifted his head for the first time.

Stephanie shook her head out of the memory. Those thoughts always seemed to cross Stephanie's mind almost daily, reminding her not to be so hard on Ian. He had a reason to want to hold on tightly to Spencer that only Ian's best friend could understand. "I'm sorry," Stephanie whispered.

"For what?"

"For... you know, telling you to back off."

"You mean telling it like it is. Don't apologize. I needed to hear that."

"But you..." she stopped, too afraid to mention the severity of Ian's past.

"I trust you more than anybody telling me what to do with my life."

"How do you do it? Have so much trust in people after all this?"

Ian paused. He fought against the pull of the memories he tried so hard to lock away.

He shut his eyes as tight as he could. *Don't think,* he thought to himself. Although time had created a gap between tragedies, the reoccurrence of the instances still remained fresh for Ian. Sure he was good at ignoring it, in most cases he felt like he fit right in. But it was always there. The reminder that nothing good lasts forever. And every morning, Ian prepared himself for a potential loss that he may face each day. The family that he had—gone. The school he frequented—nonexistent. His friendships—obliterated. The memories remained void of emotion, just fillers in his mind of some other child's life that was messed up in every way possible. Presently it all felt foreign—he felt he was undeserving of a life so tranquil that often seemed surreal and full of doldrums. With a daily routine absent of hardships, except for the occasional Pre-Calculus test, Ian felt the need to let go of the tension within his mind. However, the nightmarish reminder of the past was a constant punch that prohibited such.

After a short goodbye, the two split separate ways to their next class. Ian moved quickly, dodging students in the halls, to seek out Spencer—there he was. Taking Stephanie's advice, Ian darted into a classroom, peaking around the doorframe in attempts to spy. Now it was clear to Ian: he had a problem. It would take some time getting used to maintaining space, time that Ian could not stand waiting. Spencer was standing beside his next class talking to Desmond, a kid whose characteristic stance instantly identified him.

To Ian's relief, there was no sign of Michael or his posse. Ian took a step back, admired his boyfriend once more and then turned away to head to his next class. He knew he would have to let go one day, but even this was too much.

The three beasts trekked upon concrete into a town whose paper mill tainted the air with stench. The nightlife here was exquisite: the clubs that decked the streets were in full business, bars eased the souls of lonely men, the walkways were full of women and their girlfriends loud and lively. There was, however, the dark side to all this rampant energy, lurking in the midst yet hidden from the eye. It was there that Baal would strike.

Travius could hardly contain himself. The view of humans excited him, their exposed skins and lack of cares. Had he not been under the stringent ownership of a lord, he would seek out the lusts his twisted soul urged him to feel, breeding his deranged desires.

Baal, however, was far more learned and in control than the low-level demon, though it did not keep the lusts from crossing his mind. More than anything, he wanted to claim the emotionally unstable as his victims, feeding from their helpless cries, claiming their souls as his, then claiming their abodes and families. It was done hundreds of times in the past, something Baal never could tire of. But now he had a mission; he could not let such pleasures get in the way. That included the agendas of his Sentinel—his near-mortality proved to be a crutch—and definitely his servant, whose uncultivated habits could break conduct instantly. Baal had a job on hand. His personnel, as predicted, were in a frenzy of awe and excitement, faces pressed against windows of restaurants watching young families dine. Hazth watched intently at the family scene with eyes full of jealousy and sorrow. Travius, hungry and demonic, scratched at window glass, leaving trails of claw marks and inquisitive looks upon mankind's faces; these marks seemed to appear out of thin air.

Baal went on to explore the area. Naturally his Sentinel followed like a loyal dog. Travius, however, had to be choked by an invisible force only of Baal's doing in order to get moving.

Master sent Baal to search for the Young Ruler before the demons of other kingdoms, the Gates, were notified of this great power. If the others were to get their hands on the Young Ruler, they'd have access to an abundance of powers, an array of possibilities that could only mean destruction in the hands of any demon. Imps would use it to gain lord status. Lords would use it to gain god status. In every way possible, as Master explained, it would be misused in the hands of the wicked, but figuring out *how* to use it was an entirely different process, especially since the Young Ruler had a mind of its own. That's why he sent his trusted Lord of Knowledge to find the power, something Master saw as rightfully his. Prophecy after theory after legend after myth told of the Young Ruler for eons, yet none explained what it was capable of. As far as anyone knew, it was the ultimate power, bridging the gap between worlds. That was it. However, Master and Baal had their own theories, theories which could be tested only if the Young Ruler was rightfully theirs.

Baal held this information close, recalling every detail to carry out his master's every order. Master was beyond Lordship, ancient yet timeless, truly one of three of his kind unless the realm had further secrets cloaked. Just like the ruthlessness of intermediates and imps seeking lordship, lords sought the secrets of masters, however, far more discrete. Many lords were the servants and sentinels of the masters, holding as many as two thousand to guard their immediate quarters.

Master knew the tricks of the trade, knowing demons inside and out, anatomically and habitually. But to Baal's confusion, Master trusted him the most. Baal couldn't see why—he was like the other Lords, arrogant and selfish. And if Baal diagnosed correctly, he felt undiminishing respect for his master. That was why he had to complete this mission as swift and faultless as possible.

Once they found a remote place within the inner city, Baal turned to his Sentinel, who recoiled. "Would you stop flinching every time I look at you? It hurts my feelings," humored Baal.

"I'm sorry, my Lord."

"Hazth, I need you to complete a task for me. Probably your biggest one yet." Hazth shifted on his feet, anticipating the request. "Relax, it is not like you are killing anyone. Listen, I am going to say the incantation to release you onto the mortal plane." Hazth froze. "You need to change into a form that evokes emotion from people, say, a small child. Use that form to lead them back here. Tie them up and use the possession incantation I taught you to bind Travius and I. Got it?"

"Yes, m-my Lord." There was no way Hazth could do this. He was shaking, beyond nervous, now fearful. He had to betray a race he so recently belonged to.

Of course, Baal took notice of this. He continued with his demands, "We will have to fit in with the Young Ruler's circle, wherever he may be. I will leave this up to your best judgment to find two humans that seem fit for our present predicament. I trust you will do this effortlessly."

Baal, standing at an easy ten feet in this form, kneeled to place a hand upon Hazth's soft hair and, with the same amount of power that made other imps and intermediates cower, he spoke the words placing the pain of separation within Hazth, the same he felt fourteen years ago when abducted to the Uver.

Hazth's mind swam about a hazy void before he found himself strewn upon littered asphalt. Feeling its solidity, he smiled at the site of his hands. He could still see the two demons clearly as his sight was nevertheless supernatural. The shapeshifter, Hazth, knelt before his lord.

With a submerged voice, Baal gave further instruction. *"Do not do anything remarkably stupid out there. And for the sake of us all, do not let your emotions get in the way."*

With a smile and a nod, Hazth gave a final, "Yes, Lord Baal," probably the most enthused yet, got a running start, jumped, and in its midst, shapeshifted into a canine, running full speed towards the city. He was back home. He could feel the earth and now used her ability bestowed upon him on her surface. Shapeshifting could be done in the Uver, but here it felt pure. In that moment, every doubt trickled out of his being, replaced by the nostalgia manifesting throughout his muscles.

It did not take long for Hazth to fulfill his duties, remaining in favor of Lord Baal now adorned in his temporary vessel. It would only be a matter of days until they were to force themselves into the Young Ruler's life.

Stephanie was very much interested in the world, beyond what mainstream life convinced to be a cycle of life and death, a place where the strongest survive, where politics and economy seemed to be the only definite rule in life. She saw the world as this huge, unexplored place that mankind only grasped at. She knew there was more to such routine, which she was often ridiculed for not participating in. Her parents were higher middle class, caught up in the flow of the American rush. And for the third time this week, her parents yelled at her about grades, about college and becoming a doctor. To Stephanie, this was a

load of bullshit. All this translated to was living a currency-con-
trolled life where money was the ticket to feeling something as
priceless as happiness. But Stephanie felt obligated to do such
seeing as her fantasy world had no evident path of travel.

She sat in her room, still fuming over her latest discussion with her parents. At this point she no longer had de-
termination to sway their viewpoints—every time it was the
same result—now she just nodded, filling in responses with yes
ma'ams and no sirs. And now she felt as if they were in the right.
She began to doubt herself. The image she had of herself in a
uniform life sickened her to the highest level of disgust. And
every day, she would make a silent vow to herself, promising that
her future would be more than a systematic existence.

As for her placement in the world, she felt as if hers was
not a notable one. She didn't like sports, had slim to few hobbies,
and was known to dabble ubiquitously in any frivolous activity
that captivated her attention. Perhaps sketching was her niche,
but of course, no future could blossom from that as her dreams
were told to be "useless" by her elders. "A starving artist," they
would call her. It did not stop her—the young lady was full of
zealous optimism. Her friends often questioned how she was capable of such an attitude, something she also pondered herself.

Suppressing a tantrum, Stephanie pressed her face into her pillow kicking off her socks. Taking deep breaths to ward away the welling of tears, she bit her bottom lip, cussing every word in the book. "I hate this fucking house, this fucking place, my fucking life!" she said, all muffled by the pillow. Her words were short of hate, more of revulsion and denial. She knew she couldn't escape any of it. If she did, the fear of an impoverished life imposed upon dreamers such as herself would take over and set her back on the course of complacency. The words of the church folk led by her father, a preacher, echoed in her thoughts about how obedient and well-mannered she was—always polite, executing favors asked of her, never saying no. She realized she was too nice, and although she embraced ample kindness, it turned her into a gull, someone who would not say no. Her parents knew this; there was no chance Stephanie would ever speak out of place. Often, paying attention to the wants of others led her astray from truly knowing her own wants. She appeared content in the company of others, gluing on a smile to ensure ease within her environment, yet she longed to be left alone to swim her inner realms.

Perhaps she was used to living in this sizable house with the plentiful amenities provided by the churchgoer's tithes and offerings—perhaps she had grown so accustomed to being treated as a saint that she felt no need to try.

No, it wasn't that. Never that.

Stephanie only wanted change in the requirements of lifelong happiness and sustenance.

This way of thinking grew old to her—a repetitive rant at every moment of distress—so she reached for the remote. Browsing through channels provided for a good mental dam.

Within the next few minutes, she was fast asleep. She dreamt of dreams that would later become irrelevant, mundane, and then forgotten.

"Anything you need help with, ma? Dinner?" Ian yelled across the house while making his way downstairs.

"I've got dinner, sweetie. Why don't you find your father and see what he's up to."

The family-oriented boy searched the house for Greg, his adopted father, who ran one of the city's car dealerships. Ian found him in his study, busy with reports unmistakably for his job. Just as Ian was about to knock, Greg issued, "Come in," from his swivel chair.

"Hi, dad."

"Well, now. Ian. What brings you? Your mother?"

Ian smiled, "Well yeah. You guessed it."

Greg turned to face Ian, staring a few seconds too long into his son's peculiar eyes. "That's no problem. Come here, let me show you something." Ian stood adjacent. "So what do you think of this baby?" Greg passed a picture of a black car, a few dents here and there. Acceptable condition.

"A Cavalier. S'nice," he lied through his grin.

"She's a 2001. Old but with an almost new engine. Just got moved to our used lot a few days ago."

"Oh really?"

Greg surveyed it again, "Yep. This baby," pluck, pluck, "drives like butter."

"You sell motorized butter at the dealership too? That's a first."

"She gets twenty-seven per gallon," Greg ignored. "Not bad for an older car. Was thinking you'd like to come by the job and take it for a drive." He and his son met eyes. Greg averted.

"Sounds fun," smiled Ian. Times like this made Ian giddy, another seemingly minuscule moment to appreciate. Having moments to bond with his family meant the world to Ian. However, the giddiness refused to arrive alone, bringing with it a tinge of sorrow, reminding him of the pattern of impermanence within his life. Nonetheless, Ian smiled through the sting, leafing through the dealership catalog on the desk as a distraction.

It was obvious that Greg was trying to tighten their bond by striking up some father-son, macho-man conversation. With the expectations of bringing various girls home every other week, he brought Spencer instead to do homework or play video games with. He was sure that Greg suspected his relationship with Spencer to be oddly close, yet Stephanie's presence provided great deterrence. Ian didn't partake in Greg's world much—they barely talked. They coexisted within the same house and harbored care for one another, which was good enough for both.

Ian leaned against his father's desk, poking the dry conversation on. "I can only guess the reason you're showing me this is because you're going to buy it for me."

"You better guess again! Get yourself a job and we'll discuss it," Greg chuckled dismissively. "I hear the place down the street from the hardware store was hiring."

Gosh, he's serious. "Bee's?"

"Yes," Greg clacked the papers in a stack, put away his reading frames, and swiveled towards Ian. Ian shuffled his feet; how uncomfortable this made him. Bee's was a fast food joint with a notorious reputation for long-hour shifts, minimum wage, and below-average tasting foods. And working there was worse than visiting. "I saw an ad for a cashier in the paper. You should apply. It's only a week and a few days until you're eighteen."

"Sure thing. I'll check it out."

"Great." Greg seemed to be between apathetic and joyful. But Ian tried his best to impress him. "You might get that car if you do."

Ian looked to his right, away from his father, to ponder this exchange. Ian owed it to him—if doing what his father said to make him happy and stay within his good graces, Ian would follow that path, no less. Ian felt he owed that to his late parents, an odd moral he held when executing most of his actions. He wanted to please his parents, ensuring they'd be the permanence he sought. They would be the last without a doubt; with a birthday nearing, his adulthood would become finalized, and if the two were to abandon Ian, there would be no foster care to harbor him until a pair of onlookers felt sorry enough to take him in. Ian would be an adult in less than two weeks. The lad had his share of independence, way more than any child should. Being an adult would be no different, only now he would not get any more chances, just himself against the world.

Spencer was in no particular position to socialize this hour, as much as he wanted to. His three Advance Placement classes demanded two essays and a reading assignment due in just a matter of days. Spencer was the type to put school before everything; when he got home, after a few hours with Ian of course, he would hit the books, making sure his GPA stayed a perfect 4.1 or to improve it, on track to becoming his class's valedictorian. Betwixt the schoolwork, Ian's birthday was coming up. Spencer wanted to surprise him with something extravagant yet original, however, he couldn't think of anything that didn't scream, "boyfriend". He sighed at the thought and continued to key word eight-hundred-fifty-six for his six-hundred-word essay.

After finishing the second essay, Spencer sat back and, with another sigh, folded his arms behind his head. If it were up to him, Spencer would procrastinate as his friends did—after all, it would be easier to be carefree until the night before the due date. Then again, the recoil of improper sleep habits, along with the hustle and bustle of making his words fit seamlessly would kick his backside more than it was worth. His life was an arms race, one he just ended up in. Of course, he wanted to try for a bright future but it all seemed in vain. There was no way in God's name Spencer was changing course, not this close to the finish. Junior year had only a few months until it came to a close, and then senior year, the rinse cycle.

Spencer was what Stephanie deemed as "straightedge." He dotted every i and crossed each t; had no inclination towards nefarious activities—sex, drugs, and alcohol were always out of the question. Although the two were alike when it came to scholastic endeavors, Stephanie was always the type to flex boundaries. She would, say, arrive to class purposefully late and would be excused by simply being her. On the contrary, Spencer strived for perfection, prompting the contempt of his peers. In a synopsis, Stephanie was inviting—everyone felt comfortable around her; Spencer, the intimidating smartass that the rest use and shun.

He decided to take a break and call Ian, one of Spencer's few activities. The phone rang, and Spencer thought of the call's recipient—from his smell to his stance, to his slender body, and...

No answer. He put his phone down.

Ian's touch on Spencer convinced him that maybe a perfect GPA wasn't what determined his longevity. And often

Spencer would dream only about being touched by his significant other. Every time a different place. And each place becoming more and more discrete.

He placed a hand outside his sweats.

Spencer especially liked it when Ian wrapped his arms around him from behind at moments when the world wasn't there to witness. Ian's breath would slide down Spencer's neck, and he would hold back every gasp with parted lips. He knew Ian could tell what he derived from the act; Ian would delicately pester until the determined straightedge gave a peep.

He slipped his hand below the elastic.

Spencer's phone rang the iconic ringtone, and he abruptly removed his hand and wrangled his wandering mind. He mentally shunned himself for the act before answering, "Hello?"

"Sorry about that. I didn't get to my phone in time. Wassup, Spence?" said Ian amongst noisy shuffling.

Spencer sighed, "Nothing much, hun. Just finished a good portion of my work."

"Whooptie doo," Ian sarcastically remarked.

"Yeah, yeah, yeah. What's new, right? What about you?"

Ian moved about on the receiving end, "Dad's got me looking for jobs. He says Bee's is hiring."

"So?" prompted Spencer.

"So what?"

"You going to apply or what?"

Ian tumbled the thought for a while. "I might as well. Have nothing else better to do. Greg says it'll be good for me."

"And that's it? You don't think it's good for you?" Spencer asked, audibly placing his books aside.

"It's worth a shot."

"But is it something you want to do?"

Ian scoffed, "The same could be said to you. Make asstastic grades, get into an Ivy League college, and then what?"

The blonde boy remained silent. He pointed towards himself indirectly in that previous question, causing Spencer to stumble before proceeding with the next bit of consultation.

"I'm sorry," Ian said betwixt the silence, not wanting to upset Spencer any more than he did in one week.

"No, no, you're fine. You are right—what am I saying?"

"I honestly think you should go for what you really wanna go for. I know this is the five-millionth time I've said this but, being stuck in a career that your parents wanted you to do is no career at all. And this citywide fame of yours is only bound to last for so long. Don't conduct your life based on that."

Spencer shook his head, all too familiar with the pattern of thought it would lead to—he would ponder for too long, placing himself in a state of depression and self-denial. "What's your excuse?"

Ian sat on it for a while, then spoke, "I don't know, I just owe it to them." And it was this that influenced most of Ian's decision-making. A selfless act familiar to Ian in which he would base most of his goals on the gratuity provided by his adopted family. In fact, too selfless. Ian could not help but feel as if he owed everything in the world, including his life, to the Frances family for his adoption at a borderline-late age. By having a birthday just weeks away and transitioning into adulthood, Ian felt it only necessary to show what was reflected in his soul. Deep down, it broke his heart. To think that after only six years, he would be off to embark on a life of his own, separate from the path of adoption and confusion. It would feel odd for Ian to start over again, this time on his own. "It's just too soon for me. Being eighteen n' all, independent for good. Sounds like spoiled white boy problems, right? I'm pitiful."

Connecting the phrases together, it took no context clues to bridge the gap, especially knowing Ian from the core. Spencer took a moment to feel where it felt safe to speak, listening to the subtle changes in Ian's voice.

"I just... don't want it to end. High school and all. Years here have been the best of my life, and to grow up and leave this all behind... I don't know if I can do it," Ian concluded.

"You'll be fine. You're the strongest person I know. Not to mention cute, quick-witted, with a super-hot bod, and fantastic legs. Oh, and that butt!"

"Okay, now you're doing the most," Ian laughed. "I think your horniness is interfering with your thought process."

"I mean, you're not too wrong with that statement," Spencer remarked, embarrassed by his actions prior to the phone call.

"Like I can do anything about that, Mr. I Wanna Wait. Let's see how long you can keep this up. Your perpetual horniness will get the best of you and that waiting policy of yours is bound to be broken. You'll come running straight to me with your pants down. And I shall accept with open arms," he gesticulated. "And legs."

"Oh shut up!" said the blonde with a smile.

Every morning, over the course of the week, the three grouped together as usual by the rear staircase of the school. Stephanie had coffee and the overzealous look of optimism; Spencer, the look of professionalism; and Ian, a look of an all-nighter. As disguised as possible, Ian darted his eyes this way and that, looking for Michael.

The demons fed at night. They rested none. And they attempted to leave no ruin here on Earth, an attempt praiseworthy by their inherent nature. A week had passed since they arrived through those apertures, and within its span left twenty-nine people reported missing. Every day on various news stations, one would recount seeing five or six missing faces, each there one second, the next gone. Response teams on the lookout would not be let off anytime soon from the now high-traffic career and the near impossibility these persons were to find.

The entrails of a man were flung on a wall after a concluding scream. And then, the dusting of hands.

"I swear, why am I the one doing all the dirty work?" breathed Baal, sucking the residual gore from his fingers. The new vessel he wore was beginning its tainting process—a nice shade of red, to be exact.

Hazth dipped to fetch his lord a towel without a sound whilst Baal continued to harvest the victim, whose eyes were wide and dead with a gaped mouth. Kidnapped on his way to his son's swim practice, it was safe to say he'd be a bit late. The demons thought him to be of interest, or one of help. Either way, they weren't any closer to finding their target.

Travius sat in the background, watching his Lord labor with no thought of helping whatsoever. He'd snack on the parts that were flung his way and flip through a magazine, displaying humanity's new feats within this century, perplexed at how fat Americans have gotten. Suddenly, a fillet knife whirled by his ear, managing to nick it, slicking black blood down his neck. He whirled around, "Hey! What's the big—" suddenly remembering who he was talking to.

Baal slowly walked to a startled Travius while ringing his bloodied hands in a towel. And in one quick motion, he had Travius' jaw within a death grip.

"No! No! Lord Baal, please! I'll work! No!" protested Travius, realizing the promised consequence.

Lord Baal seamlessly scooped out one of Travius' eyes, flicking it aside. As Travius wailed, Baal left the room with his final command, "Clean this mess."

With a socket dripping poisonous black blood, Travius scrambled to the gory scene. The sentinel watched, amused, silently following behind Lord Baal. Hazth would never know how someone could refuse to heed Lord Baal's warnings.

Lord Baal sat at the kitchen table of the previous owner now scattered across the floor, motioning for his sentinel to have a seat. After a heavy sigh and a slick through his meat-suit's hair, he spoke, "After two centuries of being on a completely different plane, you forget how much the human population can increase. A week and still no sign of this Young Ruler."

Hazth swallowed down spit, drying his mouth as he forced himself to speak. "How will we know when we are close?"

"That is the question. Orders are to 'feel around for persistent, robust souls,' yet so far, all that has gotten us are more messes to clean up. Master thought being as vague as possible was a surefire way to get his ticket to everlasting power. In other words, dear Hazth, it is safe to say we 'follow our hearts.' That may only be valid for you, unfortunately."

Hazth took no regard to this and pressed on with, "But surely you must've felt this robust soul when you reported back to Master."

"And indeed I have. But it is not exactly something to pinpoint." Baal stretched by the bay window. Outside, the tree line blocked the view of the distant street and an orange sun barely tapped the horizon. "Like the onset of déjà vu." From his pocket he removed a small vile with a translucent swirling mass and held it towards the fading sunlight. He held it for a while, as if its significance accounted for assortments of recollections. Its contents contained a soul—an abstract force each individual held, the source of sustenance demons wished to obtain. Its taste was indescribable, dispersing an air of euphoria upon its digester and a rush like no other. Each soul carried with it a unique experience, a different power. A demon's dependency on it transcended a matter of addiction. Baal licked his lips, pressing the small glass onto them, gliding his gaze towards the adjoining room tinged with the red of the corpse whose soul now inhabited the vial.

"Hmph," grunted Baal, passive in thought. He then stood, popping his joints as he stretched in a ceremonious way familiar to his staff, "Well, why do you continue to sit there? Clean this mess." Travius held his gaze at the ground, hesitating to look towards His Lordship with the response, "Yes, my Lord," oozing black from the eye socket.

With Baal's gaze affixed outside, the few minutes of silence was interrupted by a slam of his fist on the table. "Damn it all!" he shouted. He turned from the window, storming past a staring Hazth.

"If I may interject, my Lord," spoke Hazth.

"Speak."

"My days back on earth years ago... as a shifter, my people were faced by a threat of merchants."

An eyebrow raised on the Lord's face. "Pity."

"What I mean to say, my Lord, is that these merchants have databases on those deemed as mythological creatures. They have reports on their residencies and extensive knowledge on capturing methods. They then—,"

"I know about these merchants, Hazth. Why do you waste your breath?"

"I was thinking... perhaps they may know of suspicious locals, something that seems different than their typical targets. Perhaps they could give us a lead." Hazth sunk down towards the end of his suggestion, preparing for the bit of punishment his Lord may inflict after being offered such a suggestion.

"You." Baal asserted, "This is why I like you, Sentinel." A smile spread across Hazth's bearded face. The sneer Travius conjured would only dare escape his mind; his lord's favoritism for that creature was beyond him, further fueling his hatred for Hazth. "Let us proceed. The nearest robust soul I can feel is north of us, again but a vague premonition. These merchants better be of use." Baal conjured an aperture and seeped through the fabric of space—the intermediate and shapeshifter followed after their foreboding leader.

Thanks to the misuse of a bathroom pass, Ian managed to slip outside on the brisk February day, a temporary relief from chemistry. It had been a stressful day—quiz here, assignments there, and an upcoming test once he was to return. He failed to resist the urge to check his phone, the lock screen flashing off and on every minute; he sent another text in urgency as his window was dwindling. Just as he set his phone down, Spencer appeared through the doors with a pointed look of frustration painted on his brow.

"I hope you're happy," Spencer started, "I'll have you know I'm skipping part of English in response to your damn texts."

Ian bent a brow and tilted his head, "Why is it my fault? You ultimately decided to come out here."

"Yeah, whatever. What do you want?"

"A kiss."

Spencer blushed and blinked blankly before responding, "Um, no. We're in school."

"*Outside* the school." Ian sauntered the distance between them and held Spencer by the waist.

"You need to stop making me skip class for ridiculous things like this!" Spencer audibly communicated his frustration, yet the beet-red streaming up his face portrayed obvious embarrassment.

"Okay, okay, relax," Ian chuckled as he pulled away. "I want the answers to the chem test."

"Honestly?!"

"Look, in my defense, I was totally unprepared. It snuck up on me! And your class took it last week." Ian put on his best face of innocence and continued to beckon Spencer.

Spencer scoffed, then searched among the papers in his bag. He handed the test off, "I swear you only use me."

"Not true, babe," Ian excitedly pressed his lips to Spencer's and dashed for the doors. "Thanks! Hurry back to class before you're in trouble!" He disappeared into the building.

Spencer again flushed red, standing in Ian's dust. "It'll be your fault anyway!" he responded all too late.

Between Ian's thighs and the chair, Spencer's test lay hidden from the eyes of the teacher. In this guise, he could, with a glimpse, nod down to copy each answer fluently.

And upon completion, Ian handed in the test without a second thought at the end of class. Stephanie gave Ian a disappointed, sideways glance as they walked out.

"What?" he asked.

"Spencer's test? Really?" Stephanie smirked.

"What? He let me."

"I mean, hey, props to you. I wouldn't call that cheating, it's more like teamwork, seeing as you had his permission. It's a great survival tactic."

"Thank you for being so logical," Ian embraced Stephanie tightly. She rolled her eyes, shirking out of the hug. "You understand!"

"But bruh! That test was the easiest thing in creation. The fact that you needed to cheat on that was kinda dumb."

Ian collided his shoulder into hers as they walked towards their next class, "Which is why I leave being smart to you and Spencer. If I ever end up jobless and homeless, I'll have you two to fall back on," he laughed.

"Riiiight. And I suspect you're returning Spencer's test to him?" Stephanie asked in passing. But there was silence and a paled look on Ian's face. "You *do* have the test, right?"

"Shit," was all Ian commented before he booked it back to chemistry.

Ian knocked on the door to grab the attention of Mr. Lyle. With a desk just across from the door, Lyle looked up and sighed before opening it. Ian stepped in looking around frantically for Spencer's test he so idiotically left in his wake of post-achievement.

"Can I help you, Ian? Anything you're looking for?" asked Lyle. Ian was sure Lyle was making a mockery of him.

"Umm, yes actually." Before he could save himself with some witty excuse, Spencer's test hung in Lyle's hand by his side. "I guess I'm looking for the remainder of my dignity," Ian shrugged, "Ah, shit."

Mr. Lyle sighed once more; the smirk of genuine mockery was evident. "And here, Ian, I thought you weren't such a dumbass. Cheating? Really?" Lyle gave the paper a onceover and added, "Not only to cheat, but to actually have the paper of Mr. Holland in your very seat. Not only are you in trouble, but you potentially endangered the status of your friend, too."

"Aw, come on Mr. Lyle! Look, it's not his fault, totally all me. I can fully take the blame, just don't involve him." Ian repeatedly forked his hand through his hair, a signature in stressful moments such as this, his face slowly creeping from neck to brow in red.

By then, Mr. Lyle already had the phone in hand, calling the office with a full incident report, all in the span of what felt like ten seconds to Ian. Stephanie, hidden behind the doorframe, gestured a thumbs up, hoping to receive the same response—however, she was met by the slight shake of Ian's head. She shook her head and saluted to the boy who needed any and every stroke of luck, then walked off. Not even five minutes later, "SPENCER HOLLAND AND IAN FRANCES, PLEASE REPORT TO THE FRONT OFFICE," was called overhead.

"Well, why do you wait? Office," commanded the teacher.

"Come on, Nathan, we can talk this out. You know I'm a good kid. Adult to adult. I realized I screwed up and—"

"Go."

Ian concluded his start of the day with a trip to the office, the walk of shame he took for the second time this month. How was he to face Spencer like this, he thought. The office's front desk personnel questioned his presence in which Ian answered honestly; they directed him to have a seat and wait to be called back to Mr. Cane's office. Mr. Cane's voice could be heard from the back of the foyer, attempting to use bad workplace humor with that cursed mug in his hand approaching the front. Stopping at the mailboxes to collect, he caught the red eyes in his periphery, adjusting his necktie before calling out. "In trouble again, are we?" joked Cane.

"Yeah, what's new, huh? Have to see you, actually."

Cane's smile faded. "Oh. Follow me to my office." Ian lazily slung his backpack onto his shoulder and made his slouched trek behind the principal. Upon entering the office, Cane gestured Ian to have a seat—he sat in the same one as last Friday—Cane did the same. "What happened now?"

Ian smiled, "What's not happening?"

Cane fought a smile, seeming more and more like Ian's ally, yet the joyful air was still in his words, "Considering you are here, I suspect another classroom disruption."

"Cold."

"Oh? A fight?"

"Colder."

Cane sat back in his chair, huffing a short chuckle, "Then what?"

"I 'maybe' cheated on a test," Ian shifted uncomfortably in his seat. Cane adjusted his necktie, putting on an authoritative guise. And one foot after the other, Spencer entered with his head down enough to glance ever so crossly at Ian. He took a seat, spacing one between the two.

Spencer pushed up his glasses before saying, "Hello, Mr. Cane. How are you this morning?"

He's such a kiss-ass, Ian thought. Ian glanced sideways at Spencer, seeing literal fumes escape the top of his head. *And I'm not going to hear the end of this... I fucked up.*

"Mr. Holland, what a surprise! What can I help you with?"

Spencer was confused at first; Cane could not believe Spencer could be potentially accused with the strange boy. "Uh, I was called here, sir."

Cane looked back and forth at the two, abashed by the shocking situation. "You mean to tell me, Ian, that you cheated off of the paper of Spencer Holland?" Ian looked to his feet, thumbing over his fingers. "Speak."

"It's not his fault," Ian's gaze was still directed toward the floor, "I took the paper from his bag when he stepped away."

"Ian, don't—" Spencer interjected.

"I didn't study for this test. I was unprepared, so I stole it from Spencer."

Spencer pleaded with his eyes at Ian. He didn't have to stick up for him this way. "Is this true, Mr. Holland?" Spencer remained quiet. "I see. Ian, this could lead to suspension, you know. Now how could you go on and do such a thing to Mr. Holland? He actually works hard, puts effort into his grades and this school." Ian looked at Spencer once more to beg forgiveness through a simple glance; however, Spencer remained upright, respectfully listening to Cane's lecture. The obvious blush was upon Spencer's cheeks—or maybe it was the welling of potential

tears. Ian looked down at his lap. *Perhaps I'm not the best for him...*
"Ian! Are you listening?"

"Huh?"

Cane shook his head, "Spencer, you are dismissed. I'm sorry for what Mr. Frances here did to your belongings. Please try to keep an eye on your stuff next time. Theft," Cane sharply gazed at Ian, "is not tolerated at Willard."

"Thank you, sir," Spencer trekked out as he came with a slight glance back at Ian. Whether it was pity or frustration, Ian would find out later.

"I am starting to think that letting you off Friday was my mistake. You *stole* a test from his bag and *left* it in your seat. And here I thought you were smarter than that."

Ian sat in silence, surrounded by the ambiance of the office—chiming phones, voices of the front's faculty, and Cane's staggered typing. It would take a huge weight off his shoulders if Ian could get through this without having disciplinary action pressed on him.

And suddenly, a certain fear began to creep through his veins. Ian was beginning to mess up. Here it was, a good five years later, rounding the edge of seventeen—Ian was beginning to see himself as the delinquent most viewed him to be.

Ian swallowed the slender lump in his throat. "So what's my punishment, Robert?"

Cane frowned at the direct title, "That's what I'm figuring out. How is life at home?"

"Come again?"

"Everything okay? Because it has been less than a week and you are back here. You are beginning to form a routine."

Ian slipped his fingers through his hair and blew out a stress-filled sigh, "I dunno, man. I really don't know what I'm doing. I'm messing up."

Cane studied the boy's eyes once more, almost forgetting his response in the process, "No, you're not messing up. You just need to garner some self-control. In-school suspension tomorrow." Cane began to text without another glance at Ian.

Ian reproachfully waited for Spencer to board the bus, and as soon as the blonde hair was spotted, he redirected his gaze out the window. Spencer took his seat beside Ian as usual without a word. They both knew what they wanted to say.

A quarter of the way home Spencer finally spoke, "So what was that back there?"

"I'll admit: I fucked up." Ian still locked his eyes somewhere outside. "I'm sorry." He mentally slapped himself for being so careless. Everything was beginning to go downhill, he just knew it. Somewhere deep down in his gut, he knew that this pattern of unpleasant events was the boulder at the precipice, beginning its descent.

Spencer searched for the right words, keeping his anger at bay for a while. He placed a hand on Ian's lap and said, "Is everything okay?" This was new to Ian, Spencer's tactic. Instead of becoming a raging ball of livid gayness, Spencer didn't entirely place the blame on him. Usually there would be a certain routine: he'd turn a few shades redder, mutter incoherent sentences, and proceed to hound Ian with whatever word crossed his mind. "Second time in Cane's office in less than five days. What did he give you?"

"In-school suspension. Could have been worse, so no complaints."

"Ah." Spencer primped his hair, adjusting a few stray hairs for the perfect bang. In the corner of his eyes, Ian caught the bluish bruise underneath the blonde. "Look, I can't deny that that was a dumb move, but there's no sense in me being mad over it." Spencer was interrupted by the brush of Ian's hand over his forehead.

Ian cocked an eyebrow. Spencer averted his eyes.

It was a routine with them; they took turns worrying over each other. If it wasn't Ian's idiocy, it was Spencer's fragility.

And by the looks of the bruise, only one name came to Ian's mind: Michael Grizzle. His posse was made of only the school jackasses, quick to make a good day bad. Lately, Spencer was on his list of attacks, Ian assessed—he sat idly waiting for Spencer to do something. He made a promise, after all.

4

VIOLATION

Ian's in-school suspension was more like the solitary confinement of the mentally unstable. It was about to drive Ian directly to that state of mind and drop him off at the door of the asylum. At the start of each period, a student from the class Ian missed delivered his assignments, each of them completed within the first twenty or so minutes at the start of the period. There was no talking. No sleeping. No remaining dormant, one always had to stay busy in the small, hot room with no airflow. It was situated in a system of halls that weren't usually busy, a cubbyhole next to the music classes and practice rooms. Ian looked to the students, faces dripping sweat and frustration, and Ian's was no different.

The instructor—Ian forgot her name—was much too tired for any of this, thus fueling her rage to critique each and every action of the students, making life as terrible as hers. She became the dictator on this island of the undesirable.

Despite Ian's comedowns, the week had its comeups. Surprisingly, Spencer never brought up the topic of Ian's mistake. They didn't enforce their system of checks and balances upon each other, letting each other breathe for once. Ian constantly fought the urge to call during Spencer's dedicated study hours, moments too unbearable to spend alone. Ian conveniently kept his latest rendezvous with suspension from the parents, too busy with their own lives to invest in their son's school life.

The air around was dry; every morsel of his skin itched for relief around the same time the first snows of the year arrived in Virginia. A sloppy mix of rain and bastard snow, slicking the roads of Willard along with its sister cities. But the snowfall hadn't reached an inch quite yet, and to the students' disappointment, the public schools were still up and running.

Stephanie, stuck in the stuffy confines of history class, sat between states of attentiveness and its opposite. She and Spencer had been planning events for the coming weekend—a birthday held for the red one, as they called him familiarly. And on her paper, a sad, shabby sheet with the edges all in spurs, were possible gifts and ideas (a good third of which were scratched out). Woodrow Wilson's story would never make it past the eardrums of Stephanie. She met with Spencer after class as routinely done, handing the list to the shorter blonde with the same quirky bounce she always had, his bangs brimming his eyelids and a tattered smile upon his lips.

With eyes weary, he mumbled, "What's this?" seemingly rushed to use the six minutes between class for its intended purpose. He opened up that sad, tattered parchment only to cock a brow and say, "Is this a haiku? A limerick?"

Stephanie shot back with playful defense, "No. Look! It's ideas for this Saturday. I had no clue this weekend would get here so fucking fast."

Spencer teetered from leg to leg, drumming his fingers against the books held in folded arms. "Oh. Well, you crossed everything off on your list."

"Which is why," she balled it up, "we gotta think of something quick. And did you get any sleep last night? The past few days for that matter?"

Eyes darting in every direction but to the eyes of Stephanie, Spencer explained, "Up studying all night. And I thought we originally planned to take Ian out to dinner."

"Too cliché, too impersonal. We gotta do something big like—oh! Since he'll be eighteen, we can, like, have a cigarette themed party!" Poor Spencer didn't even attempt to react to Stephanie's antics—just a blank, ridiculing stare. "Augh! I don't know! Help a sista out here!"

"Hey. You're the girl in my theatre class."

"Huh?" Stephanie looked to the person who so suddenly entered her realm, familiar, yes, but just another someone Stephanie never hoped to have a social life with. "Ah, yes. I am," she mustered a fidgety laugh.

"I was meaning to catch up with you. Wanted to thank you for earlier. I would have been screwed on that monologue." The girl's height barely passed Stephanie's by a centimeter or two; bright teal hair swept across her eyes. "I'm Lizzy, by the way."

"This was your first week here, wasn't it? I couldn't let you down like that," they both laughed as any acquaintance would. "My name's Stephanie. This is my friend, Spencer." He issued an uncommitted hello before a spiritless trudge to class. Stephanie noticed Spencer was out of sorts lately; he always made up an excuse as to why he appeared more disheveled by the day. She made a mental note to check in on him later.

"I had no idea she would throw me up there like that. The only lines I could think of were from Shrek," Lizzy raved, "You must have watched it a lot to spot me like that."

"You have no idea," Stephanie laughed once more, nervous at the one who so gingerly approached her with smiles and quite the chipper demeanor. "Do you need help getting to your next class, or..."

"Yes! Please! I will be lost for days!" Lizzy seemed interesting, Stephanie thought. From the chopped, teal hair to the androgynous ways of dress, Stephanie scrambled for something to say, fearing a dead moment. She leisurely walked her new friend to class, learning about Lizzy's origins along the way, catching the tardy bell in between. Lizzy's family was nomadic, learned Stephanie—she moved from a few states out west to Willard. In turn, Stephanie shared her story, which was nowhere near as interesting as Lizzy's. However, Stephanie ranted and raved about her friends, eagerly wanting to introduce them all to Lizzy. If it was anyone who could make a newbie feel welcome, it was a gift bestowed on Stephanie. After delivering her to her next class, Stephanie couldn't help thinking about their next encounter.

It wasn't until a light snowfall hit Thursday morning that Spencer fully realized he was sick. Stubborn, he refused to let his biology get the better of him and trudged to school. On the bus, Ian kept convincing Spencer to stay home and relax for "one damn day." Of course, Spencer wouldn't dare interrupt the busy life of his mother for some joke of a cold, nonetheless his own. And with a perfect attendance, Spencer thought he could survive seven hours of school easily. He was pressing his will through the sickness amongst all the stress his mind stomached, and through the fear he'd dare not tell the others about.

Since convincing Ian that he had things all under control a couple of weeks ago, Spencer fell victim to harassment by Michael and his crew on almost a daily basis. Michael would step on the back of Spencer's shoes to annoy him, and then proceed to toss the shoe back and forth between his friends. Spencer would retrieve the shoe after it was tossed a ways down the hall as their final act. He was laughed at by everyone around.

The obvious harassment was just entertainment for everyone else—they saw Michael as the charismatic, popular junior, the one who would always occlude his douchebaggery with charm, skill, and his good looks. Every school had the type that could not count past twenty, yet somehow ended up as the population favorite and managing to pass the grade. Spencer had his popularity as well, or infamy, one could call it. Most students had their personal struggle with mathematics or any subject for the matter, and directed their hate and disgust to Spencer simply because he grasped it instantly and could do it in his sleep. Instead of studying for themselves, they would much rather blame the teacher for their lack of knowledge when the answers were right in front of them. Spencer would be scoffed at as the teachers praised him for being on their level or above. And as a result, no one wanted to be close to Spencer, not unless they were looking over his shoulder for answers. He was sick of it but grew accustomed to being used. And Michael made it no better.

Being sick gave Spencer a lack of coordination. Upon stepping off the bus, he dizzily stepped too far left and was caught by Ian. Ian placed his hand on Spencer's shoulder with the same look of concern. "I'm fine. I just missed a step," Spencer said. Ian rolled his eyes and sighed mutely. "You don't have to hold onto my shoulder, you know."

Ian looked to the bruise covered by Spencer's bang, darker than last time, and said nothing. "Could you at least go to the nurse?"

"Ian, I'm fine!" Spencer jerked his arm away. "It is only a cold. I took some medicine before I left from home." They began to make their way into the building.

"Fine. I'm not above skipping class and walking you home if I have to."

"I know you're not. Which is why you shouldn't worry about me."

Ian couldn't stop worrying. Spencer's passive aggression, his bruises, tense shoulders, and dark circles below his eyelids did not convince Ian otherwise. It was obvious stress about school and life at home. For parents, Ian knew Spencer's to be very removed at times. Always eager to represent him at awards ceremonies, but quick to dismiss him when he wanted to do something non-scholastic. He was lucky to be let out of the house when he visited Ian, probably the only break he ever got.

Ian fought the urge to put an arm around Spencer's waist or a hand within his. Anything to reassure Spencer that he wasn't alone in whatever he was going through. But instead, all he could do was constantly ask questions and receive answers he knew weren't the truth. "You know you can tell me anything, right?"

Spencer laughed, triggering a cough or two, then said, "I know, *mom*. I'm fine. There's nothing I can't handle."

Ian took this with hesitation—it was then that he knew his boyfriend was lying—and laughed lightly. "Okay," he said on their journey to Spencer's class. "I'll see about that." As the two walked together, chatting casually, Michael and a friend appeared with their usual chaos, banging on lockers and attempting to rap with everyone smiling at their antics.

Spencer was quick to avert his eyes, tensing the shoulders more than they already were.

Ian frowned.

"Have you decided what you wanted to do for your birthday yet?" Spencer asked. Ian was sure Spencer was keeping him from inquiring about Michael.

"I keep telling you guys not to worry about it. Birthdays are just another day. I'd be content sleeping all day." Ian kept his gaze on Michael while delivering his response. Something was wrong. His gut kicked at him.

Something was happening that Ian took lightly before.

"It's not every day that you turn eighteen. You're the official adult of the group."

"The only thing that's going to change is the ability to go to jail if I screw up. My days of juvenile delinquency are over," but all Ian had going through his mind was getting to the root of Spencer's imbalance.

"Must you always be so cold?" laughed Spencer. "Saturday is a big day. Stephanie and I are going to figure out something to do for you even if it's the death of us."

"Or you can go to class before you end up making your boyfriend tardy." Spencer immediately looked at his watch, amazed that it was time for class to begin.

"Oh! I'm so sorry! By all means, go," Spencer apologized. Ian parted with a wink, which always managed to get a subtle blush from Spencer. He would push through the rest of the day with his sickness and through whatever other obstacle appeared, namely Michael. Spencer ran through scenarios of what Michael could possibly do today and prepared himself for the worst, all the while putting a hundred percent into paying attention in class.

And Ian would put the same effort into skipping his classes and stalking Michael whenever he had to.

Ian sat through the first period, consisting of stoichiometry and Stephanie talking about how awesome some girl named Lizzy was. He tried to act invested in what Stephanie had to say and what he was learning.

"Don't tell me your worried about Spencer again? Or is it turning eighteen? One of the two always seems to bother you in chemistry. What's up?" Stephanie inquired, the same coffee mug in hand with a different pastry every day.

Ian shook his head. "It's nothing."

"You know you can't fool me. When your leg is shaking at Mach 50, it's Spencer. When you're sighing constantly, you're worried about something else." Ian ran a hand through his hair, "You won't be in the wrong if you were worried about him. He's been acting weird."

"You noticed it too?! Thank god it wasn't only me! I was beginning to think I was an overprotective asshole of a boyfriend for a second. Now the dude is forcing himself to be in school when he probably has a temperature of one-hundred and two."

"That's Spencer for you. He's done that since I've known him. But I've never seen him in this state. I know he's taking some pretty advanced classes; we have some of the same ones. It's not easy but I'm not even stressing as much as he is."

"It's because of Michael. I know it."

"Whoa, whoa, whoa! Let's not let our testosterone get in the way. I know you don't like the guy. Don't be so quick to assume. I don't take Michael as the type to have a consistent target. They used to be so close in middle school."

Ian lowered his voice when shot a glance by the instructor. "I know it is. I just know."

"Why do I get the feeling you're going to do something rash?"

"Because Spencer doesn't like being a burden to anyone else. He'd rather keep to himself than to worry anyone with that."

Stephanie hurriedly scribbled the notes from the board she lagged in. "You're right about that. I know you made him a promise and all, but he's looking worse and worse by the day. Have you seen those bags under his eyes?"

"I can't exactly break any more promises. He amazingly didn't bite my head off with the whole test thing. I want to show him that I trust him."

"Are you kidding me? The kid can't even trust himself with most things. He doesn't want to be pitied, like you said." Stephanie received a look from the instructor and lowered her volume, "And he's too proud to admit that he needs help. This is one promise that needs to be broken. But we can't just monitor him every second of the day."

"Psh. Correction: *you* can't monitor him every second of the day."

"Ugh, here you go again. Do I need to remind you how many close calls you've had in the span of the last two weeks alone? I know you're worried about Spencer and all, but you need to focus on keeping your ass in school. Do you think your mom and dad would be happy in any sense of the word to hear about you being suspended?"

"I'm not going to be suspended, okay? Spencer runs the tech club after school on Tuesdays and Thursdays, the only days we don't go home together. I'll stay back today and keep an eye on him."

"And exactly how are you getting home? This doesn't seem like a good idea to me..."

"Relax, I can always get in and out of situations."

"Ian, you have to watch your back as well. Don't do anything reckless. Please?" Without receiving a response, Stephanie knew this wasn't going to end well. Spencer was cocky and Ian never thought of the ends to the means. In a way, she felt responsible for the two. If she could, she would resolve this issue between Spencer and Michael without having to do something detrimental to his future and begin another existential crisis.

As the principal, Cane spent his daily hours of remaining present until all after-school activities were over and that no child remained in the school after hours. School was just ten minutes prior to dismissal; he routinely rose to check his mail-box after a day's conclusion. He sorted through the junk mail on his walk back to his chair, dishing out workplace jokes and things of the cliché that made Principal Cane the easy-going guy outside of student affairs. Upon sitting at his desk, he surfaced a letter with an official seal gleaming across its backing. He adjusted his necktie before opening.

Ian waited until the halls were cleared; everyone caught their assorted transportation home when he left out of the class-room. He scanned the halls with every corner he rounded until he was in view of the computer lab. The soccer team gathered at the opposite end waiting for practice to start, a perfect crowd to be cloaked within.

"Hey, Ian. I didn't know you stayed after school," Desmond greeted, Ian accepting the familiar handshake.

"Yeah I had to, uh, finish a few assignments I was behind on. I didn't know you played soccer," Ian attempted with a false interest, trying to keep attention on the computer lab just around Desmond's head.

"You didn't? I wear the shorts, like, every day, bro. How could you not know? As I always tell you, you can be the most absent-minded person I know," Desmond laughed, shuffling a soccer ball between his feet. "I had to ask you something..."

"What is it?" Ian treasured Desmond's friendship, but he was being too much of a distraction. He tried his hardest to never miss a moment at the lab.

"Do you like Stephanie?"

"What?!" Ian's attention focused on Dez at such an odd utterance.

"I mean I always see you two together. I just wanted to know..." Desmond's gaze remained on the soccer ball.

Ian couldn't help but to laugh hysterically, tearing up and waiting to catch his breath. "No. I don't. We're just friends. Out of all the people who ask, I thought you'd know."

Dez looked the other way in a rush of embarrassment. "I wanted to make sure that I wasn't doing anything against the bro code..."

"Wait, are you telling me what I think you're telling me?" Ian asked with the hugest smile upon his face, elbowing at Dez.

"..." A blush remained on Dez's face.

Ian began to enter another fit of laughter. The very thought of Stephanie and Desmond as a couple was a mismatch waiting to happen. Ian knew Stephanie to be quite stubborn and Desmond to be rather submissive. Stephanie would walk circles around him when it came to dominance; he imagined Desmond on a leash with Stephanie's foot upon his back and let out another cackle.

"I, uh... I want to surprise her by asking her to junior prom..."

"Good luck, man. You should be clearing this with Ryan, not me."

Desmond blinked a few times in innocent surprise. "Do you think she'd say yes? I mean, am I even her type?"

"Listen man, she'll break your heart—" A close of the computer lab's door snapped Ian out of the distraction. Tech club was starting. "I have to go Dez. Text me." Ian immediately broke from the crowd. Peeking into the lab's window carefully, he saw the familiar blonde standing at the board looking tortured by sickness, teaching to the group of fifteen or so students. Ian shifted his stance to get a better look.

And sure enough, Michael stood at the room's opposing end. Arms crossed. Attending tech club.

Before he could turn the knob to enter, Mr. Cane rounded the hall's corner with, "Ah, Mr. Frances. We meet once more. Hopefully this time on better terms," Cane laughed.

Ian snapped away from the door. "Uh, yes. H-Hello."

"Thinking of joining tech club?"

"No. I actually wanted to see if I could use a computer but I'll just use the library's."

As Ian started on his way, Cane continued, "It's a shame. Mr. Holland runs a great club. Brilliant student. You should give it a try. It'll serve as a great apology from the incident."

"I already apologized. The clubs here don't really interest me."

"Is that so? Getting involved is one of the most important things a student can do. There is a club here for every interest. What are you interested in?"

"No offense, Cane, but I'm kinda in a rush. Thanks though." Ian took off before he could stand in front of the door another minute. He would not hear the end of it if Spencer were to inquire about Ian being there.

Cane, with envelopes in hand, couldn't help but think of how strange the boy was, adjusting his necktie as he popped in to give Spencer a supportive greeting before he was off to his errand.

Ian paced in the library repeatedly trying to collect his thoughts together. Ian texted Stephanie.

He's definitely there. Michael is in tech club.

Upon waiting for her reply, his mind was in a tangle. There is no way Spencer was walking home by himself. How long had Michael been attending? This was definitely beyond bullying, had to be. *I have to go back there. I can't go back there—he'll lose my trust. But he's probably dying for help. He needs help.*

The buzz of the phone brought his mind from the loop, yet his heart still pounded. She replied:

> What?! What's happening? Does Spencer know you're there?

In a flurry of thumbs, Ian responded with:

> No. I need to go back there. I need to crush whatever Michael is planning.

> Okay. Be careful. If you need a ride home just hit me up. I'll figure something out.

Stephanie knew that she'd be in a load of trouble, yet she still offered her support.

Ian found himself stuck at the computer lab's door, running through a thousand excuses to say. Until, that is, the door opened for him.

"Ian? What are you doing here?"

"I could ask you the same. You look like literal shit."

Spencer sighed in audible frustration, "This again? Really, Ian, I told you I'm fine. We're only here for two hours and then its home. I can't just cancel it."

"Uh, yeah you can! You're coming home with me right now."

Spencer pardoned himself from those in the room, turning heads growing curious. With a gentle, shaky close of the door, Spencer continued, "What is your problem lately?"

"My problem? You are sick. You are pushing yourself to limits that do not need to be pushed. As your," Ian corrected his volume, "boyfriend and someone who legitimately cares for your wellbeing, I'm taking you home."

"In what vehicle? It's not exactly walking weather."

"Stephanie is on her way."

Outraged, Spencer retorted, "You already arranged this? And what, you want all these other students to be stranded here? I can do this, Ian. Trust me."

"Fuck those assholes. You're coming with me, or I am not going anywhere until I physically see you enter your own house. Now go back in there and tell them you're leaving." Spencer glared at Ian until defeat took over, feeling depleted by the cold and by upsetting Ian. "Now."

Spencer huffed, retreating to do what Ian demanded with embarrassment intertwined through an unstable form. He fought the tears welling up, signifying both relief and the discomfort he caused. Ian never displayed this much animosity in any situation deemed unpleasant. The last thing he needed was to hurt Ian more than that life of his already had.

Spencer's eyes shifted about every attendee's face, purposefully skipping Michael's as he delivered, "Unfortunately, an emergency has come up and the remainder of tech club has been canceled." The students expressed sympathy in noticing the red brim puffing around his eyes and the shakiness of his voice. As they departed, some expressed their understanding, leaving in silence and going about their day. Michael was the last to leave; when he crossed the threshold, he caught Spencer's gaze with his and quipped, "See you next Tuesday," and with a sly smirk, Michael parted, crossing paths with Ian, ignoring his presence.

Ian had the impulse to end everything Michael here and now. Yet Spencer's reddened face and slumped shoulder's claimed priority.

Ian held him in his arms, Spencer's head buried within his chest silently choking through tears. "I'm sorry."

"What are you apologizing for? It's okay, Spencer. You don't have to always convince the world that you're fine. Here, let's get your stuff together, okay?" Ian felt the nod on his chest before Spencer pried himself away. Ian gathered all of Spencer's materials, shutting down the desktops and putting things in its not-so-proper place. It was good enough. Ian carried the weight of both backpacks on each shoulder, Spencer's notably heavier. Before Spencer could protest, Ian cooed, "I got it. Let's go."

It was 7:43 in the evening. After a long day of the same thing, disciplining students and dealing with check-ins from the school board, not to mention the stress of making sure accreditation was retained within the high school's status, Cane sat with elbows resting upon his desk and thumbs at his temples. That same letter rested on his desk with a broken seal as well as the student records of Ian Frances.

O'Neil expected proof out of him after the inquiry Cane sent. And M.E.S. wasn't exactly an organization to disappoint. Now, it was a battle between Cane and his morals. The amount of money Cane could potentially earn from this case made morals easily forgettable.

After placing those documents within his briefcase, he slipped into his suit jacket and locked up his office. Principle

Robert Cane had quite the drive ahead of him—forty-five minutes north of Willard.

The roads were slicked with rain, this type of weather wasn't anyone's favorite here in Virginia. Cane stuck to the right lane, his cruise control set to the comfortable speed of sixty-five. It was easy for Cane to be caught up in his thoughts at the passive act of driving. It seemed his conscience was extra talkative this day, and the kid's face kept popping up in his mind. What a strange thing he was. And how strange it was for Cane to relate to the student—the unintentional troublemaker, Cane's teenagehood to a T.

You could just turn back now, Robert, Cane thought. *You can spare that kid any more trouble than he's already faced. But it's either this or pull out a mortgage. Your family is more important than some kid. So what if anything happens? You need this for your well-being. You can do this, Robert.*

So Cane pressed the petal slightly, increasing to seventy, the engine's rev silencing the moral codes.

You've already involved M.E.S. To turn back now would be foolish. The most inactive member to turn in a report and then to cancel... I can't do that.

His arrival silenced his mind completely. Now he faced the challenge of presentation—he couldn't just waltz in with the same workplace humor. He had to make himself seem better, more of importance. With a sharp breath in, he entered the club.

Blues night, he noted. *How appropriate.* With a nod towards the exhausted bartender, Cane kept straight back. To the VIP lounge? He wished. Straight through the kitchen to descend the stairs into the basement storage below.

It was maybe a good twenty degrees colder below within this storage area and was probably six times the size of the club upstairs. Nervous, he quickened his pace, weaving through paths made by stacks of boxes. A door marked DO NOT ENTER was soon before him.

He entered.

The view before him was even more extravagant than the club upstairs, only he was still moving through corridors. His old shoes clacked the marble flooring. The soft lighting from the stream of chandeliers accentuated the portraits of important-looking white men that decked the halls; Cane glanced at each as he passed. The closer he approached, the louder the music got, this time, he figured, live piano.

A stoic woman stood by the entrance. She wore a skirt suit, hair pulled back in the tightest bun Cane had ever taken notice of. But her voice was something entirely of its own. "Name and identity number, sir."

Cane loosened his necktie and wracked his brain for that string of numbers. "Robert Cane. 1608452."

She opened the door for him; barely through, it slammed shut. Robert was utterly dazzled by the lounge before him. Busy as ever, occupied by business executives, scientists, doctors, lawyers—every person within the layer of the building was intimidating, important. Among the importance were individuals whose presence Cane couldn't quite process. And yet here he was, a lowly principal of some sad high school.

"Robert! So nice to finally meet you!"

Cane whirled out of his glamoured stupor in time to see who he thought to be O'Neil, the owner of this branch of M.E.S. "Oh. H-Hi there. Samuel O'Neil, was it?" he extended a nervous hand.

"Sure is," O'Neil received. "Nine o'clock, right on the dot. You're a timely man."

Cane smiled, "Well, it's the same routine every day, what can I say?"

"Right this way, Mr. Cane."

It was odd to hear the title outside of the school. To sit at a desk other than his own was how Robert expected his students to feel. He made a mental note to perhaps be gentler on those poor souls. Highly furnished, tastefully decorative—the place knew how to disguise this extravagant amount of luxury beneath the unassuming club. The man before him, Samuel O'Neil, was supposedly some big-time banker; Robert didn't know much about Samuel outside of his fame in the business world. The gentleman could retire right now and be no older than fifty. And here Robert was, amid Samuel's spare time and hobby, only increasing the green in his pockets.

Robert was well aware of how awkward he looked; he was sure O'Neil noticed too. With the relaxation of his shoulders, Robert engaged with, "A very nice establishment you have here. Almost got lost."

Without looking up from scribbling on a document, the businessman replied, "I get that a lot. I hope my instruction proved to be sufficient."

"Very."

Cane couldn't stop shuffling his ankles one over the other. The silence became almost stifling, save for the pen's track across the document. Once finished, O'Neil looked up. "So, what do you have for me, Mr. Cane?"

"Oh, I-uh, yes," Robert stuttered while fumbling with his briefcase. A slight umph was uttered with its placement on the desk. After aligning the digits, he pried opened the case and slid a manila folder upon the desk.

"A student file?" questioned O'Neil, a slight tilt of the head as he pronounced, "Ian Frances..."

Hearing the name locked Cane's muscles tightly. "Yes. A student. He is remarkable—you would think his work ethic to be in direct correlation with his personality. But the kid is strange."

O'Neil placed the papers down with a strict fop. "You bring the private records of a minor into my office and expect this to be alright?"

Cane froze up. His eyes darted every direction and he dared not to utter a sound. A chuckle caught him off guard followed by the softening of the man's features, crow's feet tightening at the borders of his eyes. "I get these a lot." Cane relaxed, but the same couldn't be said for his bladder. "I can see by this photograph that," O'Neil flipped the picture, "he seems of fae origin. Very fae indeed. Yet, the way everything is structured—his cheek bones, ears, nose—that definitely speaks otherwise."

"I know that he has to be something other than human," Cane said in a rushed tone. "The eyes, those eyes speak a language of their own and—"

"Yes, yes, red eyes. Common amongst the ranks of vampiric bloodlines, lycan too. Not to mention ghouls and sirens, yet the sirens tend to have a softer gaze..." O'Neil scanned through the file twice over before saying, "It says here that he suffers from a condition which gives a lack of pigment to the eyes. An official report," he turned a medical document towards Cane, "from several of Ian's doctors." His stare tested that of Cane's.

Almost one-hundred percent willing to submit to the authority, Cane barely pushed with, "Those are all fabricated guesses on the doctors' parts." He reached within the briefcase to pull printed documents on the disorder. "I have personally researched what the doctors have diagnosed him with. Severe *ocular albinism*. It's supposedly a rare condition in which the patient lacks pigmentation within the retinae, causing extreme sensitivity to light, painful vision, and other symptoms. However, there has never been documented a case of *ocular albinism* in which the eye takes on a reddish hue, let alone with perfect vision."

O'Neil stroked at the fine hairs on his chin. Cane was not to be underestimated. Samuel may as well have had the biggest case of the decade on his desk. "Hmm. I tell you what, Mr. Cane: I will investigate this a little further. If we happen to gain backers, then arrangements will be made for your payment, and further investigations will be carried out. This case," he plucked the papers, "is one that is not to be ignored." And with a final handshake, Cane was dismissed from the office.

Relief washed over the principal once outside of the office, finally able to take in the massive underground club. His brave and utterly idiotic venture here had not been in vain after all. He clutched the files against his chest, mustering the largest sigh of relief he could manage. It was goodbye to this place for now. Shaken to the bone, Cane made the commute home to be welcomed by the adoring family once more—their future made brighter by the sacrifice of another.

Stephanie arrived at school before the buses; her mother thought it convenient to always drop her off on the way to work, save the long uncomfortable bus rides for the other students. "Bye. Love you too," Stephanie replied to her mom, shutting the car door before her mother pulled off. Today was just like yesterday, imbued with a nasty mix of sleet and rain. The heist she pulled last night would land her in the biggest load of shit if her parents were to find out. Taking one of their cars while both were at church—not something their angel child would do. She would do anything to remain perfect in their eyes—she was numb to the discomfort caused by lying, a habit now, something good girls did to get some of the most harmless things.

Arriving before the start of school forced her to wait in the cafeteria among the other early birds. Usually she carried breakfast—a bagel or some pastry always paired with coffee—capping her routine with music jammed in her ears streamed from her cellphone.

A jolt next to her made her whirl around in surprise. She was soon reassured by the new, familiar face. "I thought that was you," smiled Lizzy, sliding into an adjacent seat.

Stephanie removed the earbuds, "Oh, hey! How are you?"

"Spectacular in the most sarcastic way ever put. I didn't think I'd be at school this early. I miscalculated. Sped here like a maniac."

"See? At least you drive. I get the good ol' fourth grader treatment. Mom drops me off." They both laughed as new friends would to keep the mood light, feeling out one another's personality. "I didn't get enough sleep. Had to babysit for a few hours."

"Oh? I didn't know you looked after kids," said Lizzy.

"I didn't know either. One happens to be seventeen, and the other turns eighteen tomorrow."

"Heh, sounds rough. What happened?" With Stephanie filling Lizzy in on the latest rendezvous with the crew, it almost felt like catching up with an old friend. Stephanie grew excited with every word that passed, a potential friendship blooming right before her. Finally, a girl she could talk to without feeling like her words were getting nowhere. "Come to think of it, Spencer looked like he was about to pass out when you introduced us."

"Yep. And now he's condemned to bedrest, and I'm forced to plan Ian's surprise party alone. It's tomorrow for goodness sake!"

"I can help you out. I usually have nothing better to do after school, anyway," Lizzy shyly teased at her bangs.

"Really?! I would love that so much!" After exchanging numbers, the two made plans to meet before parting ways to class.

Ian tried not to let yesterday's evening activities get to him when preparing for school this morning. He paced the room heavy-mindedly, clumsily fumbling through his morning ritual. The bus would arrive in fifteen minutes, yet Ian still slumped around in his boxers. After further convincing last night, Ian managed to get Spencer to stay home. That stubborn kid, Ian thought, would end up killing himself if someone didn't tell him better. And yet, although Spencer was being taken care of and finally resting, Ian still paced.

He picked up whatever shirt was in his vicinity and the same jeans he wore two days ago. Ran a hand through his hair and brushed his teeth. He slunk out the door with the sling of his backpack to await the bus's arrival. It was weird to linger at the stop sign without Spencer, quite lonely actually. Selfishly, he wished Spencer was there to calm his nerves. Ian felt like a caged animal, pacing the roads, eager to sink its claws into something concrete and stable. Nothing was going to feel the same unless Michael was removed from the whole picture.

Ian sat in class, head buried in arms, inattentive to Mr. Willis' dull droning. Being worried so much for Spencer left him to feel the debilitating crash of his own worries when they resurfaced. One could say the distraction provided yesterday was nice in comparison to what tomorrow held. It was, to Ian, judgment day. A birthday in the eyes of friends and family; a start of another ending for Ian. Eighteen. The number meant independence, something to be longed for—every teenager in this class would give anything to escape from their parents' shadow. Ian didn't want to leave quite yet—he could admit that to himself—as he never garnered closure from his harrowing past. The pain of remembrance jutted at him, reminded harshly of life's transitory nature.

5

THE INITIATE

"Now this is my kind of thing, Lord Baal!" Travius exclaimed, arms folded behind his head. The apertures opened once more, revealing the three visitors. "Just the type of place I need to refuel. Think of all the babes inside!" Ignoring the obscene remarks from that creature, Baal remotely touched bases with Master, prompting Travius to blabber at Hazth.

"So what do you think, shifter?" he beckoned at his comrade, throwing an amiable arm around Hazth's shoulder.

"I think it is wise to calm down and remain to your senses," Hazth retorted, shaking the demon's arm away.

"What's the matter? Remind you too much of the *good ol' times* with your family? Let's face it, they were probably all bought and sold here. Your mommy and daddy," Travius teased; Hazth remained unwavering. "Some old guy is probably abusing the fuck out of them while rolling in stacks!"

"Perhaps we could fetch a decent price for you, as well. I'm sure Lord Baal would gladly take currency over a thing as worthless as yourself."

For one that loved to dish out insults, Travius would never fail to take offense when the roles were reversed. Now he revved up, "You little—I'll have you know that a demon like me don't make no good house pet! I'll kill any human that dares buy me up like cattle." Hazth rolled his eyes. "What? I will turn the roles right back on them."

"Be quiet, Travius. Your mouth is sure to cause a scene."

Lord Baal was particularly lively tonight; a remarkable feeling of luck rested on his shoulder—he wasn't the kind to believe in such a thing, yet his pep proved to be out of character. The parking lot where they stood contained a few cars, nine or ten at the most, not too uncommon for this old nightclub, Perk's. For this nightclub to be in business with few to no customers was no mystery, at least for those in the know. And those aware weren't the typical audience for Perk's.

Travius picked at the dried blood around the empty eye socket, his vessel adorned with fresh, formal clothing even after neglecting to freshen up. "A nightclub? I would not think this to be your scene, Lord Baal."

Lord Baal led the way through the lot, moonlight stretching their shadows on the cracked pavement below. "My scene? Exactly what is my scene, Travius?"

"You know, dark fiery pits, torturing the innocent, reveling in souls. That sort of thing."

Baal only smirked. "How wrong you are. In the Uver, perhaps. I do not have a 'scene.'"

"I guess that's more my scene, then. Say, when can we have real fun? I know we're on business, yadda yadda yadda, but is that it? I'm dying to feel alive again!" Travius whined. "You must really be set on this mission. You were always passionate whenever Master—"

"Travius, I am sure Lord Baal will grow irritable if you keep speaking," quipped Hazth, protecting the intermediate demon from the wrath of their lord.

"You should listen to Hazth. He has not lost an eye yet." Travius rushed ahead to hold the door open for his leader.

Upon entering, Baal removed his vessel's gloves, adjusting his coat collar. The place was shaded in cool tints of purples and blues—green lights flickered about in step with the blaring techno beats. A couple chatted at a table, and by the looks of it, they were freshly hit by cupid's arrow—she giggled endlessly as he flirted. A man sat at the bar, looking at the paper, glancing up at the game on screen, then back to the paper. Baal made an audible groan at the distaste all around.

Lord Baal's authoritative stature caught the bartender off guard. The three looked almost comical—formal, commanding, yet lost in the world of modernity. "Hello, welcome to Perk's! Can I get you guys anything?" She was skittish, the bartender, a hyper, awkward little thing with tattoos descending the arms and a lip piercing to match.

Baal glided towards the bar, resting his arms upon it. He gave the girl a sincere smile, his dark eyes reflecting his amiable aim. The bartender's face grew hot, red billowing through her translucent skin. "Yes you can, dear. I'm here for business. Is there an owner I can talk to?"

For a few seconds, she was lost in Baal's air, immediately apologetic. "I-I—yes, I'll call him up for you. May I have your names?" She scampered through her apron for a pen and pad.

"You can write, 'Investor'," Baal returned. She looked a bit lost, waiting for actual names yet too afraid to ask. She nervously dialed the extension; these types of customers, the obvious wealthy ones who came here for "business" always gave her an unsettling vibe.

"Mr. O', you have visitors here to see you, an investor ...yes, right away... mmm hmm!" She tuned back to the strange customers, "He'll be right up! Could I offer you gentlemen any-thing? A drink?"

Baal silently turned away the offer with a wave of the hand, taking a seat at the bar, prompting noticeable discomfort from the bartender. Tonight, the demonic trio would scout their options; the lord would only take inventory of the people in high places, avoiding bloodshed if possible. The banker soon approached the men with a hand outstretched; Baal received him. The demon lord wormed his charm through unassuming eyes and soon was led through an underground maze—his victory rested right around the corner.

The next morning was spent in bed. Ian sandwiched his head between pillows, blocking any noise and speck of light that dared to touch his senses. He was paralyzed, in a sense, only moving to check his phone. Spencer was recovered to a point where he was running errands. Ian thought it to be strange. Only a day and the busy body was... well, being busy. That was one worry, gone. Today he was a legal adult. It wasn't today that led him to worry, so to speak, but what was to follow.

Soon, he flipped the phone over. All the birthday shoutouts were sickening.

To his surprise, the day was oddly passing fast, with neither parent home to shove this glorious day further down his throat. His two friends knew the drill—any mention of Ian's birthday and they saw the imminent change within his posture—they kept their wishes to themselves.

Again, Ian's thoughts lingered towards his parents. Why weren't they here? Was it happening?

Searching the house, he soon confirmed himself to be the only one present. Both cars were gone. He was alone and began assuming the worse.

"This is the third time this child has ended up here. Are we sure we should keep housing him? Why not transfer him to the downtown facility?" hushed voices whispered in the adjacent room. *They discussed the fate of this boy, one whose fate didn't seem to be in his own favor to the eyes of the caretakers.*

"With the budget cuts and his history, I do not think it possible to continue housing him here. He's too old. Nobody is going to want him soon enough." The child sat with his knees cradled to his chest. *He appeared as only a small grey dot in the corner of the lounge, in oversized clothing with a downtrodden disposition.*

"I'm not denying what you are saying. You speak very truth-fully, and yes, for this specific situation, we cannot afford to house him any longer. But this is a child you are speaking about! Whether or not he gets a solid adoption, it is still our job to raise every child that comes through our doors."

"We will lose this place before we can even help any of these kids! All our grant opportunities are used up, we have no sponsors, not even the state! How do you expect a non-profit organization to run? Through donations and good wishes?! Get real. I'm transferring him to the downtown facility, along with a few of the older children."

There was an abrupt thud. "You will not," he said sternly before leaving to join the newly orphaned child. There was silence before the man placed a reassuring hand on the child's, Ian's, back. Nothing was okay, as far as the man knew; there was no point in asking. He struggled to find the appropriate thing to say. For an occurrence such as this to happen... to happen to a child no older than ten at that... no, one that just turned ten on this very day.

The man simply sighed, emotions getting the better of him. "Are you hungry?" he was right not to expect an immediate answer from Ian. In the oversized grey hoodie, Ian shook his head, refusing to meet the eyes of the utterer. "C'mon," the man soothed, "Let's go get you cleaned up." Ian moved unresponsively beside the man. Those red eyes were always spirited at this foster home during his last residencies.

Yet now, a shadow seemed to be passing over them. The man was holding back anger. And the longer he held it, the more he wanted to sob in the child's behalf. From the moment the police arrived at the entrance bearing the offering of the helpless boy, his heart sank. For years, he received pictures, letters, postcards, and gifts from Ian and his family, full of smiles and cheerful days. How—what could have happened? Everything the cops said just didn't resonate with him.

And now all he wanted to do was tell Ian something to get that glimmer of light back in those scarlet eyes. But the only thing he could think of was 'happy birthday.'

"Here. Fresh clothes. Go and put these on and I'll have dinner made for you." He left the boy to change, soon to be back with a tray of sandwiches, fresh fruit, and juice. Yet Ian had reverted into the same position: knees to chest, and head to knees, still buried inside that old grey sweatshirt.

It was clear that getting him to eat was pointless. So instead, the man sat with him.

Ian bathed in the forlorn memories while the sun descended. Tears streamed, and panic settled in. His breathing became uneven. It was happening, he thought. He rushed through his parents' phone numbers time after time, through each ring he received no answer. He paced distraught. Punched the wall several times. Reality vanished before his eyes. He screamed for his parents, both present and past.

"Ian?" said Spencer from the doorway, horror all over his face. Realization set in, and Spencer rushed by his side to ease Ian out of his panic attack. "It's going to be okay. I'm here. We're all here," Spencer cooed softly, cradling Ian's head in his lap while stroking his hair. "We're here. It's okay."

The panic subsided, and a stillness came over the room. Ian lay in Spencer's lap staring blankly ahead. Spencer gave Ian the time he needed to come around and patiently waited, continuing the comforting strokes.

"I think I may have overreacted," Ian forced chopped laughter.

"We don't have to talk about it if you don't want to," replied Spencer. "Would you like to go somewhere? Let's go to the park or something."

". . . yeah. That sounds good."

Spencer helped Ian gather his belongings and tidy up the room without a word. Nothing had to be said. It was funny how they took turns looking after each other, Spencer thought.

He was careful not to remind Ian of any memory that might trigger another episode. His mother was kind enough to let Spencer use the car after a decent amount of convincing, pursued, of course, by an anticipated argument.

The atmosphere was a fragile one—Spencer cranked up the radio, bobbing his head to an upbeat song, singing along with a pitchy voice. Now Spencer began to doubt all that he and Steph planned. Right now, it seemed like Ian didn't need any more surprises. Yet all that planning... all of the organizing to get something this elaborate...

Ian did not seem completely back on this plane, assessed Spencer. To ease him back, he tried to ramble aimlessly, "Did you eat today, are you hungry?" Ian continued to gander out the window, silent. "We can stop to get some burritos or something."

"We can get some pizza. You like pizza, right Ian?"

The orphaned boy shrugged.

"Okay. Then, let's go do something fun." A lot of time would pass before Ian was to get out of his shell. And the man, the primary caretaker of the orphanage, Jonathan Fetcher, was particularly close to him—he was the first example of family Ian knew. Weeks would pass before Ian would utter a sentence. Fetcher kept track of this gradual mood change. He would have to continue providing all the support to this child; he'd put one-hundred-fifty percent effort into bringing the child's situation back to a positive standing. And soon

enough, maybe not soon but given the circumstances, Ian began to shed his first smiles roughly four months after the incident.

But it still didn't make sense... the police report detailed the corpses of the bodies found—both previous adopted parents were found with full decapitation, bodies mangled and almost beyond recognition. The cops arrived at the scene in response to a call from a child, presumed to be Ian. It was hard, almost near impossible, to get any word out of Ian when questioning. He was traumatized, never blinking, staring blankly whilst murmuring incoherent phrases again and again. There was no murder weapon, no means discovered. No traces that would ever give a hint to the forensics team. They speculated the wounds to be made by a precise tool, yet other marks and scrapes looked animalistic. There was no DNA evidence detected. And now, the kid who had to witness the death of the family he waited so long for, was back at the foster home he had hoped he would never see again.

The caretaker, Fetcher, took it upon himself to find the root, all the while keeping Ian out of the know.

The car had been parked for a while; Ian hadn't noticed, finally breaking his gaze from the window, looking to Spencer.

He returned the look, trying his hardest not to reflect the sadness in Ian's expression. He was sick of feeling sorry—he wanted to do something, at least once, for Ian. To truly bring happiness to his boyfriend.

"Where are we?" breathed Ian.

"The park. It's getting pretty late, so we're gonna trespass, break the rules a bit."

Ian looked at the time: half past seven. Time flies when one stays in their head.

"Come on. I wanna see who can swing the highest," Spencer taunted with his smile, urging Ian out of his seat.

Ian hesitantly held the swing chains in his hands, on the brink of another painful memory. "I'm winning! C'mon, you just gonna let me beat you?" Spencer tried his hardest to get some positivity to penetrate Ian's gloom. "You used to do front flips off these things, remember?"

"Yeah..." Ian barely got the word out in a hushed, thoughtless voice.

"So you gonna show me how?"

"Oh. Yeah." He pulled back on the swing. Letting go, he barely made any air, losing momentum as he looked towards the sky in silence. Spencer had to change his methods. He transferred his attention to his phone, giving Stephanie the current update of this situation. She was just as worried as the blonde.

"Hang the streamers from that window to the staircase," instructed Mrs. Frances. "Thanks again, girls, for setting this up."

"It's not a problem at all," grinned Stephanie, checking her phone once more.

"Okay, I think I can cover everything else here. You girls can head on over to pick up the food," Mrs. Frances passed a wad of cash to Stephanie. The way she rushed was reflective of the perky person she was—always up early in the day and back late at night. The free time she did have, if it wasn't spent catching up on much needed sleep, was spent on making sure the house didn't collapse in her absence.

Lizzy started her truck, glancing over to Stephanie in the passenger seat. "So? How is it over on Spencer's end?"

"Not so good. He's managed to distract Ian about the party, but he's still not in the best headspace." She breathed a sigh, resting her head on her lap. "I just hope he doesn't take this surprise the wrong way."

"I think it'll be fine, relax a little," replied Lizzy.

For such a new friend, Stephanie thought, *she expresses so much concern for us. And to boot, she jumped at the opportunity to help me at such a last minute's notice.*

"I know he's paranoid," continued Lizzy, "but to see everyone gathered in one spot in support of him—it's sure to turn out well!" Lizzy gave Stephanie a thumbs up and an enthused chuckle. Stephanie had no choice but to smile, involuntarily blushing at her.

"Did you even meet Ian yet?"

"You never introduced us, unfortunately, but you guys are the weird kids; we'll be friends in no time."

Stephanie gave a distracted giggle while responding to the latest of Spencer's texts as they made their way to the supermarket. "Well, Spencer is stalling time pretty well. Says that he's never seen Ian in a mood like this. Ian is always... everywhere. Loud, distracting... I wish I would have planned this better... now he's probably thinking the worst out of this situation, that everyone's abandoning him."

"You are doing fine, Steph! Don't stress so much." Stephanie groaned. "This is going be bomb as fuck, he's going to love it. I just know it. Who's coming anyway?"

"Desmond, Kiera, Ryan, Jasmine—they'll be on their way in a few minutes. And Mrs. Frances invited a squad of her own, coworkers and such."

"Fun. Nothing like a party with all your mom's friends."

"Ugh, you know moms; always gotta be overly social for no reason whatsoever."

The two rushed around the store gathering everything on the list.

People were going to arrive to the Frances' house in less than an hour. And Stephanie had no idea how Spencer was going to stall Ian much longer, let alone drag him inside.

Stephanie met back up with Lizzy in the toy aisle. "May I ask why you are looking at toys?" asked Stephanie quizzically.

"Don't judge, I'm trying to find him a gift. Does he like dinosaurs?"

Stephanie snorted, "How old do you think he is? Twelve?"

"Fine. Since you're so good at this, what should I get him?"

"Oh, don't worry about it. I got something for him already. You can just sign the card and I'll say it's from the both of us."

On their return, Stephanie couldn't help but to take in the characteristics of the driver: how nonchalant she appeared while gripping the wheel; the tranquil way in which she handled the road; her smell, so delicate and distinctive. Stephanie started when caught staring, fleetingly looking forward.

"What? Do I have something in my hair?" Lizzy combed through it in playful response.

"No. I was just lost in thought."

"Not you too!"

"Tell me something about you. I feel like we've been revolving around me and my worldly problems way too much," Stephanie urged, genuinely curious about her new friend.

"Something about me?" Stephanie nodded. Lizzy pondered for a moment, finger on chin, before saying, "Well, let's see... I think Willard is interesting. My whole family moved at once, so I don't feel home sick one bit. They made sure to bring their drama with them."

"I take it you have siblings?"

"Yes. Six actually. An older brother who's kind of a tool, two little sisters, and three little brothers. We all live with my grandma."

"Holy shit, that must be hell to deal with."

"I'm used to it," explained Lizzy. "My parents died six years ago in a car accident, so it's been up to me, Nana, and my older brother to raise those kids. But they're angels for the most part. Wings and all," she laughed to herself.

"Oh my god, I'm so sorry to hear that..." Stephanie had no idea Lizzy had faced such an awful tragedy so recently. She was collected and easy going, the contrast of Ian whenever he talked of his former parents.

"Hey," Lizzy beamed a reassuring smile to Stephanie, "I can't waste my time mourning after their deaths... it happens to the best of us, all of us. I can only deal with the legacy they've left us and turn that into a promising future." She was so mature, thought Stephanie. Every word that Lizzy spoke was surefooted; Stephanie could tell she was used to this way of living. It was strange to see Lizzy remain intact despite her age; a high school student, forced to take care of a sizable family.

"How old are you?"

"How old do I look?" Lizzy quickly retorted.

"I'd say about twenty, twenty-three. You have a very robust body, like you've skipped the awkward teenage stages. Then again, you wouldn't be in high school if you were that old."

Lizzy joked, "So you've been looking at my body... interesting."

Stephanie felt her cheeks well up with blood, rattled by her imagination hinting at the crush it placed upon Lizzy. "What? You have nice boobs, what can I say." Lizzy pushed her chest together—their humor aligned perfectly with one another.

The two were soon back at the house, completing the setup, getting the guests prepared for Ian's momentary arrival.

Spencer grew anxious and ultimately felt wrong for taking Ian back home knowing the dread that he felt. Pulling up, the street was already lined with cars, and to Spencer's surprise, Ian didn't seem to notice at all—he walked sluggishly towards the door with his head down, then paused apprehensively. Spencer cocked his head in question.

With Ian's eyes brimmed red, he asked, "You're gonna stay with me, right?"

Spencer beamed the brightest, most honest smile, "Of course. I will never leave your side, especially on days like this."

On the inside, the guests were in their assumed places according to Jennifer Frances' direction. Hushed, excited whispering ensued, shushing and shuffling. Stephanie braced herself expectantly, clutching her hands against her chest. The room was in total darkness, and the partygoers awaited the impending moment.

Ian stepped inside the mudroom, juggling between kicking off his shoes and maintaining composure. By hearing Spencer's words, the welling tears held a sort of promise that this life of his—the people and places within it—held permanence simply because of the patience and kindness that his boyfriend exuded. And to show for that, Ian mustered up the courage in the midst of his torment to embrace Spencer close, body pressed to body, cupping his lips to Spencer's as the door came to a close.

"SURPRISE!"

The lights flickered on, revealing the party guests. Spencer pushed himself away, caught off guard by Ian's timing. The overall conflict of joy and embarrassment frothed within, making Spencer a fair shade of vermillion. *Did they really see us kiss? Did everyone just see that?!* Spencer's heart dropped, looking to Ian for solace. Yet Ian remained sullen and pale; the cheering of "happy birthday" was lively until the guests observed Ian's demeanor, inducing the decrescendo of celebratory chants and sprouting discomforted murmurs.

Stephanie's heart bottomed. *That's it, it's over. This was a bad idea. I blew it. Ian is—*

Plump tears streamed down Ian's cheeks, intermixing with an enormous grin—he began to sob, crumpling to his knees. Trying his hardest to maintain his composure, he promptly failed in his struggle.

Ian's mother helped him up, dabbing away the tears, encouraging her son to greet everyone who attended. He sheepishly obliged, melding into the merrymaking.

Stephanie keeled over finding respite on Ryan. "I'm sooooo relieved, holy shit," she breathed, clenching her heart once more.

"Yo, you are so dramatic. Stop leaning on me so hard," Ryan jabbed. "We told you that you were over-reacting; everything's chill."

Kiera interjected, "Yeah, this is the first time I've ever seen you stressed, at least this much."

Stephanie laughed in short, fretful bursts, "You don't understand, guys. I've had a pressing feeling as the week went on. It was strange... unsettling."

"It was all just in ya head, Steph," Ryan amiably threw his arm around her shoulder, a boy who has had quite the history with her. Desmond looked away from the two, sifting off to join Ian.

"Hey, bud!" Ian was surprised to see Desmond. "How's it going?"

"Hey, bro! Oh my god, I just—I didn't know you guys planned all of this. Thanks for coming!"

"No problem. Thank Stephanie. It was her idea. You should have seen her, scared to death and all," he giggled.

"I really appreciate it, Dez. I mean it. Who else came?"

"The gangs all here, dude. Ryan, Kiera, Jasmine. And that new girl, Lesly or whatever her name is. But you look like you have plenty of friends outside of school, kind of old, though," he said gesturing at the crowd of thirty-plus people.

Ian snorted, "Please. They're mostly my parents' friends and mysterious relatives."

"Ian," called Jennifer, "Come here, I have some people I want you to meet."

"I'll catch up with you guys in a few minutes," Ian told Desmond. Mrs. Frances introduced multitudes of kith and kin, ones both familiar and new. Ian wondered why it had taken this long to finally meet them—how long exactly had Stephanie been planning this? There were so many of them, and each one received him kindly. They all avoided the question of his eyes, yet the children did not hold back their fascination.

His aunt, Jennifer's sister, was absolutely thrilled at Ian's presence. "Wow! You've grown so much!" she hugged. "It's so awesome finally meeting you. Jennifer has only sent me pictures. And you were like, this small," chuckled Aunt Lisa. She and her kids flew in from Arizona to be here, and soon enough her kids, ages three and five, already took a liking to Ian, climbing all over the young adult in a game of playful attack.

"Looks like he's got his hands full," said Spencer, meeting up with his school squad. They all looked to him in coordinated consolation and second-hand embarrassment. He reddened, being reminded ever-further. "Look, I'm sure no one noticed and will soon forget that even happened," Spencer sighed.

"My dude, everyone saw that kiss," said Ryan. "Looks like you're finally out of the closet."

Stephanie jabbed him in the ribs, "Ryan, shut up. And I'm pretty sure no one cared, Spencer. It's Ian's family we're talking about. They're open-minded." Spencer groaned. "It'll be fine. Mrs. Frances probably took the hint ever since you guys started dating—she's not dumb." Spencer groaned even louder, plopping his head into his hands.

"Why now of all times?" he whined.

"Stephanie... Spencer... you both have some serious explaining to do." Ian, with party hats over each ear, nearly tackled the two in a hug. "Payback is due. I must have my revenge." He smiled, "I really appreciate it, guys. Really. You didn't have to."

Stephanie nodded, punching him on the shoulder, "You deserved it, red." She then pulled Lizzy beside her, "By the way, this is Lizzy. You were always too busy getting into trouble to meet her. She was a big help with setting this thing up."

"Heh," he scratched his head, "Nice to meet you finally. I'm Ian. Stephanie told me about you. Welcome to Willard, the most boring city you'd ever visit."

Lizzy's features relaxed. *So this is Ian,* she thought as she reached out for a handshake, "Stephanie was right, you are handsome—you should be a model. Pleased to meet you."

Ian clasped her hand, "Welcome to the group, Liz. I'm sure you'll find us all to be the best group of assholes you've ever met."

"Yo, shut the fuck up, Ian. You love us!" Ryan retorted.

"Yeah, bitch. Calm that sappy shit down," Jasmine joined in on the play. Everyone laughed, and Lizzy immediately felt welcomed, making her job much easier. She smiled at the comical group. They all fit together so well—they flowed.

"Let's go to the backyard," suggested Stephanie, "We'll get the fire pit started. Mind grabbing the marshmallows, Ian?"

"Marshmallows, gotcha."

They were comfortably gathered around the pit, talking casually, well, their version of casual—shit talking teachers, calling other classmates out for their bull, and relating to one another's antics.

Stephanie grinned at the fact that the day had changed for the better. Seeing Ian so happy to be around family made her long for the same conduct within her household. The way Ian's family didn't seem to mind whether he got suspended over something like the test incident. They were upset, yes, but they didn't make Ian feel like less of a person, or like he was taking a turn for the worst. They had absolute faith in his ability. One could say Stephanie had a support system at home. They always encouraged her to make fantastic grades and to respect all forms of authority. So much so, that if she made one mistake, it tormented her. One C, and it was the end of even dreaming of getting into college. One tardy, and they lectured about how one couldn't be late in the real world. Not to mention the lectures they gave Stephanie on lady-like conduct. Those are the best, she sneered.

Stephanie was a simple girl; she wanted nothing more than to be who she was and perform to her best ability. She didn't mind making mistakes; she learned from them and moved on, but usually ended up hating herself whenever her parents forced their opinions upon her. Mistakes were in the no-fly zone. The perfect daughter—brings home her gay friends to a household of homophobic Christians; wears a plethora of black, displaying little interest in vanity; chooses to hang out with those considered outside of the social norm—the perfect daughter indeed. She knew her parents and relatives thought her to be the black sheep of the family. Her eccentricity left her on the outskirts of the in-crowd, yet she always found solace in the recesses of her imagination.

She found interest in profundity, thus gravitating towards the sciences; she correlated her religious environment to have fostered that mindset. Yet her imaginings inflated towards the fantastic, things she would never dare mention aloud. She wandered in her own realms, inventing a myriad of characters—hybrids, aliens, magical beasts—all with elaborate stories. Stephanie was physically on earth but lived in her mind for the most part. Something in her heart begged for a life that would never exist.

Although partially removed, she was glad to be sitting amongst the friends she grew up with, Lizzy as the newest edition since Ian's introduction five years ago. She gazed at the new girl, an unanticipated magnetism. Stephanie internally struggled against the notion of possibly having feelings for the girl. There was something about the way that she carried herself, a charismatic chameleon who adjusted quite quickly to her new life. She was one of those people who had a natural ability of making others feel included; she could easily swing the tides of the atmosphere when things grew cumbrous—it didn't take long for Stephanie's friends to open up and accept her. Lizzy sailed through topics as if she knew everyone for years; to Ryan's chagrin, his embarrassing attempts at flirting were immediately countered by the confident conversationalist.

Spencer stared into the fire, charring the marshmallow into an unrecognizable black ball—embarrassment was still on his mind. "I have the worst timing ever, don't I?" Ian asked the group as he observed Spencer's character. The friends broke out in laugher and imitated Ian's reaction to the surprise. Spencer couldn't help but to laugh, covering his face from the flush. "How the hell was I supposed to know there was a surprise party going on?"

"There were fuckin' cars everywhere, dude. Your driveway was packed and you ain't even notice?" Ryan asked, puzzled that Ian could be that shallow. "You had your man's booty all up in your hands."

"You could have given poor Spencer some time to breathe—sucking all the air out of him," teased Jasmine.

"I guess you can say Ian's good at sucking," Stephanie jested. The laughter continued, and Spencer sank lower into his chair.

"Guuuuys! Why don't you all have any chill whatsoever?! That was so embarrassing! I'm so glad my mom didn't end up coming," whined Spencer.

"Wait, you're not out yet?" Lizzy asked.

"No. God no."

She turned to Ian, "What about you?"

"Yeah," Ian shrugged, "I am now. I don't really care who knows. I care about where Spencer is at emotionally—he's got enough shit going on at home. He doesn't want to come out yet, so it's no problem keeping it a secret."

"That's very kind of you," Lizzy smirked. "Trust me, you will feel *a lot* better when you do. I couldn't keep my gayness in to save my life, so the fam pretty much made me come out," she sighed.

"You're a stem?!" Spencer asked excitedly.

"Uh, yeah! Is your gaydar broken? Were the flannel and teal hair not enough of a hint?"

Stephanie felt an involuntary blush spread across her face. She looked at the ground in fear of making an obvious expression.

"You totally fooled me. Nice."

"Back to that kiss, though!" Kiera exclaimed, demanding the moment to be revived.

"No! Guys, I swear! Stop!" Spencer yelled, failing to remove the permanence of his grin. Once more, the circle was filled with smiles and laughter as the razzing continued.

Ryan and Stephanie, as aforementioned, had a unique, complicated history with one another. They hadn't dated since the start of her eighth grade year, however, during that next summer before the start of high school, they were each other's first. Stephanie still thought nothing of it, neither regret nor denial. The two were still tight-knit, getting into spirited disputes here and there over the smallest of issues. Every now and again, perhaps a *favor* would be asked from either of the two, especially since that trust was already established. Stephanie remained unfettered by Ryan's persistent flirtations which fell on deaf ears; Lizzy was good at deflecting his attempts, soon to excuse herself to smoke.

Mrs. Frances emerged through the backdoor to give everyone a heads up; they were about to open gifts and serve cake soon, summoning Ian to lead the ceremonies.

His family, his friends... they were here to stay. Ian knew he had to protect these bonds, protect what mattered. He wasn't going to let unseen forces interfere anymore.

On the intersection of Delrose and Argonne sat Lizzy, blowing through her second cigarette, watching as the smoke drifted towards the streetlight—ash fell onto the tip of her shoe. She wore a face void of its playful spirit, preparing for what was to come. A figure lingered on a rooftop four houses away in perfect view of the party, obvious enough to be detected by Liz.

"Show yourself. It's pretty creepy for someone as old as you to spy on teenagers," Lizzy called out towards the night sky, stepping on the smoldering filter.

The figure descended silently towards the streetlight landing beside her. "I could ask you the same," his deep voice responded.

"I didn't know there were any shifters left in the area," Lizzy said, analyzing the stranger's scent. "I was told they were all wiped out in a three-hundred mile radius."

"Once again, I state the same. A shifter such as yourself could fetch a fair price these days if you remain here too long." He looked her over. "Especially a female."

"Why are you here?" Lizzy griped.

He laughed, diverting his attention back at Ian's house. "I think it's wise for us shifters to stick together. Our downfall is upon us... our pride is too great to work with one another. It's a shame, really."

"Answer my question!" she demanded, wielding a pocketknife behind her back.

"I'm not here to harm, woman. You can put your weapon away." He put his hands up defensively, edging closer with a smirk upon his lips. "And I'm sure you are aware as to why I'm here. The boy is rumored to be of interest. I'm only here to investigate."

Lizzy regained her posture, tuning her suspicion into curiosity. "The boy? You don't mean..."

"The one who calls himself Ian Frances, a weak excuse of a name if you ask me."

"But why? Why is he of interest?" She knew those eyes were bound to attract the wrong crowd sooner or later.

The man only chuckled, reconfiguring his stance. "So, I guess you're here for a different purpose then. Very well. Ian is rumored to be a missing link in a grand scheme. And I'm here to observe his situation. That's all. Now, if I may ask, why are you here?"

"It's nothing of importance," she stated firmly.

"I've shared my reasons. It is only common courtesy to return the favor."

"It's family business."

"Oh, I get it. Here to induct one of these children into your clan by force. Is that really how us shifters operate now? We have truly fallen far," he shook his head in disgrace.

"You shut up! And Ian is off-limits," Lizzy put herself under a new mission that instant. Although finally encountering another derelict shifter for the first time in years, this guy rubbed her the wrong way. She had caught his scent only a few minutes after the group decided to sit around the fire; its lingering led her to confront the uninvited guest.

"What's your name? What clan are you from?"

"Hazth. Of the Basilisk clan."

Lizzy's eyes widened—a myth was before her. "Hazth...? But the Basilisks were wiped out. And you... you were said to be one of the last surviving members... they said you died fourteen years ago."

Hazth rolled up his sleeves, stretching to break his stance. This young shifter knew nothing, yet she was old enough to be alive during the war fifteen years ago. She survived, so Hazth presumed her resilience and deemed her clan apt enough to avoid capture. He would tell her just enough information to keep her at bay. "You're right. I was one of the last ones. At least as far as anyone else knows, I'm considered dead. But, that much does not concern you." He eyed her cigarettes. "May I?"

She held out her pack. Hazth retrieved a Marlborough while Lizzy studied his movements, deciphering his intent. He struck the cigarette upon a claw, sparking a perfect light. For this missing-in-action shifter to be interested in Ian made no sense to her. And frankly, she didn't like the way this looked. She was sure nothing good was to come of this—she was not about to let any of her new friends become the object of this suspicious man's plan. So Lizzy decided to play friendly and find out as must as she could.

"I must say," Hazth continued, "it does bring me happiness to know that shifters are still alive and well."

"Those damn merchants lost their supply from the war, remember? I'm sure they're just waiting for the remainder of us to reproduce so they can do as they please. The demand for shifters is still large."

"Hmm. Wise of you to think that far in advance. The merchants are greedy after all, and their branches are growing. They're even recruiting everyday people to be their source of intel."

"They're doing what? How do you...?"

"Exactly how do you think we came this close to finding the child with the red eyes? We had no idea of its age nor gender, nor where to begin looking. Your friend was sold out. Has his own profile within M.E.S."

Lizzy clinched her fists. "M.E.S. is so inhumane as to sell out a kid?!" The look that she portrayed bore pure vengeance. "And you. You used MES yourself for info *knowing* what they did to our people?!"

"Relax, girl. MES is not my issue anymore. I realized that the shifters deserved what became of them. To be so weak for mere humans to gain the advantage and abuse our entire biology, abilities, our entire race," he laughed at the absurdity of the situation. "Shifters used to be a noble race. Hidden amongst the humans in secrecy, evolving our race into a true apex creature. But you let yourselves get weak and discovered by far too many."

"Enough! How could you say that when your entire family was captured and sold by them too? How come you aren't fighting with us?"

"I will leave the fighting to naïve ones such as yourself. M.E.S. has the technology to locate, capture, and tame something as strong as our lineage. It would be wise to lay low and save your strength for when you actually have a strategy. Besides, I have another goal to accomplish."

"Like?" Upon studying his characteristics, namely his auric field, she noticed that it was not purely shifter, but contained something else. He was something different, changed. This wasn't good.

Perhaps he would tell of Lizzy's whereabouts and… no, he seemed as if he would not support MES, despite the words he spoke defiling their race. This man was definitely up to no good either way.

"That's enough, Hazth," a voice boomed from behind her. Before she had enough time to jump away, someone had her wrist firmly within their grip. Her Marlborough's clacked to the ground. Liz turned around to meet another strange man. He was secretive enough to not be detected by Lizzy's senses.

"Let go of me!" she demanded.

He did just that.

Rubbing at her wrist, she asked, "Who are you? You with Hazth?"

The entity seared into her eyes, strict and menacing. Every bit of her will was used to maintain focus. *This man… this man is something entirely different, ominous.* She swore that she felt something familiar once more. Then it hit. "You're… " she staggered away, "You're a lord. A demon lord!"

"Hm, not bad. You are smart enough to know when to back away."

Lord Baal swung his scepter in wide arcs, whistling impatiently. "Well, Hazth? Was that man's information correct?"

"Yes, Lord Baal. I definitely saw the boy. And the energy he emits is exactly the way you described it to be," responded the shifter, putting out the cigarette butt and flicking it into the distance. She was sure of it now—somehow they successfully gave this shifter demonic prowess. That would explain the abnormality of his aura. "He's having a birthday celebration."

"I suppose it would be rude of us to barge in on his special day. Mind introducing me to your new friend?" asked Baal in reference to Lizzy, who stood nervously between the two. There was no way she stood a chance of surviving if they decided to engage her.

"She's a shifter who has had her sights on someone within the boy's friend group. Don't worry, she's not a threat in the slightest. I'm sure as long as she doesn't get in the way of our plans, we would not ruin hers."

"Fine. Your soft spot for your fellow creatures perplexes me. Let us get going." Baal directed his eyes onto Lizzy's. "If, by any chance, you decide to intervene in any way possible, do not think that I will hesitate in the slightest to make you regret it. I am sure M.E.S. would love to welcome you into their trade." And right before her eyes, they vanished into a dark shroud, leaving a murky, blue flame to engulf their perimeter.

Lizzy had inadvertently involved herself in a situation bigger than she expected. She could leave, leave and choose someone else to bear the task of bolstering their clan while she had the chance. But she was stubborn. Stephanie exemplified every treasured characteristic, the perfect candidate; she had the physiology to complete the change, and her genes were resilient enough to withstand it. From all the weeks of observation prior to enrolling in Willard High, Lizzy knew Stephanie to be someone who was worthy of the change, and someone to benefit greatly from it.

Lizzy collected herself and began to head back to the party. She had to protect her investment and warn Ian of this threat as best as she could. For a demon to be after him, a lord at that, she knew that this business of theirs was something she would not wish upon anyone, even if only just meeting them.

Ian's family bickered over whose gift Ian was to open next. He chortled, swearing he chose without bias, "Okay, okay. Everyone settle down. None of you were chosen." Instead, Stephanie's gift was in the midst of being rummaged through—Ian dug around the bag for the card. Tearing the envelope apart, he met eyes with Steph, making sure he had his friend's permission. Lizzy made it back inside, unnoticed, joining up with the others.

Ian read aloud: "'To someone on their special day, make your days worthwhile and things will be okay,'" he flipped it open, continuing. The rest was hand written. "'Dear Ian,'" he paused looking up at Stephanie again, who urged him on, "'You're eighteen now; I can imagine how scary that could be. But hey, you can buy cigarettes and go to strip clubs, that's about it'—Stephanie, really!" he laughed. "'You can also finally go to jail for breaking laws—you'll probably be there in about a week or so'—thanks, Steph. 'But I know you'll do just fine. You are brilliant and unique. Your will to make the world better is what makes you beautiful and simply irreplaceable. You will do just fine, don't let your age scare you, love. You will always be the same person no matter what. Love, Stephanie and Lizzy.' Aw, thanks guys! I'll be sure to hang the card in my jail cell after my strip club rampage while smoking an entire pack." Everyone hooted in good spirits.

Ian revealed a leather jacket from the bag, one that he had his eyes on for a while. "Oh my god! How'd you know?!"

"As if you didn't talk about it a hundred times," Stephanie remarked.

"Thanks so much, both of you!"

Spencer's gift was next. He retrieved the item from its bag. It was a necklace, handmade with a crystal dangling betwixt an assortment of shells. Attached was a note that he read silently:

'This is rainbow quartz, also known as aurora quartz. I absolutely hate to see you bothered by your past, although I don't know much about it myself, it doesn't matter. Every single one of us is here to stay. I want you to know you are loved. Which is why I got you aurora quartz. Its energies are supposed to resonate with the heart chakra so you can feel more confident with knowing that you're loved. And it's also rumored to bring out hidden abilities/talents; not so sure if you believe in this stuff, I don't, but it's worth a try. I really, truly love you, and hope to be with you now and in the future. Thanks for everything. Spence.'

Ian donned the necklace, dangling at his sternum adding a new glimmer to his presence. "Thanks, Spencer. I love it."

He perused the table of gifts, taking the time to read each card.

Lizzy felt fearful for Ian, keeping her eyes on the windows and doors. She could no longer feel their presence, but a certain air lingered that made her feel uneasy. If she could devise a way to keep an eye out for both he and Stephanie at once...

no, that wouldn't be possible. *If my brother could somehow... no, he would never agree, especially if he knew that a lord was involved.*

Lizzy's best bet was to forget about feeling scared for Ian and focus on Stephanie, the only task she was given. Lizzy could smell the sweet shea butter aroma of Stephanie's body wash, and the coconut oil used in her hair. Knowing this scent so well, even at great distances, she was sure that Stephanie was there. She felt relieved that she stood beside her, and that she could at least be able to protect her if anything were to occur. Yet Lizzy still felt the need to introduce herself slowly; forcing this friendship would only push Stephanie away, she knew this. Stephanie wasn't the type to take things for face value, cautious and observant.

Desmond bought Ian a new set of WadeTech head-phones, expensive at that. The other three friends chipped in on a gift card to one of Ian's favorite restaurants. All in all, Ian was happy with or without the gifts. He thanked everyone for coming out that Saturday night to spend it with him. The singing of happy birthday sounded like a new tune, marking its old memory with that of new meaning. After the tradition of cake and ice cream, guests began to take their leave, parting with the best of wishes for Ian—soon the house was empty, save for the core group of friends.

"Since the seven of you remain, it looks like I have my cleaning crew," Mrs. Frances sang. They groaned in unison with manners about them, commencing her request. They would finish shortly and were approaching a night's end until a knock came at the door.

Lizzy immediately grew on edge, almost answering the door herself—Mrs. Frances beat her to the punch. Lizzy relaxed as she heard the familiarity in their voices. "Come on in," said Jennifer, "I'm sure you'll be the best surprise yet."

A man entered; he was somewhere approaching his mid-forties, sporting a peacoat and scarf with a fatigued disposition.

Ian was too busy with his friends to notice the new presence. When the guest cleared his throat, Ian almost leapt out of his skin.

"No freaking way... no way. You—I—this can't be..." Ian thought he was done with tears for the night, yet another round threatened to spill. "Jonathan!" Ian embraced the man amiably, meeting each other at the same height.

"Is that you, Ian? You're almost taller than I am, my golly!" Ian was beyond glad to see his caretaker—this was the man who looked after Ian since the age of six following the tragedy of his second family. He finally got to see him on better terms.

Jonathan Fetcher stuck by Ian's side even when he didn't have reason to. He would check in on Ian throughout his second and third adoptions, each time wearing the same grin he wore now; when adopted by the Frances family, their bond grew distant. It was miraculous to see Ian this positive—the boy still had faith in others, noting the companions at his side.

Fetcher smiled widely; oh, how things have changed. The boy had truly grown—his looks... fey, impossibly striking. *It may be true after all,* Fetcher regrettably thought.

Before his adoption by Jennifer and Greg, Ian concluded that Jonathan Fetcher was perhaps the only person keeping him tethered to this plane. He was always there to reassure Ian of his place in life.

"I didn't think I'd ever see you again," Ian sniveled. "After that day, I almost didn't want to leave."

"Oh, don't worry yourself any. You were far more pleased to leave than to stick around an old man like me." A melodic female voice followed an ecstatic squeal from Jennifer at the threshold. Jonathan's eyes pulled Ian's line of sight in the direction of the excitement. "Ian, I'd like you to meet my beautiful wife, Alejandra."

"You must be Ian! I'm so glad to finally meet you!" Ian replicated her hug, overjoyed that his caretaker had started his own family. She was beautiful, youthful and bouncy with a length of dark hair twisted into a fishtail braid. Her accent was purely music—her words retained just enough Spanish to add to her overall splendor. She was so overjoyed, she embraced Ian with a second hug. "This is surreal. You are like a long-lost brother or something. Ah, you're just too handsome, look at you!"

Ian flushed, "It's nice to meet you. I didn't know Jonathan had it in him to marry someone as beautiful as you."

Jonathan chuckled, "Yeah, yeah. I may have a few grey strands, but I still got the game."

"This is so awesome!" Ian cooed at the infant in the carrier, "And who is this cute one?" He couldn't believe such a sight.

Jonathan carefully picked her up, bouncing gently. "This is Ramona. She turned one a couple weeks ago. Would you like to hold her?"

"Yes, yes please!" It was a novel experience in itself. He was holding a legend in the making, feeling as if she were his own flesh and blood, a little sister graced to have a father like Jonathan. "This is... wow. It seemed like just a year ago you were struggling with college courses, running around like a headless chicken."

"Bah, that was seven years ago, can you believe it? Her middle name is Ianna. I guess you can say you were the source of inspiration."

"Ianna..." Ian kept the name at the tip of his tongue. His friends were silent while discerning the group before them. So this was the one that looked after him in his youth, Stephanie and Spencer deduced. Ian was sparing when it came to detail about his past. And it was astonishing to see this in person, like they were a part of the history themselves. Spencer kept himself from choking up.

"We have some catching up to do, Ian. Shall we go for a walk?" Jonathan offered.

"Of course!" He passed Ramona off to her mother, hurriedly donning the jacket he received, Stephanie's gift. Rushing to get his boots on, he bid his friends a temporary goodbye and parted with Jonathan.

The brisk wintry air gave the trees their sway with remnants of last week's snow covering the ground in patches. Ian and Jonathan's boots crunched side by side in the pleasure of tonight's atmosphere. Ian was almost tempted to hold his hand out of past habit, now unable to take part in those simple pleasures that were never acknowledged. Everything about Jonathan was the same, yet age was starting to take its hold on a man who always was so youthful.

"I must say, this brings back a lot of memories. How do you like living here?" asked Jonathan, picking apart a pinecone.

"It's boring here, but I like its simplicity. I always find something to do."

"And your family? Do you enjoy living with them?"

"Absolutely! I couldn't ask for anything more. Jennifer is great—I guess I shouldn't be calling her by her first name—but yeah, she's such a patient mom, and super motherly. Greg, I mean, dad is good at dad jokes, that's about it."

"Wow, harsh," laughed Jonathan. "I'm glad everything's working out. I have some news you might enjoy."

"Hmm?"

"Alejandra and I bought a house uptown. You and I are only fifty minutes away," he beamed.

"Really?!" Ian punched Jonathan's arm, "Why do you keep surprising me like this? That's amazing! Does that mean I get to see you more?"

"Yes, it does. I just landed a job as associate for the upstate branch of CPS. Looks like those years of college paid off."

"Not only that, but your years of looking after kids like me gave you the experience to help kids everywhere now. Congratulations!" Jonathan was the biggest blessing he'd ever received. He was such a caring man—there for him in the darkest of hours. There truly were good people left on this earth.

"Well, you're a man now. So, I must ask, any love interests?"

Ian blushed, "Well, since you're married now, I guess my chances with you are out of the question. Ah man, I was such a kid back then, thinking you were going to be my husband one day."

"I'm surprised you still remember that. You had great tastes back then, but I think I was a bit out of your league," he laughed. "Well, do you have a significant other?"

"I do, actually. His name is Spencer—I forgot to introduce everyone to you, crap—but yeah, he and I have been dating for a steady three years. He's great."

"Let me guess, he was the one with the blonde hair standing awkwardly?"

"Yep! That's him down to a T. He's a local legend, a brain kid. Super smart and innovative."

"Seems like a good guy. You could learn a thing or two from him."

"Sure, whatever." The two laughed, both in good spirits. They walked in silence, enjoying each other's company for what seemed like hours. It was as if there wasn't a hiatus between the two. Jonathan went on to explain how he and Alejandra met, by Ian's request, and the bringing of Ramona into the world. Ian was super invested in his caretaker's life, which mostly sounded like it came from a storybook with all its cliché details. Jonathan was living a happy life.

After another moment of silence, Jonathan halted his gait. "Ian."

"What is it?" Ian replied.

It took Jonathan a minute to search for the words to speak. "I wanted to have a private talk with you because... shit, how do I say this?" he scratched his head. "I have some insight as to what happened that night." Ian stood, confused. "The night of your tenth birthday. But if I tell you, you have to promise me that it stays between the two of us. It is a confidential topic; others knowing may bring... complications."

"O-Okay..." Ian wasn't sure if he was prepared to recall those memories in a time like this after everyone tried so hard to brighten his mood.

Jonathan picked up on the vibes and asked, "May I see your phone for a second?" Ian complied. Jonathan proceeded to type, handing the device back. "I put in my cell number and address. I figure now isn't a good time to talk. Will Tuesday do? I'll come get you after you're done with classes and we can discuss it then." Ian looked away, nodding. "You okay?"

"Yeah. If anything, I'd like some closure. Having to wait until Tuesday is going to kill me."

Jonathan sighed, "Let's get back to the house. My hands are going numb. I hope you saved me some cake."

The night carried on the same way it had, yet it held a new mystery to it. Ian's mind could not slow down from all the possibilities it threw his way. And Lizzy's was no different, pondering the many ways the future could unfold.

The truck's rebellious brakes screeched to a halt in front of Stephanie's house. Lizzy walked with Stephanie to the front door, the nippy night bringing them close together.

"Thanks for helping out today. And being there to calm me down. Sheesh, I was a mess."

"Hey, no problem," Lizzy smirked. "I'm glad I got to meet everyone. Now I actually know people. Yay for friends! I really enjoyed chilling with you."

Stephanie couldn't help but adorn a coy smile. "It's getting late. I should get inside before I have an earful."

"Goodnight. See ya Monday."

"Night. Drive safe."

Lizzy steered her rust bucket towards home, doing her routine checks in making sure she wasn't followed, proceeding down the overgrown gravel driveway. The woods around her country farmhouse provided security, secluding her family should anyone come sticking their nose where it shouldn't belong. Once more, the old truck ground its wheels to a halt, its door protested when shut.

She unlocked the front door, taking a moment to sniff its air to validate that it housed its usual crowd. Once comforted by confirmation, she removed her coat and breathed a sigh. Before she could notify the others of her presence, two little ones came bounding down the stairs, racing to Lizzy.

"Whoa, you guys! I'm happy you're *that* enthused to see me," Lizzy stumbled as the two collided into her.

The taller one spoke, "How did it go? Will we be getting another sister soon?" The two stood excitedly waiting for the news. The taller one was female, years younger than Lizzy—twelve to be exact, still in her adolescence and impatient as ever.

Lizzy smiled, roughing her hair. "Gil, Mellori, would you two settle down? And Mel, I told you, she's not going to be your sister just yet. This is an important mission the elders gave me."

"Noctua, when will we get to meet her?" the smaller one, a ten-year-old, whined.

Lizzy picked him up, "How many times do I have to tell you, Gilvus? You have to call me Lizzy while we live here." She lifted him over her head, his endless bouts of giggles filling the house's silence. "Where's Gularis, Mellori?" she asked the female fledgling.

"He's upstairs being boring as usual. He kicked us out of his room. Man, he can be a real drag sometimes," Mellori responded.

"He is always writing in that dumb book," Gil complained with kiddish scorn.

Liz began to make her way upstairs, the two still following her curiously. "Don't you two have something better to do? Where are the little ones?"

"They were training with Nana all day. I think they're sleep," responded Mellori. "Thanks for ditching us today. Gularis never stopped lecturing us the whole time."

"Well, you are home schooled. What do you expect?" Liz teased.

Mellori pouted. "How come you get to go to an actual school? It's not fair!"

Lizzy sighed, resting her forehead on her hand. "I keep telling you both, it's too dangerous. You two don't have your shifting under control. One sneeze and you turn into a bird."

"I do not!" Mellori protested. "That only happened when I was little. Besides, I'm much stronger and I can control myself! I'm almost of age now."

"Yeah, yeah. Regardless, it doesn't change the danger of the situation no matter how strong you are. Isn't that right, Gil?" The small boy nodded, happy to respond to his older sister whom he looked up to. "Why don't you both go watch some TV? I'll be back to spend some time with you nerds."

The two raced off only to fight over possession of the remote as Lizzy joined Gularis in his room, flopping exhausted onto his bed. She sighed forcefully.

"What's got you worked up" said the older male, stopping his writing to look up. "I warned you that teenage girls were a lot to deal with."

Lizzy shook her head, dismissing his comment, saying, "I think we have ourselves a slight problem..."

Gularis defensively slammed the journal shut, shooting up from his chair. "What is it?" he demanded. "Is it MES?"

He's worked up already. "No, no. We are in the clear. It's okay, Gularis. You can calm down."

Gularis returned to his chair. "Then what is it? Everything at the school alright?"

"Everything's going well. I met her friends—they're a great bunch." He gave her a look to continue. "Remember that kid I told you about? One of Stephanie's friends?"

"The one with the red eyes or the nerd kid?"

"Ian. The kid with the eyes." He nodded. "It turns out that just as I am looking after Stephanie, Ian has unwarranted watchers of his own."

"Noctua, would you stop being so vague and get to the point already?"

"Fine. I bumped into another shifter and a demon lord today."

Gularis stood once more into action, preparing to defend his family. Yet he demanded to hear more. "A demon lord?! Here?!"

"Look, all I know is that they are after Ian for some strange, unknown reason. I talked to them and—"

"You *talked* to a demon lord? Noctua, are you insane?! Do you know how demons operate? If you even seem of interest, they *will* find you; they will do anything to get you. They're ruthless. Greedy. Oh Nyte..." Again, Gularis began to stress, lecturing Lizzy on things she was well aware of.

"Gularis, calm down. Let me finish. As I said, they're not after us. If they were, then they wouldn't let me off so easily. But that's not even the strangest part. Remember the Basilisk clan?"

Gularis nodded, adding, "Yes. They all died out."

"Wrong. I met one—I met Hazth."

"Impossible. He's dead, we have records of their deaths."

"No, he didn't die, he just became that demon's bitch. He smelled different. His blood was definitely tainted by a demon's."

"We must tell Nana. She has to alert—" just as Gularis was set into action, Lizzy blocked his path.

"No. No one can know, Gularis. The lord threatened that if I were to get involved then... then he'd blackmail us. But he didn't mind me carrying out my mission. I'm fine. I just can't get in the way of his or warn Ian of their presence."

"I knew this was a bad idea. You're going to have to find someone else."

"But I'm almost there! Stephanie is unique in that she—"

Gularis' voice boomed in lecture; yelling was only resorted to when he was backed into corners or fearful of consequences that may result. "Noctua! I will not sit by while this demon is here and have our family endangered again, you hear me? You are the one who is going to lead when Nana can no longer. What will we do if something happened to you, huh? Starting tomorrow, you have to find someone else to earn the bloodline. We are not getting close to a lord like this."

Angered, Lizzy yelled, "Do you understand how long I've had to wait to even talk to Stephanie? I just enrolled in this school. I'm not letting all that damn paperwork go to waste."

"You are transferring."

"Like hell I am! Stephanie is promising! She's smart and the nicest goddamn person—"

"We don't need 'nice' to join our clan. We need strength and the wittiness to guide our family into another goddamn decade, Noctua. We're not getting involved. I won't allow it."

Lizzy pounded the desk. "I was the one selected to do this job, not you. I will do it however I fucking please. I'm not as irresponsible to lead us to danger. I found the one, the only person who can do the job! I am the eldest daughter, I will decide whatever I please."

"Nonsense. I bet you've grown so comfortable feeling loved and accepted by those humans that you don't want to leave. You've caught feelings, I can tell," Gularis quipped.

Lizzy had every urge to hurl his desk straight at his head, to shut him up and declare herself as a force not to be underestimated. Instead, she breathed deeply and continued at a more civilized tone. "I'm going to continue this. You have to learn to trust me."

Gularis only stared for a moment, and then looked back to his writing. "Fine. But don't even get close to that boy." He sighed, rubbing his temples. "Noctua. Don't let what happened to mom and dad happen to them," he said in reference to their younger siblings.

"I won't. I'll die before I even let them get close to mine." Lizzy disappeared back down the staircase, preparing to make her leave for the night. Quickly, she slopped peanut butter and jelly onto slices of bread, finishing the sandwich in a matter of seconds, and then washed down a bottle of water. Standing at the back door, she stripped off her clothing, opening the door as silently as possible to not wake the others.

"Where are you off to, young lady?" a voice interrupted from the living room. An older woman sat in the midst of Mellori and Gil, both fading in and out of sleep. Although upon hearing their sister prepare to leave, they were now wide awake.

"You're leaving again?" asked a sleepy-eyed Gil, upset at the fact that his youth prevented him for doing what he assumed to be the exciting things in life.

"You know, duty calls and whatnot," Lizzy scratched her head.

Yet her grandmother returned a sharp gaze, demanding a talk. Lizzy sighed, wrapping up in a blanket before stepping outside. Her grandmother soon met her there, closing the door. She stood, although short, with authority that any younger shifter would not dare to argue. Still strictly looking into Lizzy's eyes, she started, "What's got Gularis worked up?"

"It's nothing, Nana. Please don't worry about it." Yet her grandmother demanded an answer, continuing to pour her authority into Lizzy's eyes. Lizzy sat on a patio chair and explained the situation, from start to finish, in much more detail than she gave Gularis. As much as Lizzy wanted to avoid spilling this information to Nana, she knew her grandmother would ultimately be the one who stirred the tides of her clan's whereabouts. Every decision was enforced by Nana, one of the elders of their ever-shrinking clan. And if her grandmother perished, it would be all up to Noctua.

Nana was approaching an age where her looks began to show the first signs of aging. Nana was just now approaching her second century. An elder who bore many children in her lifetime. However, after many offspring, only her grandchildren remained. She bore the pain of enduring through each of her children's deaths, so one could see why her authority over the younger ones was so prevalent.

Nana took a seat adjacent, and began with, "The Basilisks were close to our clan when I was growing up." She looked down towards the deck. "I grew up with Hazth's grandfather, Rufio. Hazth was born around the same time that your mother had Gularis. Whenever those two would visit one another," she smiled, enveloped in the memory, "they would fight tooth and nail one minute, and the next they would act like they were the best of friends. When Rufio was taken at the start of the war, his wife and children set out to get him back, against my protests. In their leave, I watched over his grandsons, Hazth and Hollock. Hollock was only seven years old then..."

Lizzy vaguely remembered the memory in which Nana spoke of. Fifteen years ago was when this war started. The war on shifters and the Merchants of the Exotic Species, engaged underground, beneath the eyes of everyday people, but legendary to the informed upper-class men and women who reap the benefits to this day. Lizzy was five at the time, old enough to remember every detail, every hushed conversation the adults tried to shield from their children's ears. She remembered every town they moved to, jumping house to house in order to protect the species.

"Hazth was always a strange one. It started as soon as everyone left in search of his grandfather. He kept to himself. Wasn't the best hunter, so he'd spent days starving, often giving Hollock most of what he found. I tried to help as best as I could.

"He was always quiet, and whenever he did speak, it was when he self-inflicted pain, cursing at his own body for being so weak. He was eighteen back then, and bullheaded at that. When it was evident that his family wasn't returning, I offered on countless occasions for the both of them to move in with us. But he refused each time. It came to a point where I could no longer look after the boys, you all were my priority. At that time, I received news almost every week that one of my children had fallen."

Lizzy listened to her grandmother intently, forgotten details of her memories now resurfaced—playing shifting games with Hollock, racing him through the woods; the strangeness of Hazth, his withdrawn temperament. She longed for those simpler times in abundant innocence, and now that she connected the dots, she was sure that Gularis remembered everything with clarity. Lizzy's and Gularis' twelve-year age gap proved to be the difference between their personalities, why he's so protective and she's so ambitious.

Nana continued, her tone grave and compelling, "We had to move away at that point. Every clan around, in the cities, the forests, on the beaches, everyone started to dissipate at an alarming rate. Ever since, I regretted leaving those boys behind. I thought they'd starve to death or get captured. I paid one last visit on the day that we left, only..." she swallowed, converting the frightening memory into words, "only to find evidence of a huge struggle. Blood everywhere, claw marks covering all the walls and floors, the entire place was unrecognizable. It was a fresh scene, probably happened only hours before I arrived. The scents... they were mixed with the boys and something entirely not human. I followed the scent trails as best as I could, but Hazth's wasn't apparent outside of the house."

"You said Hollock was only seven then. What happened to him?"

"I don't know, I couldn't detect a trail. I can only assume he perished."

Lizzy stood, gazing towards the fallow fields of the back-yard encapsulated by palisades of pines. "In other words, he still may be out there, too."

Nana shook her head, "The boy was only a child. He could not survive on his own. Noctua, you are positive that you met Hazth today?"

She nodded. "As much as that sounds fabricated, I was sure that it was him. I can remember what he smelled like vaguely from memory. But Nana, he seemed so careless; he acted as if he never felt affection for neither his clan nor his species. I don't even think he recognized me."

Nana pondered on a thought for a minute or two before speaking. "MES has quelled its poaching enough; we need to make ourselves blend as residents of this town. Noctua, I trust your judgment. You are as stubborn as your father." Nana smiled, coaxing her granddaughter's hair. "Get that truck of yours fixed up too; all that screeching gives me migraines."

Lizzy stood, preparing to make her leave once again. She smiled largely and shed her blanket. She was given her grandmother's wholehearted trust; by the way Nana spoke of action, Lizzy knew that her grandmother had met a sort of resolve. Nana rested her faith within Noctua.

In one swift motion, Noctua harnessed an energy which engulfed her body's entirety, shifting her form into that of an owl, soon disappearing into the night.

Nana watched Noctua soar off towards the reaches of the city. The elder softly smiled to herself—she knew now that things were going to change for the better, and Noctua housed that very hope.

6

DISCIPLES

A fit of laughter from a group of boys following a long trip to the floor was all Spencer needed that afternoon. He slid his glasses up the bridge of his nose just in time to watch Michael and his friends walk away, high-fiving one another on their success.

Spencer only sighed and picked himself up. A teacher who witnessed the situation looked away when making eye contact. *Do something, you coward,* he told himself. He couldn't. All he did was make it to class in a timely manner and hoped it didn't happen again. That's all he ever did. And with Mr. Willis gone, there went Spencer's hope for an easy day. The teacher left busy work in his wake, administered by some student teacher, who walked by every so often to check on the advanced placement class's progress.

Spencer placed a stack of completed work on the sub's desk. "First one, look at that," remarked the teacher, proceeding to read the student's name from the paper. "Spencer Holland. Hm, good job." Spencer's face bore only malaise and his abhorrence to being there. "Does your teacher let you all have a break at any moment? This work is horrendous."

"I'm afraid not, Mr. uh..." Spencer looked to the board for the substitute's name, "Mr. Abbitt."

"Please, call me Liam. Keep it copacetic. I'm only a few years older than you all."

"So, you're a college student then?"

"Yes. Drowning in debt with these false pretenses of success that these corporations known as 'universities' sell to you. But yes, teacher in training." Mr. Abbitt wasn't as generic as Spencer thought him to be. Quite amusing, actually. "Tell me something, Spencer."

"Yes?"

"Is this really what they have you doing in school now? Just mindless worksheets?" Mr. Abbitt looked deeply concerned, amused at the differences in generations, even if only a few years older.

"If I said yes, how surprised would you be? Alongside reading tasteless classics, writing literary analyses, and answering disgustingly pretentious prompts, I'd say what you see is not far from every day here."

"Have a seat, Spencer," Mr. Abbitt patted the seat beside him, "I have a lot of ranting to do." Spencer smiled and did so.

Liam went on to show the dissertation, all thirty-four pages and counting that he had to write for his master's degree, and proceeded to rant about college, answering every question Spencer asked about collegiate life. "Don't worry much about it. College is easier than this jail. Yet it still makes you want to pull your hair out."

The bell rang, dismissing the students from class, ushering them onto the next. Liam instructed each to leave their papers in a stack prior to leaving.

Spencer gathered his belongings, preparing to follow the flow of the others.

"Great conversation, Spencer. You have a head about you," remarked Mr. Abbitt just as Spencer took his leave.

It felt good that a teacher didn't throw him up front to be an example for the others. For once, he had a kinship with a teacher that had actual advice to offer, and talked to Spencer as an adult, not some unknowing kid. The fear of his future diminished with the talk—it was always relieving to meet adults who had differing advice to offer other than the repetitive warnings to stay in line. Liam made it clear that there were multiple paths to success and fulfilment than what others thought. Spencer smiled at the new insight he was given—a large percentage of his trepidation subsided.

Soon the school day was over. He prepared the computer lab for the start of today's tech club as well as the arrival of the unwanted member.

"Knock, knock," Ian entered the lab, closing its door behind him.

Spencer was caught off guard while placing papers at each computer. "Oh. It's you. Hey."

"Just thought I'd check in on you."

"You didn't take the bus home?"

Ian's demeanor was calmer than it usually was. He sat comfortably and replied to Spencer with adjusted character. "Nah," Ian took a seat. "Jonathan is picking me up."

"That's nice." Spencer sorted the rest of the papers. "It's super awesome that you get to see him more often."

Ian nodded, preoccupied by his phone—he stood to make his leave. "Will you be okay?"

Spencer affirmed, "I'll be just fine." He smirked, unsure of his own ability, especially with his inability to handle this morning's fall. "Have fun. Tell Jonathan I said hello."

"Will do." He gave Spencer a peck on the lips and parted, attendees filtering in soon after.

Principal Cane made his rounds on the bus ramp, taking account of the buses present, notifying the office to make the appropriate announcements of those absent, and finally giving signal for the buses to take their leave at three-fifteen on the dot. Back at his office, he organized the documents of the day, constantly checking his watch in order to make today's faculty meeting on time.

Paranoid. Cane was paranoid. His mind could not stay at rest knowing the act of treachery he committed a week ago.

He made a trip to his car to change into a more comfortable pair of shoes, removing his blazer. Locking his door and stepping his way toward, he was paralyzed upon gazing into those eyes, those damned red eyes! Cane could not tear his stare away from those flickers of crimson as they made their way into the passenger seat of an SUV; he nervously waved when caught in the line of sight.

As soon as Robert made it back inside, he nearly collapsed into the grave he dug for himself. He thought he'd find comfort in the reaches of his office, safe from his recent acts of treachery. Upon returning his heart rate to normalcy, it once again jumped at the knock on the office door.

"Come in," he answered.

The student teacher made his way to a chair within Cane's premises, settling comfortably. "You look as if you'd seen a ghost," commented Liam Abbitt, fiddling with the bobble head on Robert's desk.

Cane froze. He couldn't bring himself to talk.

Abbitt placed his feet upon the desk, raising an eyebrow in question. "We have to talk at some point, Robert."

"You're the teacher in place of Mr. Willis..."

"Yes. You *did* approve this, remember?"

Cane wasn't even sure he was breathing, his face sporting a stark pink. It was beginning. At this very moment. There was no turning around, even if he tried.

"I am taking it from here. As you are aware, my partner, Mr. Green and I were entrusted by O'Neil to investigate the case you have submitted. How convenient of you to have an opening for a teaching position." The casual tone, the overall atmosphere that Abbitt presented... this brought insecurity to Robert Cane.

Robert cleared his throat, pretending to busy himself by typing on his desktop. "I wasn't aware that you'd be here so soon." How did this come to place so suddenly beneath the radar? When Robert saw over the approval of the substitute, the abruptness of Willis' situation called for his quick replacement. M.E.S. never told him that they'd employ someone within his school. It was too intense for him to be outraged. Unless... "Was this staged?" Cane held his breath.

"It all depends on how you look at it, Robert," Abbitt smiled. "Now, I've been here all day and have yet to see the one you sent your inquiry about. O'Neil expects results in a month. So how will we make this possible, Robert?" Liam crossed his leg over the other.

It felt more like a command than a question. Cane loosened his necktie. "I s-suppose we could create an environment that allows for c-closer observation," he pulled up Ian's class schedule. "You teach his class tomorrow, everyday actually. He has your class for seventh block. Are you sure he wasn't present?"

"Don't you think I would have noticed him if he were?"

Robert shrunk away from his tone. "Right. Forgive me. I'm sure he must have been playing hooky."

"I don't know, Robert. It seems to me that you don't enforce rules heavily here." Liam stood, tinkering with items on Robert's bookcase. "Remember, you were the one who submitted this case. It would be wise to stay true to your side of the contract. Or I am sure M.E.S. will see that you are dealt with accordingly."

Cane was sure this man was not much older than thirty, and to have such a command about him was alarming. Abbitt took his leave; Cane sat in his wake until it was time to move for the faculty meeting.

"I think I'm gonna invent a device which allows for no bullshit. It'll be just a button. You press it when you want people to fuck off." Ian took a bite from his turkey club sandwich, casually telling Jonathan of his world-domineering plans for an easier state of living.

Jonathan frowned comically. "I guess by having that, there would be no more social interactions. Ever." They laughed. "Hm. I suppose I'd invent something that allowed for flight."

"Sorry to inform you, but airplanes are already a thing."

"Oh." Jonathan and Ian picked up right where they left off as far as their quality of conversation went those years ago. At present, they discussed preposterous ideas just to make light of their time. Truth was, Ian was nervous in waiting for Jonathan's spiel he mentioned Saturday. He wanted to get to the topic that instant; it was driving him nuts, bouncing his leg a thousand miles per hour. Many conversations passed before Jonathan was to approach the one of Ian's overall interest. It was as if it made Jonathan uncomfortable.

Jonathan took note in Ian's gradual loss of interest—the boy now fiddled with his utensils in his wake of anxiety. Fetcher began by removing a binder from his satchel. "This can become a bit graphic for you, Ian. You experienced trauma that night. Are you sure that you will be fine after this discussion?"

Ian was taken aback at the impromptu change in dialogue. He asked the same question to himself ever since Saturday, up late hours of the night pondering the answer he'd give Jonathan. He really wanted to know more than anything. The overall closure he'd receive would be worth it. That is, *if* he would receive closure. And Ian figured that time healed enough to give the imagery its numbness. Perhaps Ian's episode early Saturday was contradictory, however his curiosity and stubbornness craved the knowledge.

Ian nodded. "Yes. I'm sure."

Upon Ian's answer, Jonathan flipped the cover open to reveal a document, yellowed from age. The words NOTE OF ADOPTION headed the upper margin. "This is the note of your first adoption. Most of these fields were left blank due to the lack of information that the adoption home had at the time. It was located in Montana and sent to the one I worked at,

Goodman's Home for Children, when you arrived years later. They received you as an infant. You were not even a month old. You had no name, no clues as to who dropped you off. Just a blanket wrapped around you. You were roughly three months old when you were adopted. Do you remember your family back then?"

"Hardly. I remember how they looked, the house. My last name was Damery then."

"Right. The Damery's were the first to adopt you. They also named you. You stayed with them for four years. You were then placed in Goodman's Foster, in western Virginia."

"But why? What happened that made me go up for adoption again?"

Jonathan turned to the next page. It was more documentation, and the page adjacent was a compilation of images. "They just left." Ian swallowed, confident enough to continue. Jonathan went on, "The home was completely abandoned." He pointed to an article snippet, "It was a postman that discovered you a few days after the Damery's made their leave."

"They just left me?" Jonathan nodded. "That's so fucked up!" Ian slammed his hands on the table, causing a few customers alarm within the restaurant. He reinstated himself, looking to Jonathan apologetically. "I'm fine. You can continue."

Jonathan hesitantly turned the binder towards Ian, pointing out pictures of the Damery's with Ian in his early stages of life. "Is that me?" He stared at the pale infant, its red eyes staring back brightly. It was almost supernatural.

"Yes. I found these pictures back in Montana. At the police station in the town you lived in. I had to do *a lot* of digging to compile this binder."

"My eyes... were they always that..."

Jonathan flipped the page, revealing more papers. Ian skimmed over its information. "What do you remember about your second family?"

"I remember..." he cudgeled his memory, forcing whatever detail he could recount to the surface, "I remember they were *extremely* religious. They called me their 'angel of light?' We went to this small church with only a few members. Now that I think about it, that sounds very creepy." Ian looked to Jonathan for reassurance, but he found none. Only a look that supported Ian's last statement persisted. "I remember how much they cared for me. I mean, they gave me anything I asked for. I was fat back then, I think."

"Ian," Jonathan started, "This is where things may stop making sense, okay? I mean, things might sound horrific." Ian skimmed the papers once more, and Jonathan resumed. "Your

parents back then, Sarah and Richard Oakland, they were religious fanatics. I'm talking borderline insanity."

"How did they adopt me then? Weren't there any regula-
tions or background checks they had to submit?"

"Yes. They passed. They exhibited the qualities that it
took to adopt a child. No records or anything. However, they
attended this church called 'The Sanction of New Light,' known
for its overall bigotry and acceptance of over-the-top practices. They would boycott funerals for veterans and go as far
as to blame certain natural occurrences, like tornados or earth-
quakes, on the sinners around them. After events like such,
they would gather and perform rituals, like self-mutilation and
drug-induced sermons."

Ian shook his head in disbelief. "Wait. I remember the
strange services they had there. Every service, the pastor would
anoint my forehead with this liquid and say something weird.
Something like, 'transcend'... I... I don't think I understand,
Jonathan. I mean, I didn't get it then because I was, what, five or
six, I went along with my environment. But I don't understand
how this never occurred to me. The memories are very feint...
Why did this happened?" Ian's heart palpitated.

"This church was forced to disband several years ago. But
similar things have happened to others there. Look," Jonathan

handed Ian a small stack of photos and articles tucked away in a transparent plastic slip.

"'Local Church Attempts to Build Ship to Heaven,' 'The Sanction of New Light Protests Funeral of Governor,'" Ian read aloud, "'Prophet Rumored to be Inside 5 Year Old,'" Ian stopped abruptly at the article's description. A picture of Ian smiling cheekily at the camera between the Oaklands was wrapped by the article's text. "That's me..." He continued to read the article silently to himself. It explained of the second coming of an entity by the name of Zephulum, a figure that this church believed in. He was said to represent the being which assisted human souls in transcending to the heavens. And Ian was, in their eyes, the very being in which they worshipped.

Ian was the idol of a cult.

He covered his face, talking through his hands. "Please tell me this is a joke, Jonathan. Please."

"We can stop. I'm sorry. This was a bad idea." Jonathan took note at the redness in Ian's ears, gathering the snippets to be put away.

Ian had tears in his eyes. And Jonathan regretted his decision.

But Ian was laughing. In fact, Ian was laughing so hard, he fumbled for his next breath to engage in another fit of laughter. He struggled to respond to Jonathan through the pain of hilarity. "No, please." Insert another round of laughter. "Please continue." And another.

Jonathan shook his head, smiling. "I told you that things would get weird." He had to wait until Ian's laughter subsided to continue. "I think that this is a no-brainer as to why they lost custody of you."

"No shit! They were fucking maniacs!" Laughter threatened to make its next rounds. "Okay, okay. What happened after that?" he insisted. "To think I was a fucking god," he remarked under his breath.

"Interestingly enough, this was a factor in which they lost custody, but not the entire reason."

"You're not serious. You're telling me after all of this, they were still able to be parents?"

Jonathan paused. "Ian, they committed suicide." Ian tilted his head in question. "The Oaklands and the church's fifteen or so members all committed mass suicide inside that church."

"I only remember this huge party at the church. I was being raised and passed around. Everything after that is blank. Then I was back at Goodman's.

"Right, the police report states that they found you at the church, as a lone survivor. I met you that night. You were oblivious to everything."

"I knew something had happened. I remember seeing the foster home before, when I was four. I just don't remember everyone dying at that party. No one told me. I'm only finding out now that my parents... died."

Jonathan flipped to another page, and in its sleeve was a brown envelope. "Although most of the reports say it was mass suicide, I have my theories. I have a good friend who works for the FBI who owed me a favor—thank goodness for networking. Anyway, I asked if he could fish the coroner's reports of the members of The Sanction—memos, pictures, anything he could find. Since the case was closed, it didn't present a huge risk on his part in faxing me these items." He then pulled the envelope from its sleeve and began to unwrap its bindings. "Alright Ian, this will be pretty grotesque, okay?"

Ian gave Jonathan a firm nod, sure enough that he could handle whatever was going to transpire. Jonathan slid forth an image of a corpse, toe tag and all, during its examination at the morgue. Ian studied it closely; the man's body was covered in lacerations, various cuts along his chest. It had to be well over fifty wounds, making it look like a prop in a bad slasher film.

The most profound detail was the gaping wound on his chest, right above the heart. It looked as if someone forced their hand straight through the chest cavity.

Ian continued to flip through the stack, each corpse displaying the same number of cuts, and the exact fatal wound on the chest, both male and female. "If it was suicide, how could they mutilate themselves to this extreme?"

"The forensics team suspected a possible psychedelic may have been used to numb their pain. But here's the thing—upon testing each of their blood, nothing was detected. No narcotics, psychedelics, anything."

Ian went through each picture once more. "Correct me if I'm wrong, but it looks like their hearts are missing..."

Jonathan nodded grimly. He then slid Ian a different stack of pictures. "Here are the pictures of the Oaklands' autopsy." He kept his sight on Ian, keeping check of his expressions—he didn't seem too vexed about it.

"They look so different..." Ian flipped to the next picture. "No hearts. Did this case go to the FBI?"

"You would think it should have. But they closed it as soon as it made press and declared it suicide. No one really cared about a bunch of small-town religious nuts. However, one detective kept the case open and continued the research on it." Ian was handed a different set of images, more dated. "Something similar to this happened in Texas back in the eighties. Another religious group, but they were Baptists. As far as the reports go, their practices were no different than any other Baptist church. No obscene rituals or anything of the sort. Most were good people."

And Jonathan was right. It was the exact same scenario, same cuts, same chest wound. "What did this detective think?"

"Well, he suspected that it wasn't suicide. In fact, he thought it was the work of someone. Keep in mind that there was no evidence of trespassers on the premises during both of these cases. Their hearts were missing, completely. I mean, not even around the scene. He figured that the cuts and scrapes were a message of some sort. So, he sent it to a university to be deciphered and researched. They confirmed that it looked to be a form of writing, similar to cuneiform."

"Was it translated? Could anyone make meaning of it?"

"No university or organization the detective sent it to could make out a thing about it. The detective, Detective Melbourne, heard from my friend in the FBI that he and I shared a similar interest. We got in touch roughly four years ago; met for coffee at this diner in a small town in Mississippi."

Ian interjected, "Did you do all of this research for my sake?"

Fetcher sighed, "Yes. It just didn't make any sense to me that the adoption instances occurred as frequent as they did. My time caring for you was the highlight of my life—I couldn't live with the thought of you going through life without some sort of explanation. Someone owed it to you."

Ian had a thousand-yard stare focused on the other end of the city through the frosted window. All of this—the pictures, the documents—felt like it belonged elsewhere, not in Ian's life. Was he really this much of a mystery? He wouldn't even think to believe that something like this had any place in his past—he was content believing that he was an unwanted child with a birth defect.

It brought him great gratitude to know that Jonathan never gave up on him, despite their little time together. And to think he was doing so much behind the scenes was more than astounding in Ian's eyes.

"And now we move on to the Montgomery's. I don't have much to say about them, Ian. It's a struggle for me to even begin to explain." Jonathan looked pale, bothered by the folder he held in his hands. "No matter what, do not jump to conclusions, okay?"

Jonathan steadily passed Ian the folder. Ian stared at it, neglecting to open it at that instant, asking, "Tell me what happened first."

Fetcher rested his head upon his hand, struggling to find the words he wished to compile. "Okay." He sipped his now-cold coffee. "Ian..." he sighed, "a few days before their deaths, they witnessed strange happenings around the house. The police reports had detailed interviews with their relatives and their talks with the Montgomery's that mention their strange happenings. Sudden drafts, objects being misplaced, feelings of being watched." He held a thoughtful finger to his mouth. "They were becoming scared when things escalated. They were becoming uneasy... of you."

Ian held a steady look into Fetcher's, feeling the blood drain from his face. He pressed on. "They assumed that you were bringing these strange happenings. Ian, their relatives stated that they started to change, like, slowly shutting themselves off. They were bothered, sensitive to even the smallest things, agitated. Heather and Claude Montgomery stopped coming to work. None of their relatives could get in touch. I..." he paused, "Ian, something was in that house on that night. I do not know what or who, but it was something that avoided detection completely."

Ian sorted through the collection. There they were, in a picture-perfect moment of everything he remembered from that night, far from their original selves. Crime scene tape lined the room as officers stood to the side pondering the horrors that could have occurred. A hand flung opposite of the bodies, fingers strewn about.

Ian stopped at a picture of his ten-year-old self being led to a cop car, covered in the blood of the fallen. His hands began to shake. "Jonathan. I killed them, didn't I?"

"Do not speak that way, Ian. You did no such thing. Don't be so hard on yourself."

"Then what else? I-I can't remember anything prior to that moment on my birthday. Jonathan, I blanked out. What else could have happened?" Jonathan shook his head without answer. "Why? Why is my luck so shitty? You know something about me that I don't." Jonathan remained averting Ian's eyes. He took the pictures and papers, filing them away and closing the binder. "Jonathan. Why are my eyes the way they are? Who am I?" He proceeded to pack away the things in silence. "Tell me!" Ian yelled.

There it is. Those intense eyes that would spark in moments of forcefulness. "I don't know, Ian. I'm sorry. I just don't know." Ian fell silent, picking apart a napkin, trying his hardest to stop shaking. "Detective Melbourne is a good man who wanted to solve these cases, just as I wanted to find out for myself. And he told me of many, many more instances, just like the scenario of the Sanction. Some of these never made it to light. He knew of eleven instances total. It was unreal to the both of us. He suspected something—now understand that I thought it was absolutely ridiculous—but he suggested we turn our questions elsewhere. To the occult."

Ian was stunned. He waited those days in heavy anticipation hoping that everything would be explained, that every one of his worries could be put to rest, yet instead he only received more. Nothing was settled. Who was to say that at any given moment, that same unknown force could wreak its havoc into the lives of those around him? Ian shoveled his hands through his hair repeatedly, a frantic look upon his face.

"So where do we start?"

Jonathan noticed Ian's choice of wording. He wanted to include himself in the quest for information. "For now, you need to focus on your schoolwork."

"For Christ's sake, I don't even know how I got on this earth and you expect me to sit idly?"

"Yes. Until the summer, at least."

"Jonathan, please. I've waited years for this. I'm coming with you."

"No. You honestly think Mr. and Mrs. Frances will forgive me if something were to happen to you? And besides, I don't know what I'm getting myself into, and I would much rather be the one to deal with the consequences than to involve you. I am turning to the occult; that's something I know little to nothing about."

"That's why I am joining in on this. Jonathan, listen, you have a wife and a daughter now. You don't have to keep taking care of me, okay? You've done enough for me."

Jonathan paused in thought. He was so used to obsessing, day in and day out, over finding Ian's origins and maintaining his well-being. Ian was his little brother in a sense, the one whom he actually got to raise and be an influence to. And Jonathan knew that—the loss of his younger brother may have been the cause—his overbearing need to shelter this child was bordering excessive. He called Ian here with the intention of explaining everything he found; Jonathan fell short of that, once again wanting to shelter the boy. But in his caretaker's eyes, Ian seemed so small and innocent... would Jonathan be exposing him to things that could further escalate the situation into something worse, something more forbidden?

Jonathan threw his head back in defeat and cast a breath of forfeit. "Just don't let anyone know that I'm letting you do this, okay? Only because you're eighteen now. Man, I'm a wuss."

Ian bounced up and down excitedly, "When do we start? Can we start now?"

"Impatient as ever. We'll start next week. Now come on, let's go before you send me on another guilt trip," griped Jonathan.

Baal laughed manically after finishing his meal, smearing the red remnants across his mouth with satisfied lust. It had been weeks since they'd arrived, the season changing ever colder. And now Baal sat, arms spread and posted on a desk on the seventh floor of the city's tallest building. His smile was twisted with a dark charm, celebrating his proximity to victory.

"Yes. I sense it. It is he. We found him," presenting another euphoric laugh. The executive's body was strewn multiple places throughout the room, and Baal had just ingested the poor man's soul. "Who knew that making contracts with the company would have its benefits? An ignorant, sad little company."

Hazth stood guard beside the oak door, standing stoutly with barely a shift in the eyes. His Lordship was amongst a high in which bid his mind and body to succumb to pleasures unimaginable. Hazth studied the scene, avoiding eye contact unless spoken to. "It is as I've said; the organization only has archives of creatures that barely cover the spectrum of what's out there. They do not have feasible knowledge of a demon's existence."

Baal touched a glass to his lips, pondering the sentinel's words. His smile was great, something rare. "I suppose," he stood, "we should turn in the report. Hazth?"

"Yes, my lord. Right away."

"While you are out, check in with Travius. Something tells me he is sidetracked. As for me, I will continue my pursuit. I will leave you in charge of things around here. Complete the rest of our deal."

"Yes, my lord."

Baal wiped his mouth on the handkerchief ever so delicately before returning it back to his pocket.

Soon he was out, walking the block of the city with the harsh air hitting the face of his vessel, a very fine one at that. Convenient in its position, the vessel belonged to a man who did odd jobs for MES instead of taking the educational route for someone his age. He was a prime investigator for MES, his youth providing a great deterrence for risky missions. Kenneth Green was his name, and turning down a job was far from his repute as the money he received from the organization was gratuitous in pay off. His lifestyle was well paid for over and above. And as he sought to further his business, so too he sought to widen his pockets. See, Baal had access to these memory banks within the body of Kenneth. A smart guy who got away with his crimes in the name of MES was no match for a demon lord such as Baal. Lord Baal possessed the man only a few nights ago, caught in the middle of his loitering in the downstairs lobby of a local MES location, drunk out of his mind, in the company of gorgeous women. It took only a matter of seconds for Baal to claim his body when Green left out for a smoke. And so far it proved to be the best vessel yet. In doing so, Baal was granted access to exactly how the MES organizations operated across the nation. And his sentinel was right: the organization had extensive knowledge; however, they were missing a great portion as well.

Kenneth was on his way to his residency. Baal scoped the place thoroughly, making note of the people and personalities within the area. It wasn't hard for Baal to mock this prick.

Spencer didn't really know what he was getting into. He wanted to continue on pursuing the college of his dreams and go on to a school of tech. And the stars were aligned in his favor. Everything was in his grasp so long as he kept his mouth shut about himself. No one cared for a gay boy in this country or in this world of his. No one would come to accept him unless the Earth's largest miracle happened within his lifetime: acceptance. His parents never cared to know anything personal, except maybe how his grades were or his current standings towards receiving grants or scholarships. Perhaps maybe he was the only junior in his entire district that received three and counting. And the only one who blew the SAT out of the water. But he, in fact, felt alone. Sure, yes, Stephanie was about where his GPA was, maybe only 0.3 behind, but although she was pushed by an almost exact replica of his parents, she seemed to get the greater amount of slack when it came to expression. Spencer never dared to even show the slightest bit of interest outside of academics because that's not what the world cared about. He was so in tune with the flow of the scholastic world that he felt criticized for having even the slightest bit of interest for the more redundant things in life. He was so pent up inside of that 5'5" body and mind that he didn't know where else to turn but straight.

Truth was, it killed him. Every day he took the pill called stress and channeled it into his future, making his present, in a sense, nothing to cherish. People only used him outside of Stephanie and Ian. The parental figures saw him as the security to their futures. And God forbid he were to come out to his surroundings. Immediately, all of his endeavors, all of his accomplishments, would be neglected for one simple fact: he was gay.

So badly he wanted to do what the others did. He wanted to have a normal day out, loiter after school with friends, laugh and joke. But lately he never managed even a full-blown laugh. He kept himself in perfect line to a point where anything different would feel unnatural.

He wanted to breathe.

But no one was going to let him. Not even himself.

"Everyone make sure you have your webpages saved online. We will be presenting shortly. Remember, whoever presents the best webpage will have a chance in creating the website for senior prom this May." The class chattered excitedly; the challenge presented put them all in good spirits. He smirked, "Now don't get too competitive, guys. I'll pick probably two or three winners, that way it'll be a collaborative project. Perhaps Mr. Cane will let us all have a hand in the tech side of prom." The students began to pack their belongings in preparation for the meeting's end. "Oh, before you all leave, don't forget we need someone to do the announcements in the morning. And also, we need a volunteer to compile the slides for the cafeteria TVs. If you're interested, there's a signup sheet at the door."

Students began to trickle out by two's, chatting excitedly about the competition Spencer provided, and a handful signed off on the volunteer positions. Spencer stared after the crowd, and after the room bore no more of his attendees, he breathed a smile. It felt good to have students who accepted Spencer's teachings and were actually eager to apply such. Once more, he made his rounds, cleaning up, and closing the room for the day.

He found himself smiling as he walked down the halls. Other students sparsely walked the halls in the same direction after leaving their activities, all waiting at the front for their rides. "Yo, kiddo. How's your Nerd Herd coming along?"

"Same as always. How's your... whatever coming along?" he responded to Kiera.

"Man, I had to stay back for some bullshit. My Pre-Calc teach lost one of my quizzes and I had to make it up. Can you believe it? Why couldn't she throw an A on that bitch and call it a day? It was her fault anyway. Yo! Did you see that new cute substitute today? His ass is like the best thing to grace these halls."

Spencer was used to Kiera's rushed type of conversation, quickly shifting gears into the next subject of which he did, in fact, take note of. "Yes. His butt is very nice. He teaches my seventh block now. His smile and everything are perfect."

"Your seventh block? What happened to Willis?" she asked with a worried expression.

"Something about a car accident. He won't be back for a while, sadly. Mr. Abbitt will be here until Willis returns."

Kiera fiddled with her hair, "Well as long as that hot piece-of-ass sub is here, I don't miss that old head, Willis. Need a ride home?"

"Nah, my dad should be on his way."

"Oh, so it's dad week, huh? I know you look forward to that."

"Kiera, you know I hate going over my dad's house. Even if it's just for a couple of nights. But mom swears I need the 'male interaction.'" Spencer almost forgot about the impending drama of the split family he had to deal with. His dad was, well... every straight, white dad in this country. And he wasn't looking forward to being his designated driver tonight. It was unavoidable.

"I'm just saying. You are always welcome to come through if you don't wanna go. You know my mama love her some Spencer. She always asks about my little gay friend and how she wants you over more. Mainly because she thinks I need a tutor."

Spencer laughed, "Tell her that not even I can save your grades."

"Ha. Ha. Very funny. I'm gonna go before you end up in the hospital next to Willis," she chuckled. "See ya, nerd."

Spencer watched her hair bounce as she bounded to her car as if dodging the cold. Little by little, the hall began to clear of students, and his father grew ever-later in his arrival. Spencer called for the fifth time, once again met with his voicemail. He huffed himself onto the bench, tapping his foot impatiently. His dad used to be dependable until the divorce four years ago. Ever since the new job with this big-time sports magazine he took up, Mr. Holland lived his life carefree, wife-free, and kid-free, with the exception of days like today. He despised his father for giving up on his responsibilities. Timothy Holland made an effort to connect with his son, but after countless failed attempts at getting his son to become interested in the world of testosterone, all things sports, and as predicted, women, the disconnect between Timothy and Spencer widened the gap after every encounter.

Spencer could note that his dad at least put an effort forth when Natalie, Spencer's younger sister, came into the picture. Every fatherly instinct—if one could call it that—was involved when Natalie got remotely close to the 'forbidden': boys. Yes, even a pre-teen who had no concept of puberty quite yet was being guarded by the watchful eye of her father, who intercepted her juvenile male classmates with a glance and the clear of his throat.

Spencer shook his head; his father was every male stereotype in one, a man in his forties who still thought he could woo and court as if he were back at the old frat. His father was a child.

He couldn't help but to smile at how ridiculous his whole family situation was. His parents were separated, but it worked much better that way. His mother, Laura Georgian, still remained good friends with Timothy. It didn't provide an awkward air or anything. And Laura was back in the game herself, on the market, looking for a potential man to help her take care of her children. It was almost comical how the two went around as if they were Spencer's age. Laura was dating this businessman at the moment, Jake, who referred to Spencer as "Little Dude," as disturbing as that was. But he made mom happy, so Spencer would continue to roll his eyes for his mother's sake.

"So sorry I missed tech club today."

Spencer turned to the source of the voice and was frozen for a moment. "You didn't miss anything," he said softly, looking away from Michael's eyes.

Soon enough, the rambunctious voices rounded the corner, joining up with Michael, fresh from practice. "Hey, it's your friend, Mikey. What his name, Twinky or something?" Ivan said.

Sean jumped in with, "Ay, wassup, Twinky?" They laughed in unison.

"Could you all, like, not do this right now?" Spencer sighed.

"But Twinky, we wanted to see you!" Michael laughed. "Didn't see your boyfriend today. Did you wear his ass out last night or something?" Spencer stood to escape from the buffoonery but was surrounded and outmatched by the three. "Where you going, Twinky? Your ride's not here. Why don't you sit and talk for a while."

"Please get out of the way," Spencer stated, only met with more laughter. Spencer's mind raced for some plan of action, some sort of escape that these jerks couldn't follow. But there was no one around, and only a wall behind him. Today was the day that they'd have their way, and there was no one at his aid.

Michael pushed Spencer into the wall as the others crooned and hyped up their friend. "Fuck him up," they said. Michael pulled back his fist. Spencer could only close his eyes and flinch away, awaiting for the punch to make contact.

With the sound of scuffling and various protests, Spencer opened his eyes to all three on the floor collectively.

"You all have four seconds to leave this building," Liam commanded. They sat dumbfounded, collecting their belongings from the floor. "Three." They stumbled. "Two." And the three ran off without question before Liam could make it to one. "Assholes."

Spencer could only gawk and breathe heavily as the adrenaline made its course. "Are you alright, Spencer?"

He nodded; a hotness washed across his face.

"They will be suspended tomorrow. Don't worry. They have my third block class." Spencer could only look towards his feet. "Dumbasses only feel fear when they meet someone with more sense than they have. Do you need a ride home?" Spencer shook his head. "Okay. Let me know if anyone else gives you trouble." Abbitt walked into the main office across the hall.

Spencer couldn't get over how calmly Abbitt handled the situation. And how swiftly he dealt with three guys at his height and stature at once. He had this overwhelming authority about him, and on his first day at the job, he handled student conduct better than the tenured teachers, the ones who only watched Spencer's struggle just this morning.

Once again, Spencer was rescued from his own situation. And he hated himself for being so weak. His hands protested movement as he reached for his phone to answer his mother's call.

She spoke with a rushed voice accompanied by the pollution of background noises, "Hey, Spence. Your dad is working late today. I'm over in Petersburg, so I can't get you either. Can you get a ride to your dad's from one of your friends?" Spencer looked absently through the windows, silent. "Okay, love you. Bye."

He crammed his phone forcefully into his pocket, all but taking the door off of its hinges in anger as he made the nine mile walk towards his father's house.

He could depend on no one in his world. Self-hatred swelled within, intermingling with the sharp sting of unrelenting regret—reminders of the past tugged his psyche in all directions, an isotropic reminder of his repulsion of all things salacious. Forlorn footfalls fell infrequently along the pristine pavement before his father's fortress, glancing up through the twinkle of tears towards the starless sky. For the first time, he casted a single wish to the heavens in the hopes that something would hear his plea for power, freedom, and forgiveness. Promptly, pragmatism caught his folly as he sopped the salty specks into his sleeves and left his wishes at the threshold to be uptaken by a formidable figment.

Lizzy pulled into the yard, parking in the usual spot, yet this time, several vehicles were in the premise. Her grandmother welcomed her as she proceeded to lock the freshly painted truck, its doors no longer protesting, and its wheels properly lubed.

"Looks nice!" said Nana, resting her hand on the truck.

"Yeah, cost me an arm and a leg. What's going on here?"

"I made a few calls. They're surveying the house for the upcoming renovations. We were just going over a few details before we get started."

"Where are we getting all of this money from? You didn't rob a bank, did you?"

Nana laughed, "I have my ways, child. Once they see if everything is up to code, we'll virtually have a new house."

"Exactly how many renovations are being done?"

"No more plywood on the kitchen floor, no more space heaters, no more leaky rooves or leaky pipes, actual hot water. Ah, soon we'll be living the life." Nana read the concern on Lizzy's face. "I know, it's bizarre having this many strangers in our house."

"So, with all of this going on, where are we going to live meanwhile?"

"The kids and I have been moving our belongings to the basement. We will all live there for a month, three weeks at the least."

"Wow. Only three weeks?"

"Let's just say I have the money for the job."

"Yeah. Are you going to tell me how we have all this cash or what?"

She edged past Lizzy to lean on the back of the truck, swallowing a sip of water. The sun was glinting from Nana's forehead although the air was a chilling thirty-nine degrees. The woman worked nonstop, as usual for her. She shook her head, "I'll tell you after the renovations. But for now, how about you make some iced tea? Gularis should be removing furniture with the contractors."

Lizzy scratched her head, "Why must everyone be so complicated. I just need simple answers," she remarked before walking into the emptying house. Furniture was being walked out, most of which was already stored into the unit in the backyard. The ancient shag carpeting, matted down from years of abandonment, was in the process of being ripped up, revealing rot on its wood layer beneath. This renovation looked as if it would take longer than expected, yet as Nana mentioned, the amount of money she dished for this project was evident. Twenty or so men made up the team of contractors who ducked in and out of the house, taking another piece of it with them each time. Nana must have had this scheduled a great time beforehand; this was not some sudden decision made during last night's conversation.

Lizzy searched around for the dishes, most of which were packed and sealed. Exactly how much work did the seven of them accomplish today? She dismissed the thought; even if it was one of them, there would be a lot done compared to the average person. A house full of shifters? She was surprised that everything wasn't moved by now. With success finding a pitcher, she was relieved to see the pantry hadn't been packed.

The tea boiled as she watched the men enter and exit the house, finally realizing how bad this place looked. It was abandoned a year or so ago when they stumbled upon it, rot everywhere and critters of all sorts calling it home. They've lived in worse, so it became home quickly. They did their best to make it livable and presentable, but by looking at it now whilst the team tore into it, it looked like Lizzy and her family put not one ounce of effort into it.

So, we're finally calling this place home, Lizzy thought. *No more moving around, hopefully no more hiding.* Lost in these thoughts, the whistling of the kettle obviously didn't penetrate.

"We want iced tea, not burnt tea," Gularis interjected. "You're being a big help, lifting this stuff with your stare and all."

"Yeah, shut up," grunted Lizzy. She quickly removed the water from its flame, pouring its contents to a pitcher littered with tea bags. "I wanted it to burn you."

Gularis dusted his hands, leaning back against the counter, joining his sister at her workspace. "So, what do you think?"

"About?"

"This," he said with outstretched hands.

She poured an unhealthy amount of sugar in. "I think it's nice. The kids deserve to know that they can have a nicer state of living. All they know are shacks and the outdoors."

"Hm. Well, I wasn't expecting this. She told me about it when she scheduled this last month."

"Last month? How come I'm just now finding out about it?"

"It's called a 'surprise'. You should try acting amused for once. She wanted to surprise you since we've been working our asses off on the daily. I found out earlier, of course. Totally by accident. She thought we would like a more comfortable environment. To try and be normal for once." He was the first to pour a glass.

She scoffed at his actions. "I admit. I am surprised. I'm very surprised." Lizzy went on to pour Nana a glass, then herself. "You all did some serious packing since I've been gone."

"The kids did all of that. I went into town today. It was weird."

Lizzy continued listening while pouring glasses for the contractors. "How so?"

"You know how we try not to go out much? There were many humans and just plain rudeness overall."

She laughed, "Well, I'm required to deal with teenagers on the daily. I have to actually stoop to their level. It's gross."

"Yeah, well you try setting up a bank account. That was hell. The rates they charge are ridiculous."

"Why? You thinking about getting a job?"

"Sort of. Something to keep the bread on the table. We can't keep living from Nana's surplus."

"By the way, where did she get all of this money from? I'm curious."

"Something she's saved up throughout all these years. Probably before you and I were even thought of. Crazy, huh?"

"Yeah... I'm just so lost... I can't believe this is happening." She lowered her voice, "It's like we finally fit in, you know? It's weird."

Gularis laid a reassuring hand on Liz, "If anything, we deserve it. We deserve to be happy... with all that MES has done."

Thoughts of revenge sifted through Lizzy's mind; it was foolish for them to challenge the organization as their men were stationed anonymously throughout the country. Nowhere was safe. The Merchants of the Exotic Species recently got their start when Lizzy was just three years of age. Presumably, they existed well before that, beneath the radar, with a lack of technology needed to capture inhuman things. MES's lists included creatures that mankind was mostly ignorant of, as well as rare animals and other precious things of the sort, such as artifacts, jewels, or minerals. But the capture was only for the resale value. Older, more prosperous men would go to gentlemen's clubs or secluded societies, or perhaps even low-profile locations, such as Perk's. And with their social status, and most importantly, exorbitant amounts of money, they could virtually buy, let's say, a werewolf as a household servant. Or an elf as a sex slave. You name it, it will most likely exist as some sort of statistic.

These people, these humans, were insane, uncaring. And to be left alone, unheard of for generations—existing only as a myth for eons—creatures never thought to take humans this seriously until the last couple of decades. In the twenty-first century, they were myths to the everyday person. That is, until the humans found the taste for power.

"Remember, this whole investigation thing stays between you and I. Especially since I have information that I'm technically not allowed to have. And don't get those innocent friends of yours in this either," Jonathan parked in front of Ian's house.

"Relax, Jonathan. I got this. My lips are sealed. No mention of cults or murdered families. Got it."

Jonathan frowned, punching Ian in the shoulder, "I mean it."

"Ha ha, okay, okay! I got it," Ian grinned, saying his goodbyes as he made his way into the house.

Greg greeted Ian from the kitchen. "Well if it isn't Mr. MIA. Skipping class, are we?"

"Look, to be fair, I'm halfway done with The Crucible. I'm ahead in class. And I told you and mom that I'd be getting picked up from school."

Greg dried his hands on a towel and began to prepare ingredients for dinner. "I assumed he was getting you *after* school, not during. Anyway, how many heads am I feeding tonight? Will Spencer and/or Stephanie be here?"

Ian shook his head, "Nah, Spencer is over his dad's house tonight—it's dad week."

"And what about Stephanie? I don't see her as much as I used to."

Ian's phone began to ring. "Speak of the devil," he remarked before answering Stephanie's call. "Hello?" All he could hear was Stephanie yelling at her older brother Zeke, both going back and forth. Ian cringed, pulling the phone away.

"Oh, hey. Sorry about that," Stephanie laughed.

"Yeah, I'm not gonna ask. Wassup?"

There was more obnoxious shuffling going on in the background as Stephanie answered, "You want to go to Youth Revival with me? I don't want to suffer alone. Please say yes—Ow! Who puts a fuckin' safety pin on the floor! Zeke!"

"Sure, I'll go. What do I wear?"

"Button-up shirt, pair of jeans, nothing much—Zeke! Hurry up with the bathroom!—You are lucky you don't have a brother. I'm about to kill this ass-munch. Anyway, we'll pick you up in thirty, sound cool?"

"Yeah, that's cool." Ian waved to his father, running off to leave the house once more, leaving Greg questioning whether he had homework and what time he'd be back.

Stephanie said, "Ever get in touch with Spencer? I can't reach him. I think his phone is dead."

"I'll try calling. See ya."

Ian later returned downstairs in a salmon button-up, hair slicked back with gel. "Whoa, who are you and where do you think you're going?" asked Greg.

"It's your son, and I'm going to church."

"Church? Didn't think that was your thing, but I'm glad you are experimenting. You really like her, don't you?" Greg asked with a condescending tone, a common tactic of Ian's father to blare his son underneath the spotlight.

"What? No. You know we don't date."

"Yeah, yeah. It's only a matter of time. You marry best friends. You may not see it now, but I can definitely see you two having a future, possibly kids."

Ian rolled his eyes. "Do you mind? They're waiting for me outside." Greg stepped out of the way, still bearing a snarky grin on his face. "Word to the wise: girls like guys with jobs and cars. You better start stepping up in this world."

"Yeah, okay, I know, Greg. I told you I'm gonna start applying this week."

"Whatever. After you finish courting, dinner will be in the fridge. Have fun," he ended with a laugh. Ian detested how his father pretended that he didn't see Ian kiss Spencer the night of his party. There was an agenda Greg had in mind and Ian was not about to entertain it.

Ian sighed, smiling as he went over to the driver and passenger sides of the car to shake Mr. and Mrs. Carter's hands. They received him warmly, as always. Stephanie yelled at Zeke to move over as Ian took his place among them. "Hello, Zeke," Ian said, "It's been a while. How's college life?"

"Can't complain. It's our spring break. How is your life going? It's been, what, a year?"

"It has. It's going well, I guess. Still figuring things out day by day," responded Ian.

Stephanie, crammed in the middle, chimed in, "Did you hear about Mr. Willis?"

"No? Why, did he assign a project or something today?"

"He got in a really bad car accident. Won't be back until God knows when. I heard he's paralyzed, like, from the waist-down."

Ian squinted, cudgeling, "Wait, really?"

"Yep. Your class has a substitute now. And everyone is saying he looks like a model or actor or something like that. I have yet to see him. I wanted to call Spencer for the details, but he won't answer."

"It's nice to have you with us today, Ian. How are your parents doing?" Stephanie's mother, Jaqueline Carter, asked.

"They're great. Both are busy bodies."

"I hear you are eighteen now. Happy belated birthday." Mrs. Carter remarked, smiling brightly through the rear-view mirror at Ian. He had no choice but to smile back.

An hour into Youth and Stephanie was already about to keel over, dragging Ian outside with her to bum a cigarette. She took a long drag, "It's nice that you're finally eighteen. Now I don't have to bribe Ryan to get me some. He's such a dildo sometimes." In staggered syncopation, Ian took a drag from his. "Anyway, before I lose my patience with all of these Bible humpers, tell me! I've been dying to know the verdict—what did you find out?"

"Well, I'm supposed to keep it on the D.L. Jonathan says it's top-secret shit that could put his career in jeopardy."

"So now you're obligated to tell me. Spill."

Ian sucked in another lungful, "Basically it still isn't clear why I've been sifted through so many families. Two of which died around the time of my return to foster care, and one of which... who the hell knows where they went."

Stephanie's brows were marked with worry. She draped a comforting arm around Ian's shoulder. The boy didn't seem vexed about it at all, more excited than anything, really. He continued to spill every bean that Jonathan mentioned despite his warning, even detailing the documents, pictures, locations, and years. Stephanie's eyes brightened with the introduction of each odd fact; to her, it seemed like one big adventure. Upon Ian's conclusion, she stood up, animated as ever, and encroached on one of her spiels.

"We get to go to a psychic!" she blurted excitedly. "Or even better, we get one of those mediums who investigate murders."

"That's all Hollywood, Steph."

"Oh, stop being such a skeptic. You believed Jonathan when he said he's turning to the supernatural. And remember the reading Ryan's mom gave you freshman year?"

Ian turned his glance downward. "It's just that I don't want to believe it. When I think about it, it sounds completely insane. But Stephanie," he turned to her, eyes wide with optimism, "I feel like this could be it. I feel this close to having peace of mind. What if it turns out to be something... paranormal or evil? What then?"

Stephanie only laughed and shook her head. "I'm sure nothing evil wants to follow someone as sweet as you. I wouldn't worry about it. You got us—Spencer and I. Jasmine, Kiera, Dez, Liz, Ryan. Your mom and dad. Mr. Cane." Ian sucked his teeth and rolled his eyes. "Even if you don't get the peace of mind you desire, you still have us losers."

Ian gave her a disgusted look, "Way to make things unbearably cheesy," he mimicked gagging motions.

Stephanie dismissed his comment and smiled, "Whatever, someone has to be the optimist. Now," she stomped out the cigarette butt, "With another hour of Youth left, and a karaoke bar a block away, we must make the fatal decision: do we live or do we die?"

"Definitely live. Let's go," Ian led the way down the street towards the bar, where he'd spend his last ten dollars on a plate of honey barbeque wings and a lemon-lime soda.

Some guy with a terrible comb-over was singing "Livin' On a Prayer" as if he accidentally swallowed a fork along with his meal before setting foot on stage. The bar of fifteen or so people cheered him on, although they could all agree their ears were on the verge of tears. Stephanie continued to flip through the songbook until she recognized an artist, contemplated if the song was in her range, then flipped past and repeated said process.

"Would you just pick a song already?"

"I will if you sing with me."

Ian shoved another wing in his mouth, licking the residue from his fingers. "I told you I hate singing in public. You'd have to get a few drinks in me first." Ian fixed his gaze towards the bar whilst sipping from his glass.

"Look, it'll be a quick song. Just you and me. Let's make this school night count for something." Ian cleaned the meat from the bone, distracted. "Are you even listening to me?"

"Yep."

"What are you looking at?" She turned in hopes of finding what was so thrilling. "You know good and well that we are way too underage for drinks."

Ian's stare was met by the fellow who caught it; the stranger smirked in response with the nod of his head. Ian quickly looked away, catching a blush welling to the surface. "Yeah. Way too underage. You're right," in every sense of the word.

Stephanie looked back once more. "What are you looking at?"

"Nothing," said he, twirling his straw around in his mouth. *I could have sworn I saw that...*

Ian repositioned himself upright in his chair and slid the binder from beneath Stephanie's hands. "Do you mind? What's the point of looking through songs if you're not going to sing?"

Ian looked up once more towards the bar hiding behind the binder. Back towards the guy. He *swore* he saw a glimmer of red within his eyes. But now it wasn't there. Ian squinted ever harder, trying his best to catch this spectacle, even if it was imagined. The guy looking at his phone must have noticed, meeting Ian's glance again. The stranger attempted to play off the awkwardness by smiling and looking back to his phone.

"Ian, are you even listening to me? God, you suck at paying attention."

"Huh? What?"

Stephanie shook her head, "I asked if you heard from Spencer yet?"

"No. I mean, it's not unusual. He never really answers his phone when it's dad week," Ian hid himself behind his menu, hoping to catch this rare phenomenon he was convinced he saw.

"What... are you doing?" Stephanie looked back over her shoulder once more, following the trail Ian and the stranger made with their eyes. "Who's that?"

"I don't know, but I swear... I swear his eyes were like mine for a split second."

"Like yours? You mean red?" she asked elatedly. Ian nodded. Stephanie continued to stare directly at him.

"Don't make it so obvious!" Ian kicked her beneath the table.

"I bet you are creeping him out, Ian. Ix-ne on the ar-ing-ste. Besides, we gotta get back before my parentals find out we are gone." Stephanie placed a tip on the table. "Since you don't wanna sing with poor wittle ol' me, we better blow this popsicle stand." Stephanie nearly fell backward into the stranger when getting up from her chair. "Oh. Excuse me," she apologized.

The stranger smiled cheekily. "I'm sorry. I should watch where I'm going. Heh." Stephanie couldn't help but be reminded of Ian.

She looked to the both of them before saying, "Sorry about him, Ian likes to stare random strangers down for no reason," she elbowed him to snap out of his stupor.

"O-Oh, sorry. I tend to zone out from time to time," said Ian. He was completely diverted towards this guy.

The stranger rested his arms on their table, "I'm sorry, but I couldn't help but realize that you go to WHS," the man said, pointing to Ian's hoodie. The two were silent waiting for some sort of context. "A college buddy of mine recently started work there." They continued to stare, not sure what to say. "I dropped out of GHS years ago. Yeah, school wasn't really my forte."

This guy was quite a man, and Ian's lewd imagination saw to that. Filled out in all the right places, beyond toned, and with a V-neck tee that showed off every detail of his pectorals and biceps. Ian choked on his words, "Y-Yeah, Willard is pretty okay. Our principal is a dick-munch, but I've yet to get suspended, so I think you've fared pretty well. I-I'm Ian, by the way." Ian outstretched his hand.

"Kenneth," he received. "I'm new to the area."

"And that's Stephanie," she shook Kenneth's hand as well. "Now you know two people. Welcome to Willard." Stephanie blinked at how friendly Ian was in these type of situations—always quick to make a stranger feel like family. That big heart of Ian's made it hard for Stephanie to believe he's had any sort of difficult past. God only knew how much stuff he was repressing. "GHS, huh? I've only been there for a career fair my freshman year. Why'd you drop out, if you don't mind me asking?"

Kenneth hesitated for a moment; Ian could see how shy this was making him. Kenneth laughed confidently, "It's actually pretty dumb. One reason was because I got caught with vodka in my water bottle, nothing heinous, got suspended. I was not the brightest back then, really."

"Just in time. Maybe you could get this one drunk so he can stop being so damn stubborn and sing with me," accused Stephanie.

"Have you both lived here your whole life?" asked Kenneth.

"I have," Stephanie responded. "Willard is a shithole. You're from Georgetown, right? That's only a city over. I can imagine it's just as boring. And it's not like we can go to a bar when we feel like it. The curse of being underage."

"I guess I have it easy since I don't look my age. I'm twenty-five. Be twenty-six in two months, more or less," he gulped his beer. Ian could not make himself get over how attractive this guy was. Everything from his lax, murky eyes to his muscular frame, to his deathly-attractive face; Ian was having trouble looking away. And Ian's body responded positively—he slid his chair closer to the table, making sure he was the only one who knew what was going through his mind.

"School is overrated. Learning useless facts and figures that don't necessarily apply to life in general. It's not really my thing, y'know? I dropped out, got my GED, went on with life. You guys look smart though," Kenneth directed his glance towards Ian, "I could learn a few things, I suppose. Like, actually studying perhaps."

"We were just about to go. I hate to leave after just meeting you. But hey, you should take my number," Ian took his phone from his pocket. Two missed calls from Spencer. "In case you get lost around town."

"Thanks, bro." The two exchanged numbers, and they all bid each other farewell. The whole walk back to the church left Ian in a frenzy of thoughts. He was sure that Stephanie noticed his silence, as empathic as she was. Hell, she probably already connected the dots, giving Ian a well-informed side-glance, hinting at the way Kenneth smiled at Ian. Ian dismissed her comments, yet found his new friend to be outwardly alluring, a dark temptation. They walked briskly, too caught up with returning before her parents found out she left the premises.

Later, Stephanie tossed and turned in her bed, her mind not willing to settle down just yet. Finally, she settled, facing her balcony window. She stared at the owl who claimed her balcony nightly for the second month in a row, like clockwork. Its soft hoots always guaranteed her slumber, yet tonight she couldn't bring herself to drift to sleep. Stephanie made her way to her balcony doors and watched the owl.

"You are lucky," she spoke, a hand pressed to the window. "You get to be free, not worry about the future, a career." The owl only blinked at her, its deep golden eyes fixated on Stephanie's. "And to top it off, you don't understand what I'm saying. Nice." She mocked the owl by hooting, entertainment that was soon to be short-lived as the owl spread its massive wingspan and panned the houses across the street, soon to vanish.

Stephanie stepped out onto the balcony in only a t-shirt and panties; the chilly air was sure to let everyone know that winter had a few more weeks of staying. Yet, the cherry trees were starting to blossom, and the bees were slowly making their return. Stephanie received an earful earlier that night after returning Ian home. And of course her parents needed to critique every little thing that was in their daughter's life.

"I just think that he doesn't know what to do with his life. You need to surround yourself with friends that will have a future, that won't bring you down," were her mother's words to her. She was a dark-skinned woman with hair in Havana twists. She was fifty-two but didn't look a day older than thirty. Stephanie was always told that she received her beauty from her mother and her wit from her father. Her dad reflected the same—sixty; however, his graying beard was evident that he was, in fact, getting up there in age. Out of all her friends, her parents were the eldest, and the most critical. They correlated everything within Stephanie's present to influence her future, and right now Spencer was the only one who remained in their good graces.

"Don't get me wrong, Ian is a nice kid. I just don't think his priorities are in order. You are too nice to him, you do everything for him. Soon, he'll take advantage of that. That's what young boys do,

they want a girl to replace their mothers," said her mother, echoing in memory. And her father was no different. He cosigned everything her mother said, and added, *"I see you and Spencer trying your hardest and Ian is just along for the ride."*

"So what do you want me to do? Just stop being his friend because of what you think might happen? Ian's done nothing wrong." Her tone took on a defensive edge, but she wouldn't dare raise her voice beyond that. They would continue to dish out criticisms, and then explain the root of Ian's shortcomings as if they wrote his autobiography.

Her dad continued, *"The kid is damaged already. I've known people who have had lives almost exactly like that. Most of them are homeless and on drugs now. Jennifer and Greg can only do so much to salvage him. Everything else that goes on in his life is the result of past parenting."* Stephanie clenched her jaw. She hated how her parents thought themselves to be the final say for everything, as if they held the world's truths. But that was just it—they were older, wiser than many of the younger parents her peers had. Her father was the preacher of their church, Destiny Baptist, and Stephanie was far from the stereotype of the preacher's daughter. No one fancied her and recognized her only as the daughter of the church's leader; she just kind of existed. Every Sunday, she was dragged along to both services, each lasting two or more hours. And each time she made sure to carry earbuds and a sketchbook to draw the fanciful anthropomorphic beings that danced in and out of her imagination. If it was anyone who couldn't stand her father's preaching, it was her. He'd talk about never giving up on following Jesus, about helping and supporting one's neighbors, and then, on nights like tonight, tell his daughter that no one will ever have her back besides family.

It just didn't make any sense. She hated religion and its rigidity—she embraced the enigma, the paranormal, the supernatural, and other forces that may be at play and cringed at the idea of a supreme deity who sees you when you're sleeping, knows when you're awake, and for some reason, knows when you do something as petty as damning someone based on religious apathy. Stephanie liked to think in possibilities, all backed up by experimental proof and logic for the sake of remaining curious, maintaining her lust for life's mystery. Being told what and when to believe made no sense to her, especially if she didn't feel like she was gaining anything out of it.

Stephanie attempted sleep once more, but that didn't stop her brain. It should not be a thing for her to feel fearful to introduce her friends to her parents. Fear of impending judgement from her parents, and their end-all discussions, it just made a burden to even bring friends over, why she favored going to others' houses to avoid the awkwardness. She wanted to further her friendship with Lizzy more, especially since the two of them clicked almost instantly. But she knew the instant they saw Liz, they would automatically make inferences of her sexuality, and in turn, question Stephanie about hers.

Stephanie was coming to terms with how she felt about Lizzy—she actually liked her and wouldn't be afraid to do something *more* with their friendship. Dare she say it, she had a crush, and it deepened upon each encounter.

How must it be to touch another girl? Her lips must be soft, she thought, *and her skin must feel like velvet.* Stephanie ran her fingers across her nipples while her imagination ran free. They hardened after each pass, and the more she thought about Lizzy's features, the more her hands went rampant, navigating her body until she reached the elastic of her panties. Already there, she massaged herself until the pleasure succumbed, until finally the sleepiness settled in.

The owl watched silently until Stephanie was sound asleep, and then took flight to soar above the pines towards the old farmhouse.

7

ENTRANCE

Stephanie woke groggy at dawn, sluggishly engaging in her morning ritual. After showering, she applied a moderate amount of makeup. Searching for something to wear, her phone began to buzz from its position on the nightstand. It was odd to get a phone call this early in the morning. Probably Ian missing the bus again, or Ryan attempting to be nice so he could gain a *favor*.

She prepared to give the best greeting her said grogginess could manage. Upon seeing the name flash on the screen, a smile extended across her lips. "Hey, Lizzy!" she beamed.

"Good morning, Steph. How are you?" Lizzy asked.

"I'm great. Just getting ready to get to school and all. Same ol' routine."

"I was wondering if you'd like to ride with me today, perhaps grab a coffee or something before class?" Lizzy suggested, sounding as if this wasn't going to follow through. Stephanie was, admittedly, a bit quiet before answering. "I mean, you don't have to if you don't want to. I just thought..."

"I would love to! I know this great coffee place down the street—they have everything, and the best cheese danishes known to man. I go there at least once a week. And they're super cheap too!"

Lizzy gave a breathy laugh—the girl was rubbing off on her. Stephanie's bright and bubbly ways, the very hopefulness and optimism she spouted was the light of Lizzy's day, and also the thorn in her side. She stopped her thoughts before adding, "Well I'm like three blocks away from your house, so..."

"Wait! I gotta ask my mom first. Hold on." Stephanie threw down the phone and raced downstairs to where her mother was preparing her lunch for the day.

"It is too early in the morning to be running like that, child. You got your stuff together? We gotta leave like now or else I'm gonna be stuck in that tunnel traffic," her mom addressed.

She swallowed, knowing the storm of questions that awaited. "My friend Lizzy was going to pick me up this morning. Is it okay if I ride with her?"

"Who is Lizzy? I never heard you mention no Lizzy."

"She was the one that helped me plan the party."

Her mom continued to do whatever she did, and the list of questions proceeded. Stephanie rolled her eyes. It was as if this was rehearsed. "How come I've never heard you talk about her? A girl? You always hang out with them other two boys."

"Yeah, okay, yes, a girl. Listen, she's a block away. I need an answer on whether or not I can."

"Hold on, hold on. Does this Lizzy make good grades? Is she white or black?"

"I don't see how this is relevant, but she is white. And yes, she's an honors student," Stephanie presumed.

"Mmm. Well, I guess. But let me meet her before you go," her mother ended.

Stephanie sighed. As critical as her mom was, she was going to see how rusty Lizzy's truck was and make inferences on her income level. Or she'll glue some stereotypes together and instantly know Lizzy's sapphic nature—flannel, a truck, and short hair? In her mother's book, that was a surefire indicator. Stephanie groaned loudly, throwing her bag over her shoulder.

Lizzy stepped out of her truck the moment Mrs. Carter was making her exit. Behind her, Stephanie emerged, keeping as much of her smile at bay. "Good morning," Lizzy said to her mother. Stephanie noted the black gloss plaint that slicked

Lizzy's truck. Even the busted taillight was fixed. Stephanie was impressed.

Mrs. Carter responded with a smile, "Good morning. You must be Lilly."

"It's Lizzy," she smiled, "It's a pleasure to meet you, Mrs. Carter."

"Likewise. You two have fun at school. I have to get through this traffic. Stephanie, call me when you get there," rushed as always, her mom shot her a stern look before she pulled out of the driveway.

Stephanie and Lizzy looked at one another.

"Yeeeaaah, sorry about her. She's really protective over me. Never really lets me breath."

"No worries. I like your mom," said Lizzy. "Nana is the same way. I'm used to it."

Lizzy turned into the lot with Stephanie's direction, arriving at Ako's Café. "This place looks chic and hipster. A little too hipster. I feel naked."

"Look, the coffee is good, trust me. And yes, there are a lot of hipsters and cringe-worthy quotes. But hey, all in the name of aesthetic, right?" Stephanie laughed.

"Sure. Whatever you say." Lizzy ordered for the both of them with enough time before class to sit and enjoy the morning. "I was wondering..." Lizzy started. Stephanie looked up from her cup. "We could do this every morning. It would cut your mom a break and well, we can both get to school on time."

"But gas money... don't you have to travel a bit to get to my place?" Stephanie asked.

"It's not far at all. You can also ride home with me, if you'd like. No pressure. Only if you want to."

"I would love to. That seems like a great idea," Stephanie felt the butterflies in her stomach, quickly drinking more coffee in hopes they'd all go away. Lizzy was so... so beautiful and otherworldly. The way she seemed so indifferent about things, and the slight rasp in her voice; the way she pinched the Marlborough from the shabby pack, placing it between pale-pink pursed lips.

They both shared a smoke outside of Ako's, enjoying the crisp chill in the air. Lizzy listened to all of Stephanie's excited chatter side-by-side as the soot seeped into their threads. A maternal touch caressed the shifter's heart, the gaia within pulsing and tugging the two towards each other. Noctua knew she needed to have Stephanie changed soon, but she couldn't help but to indulge in the intimacy. Gularis' words echoed on an endless loop, yet Lizzy could not equate her kindness as weakness—the girl's perpetual giggles drowned out her mind's chatter and, in its place, left a vision of verdant pastures, soft winds carrying a silent whisper of promise.

So this is the one, huh? Abbitt checked his roster and looked up towards the class. Everyone was present and accounted for including the one he pursued. *Unbelievable... I would think there would be more to this child.* "Ian Frances?"

"Here," Ian responded to the rollcall. The rumors were right—Abbitt was the best face to ever have come to Willard High.

"Alright," Abbitt engaged. "Today's lesson involves the use of logical fallacies and where they are most commonly found. Can anyone tell me what a logical fallacy is?" Liam looked around the class at every face, each one dead and uninterested. Today's youth was problematic. Inattentive. Teaching this class was more cumbersome than getting his grasp on the target. Ian of all the students looked to be the most removed, lazy. That simply would not do. "Anyone?"

A student in the back raised her hand. "Isn't it, like, one of those things that the media uses? You know, to, like, leave out information or something?"

It was almost painful for Hazth to respond to this cretin. "Yes and no." *I see why Baal assigned me to this job instead of Travius,* he ruminated. If anything, Hazth was patient. "It is when a person attempts to reason but fails to do so. In a sense, it's a conversational scapegoat." The class was asleep for the most part. Hazth frowned—sixty percent of the class stared down at their cellphones; the other forty percent talked amongst each other. Hazth only observed, amused at how pitiful the scene was. It made his job all the simpler. When his Lordship assigned Hazth his duties for their time on the surface, the shifter thought it to be a Sisyphean task. Months of deliberation and tracking were minimized to merely weeks thanks to that damned organization, and the target sat before Hazth, drumming his fingers upon the desk. *For a being that was prophesied,* Hazth thought, *this kid is not much of anything. No motivation. No skill. No fighting instinct. Baal will have a job before him,* he chuckled deeply to himself.

Hazth carefully eyed Ian, who looked up in time to catch the substitute's eyes. "Ian."

"Yes? Sir?"

"Would you agree that your fellow classmates are unruly?"

Ian looked side to side, unsure of the question. "I guess?"

"Does it stem from boredom, educational apathy, or are they simply not motivated?"

Ian shrugged, "I guess all of the above."

"Fantastic." Abbitt stood, "Everyone stand up, stand up," he urged with the waving of hands. The class begrudgingly obliged, unsure of what the substitute had in mind. He was curious as to what he could meld these minds into, how far he could take them. Yes, they could serve some use in this scheme. "Head to the baseball field. We are going to do an activity."

They voiced their incompliance: "But it's like forty degrees out there." "I'm going to ruin my shoes!" "This is English class!" Yet Hazth remained persistent.

The class stood circled around the field, confused, and for the most part, discontent with this whole arrangement their once-adored substitute had pieced together.

Liam took center field, spread his arms dramatically, and bellowed loudly, "Freedom: is it what we earn, or what we embrace by default?" He looked a student in the eye. "You." The kid shuffled on her feet nervously. "What does that mean to you?"

"Uh, what does this have to do with our English lesson?" the class laughed in agreement, whining to go back inside.

"Everything. You see, the reason why literature exists, why these stories travel so far, is because it begs the questions that many of us, as humans, ask. Those questions never beget an answer—usually the author offers their own interpretation. And that's what makes a story." Abbitt eyed her dangerously, a look that made anyone uncomfortable. "So I ask you again, what does freedom mean to you?"

"It means that this is stupid and pointless," she sneered.

With more hoots of support, laugher, and cheering, Abbitt roared, "Silence!" as if commanding a militia. Everyone was shocked at how such a man with a charming character could turn from a good-looking god, to a foreboding leader, and the students now complied without argument. "What does it *mean?*" he asked strictly.

She swallowed, voicing her answer coyly, shrinking away from the pedestal she once stood upon. "To me? I guess we embrace it by default. That's what makes us individuals."

"Hmmm," Abbitt pondered, "Acceptable. You, boy. And your proposed meaning?"

The seventeen-year-old just laughed with his friends, "It means that this is gay. I mean, answering these cliché questions about life and philosophy won't get me a good paying job."

"Humanity is such an odd and feeble race," Abbitt responded, as if no word the boy said had meaning. Liam began to pace the inner circle of students. "And their freedom has been a concept determined by other humans. Enslaved by one another, slaughtered by one another. Yet have successfully escaped from the food chain." The class felt the impounding heavy air evoked by Mr. Abbitt's performance. Everyone fell silent to watch and listen, contemplating his words as if this was their first real experience of being taught.

"You dream, you play, you eat, and you sleep. You laugh, you love, you cry, do you not? You each have your own system of values—and I guarantee you'll find similarities as well as differences in those values. Your classmates standing on either side of you will perhaps forget your existence one day. They may even remember this very moment." Mr. Abbitt pointed around the circle, naming the students. "Garret—red hair, freckles, makes sure he never misplaces his belongings. Marcia—neat, talented, but also mistrusting. Daniel—indifferent about his studies, on the football team." They looked to one another, confused. "I can tell each of your stories by small samples of information I collect by looks alone," he said while catching Ian's eyes in a deadlock.

"So, starting today, we are dropping the lesson plan. This public school systemizes its youth in trying to shove the stories of others into your brain, but not enough in encouraging you all to create your own realities, your own novels. In this bag are pieces of papers with roles written on each. You are not to show your neighbor. You are not to tell your friends. From this point on until the end of the semester, you will become this role so long as you step foot in my class."

He made his rounds. The students frowned, laughed, a whole spectrum of reactions from their written role. Ian was next to reach in the bag. As he dug, he concentrated on the scrap that felt the best between his fingertips and craned his hand to read it.

He looked up to Mr. Abbitt and was met with that same, domineering gaze in which Ian could not decide whether to lust after or to respect.

Puppet

When the students emptied the room at the end of the day, Ian approached Mr. Abbitt for clarity of this supposed role. "Mr. Abbitt? Yeah, I don't get it. What does 'puppet' even mean? What, do I act like Pinocchio the whole time? Can I switch?"

"The purpose of this exercise is to see if people can exceed the rules they were given. If you are a dog, do your learn tricks or do you lead a pack?"

Ian clashed against the brazen instructor; it was hard not to back down from this overwhelming authority that Mr. Abbitt seemed to bear. Yet when the teacher smiled, it seemed as if he were the friendliest adult in the vicinity. "You're still not making any sense."

Mr. Abbitt towered about Ian casting his gaze downward on the boy. "You are a puppet. You are being controlled by others around you, yet are you aware of this? Some of your classmates were given roles of authority, but it's all in how they choose to be sentient of such. People will surprise you."

"So basically, I just let the other fucktard classmates of mine tell me what to do?"

"Yes."

"And I can't stop them?"

"Absolutely correct."

"That's bullshit."

"It is."

"They can't tell me what to do for the rest of the year."

"Correct."

Ian paused. "You confuse the fuck out of me, Liam."

Mr. Abbitt was tickled by this boy, and as a result, Hazth grew curious. Ian wasn't afraid to speak forwardly and he was not shy when it came to asking questions. But overall, he was weak-minded. The teacher laughed and sat on the edge of his desk. "I have faith you will figure it out. You will see once we get started. Until then, you have the assignment I gave you all that's due tomorrow: two paragraphs on what your character will be and what you expect out of this."

"It's not as hard as it sounds," said Spencer, rounding the entrance.

"Spence!" Ian was elated to see the beloved blonde enter yet was slammed with instant regret of his negligence; he had forgotten to respond to Spencer's texts last night.

He hugged his boyfriend anyway, hoping he could convey his apology with a single embrace. Spencer blushed almost purple, breaking the hug short. "We should catch the bus before we miss it again. I suspect he's giving you trouble, Mr. Abbitt?" Spencer smiled.

"Oh, not at all. I trust you'll explain the assignment from here? Ian is, well, a bit lost."

"Of course!" Spencer yipped and continued with, "I actually wanted to thank you... for yesterday," he blushed once more.

"Thank me? For what?" played Abbitt innocently.

"For... the," Spencer was caught in Ian's line of sight for a little too long, and God forbid Ian was involved in this situation again. It didn't matter if Ian was clued in at this point. The beef was over—Spencer's aggressors were expelled and dealt with, thanks to Mr. Abbitt. Spencer could not begin to express how thankful he was towards the man, yet he knew that Abbitt understood such and needed no vocal acknowledgment. It was over, finally. Spencer merely smiled largely, a smile foreign to him in the last couple of months—that bubbliness that was, by definition, Spencer Holland was restored to its full potential. "I'll see you tomorrow."

"Who are you?" asked Ian when the two secured their seat on the bus.

"I'm your boyfriend. Y'know, Spencer?" he sat closer than ever to Ian, squeezing his hand tightly.

"I mean, *this*," Ian said pointedly. "You are being, how do I say, gay. You are finally being gay."

Spencer tittered, "What? I'm overwhelmingly delighted to be with you. Is that wrong?"

"N-No, I'm just shocked. Does this mean—wait, don't tell me you came out! You were supposed to let me help you with that."

"I didn't come out, Ian," Spencer rolled his eyes, "at least not at home. But I want to be out at school. Is that okay?" Ian didn't know what went on in the last few hours with Spencer, but this happiness of his was lost upon him.

Ian stared long and hard into Spencer, "Are you on drugs? I happen to remember a certain someone telling me not too long ago that your citywide repute was at stake and all the stares that you hated," Ian mocked. "I was always okay with it, Spence. Hell, it would be fuckin' healthier than keeping all your crap in like I've always told you. The question is, are you ready, and are you sure you're ready? Because I believe you should think this over before—"

Spencer openly pressed his lips into Ian's for the first time. When pulling away, Spencer bit his lip teasingly.

Ian stood in the aisle of the moving bus and bellowed elatedly, "Spencer Holland is my boyfriend!" before taking Spencer in his arms to make the kiss more public than ever. And they were met with more support than they thought possible.

***

"In my honest opinion, I don't think it's up for debate. Carnivore is a much better band than Grinn. Their vocals are better, and all Grinn does is use power chords."

"Hey, there is nothing wrong with power chords, alright? If used correctly, they make great music, which Grinn *obviously* is."

"You mean *obviously* isn't. C'mon, Grinn *totally* stole their sound from FireSquad—you can't copy their exact sound and try to call it your own."

"Bullshit," smiled Ian. "Look, Grinn is their own thing. They copied *no one.* If you want to talk about stolen sound, Carnivore ripped their entire 2008 album from—"

"Say no more. They stole from no one. Carnivore is the best. End of story," Kenneth said, dusting the crumbs from his hands after downing three chalupas from Taco Gong. Ian looked at him with playful disgust. "I was starting to think we were bonding, too."

"Ah, shut up!" Ian laughed, "We both know this conversation is getting nowhere." He stood to toss his trash in the nearest bin, "You ready?"

"Always," responded Kenneth with the taunting smirk he regularly adorned. Ian stared a bit too long at the smile and its wearer. He ogled at just about every detail on his new friend's form. And each time his eyes would wander places they shouldn't, sending the same response to his groin he experienced upon their first meeting. Both he and Kenneth started this routine roughly a week ago of hanging around odd places, toking off a spliff, and heading in at odd hours of the night. It was a drastic change from what he was used to, and Ian was creating his new habit ever since he bumped into Kenneth at the 8-Twelve last week. Not being high in years—one can say around the time he and Spencer started dating—made him forget how much he missed it, and how much he longed for other male company.

They walked on the sidewalk comfortably silent beside one another, Kenneth whistling every now and again. The two were similar in their attractive, spectral looks—sharp jaw lines, piercing eyes, down to the silk line of their lips. And the looks they received along the way made the public think they were in the presence of luminaries—these weren't common features of Willard natives. They continued to talk at some new spot that Kenneth led Ian towards, both undoubtedly in an altered state. It was a large property, multiple factory buildings decorating the small plots of land in between manmade lakes, pipelines in neat rows intercepting in lattices.

"What the hell is this place?" Ian asked, weaving his fingers in the chain-link fence.

"Come on," Kenneth's lips taunted with the same leering grin. By the time Ian registered his words, Kenneth was over the six-foot fence urging for Ian to follow.

Ian looked at the NO TRESPASSING sign and then back to Kenneth. "You're crazy. Have you read the sign? This is private property of the city! What is this place, even?"

"It's a municipal water supply. Where do you think your tap water comes from, the ocean?"

"Yeah, okay. But bro, no trespassing—I'm assuming that means nothing to you?"

"Nothing at all," Kenneth breathed, walking deeper into the facility, hands in pockets.

"Hey, wait!" After managing to climb the fence, sporting a new hole in his gifted leather jacket, he caught up to Kenneth, sitting by the edge of the manufactured lake. "How do you find all these places?"

"I walk a lot. Explore. Fences are for animals." He handed a cigarette pack towards Ian all the while staring off into the horizon. For the moment, Ian's focus lingered on Kenneth's hand more than the object within—*how is this guy so relaxed, so cool?* It only perpetuated the whole dropout complex in Kenneth's favor, and to Ian, it came off as pretty badass. The company Ian held on any day was far from the man he was sitting beside. It may have been the first time he adapted so quickly outside of his usual crowd, and the first time he'd done something this risky since middle school. Now he faced greater consequences as he hatched into adulthood, but he was confident in their ability to escape authority if such a case were to happen.

It was almost freeing the way Ian complied against the law so effortlessly. He stomped out the cigarette butt and rolled another spliff, exuding the edgy nature he only fantasized about. He wasn't used to his company being so quiet—Kenneth could strike a conversation, and then would become engrossed in the ambience, holding still, watching, listening. For what, Ian didn't know. But Kenneth held his focus on the horizon, then stared cuttingly at Ian, who blabbed about nonsensical topics. Ironically enough, Kenneth seemed deeply interested, picking Ian's mind for hours at a time. It was nearing midnight, and the two were just beginning their night.

"So why did you *really* drop out," asked Ian.

"It didn't excite me anymore. I didn't want to go to school, so I stopped going," Kenneth chanted. "The vodka incident was just a piece of it all. After that, I moved to Wyoming with my father, worked odd jobs and made change here and there. And then I went on to bigger and better things, found a better job. It requires me to travel frequently, so my ass went back to Virginia, and here I am. There isn't much to say about me." And he ended it on a note that Ian was sure Kenneth didn't want to have brought back up.

"Ah man. Dude, that sounds cool. I'm not much of a fan for moving around." A text notification from Ian's father slid across his lockscreen—he was well-past his curfew. "Anyway, I should get going," he stood; Kenneth followed suit.

The ride back resulted in another musical debate as Kenneth blared Carnivore at full volume to Ian's disapproval, yelling his stubborn opinion above the metal. Kenneth detoured to the service station to fill his Crossfire.

Sitting in the coupe gave the Ian the notion that Kenneth was noticeably affluent. Maybe not a millionaire, but extremely well-off for someone who dropped out of school. *Someone has to be spoiling him,* Ian thought. There was no way he could afford a car like this, and the way Kenneth dressed, suave and pressed, blatantly conflicted with Ian's alternative aesthetic. Out of curiosity, Ian quickly sorted through Kenneth's glove compartment—just what type of guy was he? The vehicle was registered in Vermont upon purchase a year ago. It begged the question: why would a guy like him hang out with Ian?

He smiled to himself; maybe this guy was *into* him. Perhaps he was trying to pull a fast one by showing off his car and treating Ian to dinner these past few days. But for the most part, Ian dismounting from his high horse, Kenneth didn't come off as that desperate. And by chance falling for Ian? Not likely. Ian squirmed in his seat regrettably envisioning the taste of Kenneth's tongue—Ian promptly tucked his junk before Kenneth returned to the driver's seat.

He instantly thought of Spencer in attempts to divert his musings. His boyfriend was sensitive, so much so that Ian thought out every action before interacting; it was easy for Ian to hurt him if he wasn't careful—he had no filter most of the time. It'd been years since Ian experienced coitus, met with the bashful downcast of cerulean eyes every time Ian attempted to reach second base. It killed him, yes, but again, nothing to make his dear Spencer uncomfortable. He thought of creative ways to get his boyfriend off on the daily—Ian couldn't wait until the day he had total control over Spencer's libido. Impatience festered within, and Ian reacted quite positively to Kenneth, pheromones wafting past his senses. Smelling Kenneth's cologne, most likely expensive, the throbbing mass between Ian's legs begged for attention. With a limp grip of the wheel and reclined position, Kenneth continued to stare at the road to Ian's relief.

"So," Kenneth started, "You mentioned something about a boyfriend?"

"Spencer, yeah."

"Do I have a chance to meet him?"

"At two in the morning, no. Eventually, yes. It will be kind of awkward. He's, like, the exact opposite of you." Ian thought for a bit. "He might not like you, come to think of it."

Kenneth chuckled, "Opposite? How so?"

Ian tensed, "He's well known in this area. Even has a city award. The brain kid of this town. Already has three scholarships and he's only a junior. I could never amount to that."

"Wow. Didn't take you for the type that liked good guys." For some reason, Ian's first thought was to take offense, but Kenneth continued. "Let me guess: the 'I want to wait' type? Studying all day, doesn't like drugs or alcohol?"

Ian flushed, thankful the car was dark. "Something like that." Ian hated that he felt embarrassment.

Soon Kenneth was parked outside of Ian's. The storm door was open to the mudroom—Ian could make out the silhouette of his father sitting in the kitchen, watching the door which probably meant trouble in Ian's case. Kenneth, hands in pockets, walked Ian to the door, which made him all the more nervous. After the stunt Ian and Spencer pulled in front of everyone on his birthday, it was only fair for his parents to suspect Kenneth was a fling.

"I would invite you in, but it's pretty damn late. And I may or may not be in a shitload of trouble."

"I can vouch for you," said Kenneth smoothly, with that same easy smirk playing on his lips.

"I *really* shouldn't. It's a school night and my curfew is eleven."

"Hello, boys." Greg opened the door; confusion mixed with anger riddled his face.

"Good afternoon, sir. Or I should say, morning. Sorry for the inconvenience. Ian and I had a last-minute project we were working on and lost track of time." Kenneth was flawless at covering. It was impossible to know that he was lying.

Greg was lost in Kenneth's eyes for half a moment, then continued with, "A project? Hmm. I'm surprised you didn't let Spencer help you with it."

Ian shifted his eyes before answering. "He's been really busy these past few days. I didn't want to bother him."

"Yeah? Because he came over here looking for you twice today." Greg wasn't buying it. "Who are you?"

"Kenneth Green, sir." He offered his hand; Greg reluctantly shook it.

"Nice to meet you, Kenneth. Next time, don't wait until the last minute to do a project, okay, boys?" Greg said in his dad tone.

"My apologies. I should get going. Goodbye, sir. Later, Ian."

Ian felt the onset of another erection by the utterance of his name. He couldn't help it. Kenneth was outright beautiful.

The air began to warm, and the people shed their sleeves and coats. It was springtime in Willard, the best part of the year for many residents yet the worst for its students. For those who cared about their academics, it meant preparing for standardized tests as well as finals. This meant that every teacher would try to jam a year's worth of curriculum into their noggins in hopes that their school would retain its accreditation. Unfortunately, Willard High was the furthest thing from excellence. Its students were indifferent and struggled through the content taught, subsequently ranked near the bottom of the four high schools in the precinct.

They rarely fired teachers who needed to be replaced, and the punishment for felonious students wasn't nearly enough.

The majority of students were average—they did just enough to pass and that was good for them. Honors and AP students carried the school the most, yet they were met by the stressors of reality as these teens rushed to apply for colleges in hopes to get a drop of dosh from the scholarship-application pipeline.

Today was one of those grand days nearing the school year's end, yet the theatre class toiled on. There was little to no work to do besides watch musicals and practice for the end of the year's play. Amid the horseplay and cringy performances, Stephanie and Lizzy managed to find a dark space in the back of the auditorium that obscured them from the others. Like Ian and Kenneth, Lizzy and Stephanie had been closer than close in this past week. Every day, as promised, Lizzy chauffeured Steph to and fro in a timely manner. She would stick around until it felt as if she wore her welcome for the day, then rinse and repeat. There was an unspoken bond, a language that the two used to convey their emotions—their resonance in both gender and personality birthed a lexicon that her darling male mates never seemed the grasp.

Spencer was to join them a little later at lunch. He set himself between Stephanie and Ryan, as reserved so. Spencer tried his best to catch up on what Stephanie laboriously laughed at, to no avail. He could not hear what Lizzy was saying into

Stephanie's ear, but whatever it was, it had to be something simple and bizarre to make Stephanie this surrendered. Lizzy greeted Spencer, tapping her fist to his. "What's up, Spence?" she asked, arm draped behind Stephanie's chair.

His eyes assessed with an informed smirk, "Sooooo, what do we have here?"

Lizzy motioned for Spencer to relocate somewhere quieter, and proceeded with, "I've been meaning to speak with you. Is everything okay? Is Michael still...?"

"Everything is peachy. Michael is gone. I'm great, thanks."

"Good. I'm glad. Alright, two things: one, what do you know about Abbitt?" She read his confused look and continued with, "I was thinking about going to his class for study block. What with moving here late in the year and all, I kinda need to catch up."

Spencer replied, "I think Abbitt is all-around wonderful. He's smart and passionate about what he teaches, and what we students make of ourselves. If you want a cute face to look at for a couple of hours, I'm sure you can squeeze into one of his classes. He lets me hang out there time to time during his lunch break. I'll definitely ask him for you."

"Thanks, broski. Okay, and two, what's the deal with Ryan? Why won't he back off Stephanie?"

Spencer only sighed and engaged with, "You see, when two people have sex, especially if it's their first time, a hormone known as oxytocin is released. It convinces its producer to trust and find comfort in their partner. As a result, Ryan is still oxytocin's bitch and Stephanie keeps messing with his mind." Lizzy only stared. "Basically, Ryan is in love with her, but Stephanie only sees him as a friend and plaything."

"So a casual fuck?"

"Sure, yes, however you want to say it. But whatever may be the reason that you, Lizzy, a lesbian, would ask the gayest guy in school about his best friend? Is there a conspiracy brewing?" Spencer asked, knowingly.

Lizzy punched his arm and scoffed, "I can't help that your best friend is pretty fucking hot, alright? And maybe I was asking for advice on how to, uh, do the thing."

"By 'do the thing', do you mean, do the *do* thing or just doing the pre-*do* thing?"

"The pre-do thing. You know, like dating and whatnot," she averted her eyes.

Spencer nearly had an aneurism from the excitement he couldn't contain. "Yas! You and Stephanie? All my yes! Okay,

okay, okay, look: between you and I, Stephanie has always wanted to try being with a girl but has either been too shy or found everyone generally disinteresting. My advice would be to keep doing what you're doing. I've never seen her laugh so much in my life."

Lizzy asked, "That's good then, right?" and Spencer nodded. "Okay. Good. By the way, where's your boyfriend? Word on the street is you two are out now. I dig it."

"The word spread that fast?" he was astounded by how the school knew in the matter of a week. "Wow. I haven't seen him today. Or yesterday. Or the day before, in fact. Or before that. I'm pretty pissed at him. I mean, he could at least call me. Check up on me, make sure I'm not dead or something."

Lizzy tensed. Looks like Baal had made his move sooner than expected. That would explain the Sentinel being here. "Where do you think he could be?"

"His parents tell me he's been working with a friend on a school project at late hours. Some guy named Kenny or something. I've never seen the guy. Do you know something I don't?" his voice cracked upward an octave, imagining the worst outcome.

Lizzy's hands went up defensively, "Hey, don't look at me. I don't talk to Ian on a regular basis." *That demon lord has claimed a new body, I just know it.* "Why don't you ask Steph?"

They did just that, returning to their respective seats at the table. Stephanie, still in tears from whatever Lizzy did to make her crack, attempted to cudgel any information Ian might have told her in the past couple days. She wiped at her eyes, "Oh yeah! I texted him in class today because he left me in chemistry to suffer alone. He says he's downtown or something with Kenneth. They've been hanging out a lot."

"Why didn't he tell me?" Spencer asked, eyes about to take on a red tinge. "He's making me worried."

It dawned on Stephanie that this seemed rather suspicious from Spencer's perspective. And she, too, noticed Ian's previous absences. Something didn't add up, yet she had faith that Ian knew better than to do an act as low as cheating. Although something still wasn't right. "Look, whatever it is, I know goddamn well he wants you and only you," Stephanie wiped Spencer's tear barely brimming over. "Let's calm down and think about this objectively. Maybe he is one of Ian's old adoption friends. Or a mutual of Jonathan. Ian was told to keep whatever they discussed on the downlow." *Then again, they didn't know each other the night at the karaoke bar,* she thought.

"I'm calling him," Spencer said as he held his phone to his ear, seething. Stephanie only rolled her eyes at her melodramatic twin. When he got like this, there was no bringing Spencer back down to earth for the next couple of hours no matter how logical she was. He would continue to rant and rave about preposterous scenarios, consequently upsetting himself over it. "Don't you fucking 'hey' me? Where the hell are you?" Stephanie was surprised that Ian answered, awaiting to eavesdrop on the impending drama. "You could have at least told me. I have been riding the bus alone for the past three days. Do Mr. and Mrs. Frances know you're skipping school like this?" There was a pause, and then only the flamboyant yelling on Spencer's end. "You need to bring your ass back here immediately!... Yes, I'm mad!... Because you don't communicate with me!... Let me talk to this 'Kenneth' then... I don't care, Ian. Put him on the phone..."

"You're such a loser," Spencer was raised from his chair. He panicked internally before piecing together the voice of his attacker. With Spencer distracted by rage, Ian was able to pull a charade long enough to sneak up on him.

"Ian! What the fuck!" Spencer flailed, enraged. "Put me down!"

Ian laughed at Spencer's frustration, calling him, "Cute," and placed him down, only to be nagged at again. The others laughed at the two—the shenanigans of the couple never grew old, together as long as the crew could remember; a successful relationship in high school—quite the rarity.

Spencer pouted, refusing to look at Ian.

"Babe," Ian snorted, "I'm right here. I just wanted to see if you really thought I went all the way into town. I was outside the whole time."

Spencer tapped his foot. "That's not what I'm upset at. Why didn't you tell me? And why haven't you been home, or riding the bus with me?"

Their table fell silent as all eyes simultaneously met the figure walking their direction. Somehow, they all knew who the guy was without a spoken word. Lizzy instinctively stood in front of Stephanie.

"You forgot your wallet in my car, again," the words eased from Kenneth. He had all of Ian's peers mesmerized—graceful, onyx hair that fell in straight tresses down his chest and back, and a gorgeous face to top. This was not a face that belonged to the likes of Willard. Spencer gawked at the man; all manner of argument ceased.

"Oh shit, waddup! Why do I keep doing that? Thanks," said Ian. "I guess I can finally introduce you to everyone since you're here. This is Spencer, my boyfriend—he's mad at me right now. You've met Steph. Liz. And Ryan. Where's everyone else?" he asked indirectly.

"If you don't mind," started Kenneth, pulling up a chair and propping his feet atop the table, "I'd like to get to know you all finally. I've heard only great things."

"Actually, Stephanie and I have to get going. We have a scene to rehearse before class starts back up." Lizzy dragged Stephanie along at a quickened pace until she reached the classroom. *It's true. That damn demon is bribing Ian along!* Lizzy paced a couple of times before coming to her senses after panicking.

Stephanie gave Lizzy a weird look. "May I ask?"

Lizzy looked straight into Stephanie's eyes. "I'm not sure how to say this..."

Stephanie swallowed and felt her cheeks warming from the uncomfortable proximity the two shared.

I can't tell her this now, Stephanie's eyes simply mesmerized her, captivated by her inherent innocence as Lizzy's thoughts raced. *There is no way she can know about shifters now, it's too soon. I don't have her full trust yet. And to make matters worse, these demons are trying their damnest to screw things up for Ian.*

If anything happens to him, Stephanie will be devastated and there would be no way in hell I could carry out my mission. Stephanie and her friends are in danger if I don't do something. Anything. Dammit!

"Stephanie... I just moved here, and you probably still think I'm a stranger. I don't know if you like pecker or beaver, but would you be my girlfriend, goddammit?"

Stephanie's expression calmed into a smile, her heart going a billion beats per minute. *A girl? How do I keep one of those happy? Oh man, what do I do?!* "Yes?" replied Stephanie, awkward in every sense.

"So that's a yes?"

Stephanie held her breath. "Yes."

"Okay. Are you sure? I don't want you to feel like I've pressured you, especially since I dragged you all the way up here. If not, I totally understand. We can act like this never happened. Tomorrow will be a new day, the birds will sing—"

Stephanie silenced her with a kiss. It was a bold move, but the softness of Lizzy's touch made her innards squirm for more contact. Lizzy leaned in—she huddled Stephanie against a locker, making claims to her lips, and Lizzy's hands finally familiarized themselves with her hips. This kiss took everything from Lizzy. She wanted so badly to make all of Stephanie hers. From what was intended to be a distraction, Lizzy finally understood the reason as to why she picked Stephanie, and why she was chosen to be the one to change her—it was both beautiful and sickening to think of.

8

MIND, DRIPS

"On Spring Break, huh? I don't know. You know how my mom gets with these kinds of things," Spencer sipped the cola from its can.

Both were sitting on a bench at the park on the corner of Delrose, school just letting out for the day, and the two with nothing to do.

Ian threw pieces of stale bread into the pond responding as the ducks and geese raced for it, "Just say that you're staying with me."

"I would, but..." Spencer began to prolong the can's contact with his lips so he wouldn't have the burden of explaining.

"But what? You always do that. Remember that one party we went to in Antlerwood?"

"I think my mom knows."

"About?"

"Us."

Ian paused, "Shit, fam. How?"

"She went through my phone while I was in the shower. She hasn't asked about anything. I put my phone on my bed before the shower, and afterwards, it was on my desk."

"Why the hell don't you have a password on that thing by now, Spencer?"

"I told you, it got annoying." Spencer paused, collecting his words, and proceeded with, "I think we should tell her today, you and me. Over dinner."

"I'm not sure that's a good idea."

"Why not?"

"I just think that, well, it won't go so smoothly. I know how your mom is. When gay marriage was legalized, remember how she boycotted the stores that supported it? Plus, she already hates me enough."

"For the last time, she doesn't hate you, she just... she just thinks you're crazy sometimes. And a bad influence."

"Which is why she will never approve of you dating me, let alone you being gay. I think you should wait until you're in college, at your own place. It will save you from living in a nightmare."

"But Ian, I'm sick of waiting. I want us to be ourselves for once."

"What is your problem?!" Ian raised his voice, standing. "One week your all depressed and don't want me involved, and the next, you want me involved in every aspect of your fucking life."

Spencer only stared, shocked at Ian's instant rage. "Is everything okay, Ian?" he asked, tentative to start an argument.

"Yes. I'm fucking fantastic," Ian chucked the rest of the bread into the pond. "What happened with Michael, anyway? Heard he got expelled."

Spencer felt a pang of fear by Ian's tone. The only time he was this angry was when someone did his allies wrong, it was never towards Spencer. ". . .Yeah."

"What happened?"

"He tried to..." Spencer trailed off. Given a strict gaze from Ian, Spencer blurted, "He tried to fight me again. Mr. Abbitt jumped in and suspended him and his friends."

"And why the fuck didn't you think to tell me?!" Ian's fists were tightened. This was the angriest Spencer had ever seen him.

"I didn't want you doing anything rash. The situation was handled, Ian. Please don't be angry." Spencer shrunk away.

"No it isn't. He'll be back. And he *will* try to get back at you. Guys like him don't understand until they're punched in the face." Ian curled his fist repeatedly, brows bent and unwilling to hear any sort of reassurance by Spencer.

"Ian, I can—"

"Don't. Be quiet. I'm handling this when he gets back. There will be no next time. What were you thinking? How many other instances have you kept from me?"

"It's really not that serious, Ian."

"It is serious!" Ian yelled, grabbing a hold of Spencer's collar and tightening his grip.

"Ian. Please stop," whimpered Spencer with a shaky voice. Ian's eyes softened as he realized the fear in Spencer's. He let go immediately, backed up, and then apologized.

"Oh my god. Spencer. I'm so sorry." Ian brushed a hand through his hair, trembling. He never lost control on Spencer, ever, or anyone period. And he promised himself he would never do anything to hurt the ones he loved. By seeing the look in Spencer's eyes, he was terrified. Never once had he received that look from any friend of his. Strangers, yes, but never the ones this close to his heart. "I'm sorry. I'm sorry." Ian breathed while returning his pulse to normalcy.

"I'm gonna go..." Spencer said in barely a whisper.

Ian grabbed Spencer's wrist tightly, cramming his lips onto Spencer's, who pushed Ian away. "Stop this, Ian! It's been hard for me to figure you out lately. And I'm scared, okay? You are scaring me. What are you going to do after all of this, huh? Where are you going to go? Stop acting like a infant that still sucks on a tit and grow the hell up already!" Spencer stormed off in the direction towards his house, leaving Ian to contemplate those last words ringing repeatedly through his mind.

Ian sat on the bench alone. He felt as if he were making things worse for those around him rather than being supportive, and Spencer was the last one he wanted to lose.

"Pick me up. I don't care where we go. Just please get me out of this place," Spencer begged over the phone to Stephanie.

Stephanie was lying next to Lizzy who showed concern on her face, mouthing 'what's wrong'. "I'll see what I can do. Are you going to tell me what happened or...?"

"Please just hurry up."

The black truck arrived as the blonde one stepped outside. "Alright. What happened?" asked Stephanie when Spencer climbed into the back seat.

"I don't want to talk about it right now."

"Is it Ian?" Spencer hated Stephanie's intuition at times like this. He nodded. "Do you want me to fight him for you?" Spencer responded with a tired look. "Tell me what's going on or this car won't move, Spencer."

"I can't help but feel that Ian is getting tired of me. I mean, he keeps up with you, but he leaves things out when I talk with him. Granted, I left things out regarding the whole Michael situation, but it's handled now."

"Go on."

"We were at the park an hour ago and he was trying to get me to go to this party or something that Kenneth invited him to. And I was saying that that would be impossible to get past mom. And then it turned to coming out and how I thought now would be a good time. And he just snapped. Says I should wait until I move out. I think I just inconvenience Ian. Especially since he's an adult male who hasn't had sex in years. I think he's cheating on me."

Spencer began to sniffle; Stephanie knew without looking back that his face was all in shambles. "He's not cheating on you, trust me. Ian's balls aren't that big. Perhaps he does have... urges every now and then. Obviously, you're not ready. You want to wait; there's nothing wrong with that."

Spencer proceeded to explain the rest of the situation, detailing the way Ian's eyes investigated his, and Ian's fist balled up tight on Spencer's collar.

Lizzy gripped the wheel tighter upon hearing Spencer speak. Things were going south faster than she expected. She wanted so badly to warn the others, to get them out of harm's way. But that meant danger for her family. Her sole mission was Stephanie, she kept reminding herself. Yet they all grew on her, regrettably. This was bad. Things should not have escalated this quickly. If anything, Lizzy thought she had a year at the least to prepare for the worst. With all of this taking place, she may have to adopt Stephanie into her clan by the turn of next month.

"I don't like that Kenneth guy," Lizzy spoke after moments of silence. "You guys should stay away from him. I know his type. He will not be a good influence, especially to someone as susceptible as Ian." Stephanie and Spencer were shocked to hear Lizzy intervene. She was usually silent, observant. And when she did speak, it was in the form of a joke or something casual. "By all means, keep Ian from interacting." If Lizzy couldn't interfere with Baal's plan, then maybe they could attempt to keep Ian away.

No. What was she thinking? Nothing they could do could stop a demon lord from getting what he wanted. He would kill them without a second thought if they got in the way. "Oh, what am I saying? Nevermind. Who am I to judge?" she laughed nervously. It was bad enough that Hazth was keeping guard at the school. She thought back to a conversation held recently between the two. Hazth seemed more unvexed than ever, that relaxed way about him was unsettling considering the circumstances. He reiterated the consequences that would ensue if Lizzy tried to pester at their pursuit, also mentioning their arrangement on the contrary: if she doesn't try to be a hero, then she has no problems with the hellish duo. But Lizzy didn't know how long those terms would last. The only thing demons obey is a contract in blood, however, even still, they manage to find loopholes and get their way in the end.

"When do I come in? When do I strike? Come on, you guys are having all the fun!"

"Patience, Travius. Lord Baal told you your role countless times," Hazth tidied the condo they all resided in, immaculately clean for three demons. "Aren't you supposed to be somewhere?"

Travius looked at Hazth in relief, "Oh, right! Almost forgot! Baal would've had my ass!" The intermediate assembled his belongings, "Are you sure this is the guy?" Travius tilted the photograph towards Hazth.

Glancing over, he confirmed, "Yes. Early forties, salt-pepper hair. It would be hard for someone to fuck this up, even someone like you."

"I'm getting real tired of your shit," snickered Travius as the shifter laughed. "How come you get to stay here? Didn't Baal give you an assignment, too?" Travius' vessel was a young female, late twenties and attractive in all aspects. It was just like Travius to go for one like that, Hazth thought, but it worked for what the three were trying to achieve.

Hazth was uneasy when first briefed of the mission; for what it was worth, trapping a kid was not his forte. He could easily do the abominable things that Baal ordered. He felt no shame when tasked to kill hundreds or thousands of people, regardless of gender, background, or nationality. But when it came to children, he bore a soft spot that he'd dare not make known to his superior. Conditioned to bear no care, trained to fight and withstand the torture inflicted upon him, the abuse, Hazth still stood with Lord Baal who was among the highest-ranking lords within the Third Gate. As a shapeshifter, of course demons tried to take as much advantage of the foreign creature as they possibly could, many going as far to see how his soul tasted. For the first couple of years after being abducted by Baal, he was deathly afraid, full of weakness that every demon, no matter the rank, could undoubtedly notice. Lord Baal was patient, however not kind.

The patience Lord Baal had could be described as kindness; Hazth comprehended it to be Lord Baal's way of showing understanding. The Lord was smart. He rewarded his followers and gave them incentive to carry on beside him. Unfortunately, many demons didn't make it nearly as long as Hazth did. He guessed this was why Lord Baal took on a shifter into his ranks. The resilience the race presented made for good guards, and their sharp instincts kept their leader two steps ahead of the enemy. Travius was one of many intermediates that Baal commanded, also the foulest-mouthed and ignorant, yet he had skills that even Hazth couldn't deny. As preposterous as it sounded, Travius' strength in battle was to be admired. Despite his lack of wit, he was a tactician when he was given the right motivation.

Lord Baal saved his life those years ago. Hazth did not mind a life of servitude underneath this leader. Baal was just so long as he was respected but he would not mind striking down a follower no matter how long they were in his ranks if done a disservice, regardless of how much use they were to him.

Hazth watched the trio in their after-school routine above as a raven hidden in the treetops. Hazth knew each of their habits by heart and of the future activities they planned for the weekends. Noctua was witty and would go far as a shifter. But she was foolish to think that her plan would go so easily.

The way she plotted on the girl, Stephanie, was a plan with too many holes. And even still, she was young, naïve. It was only a matter of time until Noctua got in the way of Lord Baal. When it would get to that, there was nothing that Hazth could do to stop a fellow shifter from being wiped from this plane.

Even now, she stared at Hazth from her position twenty-two feet below, squinting her eyes and warning him telepathically not to do anything, demanding to know why he watched.

Ian grew ever impatient waiting on the promised phone call from Jonathan. It was weeks since Jonathan assured Ian that he'd be included in the search for his origins. And frankly, his impatience was composed of anger more than anything else, resulting in further confusion. With ample time to think on it, it made Ian feel more fucked up than he originally believed himself to be before learning of his past.

The night was growing frigid as the sun ducked below the trees; Kenneth looked quizzically at Ian, concerned. When coerced to explain, Ian proceeded, start to finish about Jonathan's findings and suspicions. It took this long for Jonathan to fulfil his oath, so why not tell the ones Ian deemed close?

After the briefing, Kenneth put out the cigarette butt on the bottom of his boot.

"Occult, you say? Why wait for Jonathan when we can do that ourselves?"

"Wait, what?" Ian looked at Kenneth, excitement brewing. "You're into that stuff?"

"Dabbled in it here and there eons ago."

"Is it real?"

"Of course it is. Why do you think people are afraid to get near it?"

Ian smiled, "Then let's do it! Right now!"

"You are fearless, aren't you? Don't you have a boyfriend you have to make up to? It's getting late, and you have school tomorrow, mister."

"Shut up. How do we get started?"

Kenneth's phone began to ring. He excused himself to answer. A woman's voice was on the other end.

"Lord Baal, uh, we got ourselves a problem," said Travius' vessel.

Kenneth walked further away, dropping his charade, responding as a lord. "Elaborate, Travius."

"Yeaaaaah. So I was doing what you told me to do, honest. I did everything the way you told me, my Lord. I swear."

"Travius. Get to your point."

"That guy you told me to kidnap, Jonathan Fetcher? Yeah, well, uh..."

"Get to your point!" Baal yelled into the tiny speaker, checking over his shoulder to make sure his company wasn't alarmed.

"There's another lord in town. Lord Voltaya of the Second Gate. Almost didn't make it out of there alive, sir. And he practically has that Fetcher guy at his disposal."

Lord Baal nearly crushed the phone in his palm. He counted silently and further interrogated Travius. "Do *not* let him out of your sight. Follow his every move and inform me of such, do you understand? Suppress your aura, like we have discussed previously."

Travius' voice shook as he was caught in two battles, either one meaning death if he didn't follow through correctly. "Yes, my Lord. I understand, but he's of the Second Gate. They are not as secretive as our Master's territory. I'm not sure if he was followed with more lords. Somehow, word got out. I thought you were the only one who knew."

"Do not you think I have gathered as much already? Do as I say. Report to the condominium at exactly twenty-three thirty." Baal tried his hardest not to tear apart his vessel inside-out by the sheer rage which set his very ethereal body ablaze. Even now, patches of skin were starting to flake off beneath Kenneth's jacket.

He breathed and met Ian with a smile. "My apologies." It was now or never. Baal needed to somehow claim Ian as his, instill part of his own being into the boy, beginning the process, Ian's transformation. Yes, tonight would be the start, enough to keep the greedy hands of the other demons away from what he worked so hard to acquire. "As I was saying, one thing that helps with introduction into the occult is altering your state of mind."

"Altering my state of mind? You mean like drugs?" Kenneth nodded. Ian was slightly reproachful towards the idea—he never touched anything other than marijuana, influenced by Spencer's abhorrence towards any idea of drug use. It was something Ian was willing to try, to sample various substances for the sake of curiosity, that was it—nothing to flaunt or gain addiction from. "What kind?"

Lord Baal always remained prepared—Kenneth reached inside his inner coat pocket to retrieve a clear vial with a dropper. It contained a thick, deep maroon liquid, sloshing around as Kenneth held it towards the waning moon's light betwixt his thumb and forefinger. "This," he began, "is only the most potent psychedelic for dealing with the occult. It transcends your mind into the alpha and theta frequencies. They oscillate and make it a piece of cake for communing with the paranormal. Also, one hell of a party drug." Kenneth took its dropper and plopped one drop onto his finger. "Well? Shall we?"

Ian was at a standstill. But Kenneth offered to help him find these answers immediately. The whole drug thing... was he honestly willing to do it? The anticipation grew as the night darkened. Before thinking himself into a frenzy, he mustered up the courage to hold out a finger, shrugging, "What the hell, let's do this!"

Together they licked the residual liquid from their fingertips and waited for the onset. Ian nervously checked his phone and jigged his leg, swarming with apprehension, impatiently waiting to feel something, anything from the come-up. Whatever it was, it tasted horrible; he wished he had something fizzy and caffeinated to wash the taste from his mouth. Now it was a waiting game. His metabolism seemed to take its sweet time...

The bass of the techno-music blaring within the club was the only thing keeping Ian tethered to reality. With every bump of the beat, Ian glided his extremities, rolled his hips, and dragged his hands along his perspiring body. He closed his eyes, smiling largely from the overwhelming euphoria that invaded his senses. Many emotions ghosted through him, everything at once—it felt so powerful, so invoking, that all he could do was smile at the thought of simply moving. Right now, he was a god and the club was his fortress, the people his to use however he wished. Right and wrong seemed to be such a limited way of thinking; none of it made sense. With a loss of boundaries and a full night ahead, Ian danced recklessly, knocking fellow clubbers over and smashing into countless people. He finally found his way into Kenneth, gyrating into his crotch. It all seemed so normal, as if any and everything Ian did was justified and needed to be expressed, regardless of the other's regard or personal space.

Kenneth's hands were placed on Ian's hips as they continued to grind to the beat. Ian was unaware of his own moaning, to Kenneth's pleasure. And Ian lost total control over his libido as he hung his arms loosely around Kenneth's shoulders. Ian's tongue glided along his neck, lost in the taste and the pleasure that was absent for so long.

"Let's get you some air," Kenneth laughed pulling Ian away from him.

"I'm fine! Let's dance!" Ian sporadically moved to the beat as best as someone could whilst being pulled outside. "Whoa, it's like a totally different world out here! Holy shit! The stars are beautiful! And the sky!"

Ian would be staring for hours if Kenneth hadn't interrupted his trip with the question, "So how do you like it?"

"What is this stuff? It's amazing! Is it acid?"

Kenneth laughed, arms folded across his chest, "No, no. Far from it. It's extremely hard to get your hands on, but I have my connections. It's called Goat's Sacrament. The feds haven't caught on to its usage, though. Hasn't been scheduled. So technically it's legal."

"I want to do this every day. I never would have imagined the world could look like this."

"How do you feel?" Baal's deep voice coerced Ian into a stronger high, a corrupted, piercing gaze broke through that of Kenneth's and into Ian's.

Ian climbed onto a car, arms outstretched, and yelled into the night, "I FEEL LIKE A FUCKING GOD!"

"Ugh, he's not in school again," Spencer sneered as he approached Stephanie in the hall. She was locked into Lizzy's arms—that seemed to be a normal look for them as of late, to Spencer's jealousy.

"Seriously?" replied Stephanie half-removed, tenderly clinching onto her girlfriend.

"His phone is either off or dead. I swear, when I see him..."

Ian was enveloped within silk salmon sheets, the morning rays beaming directly onto his face. His body felt worn, aching and sore. His mind swam, the high's comedown. Where was he? This room was too luxurious to be something he was able to afford while tripping out of his mind. He stood to glance outside through a slot in the blinds. Downtown Willard. Cars breezed by on the streets below, and the strip across the street was an all-too-familiar sight.

The sizeable room was barren, save for the king-sized bed and matching drapes. A chest of drawers was in a corner, next to it, a door which Ian assumed to be a walk-in closet.

His clothes were strewn across the floor, apparently the only key cuing Ian in on his nakedness. "Oh..." he breathed. Whatever it was that Ian did last night retuned to his memory in small bursts. The full story was never revealed.

"You're awake," the voice at the door startled Ian—he froze at the sight before him. Kenneth posed at the doorway, nude, with a tray of food in hand. "I thought that you might be hungry. I didn't know how you liked your coffee, so I put cream and sugar on the side." Ian remained speechless. Soon the events of last night returned entirely to mind, plain as day.

"Everything alright, Scarlet?"

"Did we have sex?" Ian blurted.

Kenneth set the tray down and laughed, "Was it so bad that you forgot?"

"We had sex..." Ian trailed off, staring into oblivion at the absurdity of the entire situation.

"And. You. Loved it," Kenneth teased with the flick of Ian's nose. "You should have seen the way your face looked when you *begged* for me to get inside you. Very hot, I must say. Don't think I could have resisted even if you paid me." Kenneth bit Ian's ear with a slight moan.

Ian remained in silence, donning his clothes, face flushed in embarrassment.

"What's the matter, Scarlet? Where are you going?"

"School."

"Hey," Kenneth blocked his path, pressing body against body and coaxed into Ian's ear, "The school day is almost over. Why don't you waste a little more time with me."

"Kenneth, I have to go. Last night was a mistake, a big one. I cheated on my boyfriend, something I swore I would never do. I'm a sack of shit—me and you never happened, and it can't happen again." Ian struggled with his jeans, slipping his arms into his shirt while navigating his way to the door.

"Are you going to walk fifteen miles to school, or do you need a ride?" Kenneth was behind him, hurriedly pulling up his boxers.

Ian stopped, slumped his shoulders, and sighed.

The silver Crossfire slowed before the entrance of the school—Kenneth put her in park. "Can I see you again tonight?" This was surprisingly the first thing uttered in the twenty-minute ride there.

Ian made the mistake of looking into Kenneth's eyes, immediately becoming engulfed in the same lust that always overtook him, his erection always happy to give the wrong impression. "No. No, I can't."

"He says otherwise," Kenneth slid his hand up Ian's thigh and closer to his crotch. So badly Ian wanted to whip it out right then and there, beg once more for the man to take him. But Ian's ego returned, and so did reasoning. Along with that, guilt.

Ian moved Kenneth's hand, responding with a weak, "No," as if he were unsure of his own answer. Truth was, he wanted it. He wanted to do it again and again. He wanted to release his load many times over, feel the rush that he'd never felt until last night. Kenneth made him feel powerful, like his own person. Unabashed and unscathed. Ian was soon to disappear into the school building, leaving Kenneth behind to only prepare for what tonight would bring.

Lizzy immediately scrunched her nose upon Ian's approach. He reeked of Baal, head to toe. The dots needn't be connected as she could instantly tell what last night involved.

Ian was dazed. The high still came in small waves, distorting light into various shapes; anything auditory seemed to be in the highest of quality. He could hear a locker close from the opposite end of the building on the second story and could smell the strong stench of bleach used to clean the floors.

The bell signaled for students to begin their lunch breaks, also the start of fifth period. He was just in time.

"What did you do last night? You look like shit." Lizzy attempted to brush Ian's hair into decency.

"I don't know. I don't fucking know."

Lizzy looked at him with honest concern. "Do you want to talk about it?" she asked. But she knew. All too well. She could smell the residual sex to the demon blood lingering on Ian's tongue. "You know Steph and Spence have been worried sick. Your phone was dead, I guess." Ian patted his pockets for his phone to no avail. It was left at Kenneth's—Ian remembered it sitting on the bed. Great.

"I lost it."

"Seriously, Ian. You don't look good at all. I can drive you home right now if you need me to." It was killing Lizzy to look at the transformation Ian had undergone in a night. It was a lord's blood Ian consumed, impossible to fight an addiction after just one taste for those that survived, and even survival was a rare case. She was eaten by frustration and guilt at once. "You have to stop hanging out with that guy, Ian."

Ian grew annoyed, offended that she'd jump to conclusions so quickly. "Can you all just piss off for one day?!" Ian yelled. "If it's not Spencer, it's Stephanie, and if it's not them, it's my parents or the rest of the goddamn world expecting something out of me!" The drugs only amplified his rage; it was the source, even. Ian was never the one to act out this way, even under stress. "If you're going to boss me around too, then you can permanently fuck off!" He began to walk away.

Lizzy grabbed his arm. "There's something you need to know," she started. She needed to tell him. It was now or never. This was only the start and Ian was falling heavy for whatever these demons were making him do. "You aren't being you right now because of these demons. These demons are trying to get you to give in and become—"

"Elizabeth. Ian. Good evening," Mr. Abbitt interrupted. "Nice of you to join us in school today, Mr. Frances. Elizabeth, Spencer told me of your situation—you are more than welcome to join me for your study block. I trust your essay is going well, Ian?"

"Y-yeah. Essay. Right," sighed Ian, receiving too much input for his senses from the encroaching environment.

Liam looked Lizzy in the eyes as he broadcasted his final warning, an instant that felt like an eternity. *"You are lucky it is I giving you these warnings, Noctua. Baal has noted your inconvenience more than once and has pondered your removal. The only reason you and your family are still alive is because I convinced a demon lord to let you live. Do not let my efforts be for nothing."*

Lizzy's hands fell limp at her sides. Defeat was difficult to swallow, especially seeing Ian fade in front of her very eyes.

***

Ian wiped the blood from his mouth, growling drunken taunts in a battle he was sure to lose. Once more, the man punched Ian square in the jaw. Ian staggered into a table, startling the bar's customers who relocated to watch and record the brawl. The pain did not connect as Ian still tried to land a few punches on the stranger. That was until Ian was forcibly removed from the establishment.

Ian laughed, sitting on a curb and lighting a Marlborough. Not once did it cross his mind that he endangered others and could possibly do the same to his future. Why did it matter? It was fun, or so the drug made him think. It got his blood running; he loved the rush he received from it.

"You were sloppy in there. Left yourself open every time," Kenneth remarked. "Don't put all of your focus on hitting the guy; you have to dodge his attacks, too."

Ian scoffed at his advice, "Yeah, yeah." He dabbed at his bloody lip, "Let's do something else. Got any more?"

Kenneth handed off the vial, halfway emptied since the first time Ian partook in the recreation. With five drops in the palm, Ian licked all of it clean, amplifying his high within a matter of minutes. Used to the taste, this became routine for the last couple of weeks. School was practically a thing of the past. He barely went, and when he did, he slept through each lecture. Goat's Sacrament became his lifeline. Withdrawal hit almost instantaneously when sobering up after a night's use. Hours after sobriety, he would get uncontrollable tremors and cold sweats. The nausea that ensued would have him hunched over a toilet for hours and any thought of food made him sick to his stomach. His vision would fade in and out, losing control of all balance to stumble in weakness for the nearest painkillers. These side-effects were serious, Ian knew, and the only way for him to stop them from happening was to continue inducing the high, resulting in a drastic increase in tolerance and dependency.

Lord Baal knew the potency of his own blood. For any normal human, a few drops would send them spiraling into lunacy and/or death, whichever came first. But Ian sucked it up like candy. It was working. Baal released glimpses of Ian's true nature with every drop. Violence, overt lust, Ian took what he pleased these days, or at least he was working towards that. Baal had a long way to go, but he was off to a magnificent start.

Ian's blood chemistry began to slowly match that of Baal. All the theories and decades Baal and his master dedicated to decoding the ancient scripts in presumed secrecy were becoming evident. This was a risky experiment—Baal had neither control group nor the ability to run trials. Whatever he did to Ian was finite and had to be executed correctly. Second chances did not exist. The fact that he and Master were able to predict the usefulness of a lord's blood was almost miraculous. This was the first instance Baal knew of that something other than a demon could stomach and metabolize a lord's blood as well as receive visible signs of transcendence.

Both Ian and Baal were playing with fire.

Spencer submitted his assignment online, slumping back in his desk chair. He sighed, checked his phone for the fourth time in the minute, and sighed again for the twenty-ninth time. "You have to stop looking at that thing. Turn it off," Stephanie insisted, taking over Spencer's bed as she fumbled her thumbs on the joysticks. He was used to this by now. The most he got to do with Ian as of late was sit on the bus with him, that is, *if* Ian showed up. "Here," Stephanie handed him a controller. "Help me fight this boss." They proceeded to play, having only each other as company like old times, before Ian moved to the area. Poor Spencer was trying his hardest not to become bent out of shape because of Ian's miscommunication. It was hard not to re-volve his life around the boy—man—since they've been involved with one another through the vital parts of adolescence.

"I guess it's safe to assume that he and I are over. Who chooses some random guy over their own boyfriend? This is ridiculous! I just... I can't even—" He pried his hands beneath his glasses to cover his swelling eyes. "Look at me! I'm pitiful. Crying over a damn boy."

"You have a full life ahead of you, Spencer. You cannot revolve it around Ian. You two are going at different paces; you both have been brought up in completely different worlds. He's my friend, too. I'm pretty fucking pissed at him, if you ask me. More worried than anything."

"His parents don't seem to mind at all. It's strange, Stephanie. They always make sure he obeys curfew. And you know how much they press him about school. Do they know how many days he's missed?"

"No idea. I wouldn't be surprised if our shitty school didn't notice. Mr. Lyle marks him absent on the daily. Not sure if he's called home yet."

"I'm sick of worrying about him, Steph." Spencer coiled his hair around his finger nervously, "Um... do you have any... any weed? I, um... need to get this stress out of me before I pull my hair out."

She only blinked at him, never once dreaming to hear those words exiting Spencer's mouth. Stephanie choked back laughter, unsuccessfully, and danced a celebratory jig to follow, revealing the small, clear sack of the pungent herb in her satchel.

After countless hours of club hopping without need of an of-age ID—Kenneth Green seemed to have connections around the area—and getting trashed by the sixth club, Ian grew anxious.

"So when do I start talking to ghosts and shit? I thought you said this was the occult drug."

"In due time, Scarlet." The nickname grew on Ian. He didn't mind. He liked the fact that he had a pet name in reference to his red irises that seemed evermore vermillion under the influence of Goat's Sacrament whenever he encountered his reflection.

Kenneth grabbed Ian's hip, walking side by side, arm around Scarlet's waist. His touch always seemed to send a jolt through Ian, always longing for their next intimate moment.

Rational thoughts were there yet instantly silenced, no fight needed. Spencer crossed his mind every now and then, however Ian would push it aside promptly as if Spencer was a figment of imagination.

Ian's sex drive was exaggerated—he and Kenneth went sunrise to sundown whenever Ian gave the word or made the move. It was addictive, just like this drug. And ignoring the urges was just as painful as the Sacrament's side-effects.

"Why don't we head in for the night. You look tired," Kenneth teased, unlocking the car doors.

"The night is still young!" Ian bellowed, beating his chest with unconstrained energy. It was nearing four in the morning. It would be safe to say that Ian never slept for days at a time. With as much energy as he had, one would think he obtained an adequate amount.

Lord Baal had Ian at the tip of his fingers; there was nothing another lord's arrival could do to defer Baal's ties on him. Baal reported to Master only moments ago while Ian was busy asserting control at the gay bar, taking advantage of the older men by flirting for drinks, never making returns on their investments. Master was elated with Baal's progress, but not with the amount of time it had taken to get this far. He sent out assassin-class lords to assess and, if possible, abduct Lord Voltaya to bring him to the Third Gate. If all else failed, an assassination. Master was not foolish enough to think that someone as skillful as Voltaya of the Second would fall into their traps—it was merely a deterrence until the Young Ruler was successfully awakened and imparted with the "training" he appointed Lord Baal to do.

Kenneth simply smiled, sly and as always, inviting. "There is something that we could do to end the night. After all, it is a school night, and your sole duty as a dependent is to graduate and get a career. I don't want to rob you of that."

Ian climbed onto Kenneth, straddling his lap, tonguing the surface of Kenneth's lips. "Shut up," Ian whispered. "What do you have in mind?"

"Well, after I take your ass again, how about dinner and a show?" Kenneth propped his seat back. Ian quickly undressed.

"A show?" Ian slowly rubbed his crotch against Kenneth's.

"A show." Kenneth guided Ian's hips with his hands. "I could tell you what it entails, but that would spoil the fun."

The car shook to their movement with luckily no one to spot them. The deeds were done and Baal drove Ian to what would determine if his consumption of a Lord's blood had done the trick. Baal could smell the change in chemistry. Ian's body was becoming both his vessel and true appearance, soon free to walk the realms as he pleased in his own flesh.

Baal had to admit: Scarlet was growing on him. He acted just like a novel, selfish imp the way Ian held things over people's heads and the trickery he enacted. It was fun to watch as Ian became kin to Baal. Already Ian showed signs of maturity—if Baal had to guess, he would say Ian would belong to the intermediate class in terms of ability.

Kenneth parked in front of a five-story building, a few cars here and there. It looked to be an official place—pristine glass perimetered the building, a fountain out front—that sat on a hill. The highway could be looked down upon from where they were.

"Doesn't look like much of a show here," Ian dismissed.

"Trust me. I think you'll like it."

"You never told me how you find all these places. I swear we go somewhere new, like, every night." Ian placed a few more drops onto his wrist. He now carried the vial, courtesy of Kenneth, and a free refill was included for Ian to do whatever he pleased. He licked his lips, "I liked the club we went to Wednesday. The one with the trance music."

"You have to be more specific than that. Shall we?" Kenneth held out his hand; Ian received it. Such old-time mannerisms were inviting to Ian many times over.

Inside, Ian was lost in a world of wanderlust. This place ranked over and above in terms of class. Situated on the top floor with an overlook of the city surroundings, the live band played smooth jazz while its guests partook in... in something. A waitress in nothing but an apron, stunningly preternatural in beauty, winked at Ian with a smile, and greeted Kenneth with a kiss on either cheek. Ian blinked, confused—he swore she had fangs.

"You didn't tell me you had friends as cute as he is!" the waitress spouted.

Kenneth shrugged, "He's new, so treat him nicely, Bianca."

"As you wish. There is something different about you that I can't put my finger on," she tapped her chin with a free hand. "New cologne?" All supernatural creatures weren't gifted with the sense, to Baal's relief. Common vampires were not the most introspective with those kind of things.

Kenneth nodded. "Well ain't you just the cutest lil' thing!" she pinched Ian's cheek. "What'll he have?"

"Lilith, on ice. Make that two," answered Kenneth.

"Will do! I'll clear out a booth for you two!" she sauntered away.

She was absolutely enthralling, with tantalizing yellow eyes. Ian stared a bit too long at her bare backside before being pulled away by Kenneth. "Don't get too comfortable yet, Scarlet."

"What is this place?" a dorky smile eased onto his face. "Did she have fangs, or am I tripping?"

"Yes and yes."

"This some kind of costume-themed gentleman's club?"

"No. She's the real deal."

Ian snorted, "Right." He followed Kenneth into an elaborate private booth, sitting juxtaposed to others. The booths were enclosed in opaque, one-way tinted glass; Ian could see the rest of the bar operations continue and no one even blinked an eye towards him. The stage where the band played had tables of people before it dressed in luxurious gowns and suits, which looked rather normal for the most part. And occasionally, there would be those who looked out of the ordinary. Ian noticed the common theme with the otherworldly people—they all had these mechanisms around their necks, even the waitress. Was this collar some type of ID? Fashion statement?

Bianca returned, "Two Lilith's on ice. Can I interest you all in anything to eat?" she said in the twangiest of accents. "We are running a special tonight on prime rib, as well as the pan-seared salmon. And let me tell you, it is delish!" She held the pen and pad ready.

Kenneth shook his head and looked to Ian. Ian was consumed by the items on the menu. "We'll give him some time," he sent her off with the smile.

"Why are they wearing those collars?" Ian asked Kenneth while sipping the odd drink ordered for him. "And not everyone is, either."

"The ones wearing the collars are not humans." Kenneth did not bother sugar-coating at this point. It was time Ian knew. Kenneth was to see how well Ian took it. "They were bought, purchased at an auction or through trade. Those collars help their owners keep control of them. It makes sure they don't grow too unruly."

"You're shitting me."

"Go ask. Although, I'm sure they'll ask you where yours is, Scarlet." Kenneth chuckled darkly.

Ian rolled his eyes dramatically. "And make a fool of myself?"

"You've been doing that all night. Why stop now?"

"You're lucky I like you," Ian punched his shoulder. "So, suppose you aren't bullshitting me and whatever you said is true. Isn't this place a little too public? And besides, it's not like a person can take ownership of a vampire."

Kenneth only pointed towards the distance. "See that there? Werewolf." There was this huge humanlike fur-creature being dragged alongside a woman by leash.

Ian pressed his face to the glass. "No fucking way! No fucking way, Kenneth!" He watched as the lady stopped at a table to converse with comrades, then proceeded to show off her "pet." They all admired, touched, as if this was some kind of slave trade. "So what, these creatures are sold as pets to rich old bags with too much money?"

"You got it."

"And how do you know about this place?" Ian looked to Kenneth until he answered.

With first a sigh, Kenneth sipped the drink and explained, "I catch them. I sell them. I make money. Easy income."

Ian looked to himself for a moment. The conclusion he reached brought the onset of rage, "You don't think I'm one of those things out there? Is this why you wanted to get to know me, take me out so much? Because my eyes are—"

"Easy there, Scarlet. If I wanted to capture you, I would have tranquilized you at first sight. Amongst various other things. Why would I take my bounty here, to scare them away?"

Ian relaxed, "Touché. I have so many questions. You're telling me these things have been around since the dawn of time and no one knows about their existence? How come I have never crossed paths with—"

"Lord Baal, I have—" the olive-skinned woman with auburn hair stopped short of Ian. "Is this...?" This was Travius' first up-close and personal encounter with the Prophesized. He froze, staring at Ian's regal looks, already becoming intimidated by his change in power. Given the look of disapproval from Baal shook Travius from his shock. "Kenneth, may I talk to you in private. It is pretty urgent."

"Wait here, Scarlet. Order anything you want." Ian only stared after the two. There it was, this high school dropout was off to bigger and better things, like trafficking supernatural creatures. That explained the extravagant amount of cash, the car, the condo... if Ian wasn't careful, this would have turned into a completely different set of consequences that he possibly couldn't escape. His guard remained up. Something rang in his mind that a guy like himself shouldn't be here. Regardless of his lack of money or status, Ian fit in, but on the wrong side. He rubbed at his neck while looking to the werewolf whose waking moments were full of resentment, fear, and longing, Ian was sure. To see those things rendered powerless, it was scary to see what people were capable of.

Travius followed his lord outside, stumbling on his words. He revealed a broken arm, bloodied limbs. "I'm telling you, Lord Baal. These lords are crazy! That succubus is here, too. His sister, Godimus. She joined up with Voltaya's ranks. It's getting serious out here." Lord Baal, finger to chin, looked to the ground, running through thousands of possible strategies. "Those are the most infamous of the Second Gate. I mean, what does a lousy shifter and a half-baked intermediate have against those guys? We're dead!"

"Any insight into the specifics of why they are here?"

"I have only gathered that they want to abduct the Young Ruler themselves. I do not believe they know about the entire awakening process you and Master were able to figure out. I think they believe we're doing the same. That, or they waited for you to do all the work so they can just swoop in and take the jewels." Travius' vessel's eyes looked to and fro, "I think Voltaya is going to use that old caretaker guy as his vessel. He already managed to possess him once and locate the major documents of Ian's past."

"Major documents?" Baal looked to Travius curiously.

"Yeah, your Scarlet has had a pretty fucked up life, if you ask me."

Travius reached into a bag, revealing Jonathan's binder, "And guess what intermediate was able to swipe them?"

"Travius, you have your wits about you. Much appreciated." Baal immediately began to overlook the documents. This was the first time Baal dished an uplifting response towards his servant's work. Travius was silenced—for the first time, he had nothing witty to remark. "Scarlet told me about his past, but there's only so much detail the brain of a teenage boy can process. The Sanction of New Light massacre was supposed to be an under the radar deal. A small group of lords put that together in hopes of easy contracts and to create an ulterior portal besides the Refract. Or so, that was what I was told. But Ian… I was not aware that Ian was the mass idol. These are questionable. Perhaps Mr. Fetcher will be more of use than we think."

"Nu uhn! No way am I going back there alone. Tell the World's Favorite Sentinel to do it."

"Relax. I am going to deliver Scarlet home, then travel to the Uver. Continue to manipulate the parents and have Hazth keep watch. I will be back in a few hours." Baal began to go back inside the MES facility. "By the way," he turned to Travius, "the blood will have fully catalyzed in the boy. If he begins to show viable signs, contact me immediately." Travius obliged and departed by the masking shroud.

Ian was working on his third glass of Lilith upon Kenneth's return. Its red liquid tinged his lips and tongue. "There you are! What is in this drink? It's the best thing I've ever tasted."

"Forty percent human blood. Thirty percent alcohol. Thirty percent artificial flavoring." Ian gave Kenneth that same confused, innocent look that started to take Baal for a fool.

"Don't give me that look. I don't lie to you."

"Fuck it! Another glass for Ian!" who figured out how to use the ordering mechanisms.

"No, no. We need to get you home. Up you go." There was more success in Baal's court—demonic mannerisms were starting to show, including appetite with a relative amount of control as well; any other demon would lose their sanity and maul the first human they could find. Ignoring Ian's protests, Kenneth piggybacked the altered lad to his car. Baal smirked at the kid on the drive to Willard; he was hopeless yet full of promise.

The lake was the perfect spot to detox on stress, as Stephanie put it. It was cute the way she taught Spencer how to use a bowl. He nailed it instantly, choking on the harsh smoke so much so that tears streamed his cheeks. It was a proud moment as the maternal figure of her boys. Spencer seemed to drag on for hours about childhood memories, including details that he swore he'd forgotten about. They reminisced on the many experiences they shared in youth, laughing painfully at their inside jokes. Stephanie missed this. Desperately. Now their days were tainted by stressors, quickly forced into responsibilities

that neither of them asked for. Real life was running them over
and high school was barely over.

"I can see why people do this now," Spencer commented,
absorbed by the gentle lapping the pond made. "I forgot what I
was even upset about."

"Romeo! Romeo! Where the fuck are you, Romeo!" Ian
yelled, approaching the two in the dark, early morning.

Stephanie and Spencer were speechless. It felt like an
eternity since they encountered the illusive. "Why the hell you
guys out so late?" Ian quipped—it was immediately obvious that
Ian was acting out. The way he moved, the various bruises along
his face. Ian's vermillion eyes only burned in the night; it was
either the high talking or Stephanie and Spencer thought it to
be surreal. "You guys have been smoking without me? Pass the
bowl." He wedged himself between the two, oblivious to the
shock of his presence. Ian never took note of Spencer's new
hobby, something he would have caught instantly on a normal
day, and snatched the bowl from his fingertips, lighting up. "It
feels fucking glorious out here!" Ian jumped up, too loud for a
suburban neighborhood at a time like this.

It was a waiting game to see which of the two would
outwardly ask the question they had on heart.

"Ian..." Stephanie spoke carefully. "What happened to you?"

He cleared the bowl before speaking, "What do you mean what happened to me? I'm living life!" Ian was covered in tears top to bottom, blood decorating his shirt collar.

"You look like you got in a fight, man. And you smell like liquor," she said critically.

He broke out in hysterics, dismissing Stephanie with a shove that was a little too harsh for comfort. "Maybe a few fights here and there."

Stephanie cautiously whispered, "Spencer, you should go home." He only nodded, then walked out of sight. It was too painful to stand by like this when his lover acted out of character. He stood within earshot. This wasn't right at all. Spencer wanted to turn back to give Ian everything that was on his mind. He wanted to help Ian overcome whatever he dealt with.

Stephanie stood face to face with Ian, pointedly raising her voice. "Alright. You either tell me what's going on with you or you need to get the hell out of our lives. Do you not see what you're doing to Spencer? He loves you, and you're acting like he doesn't exist anymore."

Ian snorted, "He's dramatic. He does that all the time. That shouldn't stop me from doing me."

"Doing you? This was never 'you.' What happened to all your fear, huh? Remember how you wanted to do things right? Impress your family? Protect the ones you love? Do you remember saying that, or are whatever drugs you're on making you deaf?" Stephanie was threatening when she was angry, an extremely rare occasion. She usually brushed things off and went on with life—this scenario was the exception.

Ian gave her a daring glare, "Do not comment on my life. You don't get to tell me how to live, alright bitch? This is me!" he laughed hysterically, managing to smoke the rest of the weed within the bowl, blowing it into her face. Stephanie stood still, taking a moment to gather herself before she reacted as rash as Ian was. Her self-control was dwindling but she maintained her grip.

"Bitch? Who the fuck do you think you're talking to, as many times as I saved your ass! You are being a dick, Ian. Look at yourself!"

"No, you look at yourself. You let others control you. You're a lost, sad girl. You don't like the way your life is going and you let others make decisions for you." He stepped closer. "Face it, Steph. All you do is lie to yourself, trying to pretend you're the mother of this so-called 'friend' group." He was directly over her, looking down into her eyes manically. "You're lucky you're pretty," he snatched her waist forward into his own, moving his lips up the base of her neck to her jawline.

Stephanie protested, heart pounding, pushing away with all of her strength. "Ian, stop!" she didn't know whether to be scared or angry, the former more evident than the latter. "Let go of me!" The constant tussling made it easy for Ian to gain the advantage, pinning her to the ground. He slowly crept a hand up her shirt while jamming her protests with his mouth on hers. It became evident that she could no longer fight him off.

None of this made sense, her brain went numb in confusion. This didn't seem real in the least.

She shut down. Accepting her fate, she was jostled around by whom she considered more than blood, someone she would have died for.

Ian crashed into the dirt meters from where he once was, regaining his stance and balance, holding his side at where impact was made. He coughed up blood, bracing himself on the ground.

Lizzy helped Stephanie up and situated her on the bench before yanking Ian into another packed punch, sending him reeling once more. Ian was dazed; his vision closed in while writhing on the ground in pain. Lizzy held him down with her foot. No one could guess this absurd amount of strength only by looking at her. Her jaw clinched, looking shamefully into Ian's eyes. The hell he must've been going through, the things he must be seeing at this moment, both must be unpleasant.

It took every inch of her will not to put an end to Ian. She knew one of his puppeteers must be watching from a distance, just waiting for her to do something that she'd regret. This had superseded her limit—she watched Stephanie tremble, who watched Lizzy frightfully.

Ian groaned and gagged until a red tinged mess splattered onto the ground. A few more rounds of this and Ian's pain began to chime in.

His head throbbed worse than any migraine he'd experienced, his mind could not piece together where he was or what was happening. He yelled out, begging for the pain to stop. He wasn't let up.

"What's happening to him?!" Stephanie exclaimed.

"Stay back!" barked Lizzy sharply. She watched as the inner turmoil attempted to consume him. Either the change was being rejected or his mind was fighting to maintain sanity. His form shuttered, and his screams pierced through the neighborhood. It was sure to draw curiosity towards this once peaceful park.

Behind the shroud of his torture, images danced and swarmed. The hallucinations of people called to him, and in the next, they vanished, only to return later with the same story and same pointed look all with different faces. They would look to Ian, they blamed him, they feared him. All the visions of these persons and their multitudes were disposed of beneath Ian's own hands. He saw a glimpse of himself, standing upon a jagged mountain with a red sky surrounding. He looked below at the bodies, not knowing which ones were alive or dead. Endless chanting. It looped over and over, these hallucinations. As fast as one came on, it vanished.

He caught glimpses of familiar places, as peaceful as his childhood memories captured it and of places he never saw in his waking life, yet they still felt deathly familiar. These visuals were tainted, watching helplessly as the ones he lived under, the ones that sheltered and clothed him, faded away. His heart ached; his brain ached; he wanted to die as the images haunted him for what seemed like an eternity.

He was granted his wish, waking up in a jolt. Cold sweat drenched his sheets. He focused on the ticking clock, looked to his desktop, to the bookshelf. The sight of his room calmed him, placing a hand on his heart to make the experience tangible. *It was a dream. It was all a dream.*

The door opened; Ian's heart began to race again.

Spencer entered, carrying a couple of water bottles. His eyes lit up to see Ian awake. "How are you feeling?"

Ian could not maintain eye contact with Spencer. He remembered everything. "Everything hurts," he said in barely a whisper.

Spencer made Ian drink both bottles. "How about some sunlight?" Spencer opened the curtains to the bright morning. "Alright. Potassium. Eat." Spencer placed a bag containing bananas and other vittles on Ian's lap. He ate without question. It seemed forever since Ian tasted food.

Matter of fact, it had been forever.

Spencer fiddled around with medication, humming an upbeat tune, one that he commonly sung. Was he pretending that nothing happened?

"Why aren't you in school?" Ian managed to croak in all its harshness, wincing at the ache in his jaw.

"Try not to move so much." Spencer returned to the bedside with a liquid medication that smelled sickeningly sweet. "Drink this." Ian made a face. "Oh, don't be a pussy." Ian stared at the cherry-red medicine reminded of the Goat's Sacrament and Lilith, triggering the unpleasant memories and the vulgar thoughts he bore in those moments.

He began to gag by simply thinking about its taste.

Spencer raced for the trashcan, holding it beneath Ian's chin in time to catch the chunks of regurgitated banana. "Okay, maybe we can hold off on the medicine." He tossed Ian another water, "Drink up."

"Did I hurt you?" Ian asked to no avail. Spencer only gathered the stray laundry into a basket, humming that happy tune. "Spencer?"

"Shhhh, try not to talk so much. Try to get some rest, 'kay?" Spencer remained facing away from Ian as the tears plopped onto his shirt. He clenched his jaw and wiped his face the best he could.

Ian held the blanket tight, shuddering. "I fucked up, Spencer. I was fucked up. It's okay if you hate me or never talk to me again. You don't have to take care of me."

Spencer didn't respond.

"Was it real? Was any of that real?" Quickly brushing the tears from his face, Spencer turned around, detecting the pain in Ian's voice.

"You shouldn't try to think of this now."

"Please tell me. I need to know." They were caught in a battle of stares.

Spencer caved, nodding.

"Did I hurt you, Spencer? Please tell me." Spencer looked away, that was enough for Ian. He tried his best to keep his emotions together by asking, "What about Stephanie? I can't believe I did that. I—" tears finally brimmed over. "Is she... is she okay?" he choked.

Spencer nodded, trying his best to be the one to stay strong. "Everyone is okay, Ian. We aren't mad or scared of you, okay? Please don't think about it." He could no longer keep his tears hidden.

"I have to! You're crying because of me. I can't live with myself knowing that—" memories of he and Kenneth sharing a bed, not only once but on multiple occasions: behind a club, in his car, the other people that Ian led on. "Oh god, Spencer I'm so sorry!" Ian was full on sobbing into Spencer's chest.

Spencer knew all along. And it weighed on his heart—it hurt like hell. He was trying his damnedest not to give into the pain of knowing his beloved was intimately involved with someone else with better looks and wealth. Compared to that, Spencer was nothing. To face the facts, Ian cheated. Having the clarity of his vulnerability and helplessness made Spencer weep irrepressibly.

Ian was used by that guy Kenneth, dragged along for what he wanted and vicariously manipulated Ian to take advantage of him. Whether it was the guise of success, or ultimately Ian giving into his urges, Spencer needed to find some way to stop the pain for Ian's sake.

Maybe this was the problem, he thought. Spencer always dismissed himself when it came to sparing the feelings of others. He played everything off as swell and sunshine and threw a fit if someone showed concern.

It didn't matter. He shook his head. He patted Ian's soft black hair, pushing the moppy bangs away, and allowed Ian to release all his regret.

It felt different now. The texture of his hair, the closeness. Why couldn't Spencer just let it go?

"You shouldn't be moving. Bet you didn't even sleep," Stephanie taunted with a weary grin.

"No, no, its fine," Ian held the railing as he descended the stairs. The aching seared head to toe—it was amazing that he was able to move, period. He stumbled a bit. Stephanie caught him instantly, no longer surprised by his weight. Ian pulled away quickly, "Thanks."

Lizzy stopped herself from interfering and kept Stephanie quite close, insisting that she'd go along with her when Lizzy heard of her plans. "I don't see the aspirin," she called from the kitchen. She utilized this moment to check the Frances' household for anything strange. In her book, strange meant demonic sigils or glyphs. And so far, there was nothing. Not even a faint smell nor an aura.

"Check in the back," replied Stephanie. "We'll be down there in a minute."

"You don't have to guide me. I can make it," said Ian.

"Right, and have you breaking your neck on the stairs? Not likely."

Spencer walked through the door from a trip to the pharmacy. "Alright, I got orange juice, ice packs, ginger, more acetaminophen, soup. Am I forgetting anything?"

"Why did you have to say acetaminophen like that?" teased Stephanie.

"Because that's what it is?"

"It's Ibuprofen, completely different," Stephanie remarked, displaying the medicine when unpacking the bags.

Spencer rolled his eyes, "Whatever, it isn't acetaminophen, but it'll do virtually the same thing."

"You still said it weird."

Ian laughed at the two's antics as they went on with their faux arguments. They all went silent when hearing his chuckle, all on guard.

Ian sensed the tenseness; he kept his eyes fixed on the tops of his feet.

The punch Lizzy delivered realistically should have broken a few of Ian's bones. This only proved that he was further along than expected. Anything they tried to feed him was immediately rejected, and he went through water a gallon at a time. His stomach was still sensitive to anything solid. Most of Baal's blood was out of his system, but it did the job it was intended to do.

He began to take on his own aura, his own demonic presence. It felt jagged, unhinged; Liz thought it to be sinister, feeling like the sharp winds of a cyclone when close enough to detect it. The innocuous aura of a shifter at least provided comfort in contrast. This was only the start of it all. Last night was rough, but what was to follow was going to be worse. Sitting here pretending as if nothing was occurring angered her down to the core, especially after last night. Ian would have had his deranged way with Stephanie if Lizzy wasn't spectating, watching silently as the owl.

To be the one who delivered Ian home last night initiated a conflict of morals. Ian's unconscious body had to be carried, piggyback, by Lizzy's strong arms. The look on his mother's face was priceless, of course. *"What happened now?"* was all she remarked, a tired mom after a long day of work. Lizzy explained that Ian had a bit much to drink, to Mrs. Frances disappointment, but it worked so much as to dismiss the horrible symptoms Ian went through, and now withdrawal. Spencer took first watch. Stephanie grabbed Spencer's homework and managed to forge a few excuse notes for him—as done in the past—and then both she and Lizzy took second shift.

Stephanie didn't let on to her emotional state, but she was a snotty mess last night. Lizzy paced all evening, trying her best to comfort her girlfriend all the while convincing herself to not go back and strangle the guy. Those punches weren't enough, she thought as she awaited confrontation from the lord. She stayed the night with Stephanie, sneaking in from the back when the parents were asleep to make sure she was alright. It didn't take long for her to collect herself, a couple of hours at most, which was why Lizzy knew that the more Stephanie subjected herself to her crowd, the more anguish she would self-inflict. The web Stephanie was entangled within would have her disregard her own inner experiences to accept the false world others would impose upon her, and deeper into their spiral she would fall.

Gaia chose her, Lizzy recognized, and it was her responsibility to make Stephanie come into her own power. There needn't be a prophecy for Lizzy to know this. That intense, inherent understanding made the change more difficult to execute. And the more these situations unfolded, it magnified the possibility that Stephanie would never escape the mistakes of other people, faultlessly accepting their burdens into herself and bogging down her limitless mind. She wished Stephanie wasn't so attached to the other two, but it couldn't be helped at the moment.

Ian was still adjusting to normalcy. The world around him had this angelic glow, even making him squint away from the bright, incandescent lights in the school. His head still felt constricted, changed, and so did his person. He felt out of place being there, felt unworthy even, as if the entire world stared at him when he made his way to class. He shifted his backpack's weight with head down and hiked to each class with little to no word to his friends. There was nothing he could say to them, even if they didn't mention his blatant deplorable deeds.

By mid-day, he stopped to Principal Cane's office to see about his ability to reach senior status with a plethora of missed classes.

Ian took a seat. "Hey, Mr. Cane," he mumbled.

Cane looked up, startled. Ian seemed, no, *was* completely different than the Ian he was used to. The boy looked tired, completely exhausted in all aspects, his eyes cold, sunken and uninviting, and the vitality that Cane admired was zapped out of him.

"Oh, hello there, Mr. Frances. What can I help you with today?" What sort of methods were inflicted upon this student? Cane found it hard to look him in the eyes; the guilt of selling a student out to an organization still lingered, his anguish amplified as the days went by, and it became evident that the men hired by MES weren't playing as he expected.

"I'm concerned about my graduation status. I missed a lot of days over the past few of weeks. Is there any way I can make them up?" There was no usual hint of sarcasm or playfulness in the boy's voice.

Cane gazed longingly at Ian. The child would never see graduation in his lifetime. "I can tell you've been dedicated to your studies," lied Robert. "You've no need to worry. You'll get to be a senior next year; you're right on track." *You will never get to be a senior,* weighed on Cane's soul.

Ian, confused, added, "But I missed the last three weeks of class consecutively. How am I still in good standings?"

Sweat began to collect on Robert's forehead. "Your records look pretty good to me," Cane scrolled Ian's profile on the desktop. A happier, brighter version of Ian's portrait smiled back on the screen when his face was full of color and vigor. "I'm sure your teachers will fill you in on the missed assignments. You have nothing to worry about," rushed Cane.

"But—"

"You should get to class. All the teachers are aware, and it is too close to the end of the year to burden you with makeup work. Your main focus should be to study for finals."

Ian did not press any further. This was all too strange. He stood and made his leave; Principal Cane finally relaxed upon the door shutting, not wanting another threat from Abbitt and company.

On the ride back Ian, stared thoughtlessly out the window. Spencer went on and on about the upcoming AP exams with Ian hardly responding at all. Spencer caught the hint and went silent, wishing to himself that he and Ian sat on opposite sides of the bus—the now-faux relationship made Spencer want to hide permanently. Ian completed all of his homework as soon as he arrived home, to Spencer's surprise, and submitted roughly six applications to local jobs. Spencer only observed; seeing Ian this motivated, it was his own version of penance. Spencer also noticed that Ian kept distance between he and his friends and was reserved when it came to conversing as well as other pursuits he used to enjoy.

Ian stepped out to shower; Spencer was left to his own devices in Ian's room. He doodled cats with hats on the covers of Ian's notebooks until disrupted by the vibration of Ian's phone—it happened repeatedly. Spencer flipped the phone over, knowing what to expect. There were thirteen missed called from Kenneth over the span of the day. Thirty-seven unread text messages.

Spencer scrolled through them all, remaining alert to the sounds of running water.

Hey

Scarlet you there?

You should come over ;)

Or not

Don't do drugs; stay in school

Or you can skip school and do more drugs.

I found a new club.

Hello?

You're not dead, are you?

If you don't answer my calls, I'm coming to check on you

Scarlet?

I know you're there

Spencer was furious. The pet names, the closeness, and drugs?

The phone rang again. Spencer answered.

"It's about time you answered, Scarlet."

". . . you should leave Ian alone," Spencer said with a shaky voice.

At first there was silence accompanied by obnoxious shuffling in the background. "This is Spencer, right?" Kenneth finally said; the confidence in his voice made Spencer immediately want to hang up.

He gulped down a lump of air. "Yes. Yes, it is."

"Oh. Well, it is a pleasure to speak with you again. School going well for you?"

Spencer shook his head. Kenneth made it hard for him not to play into his antics. The allure was definitely evident in this man if looks weren't enough. "Ian has not been well these past few days. And it is particularly obvious that you are not the best influence on him."

Kenneth laughed loudly; Spencer jerked the phone away. "Influence? Listen, Spencer. I do not know you that well. You seem like a good kid. But you do know that everything that Ian did was by his own volition, right? He wanted the drugs, he wanted the sex, and he wanted someone who actually lived a little, not some kid who's afraid of his own shadow." Hearing it said aloud was a kick in the gut. Spencer's mind raced for something to say, something quick and witty. But he was at a loss. Images of Ian being intimate with another was all that came to mind. "So, is Ian available or not?" His voice took on an edge that travelled up Spencer's spine.

"N-No. You need to leave him alone. Please."

"Until Ian personally tells me to leave him be, I will not do so. He should get a kick out of you invading his personal space. Or did he tell you to answer his phone?" Spencer immediately halted all manner of action. "I think you should run along and be a good boy. Do not impede into the business of adults, alright, Spence?"

"Don't call me Spence! It's Spencer! And it's my business, too! Whatever you guys were doing, it made him extremely sick. I just want him to be safe."

"Whatever. Tell him I'll be there in roughly five minutes." The call ended—Spencer was at a loss for words. This was the man Spencer was competing against; it was obvious he stood no chance against the likes of Kenneth.

Soon, Ian was back in the room, soggy hair leaving a trail along the carpet. "You want to catch a movie? We can take a bus to town," Ian asked. When Spencer took too long to respond, Ian dropped the conversation. "Everything okay?"

The doorbell rang before Spencer could answer. "That's Kenneth."

Ian looked down, shame riddling his brow. "Be right back."

Spencer followed.

Ian's heart palpitated upon seeing Kenneth's dark eyes investigate his. There was a sort of unspoken, obvious tether to he and Kenneth. Ian could feel his entirety respond in such a formidable manner that almost made him long for their sessions together.

Spencer hid behind Ian, frowning and tentative.

"Hello, Scarlet. Spence," nodded Kenneth.

"W-What are you doing here?" Ian questioned.

"May I come in?"

"Actually, Spencer and I were about to go somewhere." Ian avoided eye contact.

"Shame. May I talk to you for a second? Privately?"

Ian paused before nodding, stepping outside with the charming man. "Have you been eating? You look a bit thin." Kenneth asked, squeezing and pulling Ian's cheek.

Ian removed his hand, creating space. "We can't do this anymore. It was all a mistake."

"Hmm, deja vu."

"I'm serious!" Ian lowered his tone, "No more drugs, no more shady clubs. It's not me; it was never me, just that... that drug talking! We can't remain friends after what I did. Everyone here... they're all I got and I almost destroyed it. So please... please just leave me alone. I'm sorry."

Kenneth ran a thought-filled hand through his hair, looking as if he were defeated, now useless in a battle that was always in his favor. "If that is what you want, then I guess I'll see you around. Was nice." Kenneth started for his car.

Dismissing Kenneth was much like dismissing a world of opportunities full of promise. Ian never forgot a thing that Kenneth presented, clearer than any memory he could scrounge up. Werewolves, vampires... there was more to this life, the *more* that Ian was searching for all along. And here he was, turning away the only guy who was able to do so much in so little time.

"Wait."

Kenneth looked up.

"After all of this, all that you showed me, I was thinking... you were doing what I asked for all along, weren't you?" Ian looked longingly at Kenneth, overwhelmed with contradiction.

Kenneth nodded with a slight wave of his hand. Soon after, Kenneth revved his engine down the vacant street, and Ian found it difficult to cease his longing for their next encounter.

9

EVENTUALLY

Baal flipped through the stolen document for the hundredth time, expecting to find details or clues that he missed. He had everything memorized, Ian's story from start to finish, or at least what was gathered. He now had two prevailing questions: were other demons responsible for Ian's frequent migrations, or was it the doing of Ian himself? Of the two possibilities, the first seemed the more troublesome. Baal already had his imp lackeys scope out places from Ian's childhood, each adoption facility and past residencies. He had the specifics of each engrained so much so, it was as if he walked in Ian's shoes.

He would take out Voltaya himself if he had to wait another damn minute for an update to come through. Yet now that Baal had a pretty good idea of Ian's strengths and weaknesses, it was time to play on the latter. Baal commanded Travius' new role as an interloper, and Ian's heart surely would let its guard down for this.

Baal could not bend Ian's will and guide him by an invisible string. He only had manipulation of his weaknesses and suggestion at his side to drive Ian towards him. That annoyance of a plaything Ian kept around him, Spencer, became a nuisance that Baal wanted to remove from the picture permanently. Perhaps soon, but for now Kenneth would continue his pursuit. After all, no doesn't quite mean no in every circumstance, and in this one, the naysayer still felt obligated in some "intricate" way that he remained oblivious to.

Spring break was just beginning. This Saturday night left Ian to his own devices, especially with his parents out on a date. He was not in a mood to spend time with his friends, not for the last week even, although they beckoned him constantly to leave his house, the room at that. It was not because he didn't want to—it was because he didn't trust himself. His mannerisms were changing, he noticed. His breathing was sporadic around everyone much like the onset of a panic attack.

Ian busied himself on his laptop in the dark of the living room. Lights gave him headaches and weren't exactly the most comforting. The blue light of the computer screen did no justice to the sensitive pupils of his.

Ian jumped from the couch, nearly from his skin, when hearing the creak of the back door. And when it wasn't Spencer,

Ian tensed. "Why are you here?" He couldn't keep the relief from his voice.

Kenneth closed the door with curtesy, removing his jacket as if he were invited. "I wanted to see you."

"I told you that I can't see you again," but Ian's tone was not convincing—he couldn't peel his gaze away from the peaked pectorals and bulging biceps. Euphoria washed quickly through Ian. Oh, how he wanted that man. Badly.

"Too bad you leave your back door open. Shame. Could have been anyone. Nice house. Mrs. Frances really does an excellent job with decorating."

"Kenneth! You can't be here! Leave!"

"So, then let's do something! Go out, a movie, anything," he closed the distance, parting the bangs from Ian's eyes. Ian didn't flinch. Leaning into the brush of Kenneth's fingers across his forehead, he reached towards Kenneth's face, cupping his hands around and leering hungrily for more of the clandestine encounter.

"Hey now, easy Scarlet," chuckled Kenneth, "Aren't we moving a *little* too fast? I like to take things slow." Kenneth crept his hands down Ian's shoulders.

There was desperation in Ian's voice, feeling his teeth pulse within his gums and the rugae rub within his rumbling stomach. "I don't know if I should be dying of starvation or dying of immense ejaculation. I don't know what to do, Kenneth! I can't eat, I can't sleep, and I don't have anyone to hump and it's driving me absolutely insane!" Ian clenched his teeth to a point where the veins in his neck protruded. His grip on Kenneth communicated such desperation, as if he were awaiting Kenneth to sneak in. "Fuck, you make me so horny! I will literally kill myself before I betray Spencer again. I feel like my entire body is going to explode and—fuck it!" Before any of that torture persisted another second, Ian began to tug at Kenneth's belt.

"Looks like you'll have to kill yourself," Kenneth assumed his role as the dominant, propped Ian on the couch, and then proceeded to relieve Ian of at least one burden.

Ian was tight, yet Kenneth nonetheless pushed his way through the tense orifice with much spit and dedication. The incognito demon lord set the pace, intense and raw, enjoying the contortions reflected on his victim's face, transforming from agony to ecstasy the more Kenneth pumped his hips.

This was the most enthusiastic Kenneth had ever seen Ian in sex. He wanted the scratches, the biting, and the slapping—the choking; it all made him smile.

Ian returned the acts as ravenous gnawing, the sharp puncture of forged fangs protruded from both canines and incisors, sinking into Kenneth's supple flesh.

From beneath, sweat coalesced with that of his partner and his own, Ian siphoned Kenneth's blood without thought and bucked his hips as he let out yet another load to splatter above onto Kenneth's navel; Kenneth released himself into the taut rectum with little regard to Ian's preference, collapsing onto his chest as they both breathed raggedly beside each other's face.

Like clockwork, Ian's regret kicked in. "Oh god, I did it again. You really fucked me up, you know that?" Kenneth could hear the smile in his voice.

"Shall I expect an angry boyfriend calling me within the next day?" Kenneth coaxed Ian's back.

Ian loved the feeling.

"Don't say a thing. This never happened, okay?" Kenneth made a zipping motion over his lips in response. "God, I'm garbage... this time I might just disappear."

For the days away from Kenneth, Ian devised ways on how he would continue seeing the guy all the while keeping it obscured. Day by day, Ian was becoming used to the fact that he was different than the others, extremely unusual. His hearing and vision more sensitive, sharper; quick reflexes as if he were never clumsy to begin with. And inexplicable sights that he was sure his peers could not see, dismissed as hallucinations. And still, with no word back from Jonathan, Kenneth had one thing that no one else had: answers.

Goat's Sacrament was more than just a drug. Ian knew this.

Baal was assessing the entire time Ian's body was intertwined with his. Ian's spinous processes did not show any signs of protrusion just yet—no sign of horns developing at any site atop his head. To the demon's delight, the appearance of fangs had Baal grinning ear to ear within the tarnished vessel. And Scarlet's eyes glowed ever hungrier. The way he looked at Kenneth, the lord was almost certain that Ian could detect their likeness, that they were one of the same.

The Crossfire sat parked at a gas station as the night neared a quarter 'til ten. Ian was tense and pressed, springing his leg anxiously. "Spit it," Kenneth sighed, humored.

"What do I do about food? I haven't eaten in weeks, I can't hold anything down. You *have* to help me. I can't live another day like this. I don't know what's going on. No one else will be able to help. Nothing helps. Nothing makes sense. What's happening to me?"

"You are simply being the person you were born to be. This is completely natural; I'll help you through this. This is the process of awakening your awareness to parallel realms surrounding you." Ian was extremely calmed by the vow Kenneth made, sincere and almost spoken to existence as Ian attempted to relax his groaning muscles, awaiting Kenneth's next words. "Same thing happened to me."

"What caused this? Was it the Sacrament stuff? Do I have to go through rehab or treatment?"

"Listen to yourself. Stop getting so worked up. You just have to eat the right stuff. I'll be right back. Sit tight." Kenneth made his way into the convenience store. He returned almost twenty minutes later carrying a backpack Ian was sure he didn't have when he went in.

He tossed the bag onto Ian's lap. "Open it."

Ian did so, confused as to what he was looking at. The confusion turned to shock. "What is this?" he asked as calmly as he could manage.

"Blood." The look on Ian's face only communicated more confusion and horror. "You're supposed to drink it." Ian politely zipped the bag, placing it on the floor. "You didn't have a prob-lem with it the last night we hung out."

"Yeah, well, I'm not exactly tripping balls today. I'm sober enough to know that that's fucking disgusting. Yet strangely enough I'm still sitting in the same car as the person who came back from the convenience store with fucking blood."

"Shut up and drink one."

Ian removed a pack from the bag, inspecting every inch of it. "Where did you get this?"

"I have my connections. Drink it."

"And this is real, one-hundred percent human blood?"

"Yes. Now drink it." Ian still held it between his thumbs, mind entangled with decisions of morality versus now's reality. Impatient, Kenneth snatched it from his hands and tore the side of the sack, the copper-like scent immediately diffusing the air.

Ian surely lost the battle after that. The blood made his mouth water more than any other food had in a while.

And like so, the first bag was emptied followed by anoth-er until the backpack was completely demolished.

"I'm already too messed up to even ask why that just occurred. You can spill it, you know. Tell me what I am already. I've had enough stress in the last few weeks that I'm ready for anything. Trust me."

"I don't exactly know what you are, but you're like me."

"Vampire?"

"No."

"Ghoul?"

Kenneth made a face, "What? No."

"Tell me. Please." He knew it was pointless to beg to a guy like Kenneth whose only way of response was through stagnant facial expressions and vague explanations. All Ian gathered from Kenneth their whole time of knowing one another was that he was a silent virtuoso with a rich foundation and a rebellious nature.

"That's where the fun is. We are finding out together. Eventually you'll know." Kenneth backed out of the parking space and headed deeper into town.

The area grew familiar to Ian the deeper they travelled; they were nearing Kenneth's condominium. The scenery in this area changed yearly with either the announcement of some new strip mall or marketplace. Downtown Willard was a drab scene since this was where the Frances family came for any of their daily needs. There was no reason to travel into the next city or town. Not that Ian cared much for traveling—he liked staying in one place, calling it a home. And with its permanence it brought concrete security. His friends would always complain how Willard was a dull trap—they all were dying to go to colleges far away from this town and Virginia, or at least have any sort of opportunity as far from this state as they could get.

"How come you aren't with Spencer or Stephanie tonight? You all are supposed to be the inseparable bunch."

"If I'd known that human blood was the key to ending my starvation, maybe I would have known why I felt uncomfortable around them. This is going to stop, right?"

Kenneth only smiled, looking towards the road.

"Kenneth! This isn't funny. I'm losing my mind, here. I feel even dumber trusting you, let alone having you drive me around."

"You are a cute one, aren't you?"

"Stop trying to change the subject. This is insane! You told me that you had answers and I want to know them. Now. Stop dragging me around!"

"I didn't force you into the car, nor did I start undressing."

Ian grimaced, "You walked into my house. At least tell me what to expect." Ian sat for a moment of sorting thoughts and came to an arrangement. "Alright, I'm calm. I acknowledge that something's happening. I'm obviously not... not human..." Just saying those words was an uncanny feat—he came to terms with it gradually. Perhaps a side of him always knew from the start. From all the strange looks and the lonesome childhood, all signs pointed towards that possibility. He was a step closer to a truth that even he wasn't so sure he wanted to know. "If this keeps up, then that only means we'll have to stick together until I can get used to this change, huh?" He looked towards his hands.

Beneath his vessel, Lord Baal beamed. Perhaps an alternate arrangement didn't have to occur for the ball to appear back in his court. Ian was playing into Baal's hands all on his own, which meant that some form of trust had been established. Yet that burgeoning trust was fragile.

Kenneth sighed as if tired from the youth's antics. "I can only teach you what you're willing to learn and can only show you how to survive if you can accept what's to come."

"If you would stop talking in riddles, then maybe I would understand." Ian laughed, "You're so cryptic, you know that? I don't know shit about you or your past, yet there's this dark allure that I can't put my finger on... I may have said too much."

The side of Kenneth's mouth rose, "Dark allure, huh? More like a Greaser or one of those sappy fantasy romance novel protagonist?"

"Neither. You have your own breed." Ian reclined his seat a few inches, "Everything about you says dangerous, the kind of guy you wouldn't want to be indebted towards. The type that does black market deals and has his own system of 'business'. Hell, you probably have a loaded gun beneath your seat. I don't know why I thought it would be okay to start hanging with you when all signs pointed to danger. But... a part of me wants to see how bold I could get too, y'know? Part of me thinks I'm doomed to repeating cycles because of my morals. Perhaps that's what's holding me back."

"The dude with the red eyes thinks I'm *dangerous*. I bet your pretty little face that you've been called dangerous more than I have. They all told you that since you were born. And your own birth parents didn't even want you." Ian fell silent. "Some kid, some little mistake. No one wanted to even get near you. That's why you cling so tight to what you have. Because this is the closest you have been to affection from multiple parties at once. Do you think it will last? You can make one mistake and sever every bond you've ever made. Don't you think that's the biggest danger?"

Ian didn't have an answer prepared. Kenneth summed up the very thing he was running away from: the fear of isolation. He hadn't thought of this scenario since his eighteenth birthday, or at least this deeply. Ian swore he was over that way of thinking. "They won't do that to me."

"How are you so sure? It is human nature. If not betrayal, time will tell who your closest friends are. You are an adult now which means all the friendships made in adolescence will soon exist merely as memory. Besides, by hanging out with me, you're the traitor by default," he chortled.

"Not funny. I'm going to deal with Spencer tomorrow. I'll tell him the deal, that he needs to lay off a bit." Right, as if Spencer would accept any explanation Ian gave him. Ian was in for an earful.

Kenneth parked inside his garage. "I assume since you're taking care of it, you won't have a problem staying here tonight."

Ian pondered for a moment letting his carelessness take the lead.

"I'm already a sinner. Might as well."

Spencer perused the aisles according to the list his mother handed him. She was aisles away, chatting hurriedly on her cell in attempts to sort business with her coworkers. Natalie was at his heels, begging him for almost every item she passed. He loved her, but it was times like this when he wondered why siblings existed.

"For the last time, put it back. I'm not getting you anything," he said, pushing the cart to its next stop.

"You're no fun. Your friend Stephanie would get it for me," Natalie pouted.

"That's because Stephanie doesn't listen, kind of like you."

"Your boyfriend would, too."

Spencer fought the urge to hesitate at the words his younger sister always dished. "He's not my boyfriend, Nat. Stop saying things like that."

"It's okay, I know you two like each other," she skipped beside Spencer, reaching the next item she wanted for her arsenal. "You have that picture of him on the background of your phone. I'm not stupid."

He hated how keen and observant kids were. With a roll of his eyes, he switched subjects. "Okay, that's everything. Mom said to meet her at checkout. Let's go."

Spencer rested his head on the passenger window, watching the trees pass on the highway. His mother ran through several conversations on the way back, all on the cell she was glued to the entire day, arguing about paperwork, deadlines and so forth. He blotted it out, as he had always done. His mom dished commands to take in groceries between conversations. Hours passed when the phone finally rested somewhere else other than between her ear and shoulder. "I'm going to the office. Be back later," she managed to say, and without a rest, she was back in the car on a weekend. Who cared? They never spent time with each other anyways. Between her job, boyfriend, and children, the latter took the brunt of time allowance.

It was just Spencer and Natalie these days.

"Mom's going to the office," he sat next to his sister as she played her handheld game.

"Mm hm," she responded. "She always does."

Spencer patted her head. He knew how Natalie felt at times like this and he was no different. He usually left her to play her games, made sure all her homework was complete and cooked for the two of them on nights like these. It seemed to be every night nowadays. They were tightknit as a result. "Why don't you play with the other girls in the neighborhood anymore? You all used to be so close."

"Yeah, in second grade. They all think they're cooler than I am since they have boyfriends and stuff."

"Boyfriends? You guys are in fourth grade," he laughed. "What do they know about boyfriends?"

"Now you see my dilemma," she sighed as her thumbs glided the buttons. "They kind of stopped talking to me because they think I'm too childish. All of them are crazy about this new band."

"Well, screw them. Let's do something. You and I," Spencer suggested. If anything, he wanted Natalie to grow up with no worries or burdens. He could see that childish joy slipping away slowly, week by week. "We can ride bikes like we used to."

"Really?" Her face lit up happily.

"Yeah, come on. We'll even go down the big hill!"

Spencer prepared the bikes in the garage as Natalie bounced impatiently in her gear. Soon, they were off circling the cul-de-sacs, playing tag, and racing against one another. Spencer was glad that she could smile, grateful that he had a sister he could look after despite her annoying conduct. His parents were setting a pretty good example with all the time they weren't spending with them; they both shared that resentment. As young as she was, Natalie took the hint that her brother was the only dependable one in the family.

"You'll never catch me!" Spencer called playfully over his shoulder, in the lead. He began to brake, coming up towards a curb where Ian sat.

"You're having fun," said Ian, snuffing out a cigarette butt. "Watching you ride around the place like an idiot has been entertaining."

Spencer popped out his kickstand, responding to Ian's taunts with a dorky grin—the blush was always to follow. "You know I'm all she has. I wish you would quit smoking those things." Ian smiled, lighting another.

"Hi, Ian!" Natalie braked, nearly jumping off her bike to tackle Ian in a hug.

"Whoa, whoa. Didn't think you liked me anymore, Nat!" he hugged.

"Ride bikes with us!"

"Next time." Ian stood to brush Spencer's hair from his eyes. "You look cute enough to kiss." Spencer looked pointedly at his sister with a clear of his throat. "Oh, please. Natalie isn't dumb. You know that Spencer is my boyfriend, right Nat?"

"Yep. I don't know why Spencer keeps hiding it. He loves you."

"You hear that?" Ian kissed Spencer despite his attempts at flinching away from the secondhand smoke venting from Ian's nostrils. "You *love* me."

The evening faded from hues of pink to black as Spencer warmed leftovers, leaving Natalie to play her handheld games.

Ian sat on the counter, quieter than usual. Ever since the incident, Spencer noted how reserved Ian acted. He thought it
was cute the way Ian just watched everyone, smiling to himself
in silence—it was also disheartening. Ian was tense around
everyone, Spencer peeped it. This was the first Ian had been over
in almost a month.

Ian didn't know how to bring up any conversation involving Kenneth, not after what Spencer witnessed. After all, it was
Kenneth's involvement that almost got Spencer and Stephanie
hurt. They distrusted him, as much as Ian should. Mentioning
Kenneth would be the last thing anyone would want to hear. But
Ian needed the topic to resurface, because even now, Ian could
hear the slight pitter-patter of Spencer's heartbeat. And Ian was
almost moved to... no, he couldn't. Never.

"Are you hungry?" Spencer asked. "I think I have enough
if you're going to eat."

"No. I'm fine." From behind, Ian placed his hands on
Spencer's waist as he prepped. His grip was tighter than usual;
Ian fixated on the feel of Spencer's skin through his fabric.
He wrapped his arms around Spencer's torso, resting his chin
on Spencer's shoulder. He was warm. His natural scent mixed
with the smell of sandalwood radiated from the blond one. Ian
was enticed by his natural fragrance; he never quite noticed

the small things, these minuscule details that made a world of difference in his current state.

Ian's hands were at play all the while his mind was lost at the possibilities that he could be sensing. His fingertips found the elastic of Spencer's underwear and began to navigate further downward.

"Babe, we shouldn't be..." Spencer groaned, partially distracted by Ian's doings. Ian only homed in on Spencer's increasing heartbeat, hearing his blood rush to and from the heart. It was simply amazing, a captivating world yet to be discovered, all inside Spencer. The winds that rose and fell from his lungs to the saliva worming down his throat.

Ian was completely hypnotized.

Spencer was nervous, head to toe. Yet, the feel of Ian's hands in places where they never once met was an experience Spencer always dreamed of having. Spencer braced his palms on the counter, momentarily forgetting about the food, about everything. He felt the tip of Ian's member press and pulse against the back of his pants. Warm. Inviting. Everything washed over him like a spell, and Spencer was drawn completely towards Ian unlike ever before.

Ian's hand wrapped around Spencer's cock, stroking delicately in the rhythm that Spencer pushed his hips. Spencer gasped at the intensity, his legs losing function. He lost his balance, crashing backwards into Ian. The two toppled to the floor.

"Are you okay?" Ian asked through bubbly giggles, the weight of Spencer pinning him.

Spencer quickly adjusted himself, face beet red. "I'm fine," he said through a whisper. Embarrassed, his attempts at avoiding eye contact failed when locked by Ian's strange eyes. He was baffled at what to say or do.

Ian continued to laugh, rubbing his head. "I think I may have gotten carried away. Sorry about that." He noticed Spencer's contorted expression and immediately became recessive. "Hey now, I didn't mean to—I'm sorry, I just thought..." he trailed off.

"I hardly speak to you or even see much of you in weeks, and then you do this," Spencer choked through tears traveling over his cheeks. "I just don't get it, Ian. What am I to you? What are we anymore?"

"Spencer..." Ian immediately stood. In attempts to wipe his tears, Spencer flinched away. "Babe, you're my boyfriend. Don't be like this. I didn't mean any disrespect, I just assumed that, you know..." The disconnect between the two had been large. Meeting Ian outside was a gift in Spencer's eyes. It was as if they lived in different states, completely in another realm.

Ian backed away, suddenly scared of himself, abashed from what he did to Spencer, most frighteningly, what Spencer urged from Ian, the full effect of it. Everything was wrong, contorted in a mess of inexplicable happenings. To think that in the past few days Ian completely obliterated those bags of blood and more, went against his word in multiple instances; his frequent outings with Kenneth since their reintroduction proved to be no trustworthy act. There was nothing to be justified.

"You should go," Spencer said, looking away.

Ian stood there a bit longer. "I haven't been myself lately, Spencer. I'm trying to get this straightened out but—"

"But what? Was it the drugs that fried your brain or have you gotten used to having someone to fuck since I am obviously such a stick-in-the mud, straightedge freak?"

"I never saw it like that, Spencer. I would never do anything to betray you, and you know that! It's been complicated."

"Complicated? What is so complicated about keeping your dick in your pants? I tried to ignore it, Ian. I tried to just push it all aside since you were sick, you were absolutely messed up. But I can't. It hurts so damn much!" Spencer sobbed into his hands. "This whole time I've been convincing myself to trust you, but I can't anymore."

Every bottled emotion Spencer felt since Ian lost control that night spilled. It incubated until it hatched into a world of paranoia, fear, and heartbreak. Spencer wanted so badly to see Ian the way he always had, but it was as if the shades were tinted. To even think that a kind-natured boy would have it in him to do the things he vowed he would never do—Spencer began to lose faith in everything he once knew.

Ian pleaded, "I'm clean now, Spencer. I'm never touching the stuff again. You were there when I dismissed Kenneth for good. Why don't you trust me?"

"You're tense around me, you avoid me, Ian. I've noticed. We've all noticed. And every time I talk to you, you hardly respond. Just tell me if you're still talking to him." Spencer eyed Ian, forlorn, awaiting an answer.

"If you would just listen to me, I—"

"Are you still seeing him, Ian? Yes or no."

Ian looked away. It was all that Spencer needed to crumble onto the floor in painful sobbing, grabbing his heart at the tangible aching. The past three years meant nothing. Spencer felt that their entire relationship was based on lies—he refused to acknowledge the person before him as the same boy with the red eyes.

Ian placed his hands on Spencer's shoulders. "Kenneth was helping me find out my past. I never meant for us to have—ugh! Fuck, Spencer, I'm so sorry. He didn't—"

"Fuck your past, Ian! Stop obsessing over it! It won't do you any good, nor the rest of us. Leave already, and forget about everything we ever had. I'm done."

"Spencer. Please, please listen to me."

Ian attempted to pull Spencer into him, but was met with a harsh push. "Get out! Get out!" A dish was thrown, crashing at Ian's feet. "Get out of my life!"

Ian ran. He ran until he reached the limits of the neighborhood. Anger flashed through him, curling his fist over and over, blind in rationale.

He hated himself for existing—bearing the thought of hurting Spencer was sickening, gut-wrenching. His first impulse was to take out his anger on someone else. His eyes searched the streets frantically for someone to torment, using another's agony to cover up the pain and confusion the two both held although opposite sides of the spectrum.

Ian snapped to his senses, realizing his frantic condition as he stood there, teeth bared, salivating with unarresting eyes, and fingers that fluttered madly. It was in this moment of tranquility when he noticed his own reflection—the source of those terrible migraines could be attributed to the visage of hornish knobs sprouting from his skull.

At a second glance they were gone much like the other hallucinations, yet the feeling of them remained.

Natalie paused at the kitchen entrance bewildered at her brother's hands soaking in blood, shards of ceramic everywhere, and Spencer sitting in the middle of it all.

Curiously, Lord Voltaya watched as Ian roamed the streets this late at night. The bars were just as lively, and to the demon's delight, the target entered through the doors of the Tattered Wagon Pub. A time to be alive, the demon thought, making his path towards Ian in the vessel of a stranger.

Ian drummed his fingers at the bar and bounced his leg trying to keep his mind occupied. Voltaya took his seat beside him, ordering as his vessel would normally do. *This is the Young Ruler. In the flesh. Young, delectable, precious flesh! Without blemishes or scars. And those eyes! Those pristine eyes!* Voltaya grew excited, nearing his prey in the dead of night without a soul to interfere.

"Long day, huh?" Lord Voltaya initiated the casual banter. He could barely keep his excitement at bay, visualizing the reward his tireless pursuit would bring him.

Ian only looked to his right, then back towards the empty counter below. The roar of those by the pool table were a distraction to everyone in the vicinity—they rumbled and boasted, placing and taking bets to best their opponents. The night was still young in the eyes of the bargoers, and each one of them chose this shoddy place to detox from one thing or another.

The man with sunken eyes and stubble decorated around the chin ordered three rounds of bourbon, sliding one towards Ian who took it to the head without a conflicting thought. "What's eating you?" the man asked.

Ian knocked back another shot, sighing, "Ever feel like no matter how good your intentions are, you still manage to mess it up in some way?"

The stranger laughed heartily, hacking up a cough. "Don't even tell me, I know all about what you're going through. Another round, on me."

"Thanks." Ian went through his third and fourth shots without flinching at the taste.

"Retired military. I was shot three times while deployed. Got off on discharge. I get back home after two years deployment to an empty house. My wife left me for a coworker of hers and moved across the country. Women, I swear," the stranger was ahead of Ian by three shots. "Who hurt you?"

"I did. I fucked everything up. I had everything perfect, until I poked my nose where I shouldn't've. I want to..." Ian crushed the shot glass in his hand without a wince and watched the blood slicken his palm then trickle onto the bar.

Voltaya smiled. He could feel the rage seeping from Ian, the sorrow converted into pure hatred. The boy was intoxicated, yet still drank like a fish. After an hour of drowning his sorrows and getting acquainted with the man, they found their way to the pool table, cleared from its previous players. The man placed a ten on the side. "Winner takes all. Think you can handle it?" Ian fished his pocket to match.

"The adoption system is absolute bullshit," the man continued in reference to their earlier topic. Two striped balls fell into the pocket. Ian aimed the pool stick on his turn. "A buddy of mine never faced adoption. The government always cut funding to the homes, and any hope of a decent education was hopeless. Met him when I enlisted." The balls scattered around after Ian's failed shot. The stranger made another perfect shot, and Ian missed on his turn once more.

"Same thing happened at the foster home I lived in. Winter was the worst. We'd have no heat on the coldest of days. Had to suck it up whenever the hot water stopped working."

"You lived a harder life than most of these old guys I know. What'd you say your age was?"

"Eighteen." He missed again. "And not the greatest at pool," Ian slurred.

"Meh, I was younger than you were sneaking into bars. Back then, fake ID worked like a charm if you had enough facial hair."

Ian retrieved the ringing phone from his pocket, excusing himself outside to answer it.

"Just calling to make sure things are okay," Stephanie sighed on the other end.

"If you're just gonna yell at me too, let's hear it. I'm ready," Ian laughed drunkenly.

Stephanie paused, knowing this scenario all too well. "I'm not calling to scold you or beg on Spencer's behalf. I don't have to ask how you're taking it; I can smell the alcohol through the phone. This is a shocker to me."

Ian lit a cigarette. "It's not shocking. I fucked up our circle when I fucked Kenneth. Magnificent sex in exchange for my life falling apart. Go ahead and take his side, Stephanie. It will save us from any more drama."

Momentary silence proceeded before she responded, "I take Spencer's side in this one-hundred percent. You really fucked it up, no offense." They both laughed. "Just take it easy for now. I'm not going to lie; I'm very upset with you. Would think you had more control than that. Just don't do anything else stupid, 'kay? I hate seeing Spencer so hurt like this."

Ian sighed, flaccidly sliding his back down the brick exterior into a steadying crouch; the world whirled around, and his eyes found it hard to maintain focus. "Thanks. I'm sorry. I'm going to set things right, Steph. Please make sure he stays positive for me."

"I'll do what I can, no guarantee that he's going to come around. Later." The call ended.

Ian took a long draw before watching it drift up towards the waxing crescent. He fondled the necklace resting beneath his coat, inspecting its spectral crystal in the scarred hand wrapped in bar napkins. "Hidden abilities, huh?" he said to the charm. "Seems like I do nothing but drive everyone away. What an amazing ability..."

A shadow in his periphery interrupted his woeful scrying; Kenneth's eyes peered into Ian's without the treasured, taunting grin.

He extended a hand towards Ian. "You look like shit. It appears you need a ride home." Kenneth stole glimpses over his shoulders, "Come on."

"How did you know I'd be here?" Ian collided into Kenneth before maintaining his balance. "You don't think I'm a terrible piece of human waste, do you?"

"Shhh. Don't talk." Kenneth initially stood as a brace, yet the more Ian stumbled, the more aggravated Baal became—he tossed the inebriated over his shoulder, quickening the pace. Neon signs stretched across Ian's vision, his mind a topsy-turvy twisting, turning the townhouses into towering titans. His eyes shuttered at the streetlight's veil glare, craning his neck to watch the bar fade in the distance. The sidewalk stretched and warped, undulating as Kenneth's great strides jumbled his senses.

A figure stepped from around the bend just as Kenneth started for it.

The two looked each other square and mutually—a lord respected another so long as it was reciprocated. Beneath the competition, there was an understanding that came with their

ranks, yet with a prophecy to fulfill, the lords stood in direct
contrast among thickened tension to fill the space between.

Voltaya, adorning the drunkard, stepped forward. All
those hours waiting in anticipation were torture; Voltaya wanted to see what Ian's skin really looked like on the inside, a level
of insanity which made Baal look rather tame. "I would have to
say, Baal: babysitting really suits you well. Making them ripe,
breaking their cherries," Voltaya laughed loudly in the face of
his opponent. Baal glared, watching, observing. "I thank you for
beginning the awakening process. None of us thought to use our
own blood like you and your master have. Bravo, bravo. Now,
we can stay and chat, but I'll be departing with that gorgeous
marvel," Voltaya taunted, reaching for Ian.

Baal repelled Voltaya's attempts instantly; Ian tumbled to
the ground and hit the concrete with a thud, unable to comprehend the matter at hand. "How long has the Second Gate known
about the Young Ruler's emergence?" Baal questioned, gripping
the collar of his enemy with fire in his eyes.

Voltaya only laughed, "What, you thought your Gate was
the only one who knew? How much more naïve can you get! It
was the Second Gate who transcribed the writings. Your Gate
only stole those eons ago." He snatched away from Baal's hold.
"How about that, Ian?" Ian stood uneasily, looking towards the

two. "Did your friend 'Kenneth' here drag you all this way without explaining a thing, my jewel?" Baal made his move, striking swiftly at Voltaya preternaturally. Ian watched the dance ensue; Voltaya dodged every fatal move made as Baal did the same. Voltaya smiled maniacally at the game—all of this was child's play. They both held back their true potential.

"This is getting really annoying."

Ian whirled around to face a small girl, astonishingly beautiful with black tresses of pigtails held in plucked, pink bows. Before Ian could open his mouth to speak, Baal teleported Ian leagues away from the two.

"Lord Baal. We have the pleasure of meeting once more," the small girl giggled. She and Voltaya boxed Baal and Ian in from either side, closing the distance with synchronized steps. "You and I could have made the perfect team long ago. I see you and this adorable young prophet are well acquainted now. Isn't he just the cutest!" the girl squealed.

"Two against one," Kenneth smiled. "If I did not know any better, I would say I am quite infamous if it takes the two of you to take me down."

"Don't flatter yourself," said the girl. "It will take but a second to strike you down!" Instantaneously, Godimus closed the distance of ten meters, aiming a kick down onto Kenneth from above. He grabbed her ankle a split second before it landed, throwing her into a charging Voltaya. Lord Baal used the moment to play the defense and get as far away as he could—within a fraction of a second, he teleported atop the adjacent rooftop, running and gliding across each subsequent edifice with Ian held firmly within his arms.

Voltaya and Godimus were quick, extremely coordinated, and at Baal's heels in no time. Ian was beyond terrified, staring back at the two just inches behind. Baal jumped to the next rooftop when the two dispersed, flashing away in opposite directions.

"Kenneth, what the hell is going on! What is this?!" Baal continued running, coming to a stop on the next roof, waiting. "Kenneth! Seriously, put me down!" Ian fought out of Kenneth's arms; the rush of adrenaline brought him to sobriety. "Who are those people?"

Baal remained immersed in the state of battle, ignoring Ian's interrogation. He watched from each direction, listening. In an instant, Baal blasted an ethereal energy from each palm at both Voltaya and Godimus, sending them spiraling towards the ground. Ian couldn't fathom the very speed in which they moved, not seeing them until they were mere inches away from the two. Ian was swept from his feet, again in Kenneth's arms, heading deeper into the city. Kenneth jumped from the two-hundred-foot building, landing with ease and Ian clinging for dear life. "What the hell was that!" Ian shrieked.

Kenneth only smiled. "Are you going to keep asking questions or are you going to let me save our asses?" He pulled Ian along, crossing the streets and dodging traffic.

"I will gladly shut up after you tell me why a drunk old guy and an eight-year-old are trying to kill us."

Not to Ian's surprise, Kenneth ignored, replying with, "Come on. Stay close." Ian scowled, keeping close to his protector, if he'd call him that. Sure enough, they reached the edge of town without a sign of the threats, met with the freeway and fields all around.

For two miles, Ian hadn't seen nor heard a thing. Whatever it was that Kenneth neglected to tell, it was surely something he did not want any part of. He calmed his pulse after being on edge for hours, crashing down into the grass. Glancing upwards, he observed Kenneth's blank, calm expression—there was something else in the mix, something about Kenneth that knew this was going to happen. What was this guy, and what shady business was he involved in? At any rate, it was a daunting night. All Ian had in mind was safety and a never-ending sleep to ignore the rest of life's stressors and the oncoming emotional breakdown of the loss of a friend and boyfriend.

He pulled his legs close to his chest. "What now?"

"They are still close by. We wait."

How can he tell, Ian thought.

However he was doing it, Ian only grew more and more fed up with it. Agitated, he tapped his foot which seemed to be his signature as of late. Ian scrolled through his phone, sorting through every app for some sort of distraction. There were no messages, let alone anything that could hold his attention. Of course, he made the mistake of sifting through his pictures. It seemed like most of them consisted of he and Spencer, the entire crew. His thumb hovered over the trash symbol. He gazed longingly at the joy-filled eyes that were Spencer's. All Ian could think of was the turmoil that Spencer was experiencing. And by the pain in his voice, the episode replaying itself in Ian's mind—it was not turmoil born in that moment. It was there for weeks, that pain, ever since Ian met the likes of Kenneth. Ian felt like such a fool vouching for this man, making up excuses directly to his boyfriend's face only to sever every amount of trust he had in Ian.

Ian could not stand another moment of this. "I'm going home," he stood.

Before any step was made, Kenneth had his wrist. "No."

"You don't own me! Who the hell do you think you are?" Ian snatched his arm back, walking off towards home.

"Let me drive you home." Ian could not argue. He bore frustration on his face the entire trek to the car.

Kenneth parked on the curb before Ian's house, as he'd always done. "I'm going out of town for a few days. For business." Ian rendered it useless to ask why, it wasn't like Kenneth was going to tell him. He would just keep Ian guessing until something tried to kill him again. Even then, Kenneth would keep Ian running in circles; nothing was new.

Ian spat crossly, "Don't bother coming back here. My friends are right—I get nothing but trouble when you're around. You did something to me! I don't know what the fuck is happening, everything about me is changing from some shit you did to me. You can fuck out of my life permanently."

Kenneth only laughed. "Well now, Scarlet. If I knew any better, I would say you enjoyed every moment of it. You asked for it after all. What is it, twice now that I've heard this speech? I'll be back soon." Kenneth sped off. Ian watched until the taillights were a mere dot in the distance. Ian cursed into the sky until his voice grew ragged.

"Thank you. Come again."

It was a seedy convenience store called 8-Twelve, one of those service station, twenty-four hour combos where only truck drivers and night owls visited at two in the morning for a pack of Paul Mauls. The manager dished out tired commands to Gularis—she felt like she had to talk to a child the way the guy needed to learn every little thing since the day of landing the job. How to use a computer, a basic keyboard. Her patience was wearing thin, but he came this far being dragged on a leash, and his shift was coming to an end.

Poor Gularis was head over heels in trying to integrate himself back into a human's world. *Who knew this stuff would be so tedious?*

His nemeses was the Acre computer that glared at him from the register. Not once in his life had he touched a computer; these things were the epitome of everything he hated about people. As if it wasn't enough that they were destructive, now they had these cursed machines to do their evil bidding. He could feel the stares he received from customers while trying to navigate the Acre's prompts during a sale. "Hey, make sure you restock the freezers. You forgot for the past three nights."

"Yes, ma'am," he responded with an awkward squeal. He couldn't help that her voice was so cringeworthily, a Georgia twang that he could not learn to get past.

The cowbell on the door jingled just as he headed for the cold storage.

"Hey! Wyatt! Ring up this customer before you do that."

Gularis pivoted back to the counter, thankful for his surplus of stamina. "Hello, welcome to 8-Twelve—," Gularis' breath stopped short of the brash aura that seemed to punch him square in the gut. *Noctua was right,* his thoughts scurried about, *Hazth is alive! I have to talk to him. I have to say something—anything.*

With a composed demeanor, Hazth was soon at the counter, placing two items: salt, and utility cord. Gularis didn't realize his impertinent staring until the cowbell chimed with the entrance of another customer. "I-I'm sorry. Would t-that be all for you?" With a lack of response from the wayward shifter, Gularis quickly and clumsily rang up the items.

Hazth was out just as fast as he entered. Gularis struggled with his thoughts; does he dare go after him and risk being fired? He hurriedly locked the register and ran outside to catch up with his old friend.

He was nowhere in sight, but nevertheless Gularis found him leaning against the back of the shop, as if he awaited this encounter. It was just as breathtaking to encounter Hazth as it was moments ago. Gularis was speechless.

Hazth peered coldly into Gularis. "You honestly could not have found a better job other than this dump?"

Gularis embraced Hazth tightly as if meeting a twin separated at birth. Hazth begrudgingly reciprocated. "We thought you were dead. Hazth... you're alive. Thank Nyte you're alive!"

"Don't get used to me being here. I'm still dead to you." Hazth shrugged out of the prolonged hug.

Gularis only smiled largely, taking in everything that his friend had become. To be in the presence of his childhood friend, together, as men, Gularis could not begin to fathom this reality. And then he could smell it.

The tainted blood that coursed through Hazth's veins: the blood of a demon.

Hazth detected the change in Gularis' expression. "I am not here to be your friend or band together with your clan. Don't think about trying to persuade me, emotion does not work on me."

Gularis' mood encroached into a more serious one. "I know. You've been gone too long for me to try and change you. Just tell me that you're safe."

"We are never safe. So long as human and shifter coexist, you will always be on the run. You are trying to blend in?" Gularis nodded solemnly, met with a laugh, "You were better off in hiding."

"So what about you, eh?"

"What about me?"

"You obviously don't follow your own advice. Why are you here?" Gularis met Hazth at his level of intensity.

Hazth simply looked up towards the sky, its moon providing ample light for their reunion. "My Lord was sent here on a mission. As his Sentinel, I follow as I am asked."

"Baal..." Gularis breathed. "Did you ask for... for *this*?"

"In part. I was forcefully turned. Being partially demon gives me advantage over a lot of things. Then again, perhaps it was always in my nature."

Gularis had so many questions to ask his ally, but doing so was futile. Hazth clearly cut ties with him and his culture as a whole. Gularis was running out of quality time. "Tell me something. This kid with the red eyes. Noctua tells me about his presence as being... troubling. Also, that your, uh, lord was turning him. I don't get it. Why is he so important?"

"Impatient and invasive as always, Gularis. Once you have information, you run away with it only to dig yourself into a deeper hole." Gularis looked sideways. "Remember those old fables we were told as kids around the fire? Of old prophecies and lore? Those were all legends of shifter-kind. However, demon-kind has a far more potent reign over all, and the prophecies are no different. There are many things to this world that you don't know, including things about yourself. The kid with the red eyes is soon to be the Young Ruler."

"Young Ruler? So he's some sort of successor to a lineage."

"'An thou art not worthy of a world such as this. Dawn will come to bring ruin or justice, when worlds align as one, and a Ruler shall emerge. Eyes as embers, blood as oil. From the great veil of beyond, the Young Ruler will rise.' Those are the words from text dating back to the second century. I believe you can connect the dots yourself." Hazth surrounded himself with the thick, dark veil.

"Wait! Hazth, that boy... he's some chosen boy awaiting to be awakened? He's been dormant all this time?"

"It is best to mind your own business, Gularis. What you don't know can't hurt you," Hazth's words echoed as he vanished through the conjured ripple.

10

REALITY

Lizzy looked over her shoulder constantly. One could call it paranoia; in the shopping mall surrounded by hundreds of strangers—humans—no one could blame Lizzy's edginess. Before she knew it, Stephanie had her hand, pulling her in a frenzy towards a pretzel kiosk.

"Wow wow wow!" exclaimed Stephanie, pure in innocent expression. "Have you ever had one of these pretzels?"

Overwhelmed by an assortment of sounds, sights, and smells, all the while keeping her act together inside this enclosed edifice of stores, Lizzy smiled lovingly, "I'm afraid I haven't, Steph."

"You mean to tell me you never-ever-ever had one of the best, orgasmic pretzels on this Earth?!"

Lizzy relaxed her posture, attempting to remain as human as she possibly could. Staying in this guise for weeks, months now, had tired the woman exponentially. With hardly any breaks between shifts, she only grew more tense and para-noid. Not to mention the frequent arguments she held with herself when it came to spilling all of this to Stephanie. And the impending change... Lizzy felt as if she couldn't pull it off on her own, no matter how often she boasted and attested her confidence in the completion of this task to Gularis and Nana. It was Noctua's turn to contribute to the good of the clan. The elders from both local and distant clans recognized that the Avarians were shrinking, a dying bloodline. There were a decent number of shapeshifters left, however they were dispersed over the world, constantly traveling, guised as gypsies, dissimilated from society. In turn, the culture was changing—family life as shifters may as well be dead. Lizzy's clan was one of few that managed to still live as a unit.

Stephanie was supposed to have been changed weeks ago. But Lizzy kept finding herself absorbed in Stephanie's world, enjoying every bit of it, making friends and actually having fun for once. It was a foreign feeling, being able to openly converse with others. All the students were in the dark about the existence of her race and saw her as another person. Lizzy made sure that she didn't linger in their scene for too long: didn't participate in too many activities, turned down party invites, and kept to the inner circle of individuals that Stephanie introduced her to.

Being conditioned for a fight or flight response, Lizzy wasn't used to assimilating back into civilization quite as fast as she had. "Come to think of it, I have never eaten a pretzel before. It's bread, right?" Stephanie returned the most pitiful response of a stare. "Don't look at me like that."

A wait in line and twelve bucks later, Lizzy sat staring at the sugar-encrusted bow of dough. It smelled sickeningly of an impending sensory overload, her nose's sensitivity not serving her in the slightest.

"Come on," Stephanie giggled, "Just take a bite. You'll love it." Lizzy did so, regretting the decision to ignore her instincts. There was that sensory overload, combined by the excessive buttery spread that dripped from the wrapper, down her chin.

"This is disgusting. I'm sorry, there is no way I can eat this." She pushed the pretzel to Stephanie before catching the sad expression on her brow for a split second.

"You are weird! The first person I encountered who thinks these things are nasty. Whatever, more for me!"

Lizzy was hopeless. The girl was so full of this positive vigor that couldn't be replicated. Stephanie's presence made every atmosphere more comfortable, never down in any situation, there to bring love and humor when no one else could. Lizzy fought every nerve in her body to keep herself from killing Ian. It was unforgivable, for Stephanie only deserved the best for the shit that she endured. Lizzy didn't care if every member of MES was there to witness that night, she would do it a thousand times over—every time the thought crossed her mind, she thought of what she should have done, how much more pain she could have inflicted. When it came down to it, however, she knew it was not Ian's fault entirely. It was nearly impossible to shake off a demon lord if they wanted something—Baal's threat to Lizzy served as a great example. She did not take it lightly, which is why she held back so much. And already she knew she was ever closer to the top of Baal's killing list.

Amused, she watched Stephanie devour the bows, resting her head upon her knuckles. The perfect day without a cloud and the subtle breeze brought the people out by the droves. They walked their dogs, shopped aimlessly as if they had not one care in the world. Lizzy wanted to believe her life was as peaceful—with Stephanie's presence, it made it easy to forget the dangers around.

"Hey, Steph?"

"Hmm?" Stephanie smiled cheerfully to Lizzy.

Lizzy stopped short of her actions, caught in another moral war. *Will this happiness still be in her after I change her? I don't want to ruin her life for the sake of mine.* "I want to show you something. Later."

Stephanie smiled around her eyes, "Okie dokie. What is it? Tits and ass? Honestly, I don't think I can handle too much at once."

"Oh please, I have you at my mercy."

"Let's see; who's been the first one asleep after ruining my sheets? You're the one at my mercy, sweety."

"Whatever, kid," Lizzy said with a poke at Steph's forehead. Stephanie scrolled through a series of messages for the following moments. Her frame slumped, exasperated. "What's the matter?" Reading her body language came easy to Lizzy; lately this seemed to be Stephanie's common setting when no one was around to observe.

"What? Nothing," Stephanie smirked once more.

Lizzy could tell she was lying as her eyes veered left and downward. "Is it those two again? They'll get over it. Watch, they'll be back together a week from now. I swear, if they're trying to drag you into their drama..."

"That's part of it. My parents have been on my ass about this summer medicine apprenticeship. I'm supposed to be touring colleges for the bulk of the summer, alongside working if anywhere decides to hire." She snagged one of Liz's cigarettes—the trend picked up, starting to become her habit as of recent. "You ever just drift with whatever direction you were told to go, only because you had no idea yourself?" she said softly. "Ugh, we're having a good day! I refuse to talk about this now."

"No, go on."

Stephanie sighed, "It's okay. I'm fine, really."

"You're not. I can tell. Ever since I met you, you've been stressed, second to Spencer. You may be good at hiding it, but it isn't good to keep it all locked up."

Stephanie took a while to find her words. "I don't know. I feel like no one else would see the point on why I feel so distraught. I have lots of resources, a well-off family, good support system, never missed a meal. Good grades and a bright future. But I feel like I don't belong in that ideal life. And I hate myself for thinking that way."

"Why?"

"Because anyone else would kill to have that sort of stability. And here I am, whining about absolutely nothing."

"It isn't 'nothing'. You're obviously not happy. What do you want to do, your passions?"

"That's just it. I don't know. Sure, I'm good at things and have plenty of hobbies, but it's nothing to make a living from. If it weren't for my parents leading me everywhere, I'd be at a standstill, dreaming."

"Dreaming about what?"

Stephanie wrapped herself tighter in her jacket, embarrassment rippling throughout her demeanor. Meekly, she voiced, "Places that don't exist. Other worlds, adventure, traveling, existing without limits. I feel like... no matter how much fun I have or friends I make, I feel like I just don't belong here. An alien. Feels like my smiling and laughing is all empty, like I'm living behind the scenes somewhere."

Lizzy added, "You feel like you're trapped in a system you can't escape. And if you mess up, there will be no way out. No matter how well you do, you'll still be part of the system you hate... because it doesn't allow you to live how you want to. Seems realer in the imagination, doesn't it?"

Comfort warmed its way through her; something in her heart fluttered with a dim light telling her of the hidden potentials the future held with the girl who suddenly perched into her life. For the first time, someone was able to complete the thoughts she struggled to find words for. Ultimately, Stephanie wanted the world to have its magic despite the warnings that came with escapism—that light within spread an inkling of a knowing that something existed far greater than this current life. Stephanie longingly investigated Lizzy's eyes, irises that refracted the glimmers of hope that Stephanie bore. A tidal pool of deep swirling sapphire composed the bond she envisioned, swept away by the scene blooming within the confines of her mind. It felt as if they held a common space, away from everything and everyone. In a blink, the world around resumed.

She unfurled herself, gesticulating when she could not articulate, and began to vent. "It's like, hey, I never asked to be born, but everyone expects everything out of me, to assimilate into this disgusting world. When I do something unfavorable, even slightly against the norm, I'm met with critique on what I *should* be doing. People find a way to want to make me hide myself, to make me seem like I'm wrong. I don't even feel like I belong in my own culture. Being black, members of my family and my race make it hard for me to separate into my own image. If I don't keep up with certain songs or know the classic black movies, I lose my black card, whatever that is. They usually say, I 'act white' or that I'm weird. For them, I can't exist as my own individual self without having to qualify as something else.

"I can't tell you how many times I'm met with resistance when I ask for friends to come over. My parents stereotype like no tomorrow, don't even bother to get to know them. They never outright say it, you can tell. The way my parents talk to you, Ian, and Spencer versus the way they treat Kiera, Jasmine, and Ryan. I guess they have their comfort zones. I chose my friends by their quality, by what we can do for one another. I don't get why people don't see others as the same. It feels like the body is an illusion; there's something greater that ties all of us together. I feel bigger than all of... of this. I don't know... Earth is strange."

Although Stephanie's ranting was sporadic, Lizzy nodded with understanding. She wanted to unleash all of her people's lore onto Stephanie, to tell her that what she felt was gaia, an all-knowing force that guided all living things, a force that transcended individuality tying everything together. Instead, Lizzy pressed her lips into a hard line keeping the word vomit from spilling her truth. She opted for a general response, "Everyone does that to some degree, profiling, stereotyping, whatever you want to call it. Out of fear, it's a survival tactic. Just continue being you, Steph. Go on, what else is on your mind?"

"Spencer had to get stitches last night. Ian is, I assume, still fucking around with that Kenneth guy. They all promised we would do something fun for spring break. And right now, I feel like you have given me more emotional support than anyone ever has. All these things, the little stuff, everything about this world is trying to eat at me. I made it my priority to never change. I guess I'm starting to see why people do. I'm a stupid escapist."

"You're not stupid, you are what everyone else is afraid to be. Plus, you never give yourself enough validation. Stop trying to be there for people who don't appreciate your time. People change, and friendships fall apart. You are nice, sweet, kind—I love that about you. Others will take advantage of this, sadly. It's seen as a weakness. But it's right, it's moral. I understand how you want this shithole to be different; no one appreciates anything. We can only hope that one day it gets better. Until then, enjoy the present, because you never know what can be taken from you. Most of what you worry about will soon feel minute two or three years from now."

Stephanie smiled a peace-filled, broken smirk. Lizzy's two cents of interest was everything Stephanie had ever wanted. "Shitty, right? Here I am pretending like I'm the mother goose of my friends when I'm just as clueless as they are. Like, honestly! I've spent so much time worrying about everyone else, that I haven't focused on me or on us... This is supposed to be a date..."

Lizzy simply kissed her with the most innocently placed peck, filled with a lifetime of passion. Stephanie felt herself blush and give in. The realization of Lizzy and herself living a life together came into view for just an instant, the same flicker of sapphire pools came and went from Stephanie's mind.

When the kiss broke, Lizzy lightly thumbed the surface of Stephanie's knuckles as they persisted in comfortable silence. The mystery of the new girl swept Stephanie into another day-dream, thinking of their plausible future. Hopefully life would not take them too far apart—she wished she had more control over fate. Before her imagination could show her a life without Lizzy, she needed true information to stoke her visualization towards a brighter outlook. She asked, "What did you want to do like, after high school? Are you the college type or are you more of the go-with-the-flow type?"

Lizzy had to ground herself—she was caught off guard; her human identity felt so real and natural for once, and with the matter of a question, she was legitimately stumped.

Her silence was ultimately so prolonged, Stephanie began to recede, apologizing, "I'm sorry, I probably shouldn't place you in a box. You've had a totally different upbringing than I did."

"You don't have to apologize, baby. Stop apologizing. I always thought being a yoga instructor would be pretty chill, I don't really think about it much." Yet she could never tell Stephanie the truth, not yet. Why did it bother her so much?

Stephanie would be the only person alive to accept her role as a shifter, yet Lizzy didn't want to drag her into such a responsibility yet. Noctua felt as if she superimposed upon Stephanie's quaint life, forcing her clan's survival onto her. Immediately she wanted to backtrack. Gularis' warnings about how humans must be avoided at all costs echoed within her skull—if anyone, Lizzy would know. She witnessed her mother and father being killed right before her and was so suddenly jolted to a reality where she was the leader of her endangered clan. She would never hesitate to kill a human if they threatened the life of her siblings or grandmother. But seeing Stephanie and truly looking into her eyes, she realized that she was falling hard and fast for this girl. A large part of her could not bear to change the one she loved.

"Really? A yoga instructor?" Stephanie bubbled with giggles, her quick wit concocting a pun. "If that was the case, I'd think you'd have liked the pretzel a bit more, you know, with all the stretching and such." The two looked at each other damming their lips before spitting laughter burst forth until the cramps set in.

"When can I meet your siblings? For that matter, your family. You hardly mention them."

"Oh. Well, uh, I talk about you all the time." Lizzy's heart raced. Her family expected to meet Stephanie before and for the change. And with the renovation almost complete, the house seemed to take on a human normalcy. Today would be the best day to introduce her. But with that, she would have to spill everything. "Would you like to meet them? Actually, my brother works at the 8-Twelve down the street. Come on."

Gularis' senses immediately picked up his sister's presence when she turned into the lot, his overworked spirit perked up with relief. Yet hesitation held him in place noting the human beside her. The door chimed when the two walked in. "Welcome to 8-Twelve. We have a no Lizzy policy, so please exit where you came."

"Oh, ha ha. Very funny. Isn't it about time you get off?"

"Yeah, in about twenty minutes," he roughed his sister's hair. "Who is this?" although he knew the answer. His first impression of the one who was supposed to join their clan was very blunt: she was thin, didn't have much strength to her.

"This is Stephanie."

"Hi," Stephanie beamed. "It's nice to meet you." And most of all, she was too nice. She would not make it through the change. Gularis had difficulty approving most of Noctua's decisions mainly because she was too young to comprehend many of their hardships all those years ago. Noctua's strong sense of justice prevented her from seeing the severity often times, yet tradition still stood; although Gularis was the eldest, he was male, and was not the successor in their clan for leadership.

Within those first two minutes of meeting Stephanie, Gularis had everything memorized all the way down to her smell, much like he'd done to everyone he encountered.

Upon seeing Noctua's pointed, frustrated gaze, he received her transmission: "*Loosen up, Gularis. Trust me for once.*"

"So, you're the mighty Stephanie, huh? Liz won't stop talking about you, you must be pretty special. You can call me Wyatt." Out of respect, he outstretched his hand.

Stephanie received it warmly, "I'm not that special, I put my pants on one leg at a time. Nice to meet you, Wyatt."

There was more small talk, the usual cordial introductions. Gularis was uncertain about his read on the girl versus that of Noctua, and when Stephanie dismissed herself to the restroom, he expressed those concerns. "I trust that this introduction means that you're about to indoctrinate her into the clan. Does she even know about us yet?"

"How did I know you were going to say that? No, I haven't. I kinda want to take things slow, I don't exactly want to scare her off."

"Your job is not to wine and dine whatever human you think fits the ideal shifter description. You spend all that time with her, your scent is starting to rub off on her. This is taking way too long. What are you protecting her from?" Liz's downcast expression was enough to set him off, as it'd always done. "Don't tell me you've imprinted. You caught feelings, didn't you?"

The lack of an answer was all Gularis needed in order to scold her, his older brother complex was more that of a father, always wanting to protect a misguided child. The rage was there as his fists tightened around the broom handle. "I knew this would happen, Noctua." He tried to keep his voice as low and steady as possible, but the frustration overruled, "You treat this like a game. Do I have to remind you that humans don't give two shits about us? I don't care how 'ready' you think she needs to be, our clan is dying, Noctua. You need to do this now, or things will get problematic. There is no time for *love*, or whatever you want to call it."

Lizzy pretended as if his words didn't bother her. "She's coming home with us. I figure now would be as good a time as ever."

"Oh no. We all agreed that we will remain in secrecy until the right timing, remember? The contractors were an exception. I don't think the kids are ready for an outsider. Do you ever stop to think about what you're doing?"

Of course she did. That was the whole reason she chose now to get things underway. Lizzy was observant, creating plans in her head in a moment's happening. She saw how increasingly worse Ian was becoming, and she suspected the demons had something else involving those whom Ian was close to. She could sense the slight aura resonating from Spencer, and after the breakup it gradually worsened. No one was safe, but of course she would neglect to tell her brother and continue to play as if everything was fine.

Stephanie stepped outside of the bathroom. Gularis hurriedly whispered, "I think this is troublesome. I can't tell you what to do, and I can't guarantee that I will be nice to her if she's coming over."

"No need to be a douche about it, get your asshole out of a knot for once. Live a little."

Gularis scoffed whenever he looked in their direction while he finished his duties for the day. The flirtation and the nonchalant motifs of his sister angered him more than anything. For someone who was well-adjusted to acknowledging his abhorrence to humans, seeing his younger sister so removed from their reality only brought anger to his heart. Their parents did the same thing, they trusted others too much and died because of it. The resolved leader he knew Noctua to be turned into a foolish girl the moment she was assimilated back into the human world. He could hear their laughter from the truck parked outside, and he could only sort out the rest of the night. How was Nana going to take this? More importantly, what dangers were to come by being associated with this girl?

The waiter with a circular ring around his neck grinned with a flirty spark in his eye as he set the drink in front of Robert, parting to attend to the other white-haired men of the tables juxtaposed to him. With a nervous loosen of his necktie, Robert swirled its contents around with the straw, going over the possible scenarios for his upcoming encounter with O'Neil. Truth was, he knew he was in for an earful, seeming that his deeds got him nowhere but in a shabbier predicament. The men that Cane was instructed to take within his staff were so odd that he'd dare not question it. Such authority was among them, he would be idiotic to inquire about their occupations. Cane brushed his mustache a few times in thought, and jolted to attention when O'Neil took a seat opposite of him at the table.

O'Neil greeted Cane in the most formal of ways, and immediately engaged in the topic at hand. "My men have told me of their progress. It indeed looks like we have a rare and interesting case on our hands."

With that information, Cane relaxed a bit. "R-Really?"

"Oh, yes. Seems to be that the child shows an oblique case of vampirism. Looks like he will not go for a fair price; however, it will pay off decently for study."

Study? Just what kind of sick, twisted practices would they put Ian under? Cane wondered. The knot in his stomach grew larger, immediately tensing up again. "Ah. I see. That's good."

"Your case gave way to several more, actually. Liam and Kenneth notified me of several shifters in the area. They are exceedingly rare as of recent, you see, and are always in high demand. Since it was your case that brought it to our attention, how would you like it if you received a bonus?"

Cane was absolutely fearful for he did not know what this entailed nor who exactly the new subject at hand was. Before he could object and back out of what he pushed hard for, he nodded and spoke, "Yes. Yes, that seems good." It wasn't. After his agreement, O'Neil revealed a blurred photograph printed on normal legal paper. From the looks of it, the photograph was taken directly behind school grounds at the perimeter of the woods. In its corner, the blurred figure seemed to have a luminescent way about it, its eyes reflecting from the photo. He could barely make out who or what it was.

But it was a key feature that almost brought Cane to his knees. The form seemed more beastly than anything—he could visibly make out the human physique, as well as the wings that seemed to morph from its back. Long fingers were spread, almost talon-like. The face was of a young female he was sure he'd encountered plenty of times within the halls of Willard, only he couldn't put a name to her. He couldn't believe what he saw, and his panic was more than enough to process. "Listen, Samuel, I don't think that, well... this is a bit much."

O'Neil responded as if he predicted such. "It may seem like a lot at the moment, but you have to realize, Robert, that these creatures out here are not for the benefit of you and I. Those non-humans survived and evolved off the flesh of humanity, and if it weren't for the founders of the Merchants of the Exotic Species, who put their foot down and lives on the line, humanity would not be here. That shapeshifter has led you to believe she was harmless: it's what they do, their tactic for getting near their prey. Right now, she has attached herself to a select few students, Ian being involved. Might even be a part of some elaborate collaboration between the two species. Point of the matter is that we don't have the time to sit and wait for something to happen. There are students who trust you as their principal, that's what their parents expect when they go to work for the day. Imagine if those two wind up killing the students you were trusted with. Could you really deal with that?"

Cane pondered his words, responding, "Even still, what will you tell Ian's parents when the... study proceeds? What do I tell the others when their classmates go missing all of a sudden? I don't think this matter could be settled so easily."

"If you really cared about that, would you have come to my office the first time, Robert?" Cane was silent. "What matters is that your family is safe. What matters is that humanity is protected. I realize that you may only *think* you care, however, it will be a thing of the past. You see hundreds of new faces every year, even forget the names of students you swore you would never forget. How is this any different?"

Cane felt his face flush, downing his drink as a distraction from the obvious encroachment of emotions. He was in too deep for his own good and could not fathom how to dig himself out. All that MES presented to him now were well-mannered creatures that roamed about, serving the likes of the human men and women that had an influential amount of money. These creatures... when it came down to it, they were stripped of their identity, brainwashed to become some plaything of men.

He watched as they all followed their orders, all with the same device, size customized to their necks. Some danced erotically in the cages above the dining floor while others followed any request and command the members made. If it wasn't for that technology, they would overrun this place in a heartbeat, killing every human without a second thought, resuming their natural ways. And yet, for some reason, Robert could not help but to empathize. Maybe because he knew of one of these creatures and he knew Ian to never hurt a soul.

But Samuel O'Neil was right. In Robert's mind, his family out-ruled everything. What was a couple of kids compared to a bright future? The thought was completely toxic, yet not at all foreign.

Samuel placed a few papers on the table. "I have thought about it, and I know you are faced with rather tough decisions. You've done quite a bit for MES, more than most members have done in years, and you've only been active here a few months! I wanted to offer you a permanent position here as a member of the Merchants of the Exotic Species Board of Representatives for this precinct."

Cane held his hands up, politely turning down the offer. "I already have a full-time job. I could not possibly please you if I were to take this."

"Nonsense, Mr. Cane. As a member of the Board, you work as you work. In other words, you will attend only five or six brief workshops to hone your skills to identify local creatures and report them to the nearest merchants. Think of it as a second income with little to no effort."

O'Neil slid the papers before him. Cane stared blankly at the four zeros affixed to the two before signing his full name on the X.

The gravel driveway was enough to display the remote location that housed Lizzy's family. Stephanie remained quiet for the latter part of the drive, taking in the rural scenery in great contrast of her suburban neighborhood a mere twenty minutes apart. She was anxious but paled in comparison to that of Lizzy, gripping the wheel tightly as the truck bounded on its shocks down the jagged lane for a quarter mile. Gularis sat quietly for the ride's entirety, giving Stephanie the impression that he wasn't the talkative type, so she refrained from asking too many questions. Lizzy brought the truck to a halt at the side of the farmhouse. The three sat in silence—Lizzy's heart raced, as did Gularis'. The argument in their thoughts persisted, an inherent ability of shifters that provided ease of communication in forms when speaking wasn't applicable.

Enraged by Gularis' abhorrence to Noctua's plan, she turned to Stephanie with a smile, "You ready?"

"As ready as ever."

Stephanie's chipper response incited Gularis' final telepathic comment, *"Well, she's got one thing going for her: utterly oblivious to everything."*

"I get it," Noctua snapped, *"you don't like her. Now shut up."* She unlocked the door to the house whose interior smelled of fresh paint, only a single lamp illuminating the main quarters. Gularis stormed ahead of his sister to fill in the children of their guest and to further recite the etiquette that he preached to them day in and out. Nana was immediately alerted of the strange scent the moment the truck turned down the driveway and sat posted in the living room.

Before Nana could question, Lizzy spoke. "Hey, Nana. Sorry I was out so late. We have company."

Nana, much like Gularis, quietly observed the guest before greeting. A smile blossomed on her face, "You must be Stephanie!" She spoke with an accent that Stephanie couldn't pinpoint. "I have heard many things about you. Nice to finally meet you, dear." She kissed both sides of Stephanie's face after embracing her in a hug.

"Thank you for having me... Ms.?" Stephanie grinned shyly.

"Oh, call me Nana. You are no stranger here. Come, come!" Nana urged the two towards the new couches amongst the freshly furnished house. "I wish you would have told me that we would have company, Elizabeth. I would have prepared a meal. You make yourself comfortable, Stephanie." Nana began to busy herself in the kitchen adjacent.

"Your home is absolutely beautiful! Where did you get that painting?" The framed canvas of a fey woman who sat amongst a flock of doves, clad in white linen, was waiting to be hung, leaning against a case full of aged books.

"Elizabeth's mother was a painter. She was talented, that one. All of the paintings in there are her works. You like them?" Nana responded with a raised voice.

"They're... magnificent. I mean, the detail is astonishing."

"Stephanie is an artist herself," bragged Liz. "Don't let her tell you otherwise." Stephanie elbowed Liz bashfully.

More small talk ensued, and the more comfortable Stephanie grew, to Lizzy's relief. A small boy peeked around the corner, and four more pairs of eyes followed. Lizzy could hear the severity of Gularis' lecture from where she sat, and she could sense their hesitance. Mellori, always acting as the brave one, quietly stepped forward first. Stephanie jumped, startled, when she caught the small girl in her periphery. "Oh my god! Hi! How are you?" Stephanie beamed at the small one, caught up in the girl's cute, stout posture.

"You smell good and you're very pretty," Mellori said with childish frank.

"Mel, we talked about this. Don't be a weirdo. How do you respond properly to a greeting?" lectured Liz.

Mellori rolled her eyes. "Hello. It's nice to meet you."

Stephanie couldn't contain her excitement. "You are the cutest thing on the face of Earth!"

Mel couldn't help but to blush and immediately claimed the new guest as her own with a squeaky, "Thanks!" and forced a spot between Lizzy and Stephanie with barely enough room between. "Are you Noc—Lizzy's girlfriend? Do you guys kiss?"

"Mel! What did I tell you about being polite?" Lizzy roughed the kid into a ticklish fit.

Gularis made his way into the living room, followed by four other children who tried their best to remain hidden behind their brother. Mellori immediately removed herself from the closeness of the stranger after seeing the strict gaze Gularis sent her. Lizzy kept her fury at bay, sending a glance at him in return. For the younger ones, this was the first time they've been allowed to interact in such close proximity with a human; the ordeal was frightening, especially with the ideals they'd been indoctrinated with. The other four continued to peak around the corner.

Gularis was rejected for his attempts to help in the kitchen, urged to sit with the guest. He sat with an agitated huff, twiddling his thumbs and tapping his foot. He wasn't one for conversation, especially with a human whom he knew nothing of besides what Noctua told him. "So, where are you from?" Noctua snorted at his pitiful attempt—it was quite humorous to see Gularis act in a manner other than his serious, fatherlike way.

"Here. Willard has been my home my whole life, sadly. It sucks. What about you guys?"

"Out west." Stephanie looked to him expecting more of an explanation. "Are your friends from here, as well?"

She nodded. "I've been with Spencer since the crib. And Ian's been all over the place."

"By that you mean?"

Stephanie wasn't sure if he was always this blunt purposefully. She tried not to take it to heart. "He's been adopted a few times. He can't even tell people where he's from."

"How about we have a smoke?" Lizzy interjected before Gularis could make this anymore awkward than it needed to be. "I'll show you around afterwards."

Stephanie noticed the other four heads lurking as she made her way behind Liz. They scurried away before Stephanie could even get a look at them. She laughed, "Are they always this shy? I'm supposed to be the shy one."

"Psh. Don't pay them any mind. They like to play Spy on Big Sister. Especially when big sister brings her girlfriend over."

Lizzy conversed with Stephanie all the while tuned into the conversation behind the walls. Nana urged Gularis to loosen up, and as always Gularis' anger was before him, stating all of his opinions on the matter in the least censored way. ". . . and she plans on turning her 'soon', all we get is a 'soon' and not 'when'. Why do you have to cosign everything Noctua does when obviously she can't even pull her head out of her ass over some stupid crush?"

"Will you take your own advice and shut up? Noctua is doing things at her pace. And stop being so forward with Stephanie."

"Am I the only person who likes to be forward around here? I don't get why Noctua can't just tell her what's going to happen. If she accepts, cool. She doesn't, kill her. It's simple. And you know that I'm right, so why don't you tell her the same?"

"Noctua isn't like you, Gularis. It's called building trust. Unlike you, she would rather avoid soaking her hands in blood. We've surely had our fill of that!" There was a sound of something breaking, followed by Nana's sigh. "I have had this talk with Noctua, Gularis. She understands fully what she must do. I don't necessarily approve of this crush either, but I think that Stephanie could be good for her."

"It's not about her—it's about us! Suppose that demon kid goes apeshit again and gets a hold of one of the children, kills them. Then what? If she's not going to turn Stephanie right here and now, then this whole thing is a waste. Noctua has had plenty of time to get comfortable."

"The eldest-born female has the power to turn by force. Which means you nor any of the rest of us can turn a human into a shifter. Unless you want to go out all by yourself to find some shifter to fornicate with, then raise that child along with the ones that we're already raising, all the while the rest of us are barely staying out of sight or being sold into slavery, then be my guest!" Lizzy never heard Nana's voice reach such heights in years. This must've stressed her out as well. "Your sister has chosen who she wants to change, which obviously means she knows that Stephanie is strong enough to make it through the change and have the sense enough not to run rampant."

"And suppose the girl doesn't? We all know that she could die just as quickly as she could make it. Noctua is getting attached. I don't think she could handle another death, and I can't bear to see her cry again."

Nana fell silent. "You need to help her instead of being overprotective. I don't like this situation either. I do not trust demons to remain true to their word. I have taken the necessary precautions to protect this family—Baal has been known for not easily being banished. If it is the boy he wants, he will be successful, this is truth."

Lizzy's thoughts swarmed around her. She was at an absolute standstill.

Lord Baal walked the velvet halls of the chamber. It had been a while since he was surrounded by the Uver; the atmosphere was much more welcoming to his presence as he was able to move without hindrance. In his hands he carried with him a small box, containing ampules of Ian's blood as well as other secretions and genetic material. Baal kneeled at his master's door, waiting to be addressed—the massive doors swung inward. Baal remained posed. He conversed in an ancient lexicon. "Master. I have returned with what you have requested."

His master gestured from his position within the obelisk. Baal approached, arms forward, head remaining downward out of respect. The box hovered into Master's claws, carefully observing its contents. "Baal," the behemoth said, its guttural voice perilous enough to be considered charming. "Once more, you have done a service that many lords before you have failed to do for centuries. You may look upon me."

Baal looked unto his master, palms neatly crossed behind his back. "Things are progressing rapidly. The Young Ruler is accepting the change and displays distinct characteristics, as predicted. It will be a few more days before the surge will attempt to overtake him. I plan to have the ceremony commence then, with your grace." He bowed.

Master stood, towering over Baal by a longshot, and bent to clear the long, feathery strands of Baal's hair with the slight brush of those porcelain-cold, hide-like fingers. "That will do." Master unfastened the fixtures on Baal's clothing with only a nod. His garments dropped to the ground where Baal stood, remaining submissive while his master ran his beastly hands along Baal's sides. "You are my most loyal, Baal. The Uver made no mistake when it recruited your soul. A lowly imp you were. Yet, one of the only demons to reach the rank of a Lord in such a short span." The words ushered in this tongue rushed into Baal with hypnotic implications. "A soul that constantly begged to cling to his emotions." Master fondled Baal into further submission. His touch made Baal's knees give beneath him, wincing from the pain of his master's claws digging in.

He dared not make a sound.

"Stand." Baal did as he was instructed. "As you have requested, I will deliver on my end." Before him, a glass casing spawned from the dark smog, containing a swirling, ghastly, white-gold mass of anima. Baal's eyes widened, keeping himself unvexed and unmoving. Baal dared himself to move closer to the container. He could feel its warmth—it called out, beckoned him closer. Hands unsteady, he placed them upon the surface.

Suddenly, it disappeared back into the smog. Baal looked around frantically. An aperture opened beside him.

The master's deep chuckle brought Baal back into submission; animosity grew within Baal, looking away with the cross of his arms behind. "It will belong to you soon. When the

Young Ruler is brought to this plane, it shall be yours. You are dismissed."

"Thank you, Master," Baal bowed once more before leaving through the aperture beside him, arriving back on the human realm. Kenneth's body lay lifeless in the chair where Baal detached himself. The sun began to rise just over the trees—his eyes were fixed through the windows of the condo.

If there was anything Baal fixated on, it was the thought of one day being in a position where he was not made to be a pawn. His master had control over the fate of all beneath the Third Gate—it made Baal sick to his stomach at how lowly it made him feel. Baal already knew the plan Master shared with the lords beneath his banner. They had already proved their submission, their brainwashing, riding on the false hope of someday cashing into the power and knowledge that their master had, but Baal's intuition spoke otherwise. The masters would have them to believe that strength only comes with brute force, and to capture and maintain power and its rewards comes from the manipulation of the world around. All of these demons hated one another yet fought towards the very cause of what made them who they were. Here Baal sat at odds with himself even when he'd had firsthand witness to the rank he amassed underneath what he despised, a paradox.

He no longer desired to be number one; number two would never do. Nothing would suffice until he could escape the sick play of their world.

As unforgiving and brutish as they were, demon lords were puzzling entities who roamed the realms of the Uver. These entities were beasts and conscious beings who had constructed a caste system throughout their entire planet of etheric matter. It was ordered through discord, and it was exactly what the masters needed to keep their rank. The lords were known in their caste as the keepers of knowledge; of mathematics and science, of physics and philosophy, literature, art, and aestheticism. Each specializing in a field of the respective, separated around the realm as such. Their superiors keeping sure that the order be maintained, lords spent most of their time experimenting and constructing their most extravagant themes. These themes could not come into their etheric world without the system crumbling on itself, and instead, within the past two millennia, the beings discovered what would lead to its stability: the Refract.

In immortal history, it only seemed as if it were yesterday when the Refract was discovered. It was merely those two millennia since its discovery when the fresh, young Baal interrupted the ranks of the ancient demons, who were used to the old and chaotic ways at which this world was ran. Barbaric, unforgiving badlands stained by blood—this was the Uver before an entirely different shift of consciousness, and the old lords would not miss a moment to enforce the fact onto Baal, a memoire of the old ways. Baal endured, thankful for the rip in their plane that ushered in this new era: Post-Refract.

After its discovery, the entities of the Uver curiously observed it until many years later, its function was found. The entities entered a land drastically separate from their own, composed of concrete, corporeal molecular arrangements. This physical land of conscious beings was home to a diverse array of life; the most perplexing were the *homo sapiens*. Much like the demons, they were capable of intelligent design, thinking beyond their physical environments and manifesting ideas in a brutish way—the comparative advantage when it came to the demons was that they were well within the reaches of technology far beyond human machinery, equipped with fewer psychological emotions and innate means of existing in many metamorphoses and forms. The Uver was its own large, universal entity, just as Earth was; the Refract only connected the two.

Since the Refract's discovery by the demons, the humans have made incredible leaps and bounds in their own world, allowing these otherworldly creatures to become more of interest. Most beings of Earth did not have the capacity nor senses to comprehend those from the Uver. They displayed manner-isms and activities the demons couldn't help but be captivated by—they knew of no other behavior before than what they were. Coexisting moreover parasitically than mutually, the facilitated change of each plane was exponentially increased, most notably when the acquisition of human essence was found to be pos-sible. Naturally, the demons found that their material makeup rendered it possible to ingest this human essence. The demons continued to consume, bringing back the essence into their realm, facilitating widespread change throughout the species in manifested power. Demons slowly began to obtain abilities that allowed them to manipulate creatures of Earth, and the ranks of imp, intermediate, and lord were given from the least skilled to the best, distributing hierarchal attributes of varying strengths and forms.

Lordship was nothing more than a role, Baal thought frequently, more so in recent events. Things were being parsed together little by little about how the beings of the Uver operat-ed, and his mission proved the concept more each day. Humans were so simple and predictable, he could have had this mission completed weeks ago. However, Baal was not done conducting research for his own benefit. The Young Ruler was speculated to be the world-ender and creator—a concept accredited by the Master of the First Gate—and would ultimately unravel the Uver into another conquest much worse than the discovery of the Refract.

As his master awaited his return with the prize in hand, Baal was faced with an interesting predicament; contemplation took rise as Baal recognized the unique position he held. Currently, not many had confirmation of the Young Ruler's existence, and yet here Baal was with limitless possibility directly in his claws. Why oblige and hand the Young Ruler to the master, who often used leverage of desires to manipulate the lord, when Baal could use the boy to his liking? And if his personal theory was true, he could seal the Refract, free to do as he pleased here on Earth, answering to no one. Such godlessness enthralled Baal, no doubt Master suspected an outcome of the sort and would crush Baal without hesitation.

There was one thing Baal knew to ring true about both worlds: they both worked in teams, creating societal systems in order to innovate. Baal could not act on his selfish inkling to keep Ian to himself unless he had assistance—humans, demons, and other beings—nor would it be kept a secret with other parties involved. Yet Baal had a plan.

11

DESIRE

To become strong, to be a person of influence, what did it mean to Spencer? He didn't consider himself inventive nor creative; he only had book smarts on his side. Spencer stared at the stitches on his palms, drawn into deep thought. His mind took him elsewhere as he stood in the dim lighting of his room in front of the vanity. The room he kept immaculate was now unrecognizable—evidence would suggest that he'd given up, living with the gradual onset of depression. He hadn't spoken a word since he left the hospital. The days seemed to pass in matters of minutes. There were several worried faces, all with the same pitying look, asking the same questions, to whom Spencer never responded.

Yet there was always this figure in his periphery that seemed to bear the same starkness that he did. He wasn't sure of himself or the things that came into his vision.

Do you see how the others mock you?

"Yes," Spencer answered. The imagined figment stood behind him—Spencer stared at it through the mirror, unaware of the voice belonging only to his mind.

It's the same thing every time. They only care when they see blood.

"No one cares. Everyone is selfish."

The figure was the only familiar presence, had been for the past few weeks. At first he ignored it, yet now, Spencer looked to it for advice. He named it his instinct as it always said what lay on his mind. It warned Spencer of the threats around, and after ignoring it for quite some time, Spencer saw that it was right. It knew of the damage Kenneth would enact. Spencer was all too late, and now he wanted a piece of what he should have claimed at the start.

Ian was yours. You had him wrapped around your fingers, a warrior to fight your battles. Do you see what happened?

"No."

He gave into pleasure. Did you honestly think a teenage boy would obey commitment?

Spencer was defeated—there was no way he could answer optimistically as he usually had. It was optimism that led him here in the first place. He wasn't sure of any of his beliefs anymore.

No matter what you desire, they'll still walk all over you. You let them. Maybe you like that. Maybe it turns you on.

"Shut up!"

Why do you run away from pleasure? Why do you hold so strongly against it?

"No."

It was four years ago. It was a rough divorce. It's okay that you did that to him.

"Shut up! Shut up! Shut up!"

That was the first time you felt something like that. See look, you're aroused just thinking about it. Just grab it—stroke it up and down—yes! Just like that—don't stop...

Spencer abruptly snapped from the stupor, removing his hands from himself, and snuggly tied a knot at the waistband of his sweatpants. He buried himself in his comforter, scrolling aimlessly through social media in an attempt to distract himself with mediocrity. Perhaps he was losing his mind. At any rate, he had to regain it soon for he was to face the world tomorrow. He let his mind wander until worn, set his alarm, and fell into sleep.

Jonathan and Hunt were at their wit's end. Hundreds of papers lay both stacked and scattered along the floors and surfaces within the room. The coffee carafe was steaming with its fifth pot of the night. He just could not understand—every bit of evidence Jonathan had at his disposal did not lay in correlation, Ian's case laying more and more unsolvable as the night grew on and the fatigue set in.

Hunt refilled his mug with a disgruntled sigh. "You know, Jon. When you first told me about this, I was convinced that we could solve this thing in a few days, give or take. Perhaps we're approaching things wrong."

"What do you mean?" Jonathan ran his fingers through his hair, fighting a yawn.

"Honestly, I'm not supposed to be working with you, and I could've lost my job by handing you those reports." Jonathan urged him to conclude. "I know you've practically raised Ian, but have you considered that he may be... I don't know, keeping some vital information from you?"

"He's not," Jonathan said sternly. "I'm telling you, Hunt. Nothing in the realm of scientific information is going to solve this. You even said it yourself—Detective Melbourne said we have similar interests."

Hunt looked away uncomfortably. "I merely suggested it, not saying it exists or if it would help us. I think that's going a bit off the deep end."

"Now is not the time to become skeptics." Jonathan quickly became a believer when he returned to his office; his binder full of photographs and articles went missing while nothing else was touched. "It's our last resort."

"We can't go by what some religious fanatics did a decade ago, Jon. They were psycho. Yeah, Ian was involved but... " he paused, "Ian will be fine if we don't intervene. I'm sure you're just paranoid. After all, it is that time of year."

That time of year, Jonathan's thoughts echoed. It happened like clockwork every few years the way Ian would reappear, without family or bearings. "You're beating around the bush. You know there's something else we can do. Why else would you commit to hours of research with me?"

Hunt scratched his head, "Okay. There is something. I am absolutely *not* cleared to speak about this at all. I can't even tell my own wife about this. Anything I tell you did not come from my lips." Hunt sighed deeply. "Now, I don't know one-hundred percent about the 'other' things out there, paranormal or supernatural or whatever. But there is this organization called the Merchants of the Exotic Species. The CIA and us at the FBI keep this under wraps, you could blame money for this. It's a big-time business, extremely underground. Even the government and multi-billion dollar corporations invest in M.E.S."

"'Exotic Species?' You mean like rare or endangered animals?"

"See, that's how they maintain quite a cover to the general public. No, its main purpose is to find, capture, and sell *creatures*, cryptids, artifacts, mythical beasts, things of the sort. I don't have much on it personally, but what I managed to gather is that they have definitive evidence that supernatural or mythological creatures exist and the means to capture these beings."

"What?! Why is this being kept under wraps? They have evidence of what everyone has been searching for for millennia?"

"Yeah. Except they exploit this information by being actual vendors. Apparently, most of their profit comes from the scientific research and donations from an ignorant public and wealthy investors, and then they usually sell these creatures to the highest bidders. Their silence is part of the negotiation. The creatures are kept as servants, pets, sex objects, you name it. Even broadcasting companies use the mythical for influence over the airwaves, sirens I think."

Jonathan had to sit in silence to process what he just obtained. Ian's case was not as farfetched as he thought, seeing as though an entire, separate organization existed specializing in common human ignorance and serving the wealthy. Who was to stop someone from making the assumption that Ian could be profitable? What struck him as even more ludicrous was how his mind didn't give a second thought to the validity of the scenario. It was all he could run with.

Hunt pressed on, "They use the lower and middle classes to obtain information of possible cases, and in return, pay them a small fee, say around $2,500 minimum, depending on the creature. It's a very anonymous system; anyone could sign up or be recruited as long as they take a vow of silence."

"Why hasn't anyone shut this down?"

"Is that even a question? Think about it; the info that MES has could be an advantage if needed for a major world war or world superpower scheme. Remember the threat of weapons of mass destruction in the Middle East? Exactly, you don't remember them finding any weapons, but that area *is* the Mesopotamian basin, the cradle of civilization as they call it. Makes you wonder how we humans became civilized in the first place. There's politics behind it, Jon. I really shouldn't be talking about this. Look, I gotta get going." Hunt gathered his briefcase and other belongings.

"Thanks, Hunt. I really appreciate it." Jonathan raced home, hitting eighty on the highway.

Alejandra was surprised to see him. Ramona cooed at her father, arms outstretched. He took the infant from his wife's arms, kissing her on the cheek. "You're home pretty late."

"My apologies, sweetheart. I had to get a few things together before the middle of the week. How was your day?"

"It could have been better," she organized the shoes at the foyer, adjusted a few frames here and there. "The babysitter quit today. She is starting community college tomorrow. I wish she would have given me an advanced warning. Teenagers," she shook her head. "I have to find another babysitter. I can't take the whole week off."

"I'm sure we can work something out, isn't that right, Ramona?"

"She's had her bath. If you would just put Stinker in bed, I would deem you husband of the year."

He smiled, kissing her lovingly. "Of course, babe. Anything for my lovely wife."

"Perhaps you can put me in bed when you're done?"

"We'll see about that," Jonathan began his chores. As he tended to Ramona, he never would have imagined he would be a father. He was so used to looking after those without family, and with a second on the way, he wanted to ensure his family was safe and secure. It honestly made him paranoid after what Hunt told him. He closed the blinds in every room after settling Ramona, first peeking out and glancing in each direction. Every house around was a good acre or two apart, separated by trees, so Jon did not have much to fear from people. He armed the security system as he'd done nightly, undressed, and then posted himself in his office for more research he was bound to regret.

He discovered that MES had an official page, a .org domain, with a write-up that made it seem simply a research foundation. Anyone was bound to fall for it, official in every aspect. There was even a link to donate and one to register. Jonathan clicked around the page, invested in what he believed to be the sickest organization he was faced with in years. There, at the top of the page on the banner, was a link to office locations. The locations of each precinct shook Jonathan to the core. He stared blankly at the screen. There were at least five offices in Virginia alone, the main office only a mere five miles from Jonathan's occupation. With the anonymity of its members—an organization with twenty locations on the east coast, roughly four-thousand worldwide—Ian could very much be their target, or MES could be the very reason Ian was displaced so frequently. What was Jonathan to do? Questioning the organization directly was too risky, unless he acted oblivious to their real motives. They kept a guise that could easily be shown to the general public, using data from real statistics involving truly endangered animals; probably an entirely separate branch dealt with that.

Alejandra rubbed Jonathan's shoulders, further startling him. "Oh, Alejandra. You scared me."

"Everything alright? It's almost two in the morning," she massaged his tense shoulders, concern about her face.

"Yeah. I was thinking about having Ian over tomorrow or something. I haven't heard from him in a while."

"I'm sure he's fine. You two spent years apart before. He's probably found a life of his own now."

"I know. It's just that... I don't know. Something doesn't sit right."

"This again?" Alejandra laughed. "Look, you need some rest." She peaked over his head at the screen. "'Merchants of the Exotic Species'? I haven't heard of that in a while."

Jonathan turned to her urgently, "You know MES?"

She nodded, having a seat on his lap. "Yeah, mi tio used to work there before he passed away." She crossed herself. "My papa swore he was missing a few screws here and there. My uncle was real heavy into conspiracies. We all thought he was crazy."

"I think I remember this story. How did he pass?"

"Well, long story short, the police called it a workplace accident; that was the only thing we were told. My papa demanded to know more, said it was caused by equipment failure or something. I was only a small niña then—I only remember everyone whispering about it whenever I was around."

Jonathan was amused. "What exactly does MES do?"

"Hell if I know. My papa swears they're no good, like PETA. Apparently, it's a research foundation. One of my coworkers wears a MES pin like it's something glorious. I think her husband is in it or something. He's one of the representatives."

"What's her name?" Jonathan readied his fingers at the keyboard.

"Hannah O'Neil. Why?"

Jonathan did a search on her name, which brought up six articles with the search term highlighted, all of them about her husband, Samuel O'Neil. Jonathan read through them carefully, Alejandra's interests peaked enough to do the same. He gathered that Samuel was supposedly the son of a banker who inherited most of his father's wealth. Although Samuel took over the banking business for about twenty-seven years, he started working with the researchers at MES in Nevada around fifteen years ago. He then founded one of the first branches here in Virginia and was the reason why so many branches existed in the area.

"I knew homegirl was a gold digger, but not like this! She's married to a millionaire! And here I thought she was the breadwinner of the family—she's an excellent nurse." Alejandra found the article amusing; this was someone she had known for years and had no idea how influential her last name was. "I'm her boss and she's making more money than me? I am a little envious," she giggled. However, her beloved husband was in a world of his own, printing out the articles page by page. "Honey, what are you doing?"

Jonathan scribbled a name and number down vigorously, typing multiple searches, printing out numerous sheets that drifted to the floor. "This is bad. This is not good."

"Jonny, can you please explain to me what's happening? You're scaring me."

Jonathan picked up the papers, organizing them into his briefcase. Alejandra looked back to his screen. "A bruja?! Have you lost your mind!"

"She's a medium, not a bruja, mi bonita."

"What are you thinking about doing? You better tell me, or so help me God, you will not leave this house." Her accent thickened as her volume rose. "What are you doing that involves witchcraft? You know how superstitious my family is. I don't like to play with this stuff, regardless if it's real or not."

"I'm only trying to find out a few things regarding Ian. It's nothing to worry about, dear."

"Oh, no. No, no, no. This is too far." Alejandra nagged at her spouse as he walked to the bedroom. "Witches, mediums, brujas, I don't care what you call it. Don't get mixed up into that."

"I happen to recall that your grandmother was a bruja. What's your damage?"

She corrected him, "She was a doctura with a gift." Jonathan gave her a side-eye. "Okay, she was a bruja, but that was mi abuela, I trusted her."

"Then why are you so afraid?"

"Because." She lowered her voice, "She once told me what other brujos do, the bad ones. They talk with Satan."

"That's assuming that I'm religious and that I give two shits."

Alejandra swatted at his back. "I'm serious, Jonny. It is better to remain ignorant about this stuff. You know what it did to my uncle."

If Jonathan was to make any progress with this, it would take dedication and anonymity—he couldn't just waltz into any MES location for information. He would start simple, with a medium not in league with any organization. "Get some rest, babe. I will find Ramona a sitter tomorrow, maybe take the day off."

"Promise me you won't do anything stupid. I don't want Casper in my house, stalking me and Ramona." She slid into bed, Jonathan following.

"I promise," they laughed, "I just need information for a few things, baby. That's all."

Jonathan woke at the same time his wife did, looking after Ramona's morning care as he watched Alejandra rush around the house, running on four hours of sleep. He kept her in check; as she scrambled to look for her keys, he handed them to her—when she ran around searching for her badge, Jonathan dangled it above her head while holding the child in the other arm. Alejandra grinned at him, slapped his butt, and then she departed after their signature double kiss. When the door shut and her car backed out of the driveway, Jonathan settled to feed his daughter while he called around for sitters.

It was a tiring process. Review after review left a bad taste in his mouth, unsure of whom he would leave his child in the care of. With only one seeming to fit his needs, he left a message to set up an interview this week and cursed under his breath. "Looks like you're with me today, Ramona. Wanna go on an adventure with daddy?" Ramona looked up at him, wide-eyed, food drippings along her chin. He laughed, "I can't have my princess looking like this, now can I?"

Jonathan arrived at the city-limits of Willard, Ramona attempting to sing along to the radio in the car seat. The forty-five-minute drive did not seem as long as it used to. The city's blossoming trees by the roadside gave Willard a different character—it was usually around this time of year when the tourists came to Willard's rural areas for nature walks or down-town to the various antique and art galleries, not to mention the great local cuisine. Jonathan was sure that the main branch of MES attracted its fair share of tourists, provided they had enough coin to be deemed worthy.

Perhaps he was in over his head. What could he possibly do to help Ian if it turned out he was in danger? Jonathan had his own family now; if anything were to happen to him, he'd leave an expecting wife and a one-year-old completely alone.

Ramona screeched and pointed excitedly at the dog park they passed. "Doggies," she repeated. "Dada. Doggies."

"Doggies!" he responded cheerfully. He was way too early for his appointment, the excitement got the better of him, so he turned off towards the park. Ramona grew ever more excited as Jonathan unbuckled her, taking her to the dogs. It was directly connected to a shelter.

Ramona clumsily tried to keep up with the other children as they played. Jonathan kept a watchful eye all the while sifting through his phone impatiently. He threw Ian a few texts, telling him of his whereabouts.

He took Ramona inside to look at the animals; she pointed at each of them, demanding her dad to "Look!" After about a half hour, he received the call he was waiting on and continued down the road.

He parked his car on the curb in front of the house he never thought he'd see again. He hadn't been here since high school, to the house of his best friend. He would never forget about Patrice and the many adventures they went on eons ago. He rang the doorbell.

Patrice answered the door with such surprise, looking as if she hadn't aged a day since. She still had those large frames that always slid down her nose, and the shells that decorated her dreadlocks. She hugged him tightly, "Isn't this a sight to see! When you called me earlier, I wasn't sure if it was really you!" She greeted Ramona and invited them inside. Her house was clad in tapestries, candles on every surface, and an entire cabinet of figurines depicting deities. There was incense wafting a smooth fragrance from a small table in the corner of the room with more candles upon it. "How have you been, JJ? I see you've been busy," she said directing her attention to Ramona who managed to find the sleeping cat.

"You could say that. I got hitched and I'm living the American dream. I work in social services now. How about you? I don't see a ring on your finger."

"Yeah, yeah. Marriage is a bitch and divorce is a cunt, pardon my French." She proceeded to set up for their meeting. "Devin and I weren't working out. Claims he got freaked out about my alternative lifestyle. He knew what he was getting into when he got on one knee. Couldn't stay in the kitchen when it got hot. But hey, I'm still on the market. It's been so long—you remember my son, Ryan, don't you? Ryan, bring your little butt in here!" she yelled. "He's supposed to be in school today but insisted that he was 'sick.'"

In walked a handsome boy, who surpassed his mother in height. "Damn, ma. You gotta stop screaming like that."

"Mmm hmm, 'sick' my ass. I want you to meet my best friend from high school, Jon."

Ryan recognized the guest immediately, "Yo, I know you! You're Ian's whatchamacallit." He shook Jonathan's hand.

Jonathan smiled, unsure of where he encountered Ryan before. The memory resurfaced once he sorted through the events of the recent past, "I remember you, too! I thought you looked familiar, holy crap! You're Patrice's son? Wow, how the time flies."

"More like Patrice's servant. This woman is bossy. I didn't know you two were friends. Small world."

She rolled her eyes. "You didn't tell me you met JJ, Ryan." She darted back and forth, apologizing for her unpreparedness. "Ry, help me get set up. Get the tablecloth from the closet and dowse the room, you know the drill."

Patrice was born with the gift—Jonathan was the only one she told when they were kids, and it took some time for him to come to terms with it. He couldn't believe how time and separation led him to forget about the detail, but after tossing and turning restlessly last night, the epiphany clashed into his fitful mind and he couldn't put the thought aside. Naturally, he acted as soon as morning hit, adding a call to Patrice among the calls to babysitters. She was delighted to help after hearing Jonathan's dilemma. Now, she worked as a consultant medium, working from home and was extremely successful to Jonathan's astonishment.

"How's Ian these days," asked Fetcher, taking a seat on the couch.

Ryan shuffled about, helping his mother. "It's been a while since he and I chilled together. Stephanie told me that he was going through a tough time. Apparently he went through a bad breakup."

Jonathan was shocked, "Breakup? He didn't tell me. Oh man."

"Yeah. I gotta admit, they've been dating for three years, going on four, without a problem. It bummed me out when I heard the news. I don't exactly know the details, but Stephanie has been keeping them cool I guess."

Patrice brought over a glass bowl filled with water and set it in the middle of the kitchen table. "Ryan here still is in love with that girl. Stephanie is such a doll baby. I keep telling Ryan to gather some pride and wife her one day."

"Ma!" Ryan exclaimed, embarrassed. "I keep telling you she's got a girlfriend now."

"It wouldn't hurt to take her to junior prom. You guys are still friends. I miss Steph." She placed five candles of assorted colors around the bowl. "Stephanie used to love helping me in readings when they were in middle school. You should have seen Ryan trying his best to flirt when he thought I wasn't looking."

Jonathan laughed, "I'm sure Ryan is not that bad at flirting. And don't give up, Ryan. Women can be difficult, believe me. Your mom would know."

Patrice sassed with a hand on her hip, "You were my best friend, JJ. I knew that if we dated, it wouldn't work out. Take it from the psychic." Ryan looked between them, bewildered and discomforted. "You ready? Have a seat over here." Jonathan did so, taking a chair across from her. Ryan sat on the side, usually his mother's assistant when she had readings on the weekend. He served as her anchor and knew the protocol when things went south.

"Alright, Jon. I know you are aware of how my gift works, but since this is your first reading, I'm going to walk you through the process as one of my clients. Many people think that what I do is superstition, or that it's a curse from Satan, or whatever the hell they say. In reality, it's a state of awareness. Everything possesses its own vibration as they have their own energy. From this vibration, everything produces its own frequency, and some things with higher or lower frequencies exist on different planes that the human senses cannot detect. However, those blessed with the gift are able to detect those frequencies and have specialized abilities from such. My gift consists of clairvoyance, clairaudience, clairsentience, and scrying. Any questions so far?"

Jonathan shook his head.

"Remember that I can only tell you what to look out for; the future is always subject to change. It is you that must act accordingly with what I tell you. I will hold your hands in mine, go into a trancelike state, and will communicate what I see, hear, and feel. These candles represent the cardinal directions and the five elements, and when I light them, the circle will be closed. Under no circumstances should the circle be broken as long as there is a reading in progress. If at any moment you begin to feel uncomfortable, let Ryan know, and he will begin to bring the session to a close. Got it?"

Jonathan smirked, "This is exciting. I understand."

"Good. Let's distract Baby-JJ with some cartoons. Is that okay?" Patrice was mothering in the way she coaxed Ramona into the next room, right in eyesight. She returned to her seat.

"Now, before we begin, what do you hope to obtain from this reading?"

Jonathan took a moment to think. "There are many things that I have been uncertain about as of recent. It revolves around Ian. I have my concerns about his well-being." Patrice urged him to continue. He embarked on the explanation from start to finish, then onto his concerns with his inability to draw any conclusions, including MES—passing down his warnings of secrecy he received from Hunt—and the unsettling vibes his intuition led him to feel as of recent.

Patrice listened closely with common concern. Ryan was at a complete disbelief about the life one of his friends had led. He listened as well, moved to deliver any help he could. It was a wonder why Stephanie looked so stressed nowadays; she always had the heart that made sure her friends stayed happy, and it was apparent that her efforts weren't doing much for anyone, not even herself. He hated how she had no regard for her own needs.

"If you are ready to start, we can get this underway. Do you have an item belonging to Ian?" Jonathan reached into his satchel, removing the grey sweatshirt of Ian, torn and tattered from heavy usage throughout his childhood. She held out her palms for Jonathan to place his and closed her eyes.

Ian slid his lunch tray towards Stephanie, head down on the cold table. Stephanie informed the others at the table of the break's antics, and none of them made the mistake of bringing it into conversation at lunch. It was hard for everyone to maintain a normal talk with Ian looking so depressed. Kiera and Jasmine rambled about, blaming one another for the flat tire Jasmine received on their way to a theme park over break. Desmond sat uncomfortably, looking up at Stephanie and Lizzy, then back down to his tray.

Stephanie didn't like the atmosphere one bit—whether it was from the girls' cheerful demeanor or from everyone else's inability to resonate with one another. Spencer ate his lunch in the library, Ryan was out sick, and Desmond stared at her uncomfortably when he thought she wasn't looking. Ugh, she was sick of it. Lizzy caressed her shoulder knowingly—she recognized it, too. If it weren't for Lizzy's presence, Stephanie wouldn't be able to contain it. When the PA system called for "Elizabeth Stanton" to report to the office, Stephanie looked at her, confused.

Lizzy shrugged. "Be right back, I guess," she said, leaving Stephanie to confront this situation alone.

Lizzy ran through every scenario before she reached the office's main doors. She informed the front desk personnel of her summons, sending her back to Principal Cane's office. She knocked, and Cane permitted her to enter.

"Elizabeth Stanton. I was called," she said.

Cane smiled after setting his mug down. She snorted at his Number One Dad mug and took a seat per his instruction. "Good afternoon, Elizabeth. How's your day so far?"

She carefully took note of her surroundings. This summon was out of the ordinary. If anything, the office found inconsistencies in her record, but Liz was sure she made it as foolproof as possible. She memorized each feature of Cane's face, listening intently to his unsteady heart rate and the sweat glinting on his forehead. "It's good." Like her brother, she spoke few words.

"Do you like Willard so far? These two months sure have flown by."

"It's nice."

The short answers led to an increase in his heart rate. "That's good! Now, I couldn't help but notice that there is no valid address listed on your profile. We usually make sure every student's address is updated before we send out interim reports. Would you mind providing yours?"

"I have been staying with a friend when I moved here. I don't really have a permanent address, not until my mom moves here from Nebraska," she lied.

"Ah, the joys of a military family. Your current address should do. When you and your family get settled, we can update it accordingly." Lizzy obliged to avoid suspicion, listing a neighborhood she saw on her daily drive to school, not too close nor far from the school's zoning. Cane typed as she spoke, reading the address back to her. He shifted his chair enough for Liz to see the rest of his body from behind the screen.

She balled her fist. A bronze broach was pinned beneath his left shoulder of a shield and crossed swords that Lizzy had burned into her memory. She could never erase that wretched symbol from her mind, the same symbol that represented the hands at which her people were taken by. And now it all made sense—everything from the strange happenings to the demons' appearance. Cane was responsible for all of it, allied with the organization M.E.S. It took every ounce of her will not to dispose of the principal right then and there. She clenched her jaw tightly, feeling her canines elongating into those of a predator. Her anger wanted to inflict a shift. She hadn't been a victim of her emotion since her younger days as a shifter. The control she gained along the way ensured that her emotions would not overtake her body.

Lizzy remained calm, managing a friendly grin. "Definitely. I'll keep you updated. Is that it?"

"Yep. That's it! Thank you, Ms. Stanton."

Lizzy kept her hands in her pockets and walked with her head down, running through a million scenarios. MES knew about her, possibly her siblings and Nana. They had to leave again. This was it. All of this effort in order to run. She spotted Abbitt talking casually with another teacher and had to fight both inside and out not to confront him. For some reason or another, she wanted to think that Abbitt had a lot to do with it, but did not think Hazth to stoop that low, regardless of the demon that commanded him. She would wait until she gathered more evidence on her own before she involved him.

Upon returning to her place, Ian looked at her curiously. He blinked a few times in confusion, convincing himself he was sane. He stared again, squinting his eyes.

"Everything okay?" Stephanie asked.

"Yeah. He just wanted my updated address." The change had to happen tonight. Lizzy had to do all of it now. She felt sick to her stomach, keeping her anger and fear at bay.

"Liz," Ian's voice startled everyone. They did not expect him to speak so suddenly. To Noctua, his breath reeked of human blood—she was in such discomfort, begging her body to maintain its form. "Did you just... never mind." Ian put his head back down. He swore he saw another form in the place of Lizzy, her form superimposed onto another. She clenched her hand tightly in the other, counting backwards from twenty.

Before she could excuse herself, Mr. Abbitt approached. "Ah, here you are Elizabeth. I would have asked Spencer if he was around, but do you mind helping me get my computer online? The damn system won't seem to work. I don't mean to interrupt your lunch break."

She nodded, walking beside him in the most normalcy she could manage. After rounding the corner of the empty hall, Hazth pushed Lizzy into the classroom, locking the door and pulling down the shades. She still fought it, yet her nature over-ruled as she grunted in pain, short of screaming.

Hazth leaned against the door, cross-armed, watching the girl struggle in the battle with herself. It wasn't long until she managed control regaining her human qualities, her breath staggered and palms sweaty. She gritted her teeth, challenging Hazth with a glare. "Don't think I trust you one bit for getting me out of there."

"You should be grateful that I was there." After reaching into his pocket, he tossed a small sack her direction. She sniffed it curiously before picking it up. "It's foxglove. It will help you to keep from shifting if you have it on your person."

"Never heard of it," she spat. "Stop trying to help me, you sold me out!"

He raised an eyebrow in question.

"Don't play dumb. It was you. You sold me out to Cane!"

"I did no such thing. Perhaps you weren't careful enough. I warned you the night we met that I would not interfere so long as you reciprocated." Her expression softened, unable to draw conclusions. "I warned you, didn't I? You were sloppy and let yourself get discovered."

"Bullshit! I was careful. I watched my surroundings, even covered my tracks. Impossible."

"You were better off going elsewhere to choose an heir. Did you honestly think you would remain undiscovered in a place so populous with MES branches in practically every city?" She didn't have the words to respond. "It was pretty humorous watching you scramble after that girl."

"Shut up! Now tell me what's happening. I want everything, everything you and your owner are up to."

Hazth had her by the throat in a matter of seconds. "Do not dabble in our affairs. You were spared thus far. You did not even have the sense about you to keep yourself in check." She collapsed when he released his hold, grimacing with anger. "If I did not know any better, I would say you were afraid to change the girl. That, or perhaps you do not know how."

Noctua stood, casting her glance downward. "What do I have to do?"

"If I were you, I would hightail it out of town. Gather that family of yours and stay on the run until you actually have a solid plan. However, a stubborn girl like you won't take another's advice if it was not your original idea."

"I know... " she continued to stare at her feet.

Hazth laughed. "So why do you continue to fight an uphill battle?"

"How do I go about the change? What if she rejects it?"

"She dies. You should know these things. Were you not informed on how to invoke the change?" Her silence was taken as a negative. "Shame. I wish the goddess Nyte's blessing upon you." She wanted to believe she could finish this, and now with Hazth criticizing her shoddy plan she felt stupid. Gularis never missed a beat to reiterate this point. She didn't want to believe it.

The bell signaled the return of students.

She brushed past Hazth, rushing to meet up with Stephanie. She owed it to Hazth, to her regret. It looked like Noctua had to figure everything out on her own, and felt her stomach drop at the thought of mentioning the news to Nana. She had to watch the others fall apart again; this was supposed to be their home, the last time this had to happen.

Stephanie looked to her, smiling largely. Noctua barely held her tears back, refusing to let them spill. Instead, she smiled back. Noctua refused to let them win. She was the leader now, and she would be the change that led the shifters forward.

Wax pooled at the base of the candles. Jonathan looked to Patrice, listening intently. She sat, chin up, eyes closed. She spoke softly between long intervals of silence, gathering her sight into words. "Ian is in a state of confusion... " she paused. "He seeks answers... demands to know his origins... wonders why his life was unlike anyone else's... he is troubled?" Jonathan could see her eyes flitter about behind the lids. "I can see a fire... a previous family... I see his friends; they are all concerned and afraid... " She frowned. "Mr. Cane, the principal, holds documents, Ian's records... he takes them to a club, no... MES."

"What happened?" Fetcher blurted.

"Shhhhh," she softly silenced. "There is a wealthy man in charge, his badge reads 'O'Neil'. He appointed men to carry out his orders to keep an eye on Ian. They—" she gasped, one of the candles flickered out. "Everything is fuzzy now. These men are not what they appear as."

Jonathan's hands trembled in hers. He fired question after question, only met with her shushing his demands.

"I can only see Ian when he is not along the company of these two... he is changed... Ian is in the hands of something evil and dangerous. There is a shapeshifter in his company, she doesn't seem to be hostile... "

"Shapeshifter?"

Patrice was suddenly pushed out of her vision painfully. She screamed out, and every candle in the vicinity was snuffed. Ryan quickly jumped into action, closed the circle, and attended to his mother. Jonathan was shell-shocked. He could only sit there and watch.

"I'm fine, I'm fine," she blurted. She looked frightened to the core, and spoke in a rushed, low tone. "JJ, my vision was cut off. This normally never happens. This is bad."

"What going on? What's happening? What does it mean?" Jonathan stood abruptly.

"Ian is under the influence of an entity. A strong one in particular; the reason why my vision is not permitted to see beyond is because of its involvement. I could not see any further—everything is blurred. Now, listen closely. It is wise to assume that Ian is not of this plane. The reasons why he was put up for adoption so many times were also blurred as well. There are entities in control that do not want to be discovered."

"What type of entity, Patrice?"

Ryan rushed to give her a glass of water. "Demons, Jonathan. Ian is not safe. Even my vision of him is starting to blur. I assume they are enacting some kind of change into him. This isn't some low-level runt or imp, I would be able to see what occurred. But this demon is of a lord's status, the high-level entities of hell, if you would call it. They have strong magic, for lack of better word, extremely powerful." She stood, unbalanced in the rush, catching herself in a swoon. Ryan braced her, instructing her to take it easy. But Patrice was as concerned as Jonathan was. She hurriedly cleansed the house with sage, dowsing each corner with a saltwater mixture. "There was a shapeshifter there, a female. By the look of it, she had her own motives, separate of Ian and the demons. Her name is Noctua, underneath the moniker of Elizabeth."

"That's Stephanie's girlfriend!" exclaimed Ryan. "Holy fuck! What does she want with her?!"

"Watch your mouth, boy," Patrice swatted him. "She wants to make Stephanie one of her own. A portion of shifters were wiped by MES a little over a decade ago, an attempted genocide. If I heard correctly, it was around the time O'Neil assumed his position in MES. As for Ian... I'm sorry, JJ, but you will only be killed if you get yourself involved."

He slammed his fists on the table. "No! I will not sit idly while some 'demons' or whatever the hell they are try to get their hands on Ian. Are you sure you can't use your vision? Please, please, Patrice, try again."

"My vision was completely blocked. If I try again, we risk the chance of becoming discovered."

"You have to. I've spent most of my adult life trying to figure out what went wrong in Ian's life. You are my last option, Patrice. Please."

"I'm telling you. One more push is all it takes to set those demons after you. Ramona, Alejandra, and your unborn will die. I'm not saying no because I don't want to, I'm doing it because

I'm protecting you. Don't forget that I can see this future. This isn't what you want."

Fetcher cursed repeatedly in defeat, pacing the kitchen without the stability and wit he always had about him. Unbeknownst to him, Patrice's head writhed in pain. She winced, proceeding. "You have another option, it's not over. The shapeshifter is the only one in the know who is not aligned with the others. Ask her. Don't be alarmed, she will be defensive at first, but be persistent, she will hear you out. MES has recently been notified of her existence, so proceed cautiously. Both of you can benefit from each other's help."

Ryan yelled, "What about Stephanie? Are we just going to sit here and pretend she's not in danger too?! Why does that... that *thing* want her specifically?"

"Calm down, Ryan. You will not get involved, you hear me? Jon, the same goes for you. If you value your family's well-being, you will stay out of it. But it's useless for me to tell you that," she concluded with a downtrodden expression. "Get you and your child home. It will be selfish of me to ask for payment after this. Your safety is more important."

"No, no. You've been more than helpful." He placed two hundred and fifty dollars in cash before her and gathered his belongings. "The same goes for you. Ryan, listen to your mom. I will make sure both Ian and Stephanie are safe. Thank you."

With that, he gathered Ramona and bid them farewell. Jonathan drove back home to the best of his ability. With the success of finding a sitter, he scribbled a note to Alejandra, pinning it to the fridge, and would depart once more to Willard the next evening.

"A dirty animal like yourself will die the death of one." The constrained lord, Voltaya, continuously cursed at Hazth from his constraints.

"Give it up, Voltaya," Godimus said, in the same predicament as her brother. "You have to give Baal credit where credit is due. I haven't been tied up like this in decades, let alone by a shapeshifter. Baal taught you well."

Hazth did not utter a word from his position outside of the salt circle. The bound demon lords, frustrated and embarrassed at their outdoing by a mere shifter and intermediate, would not be able to ever live down such a defeat if word got out. They had been trapped in the shack for days.

"They could have trapped me in a more handsome meat-suit. Like a young, rich lad. Pretty enough to land every human who looked in my direction."

"You sound like an idiot when you complain about the small stuff."

"Easy for you to say! You always get the vessels you want. That's the last time I let you choose for me, Godimus!"

"Oh, shut up, you pansy. Hey, shifter. If you let us out of here, I'll make it worth your while," Godimus taunted. "Get these seals off of us and we will be out of your hair for good. Besides, the Young Ruler isn't what we expected. He's weak. Uninteresting."

Hazth continued to lean against a workbench, arms crossed and eyes closed.

"Ugh! This is so annoying! It's all your fault, you know," she nagged.

"My fault? You're the one who walked into the trap!"

"Yeah, well how was I supposed to know? We had the kid at our fingertips and you and your big butt just had to go and show off."

The door to the shack opened. In came Baal, adorned in Kenneth, per usual. He whistled his way past Hazth and his prisoners to the tool bench. "My, how the tables have turned. If I

did not say so myself, you two do not live up to your reputation."
Baal shined the knives in a towel. "As always, Hazth, you have
outdone yourself. Travius as well—where is that mongrel?"

"He is doing what you asked of him, my Lord. MES is
being subdued for their bounty."

"Ah, that is right. I almost forgot about them." He
chucked a knife into Voltaya's sternum. He did not flinch from
the impact, only to laugh in the face of Baal. "Now. Lord Voltaya,
Lord Godimus. What pleasure do I owe this reunion?"

"Baal, my love. I finally get to be up close and personal
with you once more," moaned Godimus. "Let's say you and I
forget this beef and have ourselves a good time, hmm?"

"Our partnership has long ended, Godimus. You were
remarkable in battle those years ago, I will give you that. I will
forcibly take you if the urge crosses my mind."

She scowled, "I see that this mission of yours has gone
to your head. We all know that us lords are expendable as far
as the masters are concerned. And your Gate has always been
unmatched when it came to wits."

"If you hope to flatter your way out, it is not working. At
any rate, we have an exorcism to get underway." Baal cracked
his knuckles.

"Did you taste his flesh? Is it more pink than red on the inside, or vice-versa? That marble skin would look great stretched across one of my canvases," raved Voltaya, fixated on the Young Ruler's mechanics much before the mission.

"Would either of you care to spill the information? How did the Second Gate find out about the Young Ruler's return?"

Their silence wasn't deemed appropriate, and with Baal's command, Hazth worked his spellcasting to torture the demons within the vessels, forcing their essence into a frenzy of agony. They could feel themselves painfully separate from their vessels to be tossed back into the Uver. It stopped just as suddenly as it started. Through gritted teeth, Godimus cursed, "I will rip your spine from your wretched filth of a body!" at Hazth.

Baal shined yet another knife. "We can keep this up all day." With that, the cycle of torture kept up for hours until one would answer.

"Fine! The Second Gate knows about the era of the Young Ruler's return, but they don't know it's happening now. Sheesh, lighten up, Baal."

"Good girl," Baal rubbed her hair in downward strokes. "As you were saying?"

"As I was saying? I'm saying that we're here on contract. No one sent us."

"I do not believe you. Hazth." Hazth enacted the torture once more.

"It's the truth!" Voltaya yelled out. "It was that detective. He summoned us. He wanted answers, to find out if there was any myth behind that kid of yours. To fill in the blanks."

"And what did you all agree to as payment?" asked Baal.

"Agree? Ha! I was sick of the Uver. I honestly just wanted to stretch my legs up here for a bit. You know I take what I want," Godimus responded. "But then it turned out to be more interesting than we thought. When I saw you tagging along with the kid, I knew that the Third Gate was up to something. I did what any other demon would do and followed you around for the dirt."

Voltaya added, "He offered us a few souls in return."

Their story was off. If the detective wanted Ian so bad, all he had to do was show up and take him for himself. And why was this man so obsessed with the past of some delinquent youth? Baal would have to question the man for himself, maybe in a not-so-diplomatic way. The mortal knew something, a missing piece that neither Baal nor his fellow lords knew of. And the more information Baal could piece together, the better.

Godimus added, "If you ask me, Melbourne seemed like a newbie to this whole thing. He paid someone else to do the summoning and bloodletting. Wasn't cheap, either."

"A name?"

"Ugh, you better let us out of here, Baal! I don't just go around asking every human their name. He was one of those real-deal occultists. Now will you let us go?"

Baal unfixed the rope from their wrists and waists. Removed the seals that bound them beneath the pentagram painted on the rafters. He placed a finger gently under Godimus' child-vessel's chin. "Only because I know how you operate," he said seductively. "I may want to use you some more one day."

From the girl and the old man, a dark, ghastly ectoplasm rushed from their orifices—eyes, ears, mouth, and nose—making a deathly shriek until the lords themselves were emptied out, standing amongst the others beyond the veil. Their digits of stag, and stature of mobility, with horns that spiraled about their shoulders. One would say they were of some alien creature, romantically spawned in a void of paradise—a look that all lords had about them, a dangerous beautiful that spoke of omen and death.

Godimus' voice was no longer guised as a child. It was sultry, a vixen herself that knew the rules of the rodeo. "My precious Baal," she moaned, cupping Baal's crotch with her hand, and a wicked grin spread on her lips, "I look forward to the day that you and I finally make a world for ourselves. That is what you told me those centuries ago." She pressed her lips to Baal's, gliding her tongue across his, "I see now that your master has made a bitch out of you. And I used to think you were different."

She and Voltaya vanished, their mist diffusing until no trace of them showed. "Discard of their vessels, Hazth," Baal commanded, seemingly irritated by Godimus' last remarks.

"Of course, my Lord."

Hazth dug two pits for the lifeless vessels the demons left behind. As of late, Baal wasn't as harsh as he usually was. Hazth did not know of the past that Baal bore, nor did he care. By Hazth's silence, always watching, he picked up on many hints. Lords and other demons were not sensitive to emotions as other earthly creatures were, in fact, they were the most ruthless. Hazth could detect the slight differences within his Lord's aura, which Baal took precise care in masking while in the human realm. But often, ever since initiating the change within Ian, Hazth would note a fluctuation in his lord, something Baal himself was unaware of.

Hazth tossed the body of the drunkard into the pit, covering it without a single thought. Grabbing the ankle of the small girl, he could feel the soft pitter-patter of blood flowing to and fro. Hazth stared into her face, her eyes barely focusing. She would die anyway, Hazth thought, but he remained a bit too long trying to reason.

12

LOST WAY

The mess that cluttered Spencer's room was a chaotic good, for a cram session was in commencement. It was a quarter past ten as Stephanie called through the flashcards. Spencer took longer than usual to answer, visibly displaying frustration through brow and posture. Stephanie put the cards down, "Hey, now. We can stop. We've been at this for hours."

"The AP exam is tomorrow. I'm not ready, Stephanie. What if I... "

"You're not going to flunk, alright? And if you do, so what? You still passed the class with an A." He sighed into a pillow, tears welling. "Spencer, look at me. It's going to be alright." The chime of the doorbell forced both to look at each other quizzically. Spencer, Stephanie following, set off to check on the late-night visitor. Unless his mom was locked out again—not an uncommon occurrence—he wasn't expecting any company at this hour.

Ryan stood impatiently on the other side of the door, shuffling his weight to either foot. With a short, "Hey, Spencer," he immediately targeted Stephanie. "Steph, we gotta talk."

She frowned, his urgency seeming a little on the desperate creep side, uncanny for him, but regarding their past, she could only take that into consideration. "You could have called me, you know, like a normal person. It's rude to show up, unannounced, to another person's house."

"Can I come in?" He looked to Spencer, "Please?"

Spencer gestured inward. "I'm going to shower," he said, removing himself from the drama he knew Ryan to invoke whenever Stephanie was involved. It was bad enough that he was the last to find out about her relationship with Lizzy, cornering Spencer with an avalanche of questions. The nice guy complex Ryan adorned was almost pitiful.

Ryan pulled Stephanie into the living room; she jerked away. "What the hell? Ryan, why are you here?"

"I know it's weird. Sorry for intruding. But you gotta hear me out. You're in danger."

"What?"

"Lizzy. She's using you, bruh. And Ian is being sought out by some real bad dudes."

She crossed her arms defensively. "If this is about you being butthurt about her and I, then I don't want to hear it."

"That ain't it," he scratched at his arm in embarrassment. "This is going to sound crazy as hell, but stay with me." She cocked an eyebrow, ready to deliberate his reasoning. "She's a supernatural being called a shapeshifter."

"Who?"

"Lizzy."

"A what?"

"Shapeshifter." Stephanie snorted. "I'm dead-ass serious, Stephanie, please."

"I knew this wasn't going to be serious."

He gripped her shoulder, giving her a forceful glance, "I'm trying to save your life, for fuck's sake!" She was only seconds away from losing her containment. "She is a shapeshifter, a *thing* that can change into anything. She is only with you because she's trying to change you into what she is!"

"Wow, it's almost as if you pulled all this out of your ass. You could have said anything else stupid and it would've made more sense."

"Call her." He shoved her phone into her hand.

"To ask her a dumb question and waste her time like you did mine? Nope."

"Goddammit, stop pretending you know everything for a fuckin' minute, aight? Call her."

She angrily snatched her phone away, proceeding to dial Lizzy's number. "You're really fuckin' pushing it, Ryan." The phone rang until the voicemail picked up.

Ryan paced. "Notice how she didn't answer you. Coincidence?"

"That doesn't mean shit. Apples and oranges, Ry."

"And Ian is under the pursuit of demons. It's that dude Kenneth that's makin' him do all that crazy shit. He's using Ian in order to control him... or somethin'. Point of the matter is, this weird shit ain't happenin' for no reason. You've seen my ma's work, you know she knows stuff we don't."

She remembered the times she couldn't wait to visit Ryan to see Patrice's gift in action. There was no denying her ability, as much as she tried to debunk it. In fact, his mother's gift helped her more times than not. Stephanie paused for the moment and took in what Ryan had to say. He repeated himself several times per her request and begged her to trust him. She took Ryan's words and affixed it into recent events. And the more it became less farfetched.

Later, she mulled over even more connections. Never could she have thought of things becoming more severe than they already were, but there was truth to Ryan's story. She could never forget the day Lizzy saved her from Ian—she hated seeing it in that light. Stephanie wanted to forgive and forget, yet there was no way she could neglect to acknowledge Ian's actions for what they were. He probably wouldn't have stopped. He forced himself onto her and would have gone further if Lizzy wasn't conveniently around. Stephanie never brought it up since. So much was unanswered, and Stephanie thought it to be a favor to herself by letting it be.

When Stephanie rode alongside Lizzy on the way to school, she did not allot time for silence. Before she let the ridiculousness of the scenario silence her, she spoke. "If there was someone who held a grudge against me, you'd tell me, right?"

Lizzy made a face. "That was out of the blue. Let's see. I suppose I would settle the issue before you even realized."

"What if they had justified reason?"

Lizzy poked Stephanie's cheek. "You know I'd take your side. You're my girlfriend."

"Okay, so what if I was really, really in the wrong? Like I stole money or something?"

"One, you wouldn't do that. And two, if you did, you'd be buying me something nice with it. My lips would be sealed."

"Can I do any wrong in your eyes?" Stephanie asked. "Don't you think I would deserve some form of punishment? Or do you tell me this because it makes things easier for you?"

Lizzy laughed, "What are you talking about? Easier? In what aspect?" Stephanie wanted to retreat. She was too deep to turn back.

"Why do you do so much for me?"

Lizzy looked confusingly towards Stephanie then back to the road. "Isn't that what couples are supposed to do?" she answered, smiling as deterrence. Stephanie looked towards her lap. "Am I too clingy? Do you need more space?"

"Not clingy... you're just really protective. Almost like I'm in danger or something. But that's crazy."

Lizzy clenched her jaw, tightening her grip on the wheel and hoped Stephanie didn't notice those small inflections.

"You always seem to be around whenever something's awry. Like... that night when Ian... you were able to hold him down."

"What do you mean?" She held her breath.

"I know that Ian was acting weird, we all knew. But do you... do you know something we don't? You tense up around him. I feel like you really don't like him."

"Well, duh! After what he did to you, I'm still surprised you call him your friend. I really don't like you around him."

Stephanie felt herself blush at her own stupidity. "How were you there that day?"

Lizzy was caught off guard, no excuse readied.

Stephanie held her breath. "Are you a shapeshifter?"

Lizzy wanted to laugh it off, pull into the coffee shop's lot, and carry on as if Stephanie didn't utter something that Liz took careful effort in keeping hidden. Her first thought was to deny everything. She caught the light, and at a full stop, she felt she couldn't keep pushing the charade forever. All this time searching for a way to come forward, and here she was, casually being asked about her best-kept secret. Someone was going to have to die for this. And so, with much discomfort, Lizzy nodded.

Stephanie had a million questions. She let the atmosphere air itself out, cueing for Lizzy to pick up the slack and give her answers. Lizzy's knuckles went pale from the grip, jigging her legs restlessly. "I was going to tell you, babe. I really was. I didn't know how."

"Honey, it's okay. It's fine. We are talking now." Ryan was right. Stephanie thought of the worst possible scenario, immediately wanting to backtrack and apologize, yet she stifled her kneejerk reactions until she received more answers. "So what exactly is that? Sounds like some sort of factory job to me. Do you fold cardboard into shapes or something?"

Lizzy appreciated her playing innocent to spare Liz the discomfort, but she would have to tell everything. She couldn't keep any more to herself; this was the window she was given. Her instinct knew that there was no way that Stephanie would accept any of this. Someone had to clue Stephanie in, someone who knew too much and was able to slip beneath the radar. MES? Cane? The demons? No longer was she safe. She had to get her family out of dodge. Everything hurt.

Lizzy inhaled before speaking. The red light felt like an eternity. "A shapeshifter is... " *If she doesn't accept, she has to die.* "A shapeshifter is a being that can change its form at will." *The last time you told someone, you paid in blood. You're stupid if that happens again.* "Promise me you won't tell anyone, Stephanie, please." She promised. "My people aren't exactly... welcomed here. Kind of like a mass exodus-slash-genocide kind of thing. We're a dying breed, sold as slaves for profit and research."

"I'm assuming that your parents... they didn't die in a car accident, did they?"

Liz shook her head, "No. They were captured right in front of us."

"I'm sorry."

"It's the past."

Stephanie cleared her throat after some time. "And where do I fit into this puzzle?"

Lizzy pushed her truck into its usual space in the empty school parking lot with a small twinge of guilt for not getting Steph any coffee. This was it. She was hoping for a better setting than this. But this was it. "My clan is ever-shrinking. The shifter bloodline is dwindling. I figured you would make for a good addition—you were sharp, alert, smart, and robust. Your immune system is strong. I wanted to change you, so I enrolled in Willard." Stephanie was speechless. "I knew you before you knew me. I knew your habits, your routines. I knew most things about you before you told me."

Stephanie didn't want to believe it.

"You were on vacation in the mountains. In December, on a trip with your family; that's when I saw you. Came here for you. More specifically, to indoctrinate you into my clan and change you into what I am. Against your will if I had to."

Stephanie could feel her heart sinking.

"I was prepared to do so long ago, but then things changed. I... didn't want to do it without your permission. I fell for you pretty hard. And that distracted me from what I had to do."

"What changed? You empathized all of a sudden? Bullshit. Tell me the truth. You don't love me. Something else threatened you, didn't it?" Fat, hot tears fell into Stephanie's lap. She couldn't bring herself to look up. "This whole thing between us was a distraction, wasn't it?"

"Steph, listen, I didn't mean it that way. It's because I started caring so much that it took me this long to tell you."

"'Started caring?' Basically I'm some human to tug around, huh? I had to drag the truth out of you. You weren't going to tell me, were you?" Lizzy shook her head regrettably. "Then you would forcefully change me? Have me believe in some intricate love story only to manipulate me?"

"It's not a lie. I *do* love you, Stephanie. I did it to protect you. When you told me you wanted your life to be more than it was, I figured you would understand where I was coming from."

"Protect me from what? You were going to do it whether I wanted it or not, weren't you?"

"Don't be mad at me, Stephanie. Please."

"Are you going to answer me or what?"

Lizzy remained silent. Stephanie knew it was affirmative.

"Show me."

"I can't show you right now. I'll be seen."

"No one is around. Show me." Stephanie stared at her sternly, a look that Lizzy never knew her to wield, ever, with eyes tinged red and the consistent stream of tears. Lizzy gave in, removing her jacket. The shift started with her hair, turning from its teal to a stark, shimmering white, gradually flowing from root to tip. Her complexion took on a brilliant bronze from its usual paleness, glistening and healthy. Feathers emerged from her skin, smooth, dispersed here and about her extremities. Eyes, sharp and electric sapphire. Breathtaking markings spread from her high cheekbones down her face, down throughout her body. A humanoid figure sat before Stephanie as if some brilliant, angelic presence took the driver's seat. Lizzy's ears came to a dramatic point, and her sharp predacious teeth intimidated from her parted, full lips.

Stephanie searched for the words to say but she could only reach out to touch the presence before her, tears chasing one after the other. "What now?" she choked. "What are we supposed to do now?" Lizzy could only stare forward, clinging onto the word "we" as her lasting hope and phasing out, too contorted to even know how to fix anything else. For all she knew, she just guaranteed the death of everyone. *Do it now, while she's weak*, she quickly shot the thought away. She couldn't. *This is exactly why everyone will die—because you are weak.*

Jonathan would need more information before he was to approach Ian face-to-face, heeding Patrice's warning, which landed him only a few blocks away from the school grounds. Lots of decisions that went against his character were made today, as his return to Willard at a quarter to nine required that of him, with a toolkit situated within a backpack, flashlight within gloved hands. He shifted the balaclava to cover his chin. For a few more minutes, he sat against the hood of his vehicle trying to keep himself from pussing out of his plan of breaking into the high school. If Alejandra found out about this, Jonathan would not know how to explain, let alone if he would. And if Jonathan was caught in the act, well, let's just say that his criminal record would have irrevocable changes applied to it. Being labeled as a criminal was the last thing Fetcher wanted, however one wrong move on school grounds would usher that into existence.

He sighed once more before tricking himself into action, sifting through a thin patch of forest leading to the clearing behind the school. He stopped right at the perimeter, removing a small black box from his pocket. Hunt's face haunted his mind—the man was already defenseless when dealing with Jonathan's requests. Despite all of Hunt's warnings, Jonathan would not let up on his pursuit, causing Hunt to grow evermore irritated with Fetcher the more he poked his head into this nonsense. Hunt, aware of what repercussions might await from treachery, was becoming somewhat invested into Jonathan's curious case; so much so that the little black box Jonathan now held was temporarily gifted to assist. Said box was a small, slim digital EMP with an LCD that only displayed monochromatic text. Remembering Hunt's instruction, Jonathan waited until he was fifty yards from the premises before he activated the device, and almost exactly how Hunt described, Willard High's armed systems and surveillance went offline. Jonathan was granted a twenty-minute window to get in and out.

He tapped the device against the electronic keypad just outside the gymnasium doors. It was fascinating how easily the mechanisms unlocked, making Jonathan wonder exactly how much the FBI held from the public—it would be decades before this tech would surface in the civilian world, if ever. He considered himself lucky, then slid into the building, arming his flashlight, whose beam flooded the halls almost too perfectly. The echo of his footsteps gave him slight unease, remaining anxious even after reassuring himself of his isolation. He followed the signs to the main foyer, and shortly after, he arrived at the front offices, set sure of his location when he illuminated the placard hanging right outside the preliminary door listing the faculty.

Carefully, he set his pack down, deriving a lockpick from the toolkit. Jonathan took deep breaths as he tinkered with the door, mindful of the time he had left. Sixteen minutes was plenty, granted he wouldn't have to do a lot of digging around. With a satisfactory click, the door opened with ease. Jonathan prided himself on his criminal skill, making a mental note to learn more of these illegal-but-useful tricks.

He sidled close to surfaces large enough to hide his presence in case the surveillance came back online. Cane's door was in sight and only feet away. But Jonathan noticed that something was off—the door to the principal's office was ajar. Jonathan sat starkly silent and still, cursing under his breath. Someone was here. He swallowed, inching forward.

Wham!

Jonathan was slammed into the floor, feeling weighed by a boulder. He was frantic. Bright, sapphire eyes peered into his. Quickly, he reached for his bag to no avail, having his hand stepped on. Without an interval between, Jonathan was snatched by the collar into the air. "W-Wait!" he called out desperately. "Lizzy, it's me! Jonathan Fetcher!"

She flinched at her coined moniker, removing the balaclava from the intruder.

Unwavering, she asked, "What are you doing here?"

"I was going to ask you the same," he laughed nervously. She didn't blink. He raised his hands, defensively, "Some weird stuff has been happening. I have reason to believe that someone here is pulling the strings. Do not worry, I mean you no harm."

Lizzy put him down. "You're Ian's caretaker. I remember you from the party."

"Likewise. It is nice to see you again, despite the circumstances." She only watched him with an expectant scowl. "Er, I'm here to collect any info on Ian's principal. I think he sold Ian out to someone. I don't know who or what, but it can't be good." Patrice's visions were so accurate that it was scary. He shoved the thought of imminent death away and pressed on. "Come on, we don't have much time."

"What's this 'we' business?" she blocked his path. "For all I know you could have something to do with this. How did you find out about this?"

"A psychic. I also know about you and your family." He picked up his belongings, pressing forward only to be blocked again.

Lizzy's form was intimidating. "A psychic told you this?!" she said through clenched teeth. Jonathan swallowed, nodding. "How many people know?" He could sense the desperation in her voice, appearing almost wild in nature, tightening her jaw as if trying to hold herself in.

Jonathan forced himself to see past the fear she evoked within him to the bigger picture. They had ten minutes. "Listen, Lizzy. I will tell you everything I know. But for now, we need to hurry and find something on Cane. I took the surveillance out. We have less than ten minutes before systems come online. Now you either help or we both risk getting discovered."

She conceded after another minute of thought, stepping aside but not without dropping her guard. Inside, Jonathan was faced with a mahogany shelf, and two maroon leather single-sitters that faced the executive desk, cluttered with documents, pictures, and bobble heads of sports teams that haven't won in years. He scoffed at the Number One Dad mug placed to the left of the monitor.

"I searched through the desk drawers already. Nothing," she spoke while sifting through the bookshelf.

Jonathan woke the monitor to a login screen. "Did you check the desktop?"

"There's nothing on the desk besides crap. No papers."

"No, not the… " he smirked, realizing that she probably wasn't familiar with the last decade of technology, "The computer."

She shook her head. "Couldn't log in." Without response, Jonathan placed the same black box next to the CPU tower, and with the slight press of a button, the encryption process welcomed Mr. Cane to his desktop background. "Where did you… "

Jonathan locked in, starting search queries with any keyword he could think of. Lizzy watched, intrigued, over his shoulder as he tried his quickest to dig up even one tidbit of information. Suddenly, several results popped up as the search ended, three to be exact, dating from January to just last week. Jonathan skimmed over each one, appalled at what lay in the text. He didn't have time to review. Instead, he printed two copies of each, collating a stack for Lizzy. He pocketed the device, counting down from four minutes on its display. "This is as good as it's going to get. Let's get out of here." Lizzy did a careful once over of the area, making sure to leave nothing out of place.

As soon as they made it from the premises, Jonathan saw the system come back online with several flashes of light scattered around the campus. He finally breathed into his cold, clammy hands, eyes nearly brimming to tears from his fearful frenzy. Lizzy stood still, watching Jonathan with a side-eye as if awaiting explanation. He took the cue for what it was. "Don't worry, I'm going to tell you all that I know. It's clear that you don't trust me one bit. And I don't blame you." He navigated through the trees, making the trek back to his vehicle, Lizzy following behind. He did not make mention of the obvious—Lizzy walked about naked, without a second thought. Now this *really* made Jonathan look bad; if anyone had seen this occurrence, he was guaranteed to end up on several watch lists. But he couldn't deny acknowledging how nice of a body it was, less in the perverse sense, moreso in the field of aesthetic complexity. It was as if she were the counter piece to Michelangelo's David, having muscles that protruded flawlessly, and a stature that human physiology could envy. Jonathan was absolutely intrigued, many questions fumbling for dominance on his tongue. He blindly held out his jacket towards her.

Lizzy did not want to waste another second and demanded Jonathan's explanation as soon as they reached his car. She listened intently, mistrusting, yet understanding of his position.

He ended the explanation with his research regarding the Merchants, being sure to mention that Mrs. O'Neil happened to
be a close acquaintance of his wife. He used the moment to
push, asking Lizzy who Mr. O'Neil was and what *exactly* M.E.S.
was. She described O'Neil with one harsh word and gave a
small synopsis of the organization. Jonathan listened intent on
hashing out a plan before the end of the night.

Lizzy pointed at him, "Let me see those reports."

"Oh yeah," Jonathan nearly forgot the reason they were
there—who could blame him? There was so much for his mind
to take in, comprehend, analyze, and construct a frame of reference around. Even after seeing Lizzy, he still remained a skeptic;
he was sure that somehow this entire situation still lay in the
realm of implausibility. Jonathan started the car, warming his
hands in front of the vent. "Okay," he said finally, "Let's see what
we are dealing with." He read the emails aloud.

Baal spun the knife in his hand mindlessly, patient as
ever. On his left shoulder a messenger bag hung, completing
the studentesque appearance of his vessel—although Baal did
not particularly care for keeping appearances, he took careful

investment when grooming Kenneth Green having spent a great deal of time occupying him. He wore a pea coat with a snug fit, neatly pressed faded denim, and a pair of Doc Martin boots. He leaned against the brick of the bistro on this busy college campus, students constantly filing in and out of the restaurant, some drunk and others a little too lively on an evening like tonight—Baal figured an event was taking place. In the time that he had been standing there, the eyes of many young women were caught in his; they were quick to look away, abashed and conflicted by the striking man. Baal would smirk in return, and that did them in. To amuse himself, he would wink at his onlookers. To see and feel the reactions of their significant others was nothing short of envious—it was obvious the parked silver Crossfire belonged to him. To everyone's dismay, those who were brave enough to still be watching the illusive rich man immediately lost hope as the curvy woman approached.

"If I wouldn't have known any better, I'd say you are trying to show off," she sneered through a grin. She placed an amiable hand on his shoulder, placed a kiss on his cheek, and whispered into his ear, "If this is a trick, the next time I see you, you're dead. Got it?"

Baal lifted her chin with a finger. "Godimus, now you know I am not the type to double-cross reliable allies. You have my word."

"Like that ever meant much to begin with." This time, her vessel was well-matured. She wore a fitted maxi dress with a fatal-looking high heel that accentuated her bust and hips. Her makeup was flawless, sharp contour that brought out her cheekbones and a polished set of nails. "What are you waiting for? You going to walk a lady inside or what?"

Baal blinked. "What? Here?"

"Yes, moron. Here. Do you have another place in mind?"

"I was hoping for a more discrete location. These are affairs I would rather keep unknown."

"Oh, stop being such a baby. I casted a field over a five-mile radius. If anyone tries to eavesdrop, I'd know. When did you become such a pansy? Oh, right. Isn't it your whole thing to stay invisible or whatever?"

He ignored her and headed into the bistro. It was packed, almost to capacity. Godimus paid off a few students for their seats; they were happy to oblige. The bistro was full of chatter and the clinking of cutlery against plates, the soft mood lighting was a redeeming quality. Baal sat starkly straight on the edge of his seat, looking her square in the eyes; Godimus, on the contrary, rested her head in her hand, twisting a ringlet of hair around her finger. The waiter approached, "How are you two doing tonight?" slightly confused at the new seating arrangement. His eyes lingered a bit too long on Godimus' cleavage.

As the seductress that she was, she played into it, leaning just enough for him to capture a better view. "I could be better," Godimus responded in her sultry way.

The waiter turned bright red, immediately turning his attention to his memo pad. "Are you two ready to order?" Baal declined with a dismissive gesture. Godimus knew exactly what she wanted, never skipping a beat to make the waiter flustered. He walked their order to the kitchen with broken attentiveness, nearly crashing into other servers and customers in passage.

"Well?" she clasped her hands together. "We going to discuss this important matter of yours?"

Baal nodded. "If you as much as utter a word about this, I can assure you that you will permanently be removed from both planes."

"Alright, alright, I got it, Baal!" she responded, annoyed. "That first time wasn't even my decision, and you know that. We can make a sigil if you still don't trust me."

Baal took her up on the offer, branding his and her vow onto their arms. They bore matching sigils on the inside of their wrists, then it quickly faded away. A sigil such as this was strong magick, a sort of tether from being to word that bound the recipients to the respective oath until its completion or the death of either.

"This is rather risky. Any amount of careless mistakes *cannot* be tolerated," he commanded, the ancient air about him resurfacing. Godimus leaned forward, intrigued. "Doing all this research for Master has left me troubled. I have kept a great amount of detail to myself in the reports. I do not think he has any idea of the gravity of options we have at our disposal with the Young Ruler. To even use that title begets its severity. The Young Ruler is a perfect union between the mortal and immortal. I am not entirely knowledgeable on exactly *what* that could accomplish, however I know this is too valuable to turn into the hands of Master, which would practically ensure my servitude to him for the rest of my existence. Therefore," he projected the three-dimensional, ethereal imagery with his demonic essence, unseen to the human eye, of several instances within Ian's growth, "I propose a partnership in which we will see to the research ourselves, thus keeping the power to ourselves. We could practically surpass the masters."

Godimus pondered his words thoughtfully before speaking. "You seem to have a lot of confidence in this whole prophecy thing. How are you so sure that the kid is the real deal? Just because he's survived your blood for so long doesn't mean jack shit. He could keel over any second."

"All this time knowing me and you still gravely underestimate my abilities," he teased, smirking. "I have reason to believe that the prophecy is wrong about the Young Ruler being the creator of worlds. Rather, he is some form of conduit between planes. An ambassador between dimensions. I am not certain, but I have a feeling that this connects to the Refract's origins. Not even the masters could explain that sudden rip between here and the Uver. They fight for possession of the Refract yet have not even scratched the surface of its mechanics."

Godimus mused, "It seems like suicide. I mean, it sounds very tempting, but how do you plan to get this one over your master?" Baal clenched his fist, angered at how easily he was manipulated by Master. The last encounter was enough to send Baal into a rampage, a first in centuries of servitude. Baal was certain that the white-gold mass of anima would be within his grip; now, that reward seemed ridiculous compared to the one he had all to himself.

"If we get a grasp on how Ian's power works and see to its development, I am almost certain that we can become invulnerable from any sort of contact from the Uver. No master could lay their hands on either of us if we manage to harness other planes of existence."

Godimus bit her lip in contemplation. The offer was too good to pass up, and it had been a while since she and Baal engaged in conquest with one another. Baal admired her, even though he would never admit it. Despite Baal's serious demeanor, Godimus enjoyed Baal's company, probably to have someone to tease, he was sure, and he may have been the only demon that could tolerate her presence for extended periods of time. Yet they would never admit to one another about how great of a team they made; this was as close as it came to showing admiration for the other and Baal struggled hour after hour convincing himself to involve the succubus. "You're shooting yourself in the ass if this falls through. This is all theory—to think that this would work... "

"It will. I know it will. Imagine what we could do, Godimus!"

"And when you get your power, how long will it be before you find my involvement annoying and you decide to get rid of me? Let's face it, this partnership is not going to be in place for the rest of eternity."

"Wise of you to assume such, however I will enact the contrary. I will award you handsomely when the time comes and we determine an outcome. So long as you respect my thoughts and presence, I shall do the same for you." He gently kissed her hand for the sake of antics.

"Fine. I'm in. I'm ready to start when you are. What's your first move?"

"I want to test Ian's threshold for extreme stress. He is strong-willed, somehow convinced that friendships made in adolescence will remain for a lifetime. It is ultimately these trivial connections that prevent me from converting his emotional state to one like the Uverlings. He is so optimistic, it is almost sickening. I decided to force him out of that environment. So long as he remains close to them, I am afraid our research will be stunted. We must shatter that innocence."

The waiter returned with Godimus' meal, and she asked for a to-go box. The waiter gave up on any chance of tips at this rate. That was until Godimus placed a twenty into his apron along with her phone number then proceeded to walk out, giving plenty for all to look at. Once inside the car, she shimmied into comfort. "What? You're staring."

"Nothing."

She grazed Kenneth's bicep with her sharp, manicured nails, "I have to have a hustle somehow. Not my fault men think with their dicks."

"So cruel. A man simply wants to enjoy the pleasures of a woman's body, but instead she robs him of his soul. You are quite the succubus." Baal recognized how easily Godimus assimilated into human society, and asked curiously, "How does your master allow you to access the Refract so freely?"

"It's my job," Godimus raved, letting the window down. "I bring the bulk of souls from here to the Uver, remember? It's a very lucrative job." She ran her fingertips along the dash. "Take me to see Ian." Kenneth smoothly rounded the car left at an intersection, unresponsive. "Don't tell me you still don't trust me. We're partners now."

"It is not that. As a matter of fact, I would love to show you the progress I have made. That will have to wait, however. I have to report in to Master." She sighed in frustration. "I will be back soon. Until then, you should get to know the others involved; I think that you will find great interest in the one called Spencer. His mind will be a carnival to you. And make sure Voltaya does not poke his nose in our business."

"I knew you would say that. For the last time, relax. He's here on contract. He won't bother, he gets too involved in his work."

"What are the specifics of this contract?"

"A man by the name of Todd Melbourne summoned Voltaya in order to get some power, you know, the usual. Wanted info on some old demonic practices and use them for his advantage."

"Which means that both you and Voltaya know quite a bit, maybe more than I know."

"Calm your tits, princess. I came to an agreement with Voltaya before we met up. Leased a few of my devotees to him. I don't like letting him treat them however he pleases, so I keep tabs here and there. I like to treat my devotees with respect."

"With good reason," agreed Baal. The networking Godimus excelled in was in stark contrast to Baal's independent approach. He knew he made the right decision.

The hooves of the buck progressed one after the other through the young pine woods. A little girl lay barely conscious across its back, silent and unmoving. Hazth stopped once he approached the perimeter of the woods juxtaposed to the wooden fence surrounding Strawberry Acres, another one of Willard's many suburban estates. Hazth lowered himself just enough for the girl to slide onto the ground and began to walk away. One last glance back and Hazth knew instantly that this would play out badly in the future. Hell, he was sure his lord knew what he was up to this very moment. Baal was right: Hazth let his earthly heart rule over his decisions. He shook the thought from his mind, galloping back into the woods, and when deep enough in, shifted into a hawk mid-stride. Aimlessly he circled the great sullen sky in arcs, passing the edge of the woods a few times to verify if the girl still laid there. After the third pass he continued forward, propelling himself higher and higher until the neighborhoods below lost detail.

He was already a monster, full and through, responsible for the deaths of many regardless of age. He knew exactly why he spared the girl yet did not want to give his mind the time of day to accept his emotional response. The small frail frame, the tattered, fleeting lifelessness of the girl made him regret the decisions of his past which tethered his leash of servitude to the demonic noble. Hazth was not the most responsible then, ignoring what had to be done for the good of his clan to pursue something greater. And that reckless thirst for knowledge was exactly how he ended up assuming the position of Sentinel with no out, aiding in his brother's disappearance.

Getting Baal and the supposed Young Ruler out of dodge was priority, so capturing the demoness without damaging her abducted vessel placed second. It wasn't a successful effort, and at the very least Hazth did not hound himself for those damages. Now with Baal away, Hazth made amends the only way he could think of—he imparted his lifeforce unto her, bestowing what could be considered a blessing or a curse. Either way, her survival far-outweighed its opposite. His clan would live on through her.

The girl remained with teetering consciousness alone on the cold ground a mere twelve miles away from Ryan's residence. He was sprawled on the living room couch blaring his music as loud as he could to keep his worry concealed from his mother's prying abilities. Patrice knew all too well about Ryan's current state; she was familiar with his vibe whenever he had Stephanie on his mind. She was sure that her divorce and his constant rejection gave him zero ideation for romantic love. She called his name several times before removing the headphones from his ears. Dismissing his repugnant bout, she spoke, "You're going to ruin your hearing like that, boy." He replaced his headphones; Patrice removed them once more. "Let's watch a movie together. It will take your mind off her."

"Ma!" he exclaimed, insecure and rustled from his bubble of comfort. "I'm not—" he paused with a sigh, "Yeah, let's watch a movie."

Patrice fiddled with the remote through the genre, "She will be alright, Ryan. You should start talking to other young women." He remained silent. "Stop having sex with her. Sex always leads to unwarranted feelings. You are using protection, right?"

"Ma, okay. Can we not talk about this?"

"These feelings will fade. Life always goes on."

"Yeah, you and pops are a fine example. I know."

"Your dad and I ended things before they got worse. Love is like a garden; it flourishes for several years before all the nutrients get sucked from the ground, preventing life from ever happening again. You either keep adding nutrients or farm new soil."

"Wow. Quite the advice, ma."

"It's the truth. You gotta till the dead stuff into the dirt for something new to grow. My job as your ma is to tell you the truth so you won't be taken by surprise. What do you want to watch?" Patrice sorted through the cinematic thumbnails.

Ryan shrugged. "Robotron Versus Sharkzilla Five."

Patrice scrunched her face in disapproval, "Five? That should've stopped at one."

Ryan sat next to his mom, enduring her commentary throughout the entire exposition. She asked questions that could be answered if she'd just shut up and watched. Eventually, Ryan relaxed enough to enjoy picking fun at the movie with her, making bets about the identity of the mysterious antagonist and the fate of the brave hero.

Halfway into the movie, Patrice paused it. She craned her neck, peeking through a slot in the curtains. "Lord have mercy," she breathed. "Ryan, do me a favor and go to your room for a few minutes." Instead, Ryan peeked outside of the window just in time to see the headlights of the black truck flick off. Out from the vehicle stepped Jonathan and Lizzy. "Go, Ryan."

He ignored his mom, answering the door right as the guests reached the steps. Before Lizzy could speak, Ryan interrupted with, "Well? Did she survive?"

Patrice pushed past Ryan. "Ignore Ryan. Come on in, I'll make tea." She braced herself for whatever crazy request Jonathan would ask for. As she predicted, he allied with the shapeshifter; it was almost surreal to see her in the physical. She urged her guests to get comfortable around the table as she prepared the steaming brew. As stubborn as she knew her son to be, he remained in the kitchen, inserting himself into the conflict.

"I really do apologize for bothering you so late, Patrice. I hadn't expected to be here myself. Uh," Jonathan awkwardly gestured toward Lizzy. "Here we are," he laughed nervously before engaging in the details. "I found her inside the school. At any rate, this is what we dug up." Jonathan placed an assortment of pages, already dogeared and crumpled, atop the table and readied a highlighter as he spoke. "You were right. Robert Cane, the principle, he initiated this." He circled a phrase on the first page. "Elizabeth and I assume that he submitted this before the demons arrived. The next few pages are Robert and Samuel discussing routing the payment. Here," he shuffled to another page, "is what MES classified Ian's case as: a vampiric, fae consort. This means that either the Merchants don't know about demons or they do, yet they haven't figured out how to trap and contain one for their own benefit."

"You tellin' me that bitch Cane sold my nigga out to some dudes for bread?!" Ryan interjected, taking his place at the table. It was useless for Patrice to try and keep Ryan out. "That's fucked! This motherfucker gotta go."

Jonathan agreed, "Yes, but we have to be smart about it. That's going to take some time. For now, we need to focus on getting Ian off their registry and out of harm."

"What about Stephanie?" Ryan asked Lizzy.

They challenged one another with a stare. Lizzy did not bat an eye, beyond giving in to the demands of some sprung teenage boy. Jonathan could feel this tension after being informed of Lizzy's motives and crudely introduced to this new world of his. He didn't exactly approve of them, yet neither did she of his. On the way here, she tried to convince him that it was pointless trying to get in this and suggested that he should just let Ian deal with what's to come. As emotionless as her words were, he could tell that she had a soft spot for Ian, assuming it to be the countless hours she spent in the company of Stephanie and her comrades. She had also agreed to help Jonathan, although it wasn't easy convincing her to do so. She needed help as well, and Jonathan had the tools.

Lizzy ignored Ryan, filling in the cracks for Jonathan. "We also found my name listed on the registry." The next paper had 'Elizabeth Stanton: Shapeshifter' written plainly above a paragraph which estimated her age, height, and threat level. Neither Cane nor MES made mention of her family to her relief, yet she still assumed the worst. "That leaves two of us under MES's radar in Willard. They would need some way to monitor, which leads to," she pointed, "this: Liam Abbitt and Kenneth Green. Jonathan did some digging around and it turns out that they are agents for MES. They were appointed this mission after Cane's request—this was around the time the demons appeared."

"So how did the demons find Ian?" Ryan asked in his mother's stead.

Lizzy fought the urge to berate him. "The demons have a shapeshifter with them that was taken during the war, so he knew of MES, an entire database that archives strange things. The demons found out about the case. Baal possessed Kenneth Green and Hazth assumed Liam's identity."

"Which means the real Liam is either dead or is being kept hoe. If we find him, we can probably get Ian and Lizzy off MES's registry. That solves one problem, hopefully," Jonathan concluded.

Patrice weighed all of this thoughtfully; it lined up with most of her vision. She feared for the worse and proceeded to garner as much information as she could. "Have you spoke with the demons before?" she asked Lizzy.

Noctua nodded. "Only one of them. The shifter too. Turns out he's a family friend."

"Wait wait wait wait," Ryan interrupted. "You knew that these... these things were in the school the whole time?! And Mr. Abbitt is—then I'm guessing that Mr. Willis didn't get into a car accident, he was set up. I knew something didn't feel right."

This was news for Jonathan—he wrote it down. Lizzy continued, "Most of what they told me was to stay out of their business and they'll stay out of mine, which was good enough for me. Until I saw exactly what they were doing to Ian." A silence fell upon the kitchen. No one was prepared to hear of the horrors. "To put it simply, he has taken on demonic behavior. Got a taste for blood, heightened senses, and a stupid amount of strength. He's been acting like a shitlord, lusting on everyone and everything. Almost took advantage of Stephanie. Gotten physical with Spencer. Definitely has been dicked down by Baal. It's all a shitstorm." Ryan couldn't bring himself to say anything. Jonathan hung his head, rubbing at his temples to try to make sense of it all. "It will be a few weeks, give or take, before he gets a taste for flesh and starts killing. No physical changes just yet; I assume that Baal has some ceremony prepared for that. That will make it all permanent."

Patrice broke the atmosphere, "And what about Ian's parents? How has this gotten past them?"

"Easy. The other demon is being the puppeteer. Most likely Baal has the intermediate working behind the scenes. I've definitely felt the presence here and there, never seen him though."

"And the shapeshifter is Baal's eyes at the school. Interesting," said Patrice. "So I'm guessing you want me to give you a window while you do something reckless, right Jonathan?"

"You're right as always, Patrice. Is there a wish or a conjuring you can do to, you know, blindside the demons for a few hours?"

"A spell, you mean?" He nodded. Patrice sighed knowing what this could entail for her. "Jonathan, this is... " Before she could talk herself out of it, she agreed. "I am *only* doing the spell. That's it. This is not a safehouse and I am not providing the escape car. Jonny-hun, this is a lot for you. I told you before that this can end badly. I'm concerned that this can invite a lot of things into your life that you do not want whatsoever. You've always been a fixer, but you're just one man. You can't save everyone. Are you sure you want to risk your life for... "

"Yes. I'm positive. I made a promise to Ian a long time ago." He looked down to his hands, "I told him that he was just like everyone else and one day he will have a great life. That he'll be safe and have lots of friends and a permanent family. I can't just take that from him again, Patrice. Imagine what it will do to him."

"I can tell you what it will do, psychic or not. It will make him a psychopath whether you save him or not. Salvage all you can, he's too far gone." Lizzy detracted from their optimism, drinking the rest of her chamomile tea. They all looked at her with frowns. "Well, are we going to get this spell going or not?"

Patrice retrieved an old book from another room, flip-ping through its contents on her return. She sat the old, leather-bound book on the table for all to see. This was Ryan's first time seeing this, and he wondered what other secrets his mom held. She skimmed the fine text, stopping halfway down next to a sketched image of a vile behemoth of a creature. Its head was the size of car tire, depicted with nine black, bulbous eyes, and a mouth full of three rows of needle-sharp teeth. From its head sprout two-meter high bull horns, long, straight black hair adorned around them and down its back. Its humanoid figure was disturbed by the animalistic digits, hooved feet and from long arms hang hands with claws like talons. It was alien and completely terrifying. The caption below the image read: BAAL, DAEMON REX.

Hazth returned to the condominium, closing the door softly as to not disturb his Lord. He cordially greeted Lord Baal and apologized for being untimely with his return. Hazth was beginning to become familiar with Lord Baal's vessel as he never left it throughout most of the entirety of the visit to this plane, except when he reported in to Master. At least in that form, he could look upon Baal at equal height, no longer feeling weak with the malignant being towering over him, just as a pet would feel.

"Ah, Hazth," Baal's voice resounded throughout the foyer from the floor above, "Come." Hazth knew he was to be punished for his chivalrous actions. Nothing of the sort happened, and instead a woman accompanied Baal.

Hazth knew the scent to belong to Godimus—the little girl reeked of her.

He bowed below both lords on one knee, humbly inviting them to use him as they wished. Baal commanded him to stand. "How does it feel to know you have triumphed over Lord Godimus, Hazth?"

Unwavering, he answered, eyes affixed onto Kenneth's, "I do not feel any particular emotion to our victory. I simply did as I was instructed, my Lord."

Godimus circled Hazth, using the opportunity to familiarize herself to the anatomy of a shapeshifter. "I never saw one of these things up close before," she said admirably, further enjoying the feel of Hazth's taut, brown skin. "No wonder your sentinel beat me. He's truly distracting. Beautiful... " she breathed, stroking his face delicately and peering into his eyes, captivated by the sapphire irises. "How do I get one of these myself? Are they really extinct?"

"Not in the slightest, they have gotten better at hiding. Tell her, Hazth."

Hazth did not like discussing the matters of his kind. They've been exploited enough. "Our numbers have greatly declined, perhaps two-thirds remain since the nationwide exodus, the east coast responsible for most of those numbers."

"This thing is like a walking encyclopedia. Tell me, Hazth; where can I get one as cute as you?" Hazth did not respond to Godimus. She pouted, "I think I broke him, Baal."

Baal was fixated on his workspace, most likely concocting another substrate with alchemy to urge about Ian's change. "There was that one bullheaded female. Tell her."

Once again, Hazth found himself within the conflicting tide between obeying and protection. Merely a week away from completing their work and returning to the Uver and he could not keep Noctua from the fire of Baal. There was bound to be a catch, perhaps his punishment for leisure. Hazth was sure that Baal knew of the pitiful attempts Hazth took to assist the young shifter—Baal made sure Hazth accompanied him to report to MES about Ian's condition, subsiding the greedy bastards by telling them about Noctua. Of course, this bought Baal a great deal of time, averting their attention to the rare breed. Hazth learned that their genocide had led to a period of rarity, and now shapeshifters were an exotic commodity. Talks of weaponizing the shifters for political use was in its alpha stages, having made plenty of headway towards the future with the sacrifice of many more of his brethren. At least now, Hazth regrettably thought, the shifters had more anonymity and weren't being wiped out in droves.

Hazth spoke, "There is Noctua, however I'm afraid you wouldn't find her as useful as you think. Her lineage is only able to shift into avian species."

"Awwww, no panthers? No pythons?" she flopped backwards onto the couch. "You're right, that is boring. Can't you just make one for me?"

"I'm afraid I do not have that ability, Lord Godimus," Hazth lied.

Baal swirled the concoction, its hue cycling through the spectrum until settling on a silver-purple. "We have much to discuss, Hazth. I need you to find a disclosed location far from here, off the grid, if possible. There should be no human life within a twenty-mile radius." Baal gave the shifter a list. "Gather these items. I want the correct installation of each. Once Travius has finished his tasks, we will meet you at that location five days from now. Until then, update me on your progress. Under-stood?" Hazth affirmed. "I will be reporting to Master tonight. Keep an eye on things here until I return in a few hours."

Godimus found Hazth's hand and rubbed it against her cheek. "You wouldn't mind if I borrowed your sentinel tonight, would you Baal? I would like to study his physiology some more."

Baal removed himself from the vessel, responding with, "Go ahead. Just leave him intact, he has a job to do," in his guttural demonic lexicon before fading through the aperture.

Godimus guided Hazth into her, guiding his hand across her vessel's back and waist, then cupped his hands around her breasts. She gave a vigorous push of lustful influence into Hazth; it didn't take much for him to succumb, to her satisfaction. She observed the wild, animalistic behavior emerge from the creature while he tore her clothing off with just a finger, and had her body hoisted above his waist, erect as a bull, barely able to contain himself like an beast in heat. There wasn't much she could do to tame him, or rather, she wanted to see how a shapeshifter handled itself during nature's call. She was over-taken by the beastly man within an instant, feeling his form twitch and shift on hers. She watched as his behaviors went from civilized to feral between the snarls and growls of his thrusts, his cuspids elongated and ready for a kill, and to her amusement, a bullish tail which bound her feet together.

The intermediate was having his share of fun that night with those he tormented. Baal knew what would keep Travius focused and away from sowing seeds of mass hysteria into the public. For months now, Travius got a kick out of toying with Jennifer and Greg. The parents were not an issue; Travius could damper their intervention without conflict, taking his innate influence over the human soul to mindfully control how they perceived their environments. He was meticulous in this, coining unique daily routines and keeping the form of the individuals unharmed, however the self was entirely repressed. Whatever consciousness lay within was replaced by a mere replica, a general feeling of the person they once were. Travius kept the busy-body, family-oriented traits of Jennifer, except now she became more tolerable of her son's actions, and lengthened the leash Ian was given. Greg did not need much change; there was the stoic dad, witty with unamusing jokes and a dry routine, day-in and day-out car sales. Ian was unaware of these changes—for all he knew, his parents were as normal as ever. Slowly their souls were being imprisoned and stolen; Travius did not find the need to keep them intact. Besides, it made for nice collateral, fruits of his labor.

Travius could multitask with ease when given an order, otherwise Willard would have been turned into a wasteland without the strict demands of his Lord. Throughout their mission, Travius carefully sowed his influence into Spencer, and it now began to sprout into glorious despair, he could almost taste the soul he slowly cooked. Travius was approached by the demon lord Godimus after her agreement with Baal and she proposed, no, demanded that she take over Spencer, and in exchange, she enacted a deal that he couldn't resist, a deal that would grant him rulership over potentially hundreds of souls. He agreed immediately, and soon Godimus played on all the hidden desires that coursed within Spencer, except now it was amplified by her mastery of lust. The kid had much pent up, becoming Godimus' playground. And she would play this well.

Spencer was entangled within a web of his own making—why did he consistently drag himself for the action of another? Ian was surrounded by new faces in new expensive clothing, loitering outside of a bar and grill he used to take Spencer to each summer. Spencer halted his tracks and stared like a creep thinking of what to say to him, or if he should say anything at all—he was the victim. Shrouded by a hood and hidden behind a tree, Spencer watched from across the street. He was able to get a good look at Ian's company; they were all drop-dead gorgeous and wealthy—Spencer couldn't even fathom how he could compare. Everything about Ian contrasted the way he used to be just months prior. Where did he get all this money from, he thought. The answer didn't waste time, punching Spencer's heart once more at the thought of his name: Kenneth. It was always Kenneth. Spencer did not think it possible to hate a person until he met Kenneth and sat in the wake he left.

Why couldn't Spencer bring himself to say how he felt in a burst of emotion? He felt compelled to beg Ian at his feet to love him and only him, to allow Ian back into his life to fill the void that Kenneth created. Simultaneously, he wanted to give Ian the very hell he was experiencing, yet he could never bring himself to that conclusion no matter how often his mind suggested it. Spencer would always suffer by the hands of others, never to return the act simply because he couldn't bring himself to do anything vindictive. He was a coward. He clutched his heart, sliding against the tree to the ground, not sure if he could sob silently this time.

Ian's laughter roused Spencer from tears as he wiped his eyes to make the mistake of peaking around the tree once more. Ian straddled some girl against the bar's brick exterior, gliding their tongues together and caressing about each other's body. She pulled his hand away from the group and they bid the others a good night; those left behind cheered Ian for his success. Everyone knew how their night would play out.

Kill her, Spencer thought to himself. *Make her regret looking at him.* Spencer followed them at a distance clinging to the shadows as best as he could. They did petty flirting back and forth until Ian unlocked the passenger door of a champagne Lexus for her; he got into the driver seat, disappearing down the street in seconds. *A car... Kenneth gave him a fucking car.* Spencer pivoted back towards his father's house, dragging his feet, looking into nothing.

Ian didn't go far before he parked the vehicle in an empty parking lot. He was on her within seconds. Ian tilted her seat back while kicking his shoes onto the floor, pants halfway down his thighs. He had the mechanisms of her clothes figured out in no time—Ian had his tongue busied on her nipple before she could comprehend how he got her bra off that quickly. He was strong and had that scent that made her crazy, the kind of scent that went along with boys of his stature and swagger. She was coaxed into a wave of submission, unaware that her moans made it outside of the car's safety as she drifted into sexual stasis. Ian barely slid one finger inside of her before she gushed. He'd only been touching her for all of five minutes and her fluids were pooled in the crevice made by her thighs. Ian licked the drippings from his hands and honed in, flicking his wet tongue over her clitoris rhythmically. She screamed and pulled away from the intense pleasure, but Ian held her in place, forcing her to succumb to the feeling. She fell deeply entranced, as if her entirety became one with his—she was completely at his control.

Ian knew he had her. This talent of his, he realized, was becoming a skill. She laid there trembling as Ian pulled away. There was this silver, ethereal tether that Ian could see, intangible but beckoning. He followed the tether with his eyes, emanating from his chest and settling on the center of hers where it shimmered. It was remarkably beautiful nestled between the girl's breasts, dauntingly irresistible. He fought against the call of the curves, the flesh, the pussy, the blood.

Blood.

There, the forbidden word he wanted to avoid was on the forefront of his mind. There was more that he derived from his fantasy, a certain quality that he couldn't think of, only feel the thought's presence. Was it her warmth or her smell... the way her facial muscles moved in all the right ways? Oh yes! He could almost taste it, twirling it in his mouth before swallowing to make it become one with him. What was it? What was it?!

Blood was as close as he could get for now. He needed it. His eyes darted this way and that. He could smell it coursing through every vessel. She beckoned him to dominate her through the energy's call, the smell of her liquids, her dripping pussy, her pulsing heart and protruding veins, her screams... all the blood he could ask for!

Between her moans she peeked at Ian, at his eyes which fixated on her body as if he were redressing and undressing her over and over. Ian felt his patience dwindling; waiting for Kenneth felt less and less rational as he could easily do this on his own. It was fresh, from the source, warm. And Ian knew he had complete control over it. He could feel the pain within his teeth begging to feel the puncture—he tongued over their sharp surface, fantasizing about the moment.

"You have a condom, right?" she asked, snapping Ian out of his haze. Her naked body was sprawled open, anticipating Ian's entrance. He nodded after contemplating her question, and clumsily rummaged through the glovebox. He removed his shirt, feeling the cold of the crystal on his chest. The rainbow quartz dangled below his collarbone, scattering the orange streetlight that shone through the window. It bounced rainbow rays around the car's interior. He wrapped his hand around it, encumbered by the events that led to his possession of the jewel.

Hidden abilities, huh? Ian snickered to himself, the crystal, and to his current predicament.

She sat up on her elbows, "Are we doing this or what?"

Ian's gaze was fixed elsewhere, all interest and motivation sucked away by the pendant. "Sorry," he muttered. "Next time."

She noted his current condition, "But we just got started." She snaked her hand over his crotch, "And you're still hard. I can help you out." She reached inside his underwear; Ian held her wrist.

"Next time," he sternly repeated. He replaced himself in the driver's seat, pulling his shirt back onto his body, and reversed the car out of the lot.

"I'll drop you off at home."

She caught the hint. "Recent breakup?"

"Something like that."

"Ah." And it was left as that. She was stepping into her house just as he backed out of her driveway.

For Noctua, the image of Baal was less than accurate, yet it managed to capture the more prominent characteristics. Whoever lived to draw the image with enough detail was amazing on its own. The text inaccurately depicted his wingspan; it should've read seventeen meters instead of ten. "This book. It's got some secure magic, bound in fairy skin," she said.

Patrice examined the outside, surprised, "So that's what this is. Hmm. This was in my family since their immigration from Jamaica. My mom gave this to me when I turned twelve to help with spell making." She smiled at the memory and rotated the book for the others to see. "It has information on common demons. This is Baal. Demon Lord, resides under the Third Gate of Hell. Let's see here." She slipped her reading frames onto her face, delving into the text.

She read, "'Baal is the Lord of Flyers, recorded as having a wingspan larger than most known Lords. The first written record of his appearance on Earth was during the Middle Ages. He was known to grant knowledge to scholars that summoned him, as well as grant wealth to those willing to do his bidding. Baal is not easily banished by traditional means suited for intermediate banishment. Like most Lords of demons, a direct encounter will often resort in death before the weakness is found. Baal has not successfully been banished nor contained within sigil nor bound to object. Instead, a sigil—depicted left—known as Baal's Brandish in the Middle Ages, was used to mark old texts deemed sacred and valuable, which often served as a means of offering. Texts marked with this sigil were also said to keep information private, useful when transporting over long distances. When marked with mortal blood, it is said that Baal will be summoned and will not be allowed to surface into the mortal plane unless a contract is agreed upon, however the summoner may talk with and hear the entity. Mages and those with the Sight have used this to grant temporary visual of the demon. If Baal is summoned within a devil's trap, he will remain hostage for a maximum of thirty hours before it begins to weaken. After thirty hours, the summoner will have between three to five hours to reconstruct the trap before Baal is released back to the Third Gate.' Huh, sounds easy enough."

"But he's already on this plane, which means that the trap may be completely useless. And then we are definitely dead," Ryan concluded, cudgeling for as many solutions he could think up. "Is that all we got to work with?"

Patrice turned the page over, revealing more text, lists, and images. She continued, "'When unleashed upon the Earthen plane, Baal typically inhabits a vessel with a background of wealth, political power, or other influential positions. Non-human vessels include cats, crows, rats, and frogs. See Index 4 for auxiliary spells used in capture of Baal.'" Patrice skimmed the index, seeing which items may be the most difficult to retrieve and which spells were the safest to do. She frowned, "Well, unless we can take a flight to Egypt and back, we can't do these spells. But I think we can bind him to something, or someone. I think I can manage this, but not alone."

Jonathan raked his hand through his salt-pepper hair knowing he was in for it. "What do you need me to do?"

The four stayed up throughout the night preparing the garage as a devil's trap. Jonathan labored, moving heavy equipment about with Lizzy's assistance, although he would admit that she did most of the work. Ryan learned much more than he would have ever imagined about his mother, watching as she enchanted and consecrated the structure, top to bottom. He had no idea his mother could use magick, nor that she had spent a great deal of time in her early twenties selling sugar pills charmed with spells as study aids in college. Not only had she cornered a drug market, but she also enacted her craft beneath the unassuming eyes of the public. Her youth was unlike any other, yet grossly akin to an average young adult when it came to hormones, to Ryan's disgust—he spent much effort trying to ignore Jonathan's and Patrice's rendezvous of the past.

It was a time for serenity, a calm before a storm that no one really felt prepared for. They had a plan.

13

RUNAWAY

Spencer's eyes were fixed on the sidewalk as his walk home from tech club was nearing its completion. He wandered about lost in thought as the cracks passed beneath his steps. Dad week always had a sullen atmosphere attached to it. Now, the air was humid and muggy, but the winds were growing stronger as the threat of a thunderstorm made itself heard southwest. At least it felt nice outside, he thought. It was finally feeling like spring.

The shortcut to his father's house was full of scenic beauty, pompous displays of the area's income bracket that Spencer couldn't appreciate in the moment. Everything had this dull filter over it; the bike trail encircled a manmade lake, the billowing pines went on for miles in either direction except due north where the classy suburbs of Vapor Lakes lie. He hated it here. The people pretended to respect their neighbors, a faux sense of community tied together by commonalities in income; however, do something slightly out of the ordinary and the army of Susans were always there to play neighborhood superheroes, never the ones to mind their own business.

Not wanting to become imprisoned within his nihilistic thoughts any further, Spencer took a detour through the natural paths. Perhaps some fresh air would keep his mind from daunting on the ridiculous plots of revenge. The serenity of it all was more than suitable for his current state of mind. And nature served its intended purpose, bringing with it winds of tranquility.

Maybe things could get better... he thought. But of course, the grounded intellectual pessimist would persist as well to counter and guard against any fantastic approach, rearing its stark nature and commanding the floor as usual.

Spencer felt something akin to a tickle in his mind; it was an itch he couldn't scratch. Times alone, when left to his own devices, this feeling would arise—pestering, prodding, poking. A fragrance of lilac accompanied it, the sudden glimpse of fuchsia fairies flittering at the corner of his vision. He twisted and stretched his neck to make the feeling dissipate. It gradually worsened the more he thought about Michael—now it manifested as a translucent silhouette posted at the corner of his sight, guaranteeing safety from anyone else that would dare try to rustle Spencer. It was the only reliable figment his mind could recognize.

There was an intoxicating giggle that reverberated after it spoke, yet it did not admonish him for his way of thinking. Instead, it prompted him to dig further, to investigate the influences that led to his current predicament. And often, this investigation always concluded with a sexual connotation. He tried to ignore it, yet each time he fanned away those lustful flames, his body would react in ways he could not control—roaming hands and rushing fingers.

Don't be foolish, it said. Spencer kept his head downward, walking with consistent strides. He observed the figment keeping pace. *You need to show your pain or else it will never stop. All you do is cry. You think that's enough to make anyone pay attention to you?*

Spencer responded aloud to his figment. "You don't think that Ian and I can work past this? I mean, it's worth a shot."

You fool. He knows that you still love him. And he'll use that against you. Make him need you and only you.

"H-How do I do that?"

Change yourself.

Spencer stopped in his tracks to finally look onto its formless face, eager to hear this advice. So far it hadn't led

Spencer wrong. For weeks he experienced restless nights as his phantom instinct guided him through sweat-filled discoveries of pleasure. Spencer, at first, was opposed to using his hands for deeds such as these, but the more he delved into it, the more he realized how foolish his vows of purity were. Soon, Spencer was to fill his chambers with his own moans, leaving hills of discarded tissues to pile around the trash bin. Spencer began to understand Ian's needs of pleasure with the clarity of experience. Once they were back together, he would give himself to Ian—anything to make him stay.

Let me change you. We are invincible together.

Spencer smiled, nodding. To any who would look at this externally, they would see an infant bout of madness brewing. Spencer murmured to himself in the isolated woods. The instinct went silent, affixing itself into Spencer.

For moments now, Spencer sat in brown leaves, chin tilted towards the sky, mouth agape as he stroked himself, reveling in the intense indulgence, never feeling as if his wrist were going fast enough. He fantasized about the touch of Ian's lips, the way their bodies would meld when they were finally back together. Yes, everything would return to normal once he gave Ian what he wished for.

Intrusive thoughts of his initial introduction of hedonism worked their way to the forefront—his mind began to waver, fighting the thoughts of *him* and focusing more on Ian. He began to lose steam as the unwarranted imagery of *him* worked their way to prominence. Spencer stopped himself as the arousal dwindled, again mentally sabotaging himself, wishing that his instinct would return to offer more advice to make the torment disappear. If only he hadn't have done that back then—if only he had been more honest with Ian...

The snap of a twig behind brought Spencer to, whipping his head with a startled take towards the direction of the noise. They seemed to have realized each other at the same time, and it seemed as though the same thought dawned on the two simultaneously. Spencer's body locked up. Soon his face was on the ground before he could register what was occurring.

Michael managed to get Spencer's shoes off and his pants midway down his legs. Michael worked at his own zipper with a smug grin, payback in the purest form. "Sorry I hadn't been to tech club in a while. I've been expelled. No more football, no more scholarship. And I have you to thank." Upon seeing the flesh hanging from his attacker's pants, Spencer kicked, screamed, and scrambled his way out of Michael's clutches, stumbling a few steps, tripping over his pant legs. He had an exact window to try again, getting his jeans up, and running. He pushed himself as much as he could. Ran through the system of paths solely from muscle memory, tears streaking his face. With phone in hand, he tapped the contact amid trembling hands, no time to key in a thing. He did not hear the first ring as he was slammed into the ground. Usurped from aside, Spencer had his wrists firmly bound by Michael's massive hand, the other ripping Spencer's jeans off. Spencer yelled and bellowed for help. He begged Michael to stop. In between the screams were chokes.

The more he tried to fight, the weaker he got. The two-hundred-twenty-pound quarterback treated this as a game; Michael pried his body through Spencer's clinched thighs, a useless defense. Michael relentlessly forced himself in and out of Spencer, tearing the tissue now welling with blood. Spencer screamed as loud as he could for anyone to help, until his mouth was stuffed with his own socks and covered. The screams turned to muffled sobs, then to whimpers as any hope that remained vanished in the following instances. He stared blankly at the sky, watching it fade from its clouded gray into the beginning drizzle of the storm. Soon it was only the waxing gibbous that bore witness to Spencer's agony. And the moon never told its secrets. The lone watcher cast a pale milky light over the canvas of his marred, naked skin. He was covered in this beautiful light he hoped would comfort him as it always had done, to end every thought or emotion, anything to keep him from bearing witness to nature's ugly face. He would never understand what he did to deserve this life. He didn't care. Only the sounds of grunting, the squish of the thrusts into his buttocks resounded in monotony. He felt himself getting filled with Michael's semen—Michael showed no sign of fatigue.

Spencer was dressed in only moonlight, his nails dug into the cool dirt when Michael grabbed Spencer's penis in rhythmic hydraulics, akin to his thrusts. Spencer was able to only squirm in abhorrence to the touch. Flushed from head to toe, Spencer's voice trembled in gasps as he tried to reason once more. "S-S-S-S-Stop... p-p-p-please... " his voice shrank with tittle. Michael quickened the pace, aroused by the satisfaction of revenge.

He gave a forceful thrust and froze, his stature poised merely centimeters away from his victim's chest, sweat dripping and rolling onto Spencer, into his hair and face.

A relentless two-hundred-twenty-pounds collapsed onto Spencer's chest, unmoving. Spencer felt something trickling down from Michael's naval, down Spencer's sides, puddling around him and soaking the leaves. It was warm, the fluid—following was a tangy, metallic aroma.

Spencer's mind raced to comprehend as the weight was lifted, and his midsection glistened speckles of moonlight, reflected in Michael's blood. Spencer began to process, eyes coming into focus. Innards plopped onto the ground and a bloody hand projected from Michael's naval. It withdrew from his midsection, onto his member, which was then ripped from its housing, leaving bile and other foul fluids to gush out of the new fissure.

The light flickered from Michael's eyes, body going limp, as Spencer bore witness to each limb being forcibly removed.

Michael was being ripped apart with ease.

Ian panted profusely over his work. He felt as though it wasn't good enough, proceeding to maul Michael's face into unrecognizable scraps. Whimpering from below drew him from his thirst for blood—immediately, Ian shed his jacket. Without word, he dressed Spencer, securely covering Spencer's body.

With a blank stare and mouth ajar, Spencer struggled to make words. Ian picked him up, moving as quickly and silently as he could manage, looking back onto the mound of skin, bones, and organs. That was his doing.

Spencer couldn't comprehend time. Soon he went from the wood's edge of Vapor Lakes and ended up at Cyrus Corner, a ten-minute drive yet there in a matter of seconds on foot. Ian constantly murmured something the entirety of the way there; Spencer couldn't comprehend until now. "You're going to be alright," it sounded like, but tainted in anger, guilt, and at the forefront, panic. He kept murmuring the phrase as he fumbled through his phone, pacing in the shadow of the familiar house.

Ian was talking elatedly... what was he saying? Spencer didn't care. He continued to stare blankly ahead of him. Stephanie was there. She was crying. Saying something that Spencer couldn't understand. He was inside Stephanie's room. Ian paced anxiously; Stephanie placed blankets around Spencer's shoulders. They yelled at each other. Spencer only watched from behind his eyes.

"Ian. Listen. We *have* to get him to a hospital. There is no other option!" Stephanie yelled.

"I. Killed. Michael. His blood is all over Spencer, all over my clothes. My hands. We tell them that Spencer was raped, they're going to find out it was Michael. He's dead." Ian began pacing again, "Oh my god. I killed Michael. I killed him. I killed him. We... we gotta go back and hide the body."

Stephanie lent her comfort to Spencer who was unable to register this moment's severity. Ryan's words echoed distantly in her mind. This was real. All of this. For once, she felt completely helpless. She didn't know where to go from here.

"We *have* to run. That's the only way," Ian said through clenched teeth.

"Are you out of your mind?! We can't! We don't have enough money to make it, not even to hail a taxi from here to the next state!"

"We don't have a fuckin' choice! I killed him, Stephanie, I ripped him apart. You were fucking right, I've changed, I changed into a fucking monster! I don't know what the fuck is happening to me!" He clutched his hair in fistfuls.

"We can't just abandon our families... we won't make it far enough." She was scared to death, her voice pressured to break from dammed sobs. "The cops will find us instantly, you'll automatically look guilty, and you'll definitely get caught."

"Fine. Then you stay here. Let's go, Spence." Ian started for him but was met with retaliation.

"You're not taking Spencer anywhere, you hear me? He's staying here. Unlike you, Ian, we can't do whatever the fuck we want, okay? Don't drag Spencer any further into your fucked up world!" She drove herself breathless. "Spencer is the victim here.

He *needs* to go to a hospital, now. If you're so concerned with having a clean record over Spencer's well-being, then just run away by yourself."

"Stephanie," Ian reached for her.

"Don't touch me!" she screamed.

Ian felt his heart shatter. *It's happening.* Ian pressed, "I am sorry. I don't know what's going on. I'm sorry. Please don't hate me, I don't know what I'm doing, I don't know why this happened. Can we just... can we please... " Ian gestured toward the bathroom and Spencer.

The two worked together in silence, and as compassionately as possible, they stripped Spencer and washed the night away from him. Stephanie sat with him in her bedroom until Ian was finished washing himself clean; the remainder of red slid down the drain. Stephanie avoided eye contact with Ian as he dressed in borrowed, oversized clothing. She sobbed at Spencer's trauma quietly; Ian bagged the bloody clothes and threw whatever he deemed a necessity into several backpacks. What could she do? All evidence the hospital would need was washed into the drain. No one would believe Spencer's assault otherwise. To do nothing would get her roped in. Ian could leave with Spencer, and Stephanie would crack under the immense pressure.

They never had you in your best interest, her parents' words echoed.

Ian reappeared in the doorway, "Stephanie, we have to move. Staying here won't be good for any of us. I get locked in some nuthouse prison, no one will ever hear Spencer out. He'll be forced to live in silence, and you will have to be here to bear the guilt of seeing it unfold. We don't have a choice. We can run and try to change our outcome, or we can sit here and let others decide for us." She stared at her lap, tears soaking into her jeans. "You have a choice, Steph. We don't. You can stay here, I won't blame you. None of this was your fault... I should have listened to you. But... but Spencer and I have to go."

She was running out of time to decide. Ian donned the bags and lifted Spencer from Stephanie's tight embrace.

"I'm coming," she said, just barely audible. "Fuck it, fuck it all. I'm coming." Part of her did it for her values, yet most of her mind screamed against it. There would never be any good in either case.

In total they carried four bags; in a rush attempt to certify their safety, Stephanie threw emergency supplies, clothing, and canned goods into the bags' capacity. She dumped the contents of the shoe box beneath her bed into another bag—$2,126 total in cash. The bags' weight was nothing in comparison to the weight that rested upon all of them, the atmosphere tainted with regrets, anger, pain, resentment, fear, contempt. They were now several miles away from the residentials, a few more away from the city. Ian led as she followed, screaming at herself to turn back with each step.

One look at Spencer kept her feet following forward.

They rested at an abandoned service station next to the idle street. The minimart's vacancy became their brief moment of relief. Ian sat Spencer on the counter, unloading the other weights from his back. Stephanie stood anxiously against a dusty shelf, realizing how vast Ian had changed in the last few weeks. He became something entirely different—a demon as Ryan called him, was beginning to take shape around Ian the more she looked onto him.

Ian fiddled with his phone every few seconds. Upon holding it to his ear, another voice picked up. She knew who it was before they even spoke, shaking her head in disbelief. At this point, there was no say in the matter.

Her finger hovered over Lizzy's contact.

She put her phone away.

It took no time for the blinding flash of headlights to blare into the minimart. She ducked out of its path. The door opened. She followed the Doc Martins in to reveal Kenneth, who was already inquiring about the situation. "What happened?" Kenneth mimicked great concern.

"Can I explain on the way? Help me get everything in the car." Ian buckled Spencer in the back seat of the Lexus, aware of the hot tears plopping from his face and avoided eye contact. Ian knew what Spencer wanted to scream at him, that Kenneth was the whole reason they all sat here currently and yet time after time again, here Ian was, playing into Kenneth's hands. Kenneth loaded their belongings in the back. He and Ian looked to Stephanie; she stood hesitantly a safe distance away. Ian knew what she thought too, that look of betrayal shooting straight through him. All he could say was, "Please." He knew she wouldn't come to trust him ever again.

Kenneth sighed, "You're guilty by association, darling. You can stand there if you want, but we're leaving." Kenneth climbed in and started the engine.

Ian hesitated, pleading with Stephanie to trust him. No longer finding the words to combat, she conceded if only to comfort Spencer.

Kenneth drove them outside of the city limits. He disposed of the evidence, destroying their phones, soiled clothing, and identification in a fire constructed out of discarded receipts and gasoline on the side of a rural shantytown—no one opposed.

Their identifiers were reduced to ash and their tracks were covered. They returned to the road. Where? They didn't dare to ask. They were in it for the long haul.

Blinding sunlight shone directly upon Hazth's face, arousing him from his slumber. He looked around in a haze, still not fully conscious, noting his nakedness and isolation. He jumped into action once it dawned that both Godimus and Lord Baal's vessels were missing. He cursed loudly—he needed to fix this before Baal was to return from the Uver. Without his vessel, the remainder of their time would be rendered impossible.

Hazth gave Baal's list a onceover. He noticed Lord Baal's sigil watermarked behind his handwriting. He activated it; they were instructions that contradicted all of what he was issued prior. He hustled to his usual spot to shift in confidence, shedding his cloak and soaring above in the brightening sky. It was in this moment that Hazth knew Baal was not as selfish as he once thought the lord to be, and with conviction he set out to make sure his lord's will would be achieved at all costs.

Lizzy made it to school earlier than normal that day. She was ready to do what she intended; grab Stephanie and Ian, get out of dodge while Baal was distracted. If Patrice and Jonathan's plan went correctly, they could hex the demons temporarily. In that window, she could make an escape with Stephanie and Fetcher can make his with Ian. They agreed to help each other thus far, then go separate ways—the rest was up to their individual decisions. It was almost time. She knew when Cane arrived on the daily, knew every blind spot including those of the surveillance. If Cane or anyone got in the way, she would have to run through them and keep running. Of course, Patrice and Jonathan wanted no casualties during this plan, no kids in danger, however Lizzy made no promises.

Wait for Stephanie, stall her, wait for Ian, grab the two. She pondered the form she would take as she went over the plan religiously until she dared not to dwell on it any further. She committed to it. Noctua had to break the hearts of her siblings when she told them she would disappear for a while. Gularis did not hesitate to tell her how stupid her plan sounded, getting into their usual screaming fit which led to a physical fight at the farmhouse aerie—the gnashing of beaks and talons left a mess of feathers scattered about; the children watched with unease, frightened by the increasing tension within their family that was supposed to be a haven of peace. Nana became grim, saying little to nothing in response to Noctua's impulsive decision. She knew without a doubt that Nana lost faith in her.

Noctua was grave while fighting against giving attention to the aches and stings left over from the brawl, instinct at its peak. Eagar as she waited, her target never arrived at the usual hit time, and Noctua grew anxious.

She answered Jonathan's call. "Are we set?" he asked.

"Not yet. She's still not here. And I didn't see Ian get off the bus. He might be skipping again," she said in suspicion, running through every scenario possible.

"The spell is ready. Just tell us when."

"There's something wrong. The students are arriving and school's about to start. I'm losing my window."

"Shit," Jonathan spat. "I'll try to call Ian. You see if you can get a hold of Stephanie. Maybe we can bring them to us."

"Good thinking." She immediately dialed Stephanie's number, going directly to voicemail. She came to this several times before giving up.

Now she began to worry. She took Jonathan's call.

"I can't get through to him. Voicemail."

"Same here... she has an exam today. I'll call Spencer." As she did so, she was met with the same result, no answer. Noctua almost crushed the cheap cellphone between her fingers. She persisted just until school declared its session. "Jonathan... I think we've been outsmarted."

Jonathan cursed on the other end. "How could they know? I was sure we had this... "

"We'll rendezvous at Patrice's. I'm going to see if I can pick up a scent trail."

"Right. I'm arriving at the real Liam's address. I'll call you as soon as I find something."

Noctua let herself into Stephanie's room in urgency, immediately assaulted by the scent of hours-old blood, human blood. Empty shoeboxes, drawers sprawled open. She remembered Stephanie saying something about her parents going on a spiritual retreat in Florida as she detected their faded scents. Stephanie, Spencer, and Ian were here mere hours ago. She locked on to their scent and left as quickly as she came.

Spencer's scent and that of the blood led southeast, not too far from Stephanie's house. She landed on the outskirts of Vapor Lakes. The scent of blood became palpable the deeper into the woods she ventured—as she traversed the treetops, Ian's essence intermingled, entwined with a thickened atmosphere. Dispersed among the leaves were scraps of shredded clothing—she followed the specks of blood to their source. Below the branches she roosted on was a mess of guts and the mangled face of Michael.

Jonathan knocked on the door of the Abbitt residence with no luck. The doorbell didn't serve its purpose either and left Jonathan in a conflict of morale. Without wasting another minute, he scanned the premises for something useful—he checked his vehicle. He scattered all the toys in a rush, bewildered at the amount of such and the lack of utility. It was then that he remembered the small toolset he received on Christmas, new and unopened. He used the hammer to break the door's embedded window, then, with a turn of the knob from the inside, he was in.

It was late enough for most of the neighborhood to be at work, early enough to stay out of the limelight yet a gamble for Jonathan. One false move and he would never be able to see to the end of this case. A few steps into the foyer left Jonathan awestruck. The vaulted wood ceilings and the crown moldings complimented one another perfectly. Just above his head he could see to the second floor; it only added to the grandeur of it all. Fetcher guessed that this was where Willard housed its wealthy, Willowhedge, as the surrounding houses did not fall short. He swallowed, took a deep breath to calm his nerves, and then proceeded to riffle through the house.

It brought him an odd sense of joy for some reason, ripping apart and destroying valuable things in their perfect form, yet the adrenaline kept him from enjoying his visit. The pressure was on.

Upon his trek up the stairs, he noticed how undisturbed everything was. Dust collected along the banister and in the right light he could see it on every surface. It was obvious this place was abandoned—it smelled empty, stagnant. Jonathan became uneasy in the silence. Slowly, he continued his progression up.

He became more on edge as time went on. As much as he thought he progressed, he found nothing. He was running out of things to check. Just knowing that Abbitt hadn't been here in months would be enough evidence to suspect the worst.

Upon entering the last room in the house, what he presumed to be a lounge of some sort, he was bombarded with the golden crest of the shield and swords, the symbol belonging to the Merchants of the Exotic Species, hanging from the wall on tapestries that hung sequentially around the lounge. In the center of the room was a simple pedestal, showcasing a golden vase with the crest.

Jonathan guessed this was where meetings took place. It was small, but large enough to stand six or eight people. Jonathan looked for any other clues besides the obvious vase that he could test. *Anything but that,* he detested. *If I learned anything from movies, never go for the vase. Or... perhaps it's hiding something in plain sight.* He posed his hands in the space above, taking a firm stance and a concentrated breath. "Okay, Fetcher," he breathed shakily, "You can do this."

Without another thought, he tricked himself to lift its lid. It was stuck, formed to the vase itself, faux. "Didn't see that coming," he said, manipulating the vase any way he could with gloved hands. Defeated, he braced himself on the pedestal, thinking of anything he could try. He was short of having a breakdown.

The pedestal slid an inch from his weight. Jonathan grew curious. He tried to push it again in the same direction, but it was as if its weight had multiplied over his own. Jonathan tried at every angle, and when the pedestal moved to the right with ease, that's when he knew he was on to something. The pedestal was on some sort of mechanical track, although no evidence of such could be seen. "Magnetic," Fetcher thought aloud. He wondered if he should merely wing it as he was or search for clues. He chose the former; time was of the essence.

Jonathan felt a sort of regret when the pedestal arrested with a click. The floor rumbled alive with the unseen mechanisms. The south wall lowered revealing another made from burnished copper—smooth and cold to the touch. The pedestal was anchored flush into the wall; the vase, on its side, turned clockwise, counterclockwise, then clockwise again, finally settling on a click. A corridor was formed before him.

Jonathan swallowed. "I'm going to regret this," were his last words before entering the tunnel. Darker and darker it grew the further he descended. The light from the house was beginning to fade. He used his phone's flashlight, not the brightest but the best he could get. He rounded a sharp corner, the walls seemingly growing thinner as his mind feared for the worst. Soon, the corridor abruptly ended into a great room. Motion sensing buzzing bulbs flickered on, startling him.

His eyes adjusted to the brightness. He fell completely still. Entire lengths of holding chambers lined the great room full of aquatic, humanoid creatures. They were riled by Fetcher's appearance and studied him with black, unreflecting globes, banging against the glass with webbed, clawed phalanges. They swam about in their still confines anxiously. Jonathan knew he had to make a run for it, unable to tear his eyes away. "What on earth... " slid over his lips.

When he finally convinced himself to move, he turned his attention behind him. There was a lab bench that stretched on with specimens, both wet and dry—Fetcher didn't have the slightest idea of what they were. He captured as many photographs as he could manage amid trembling limbs, being sure to back them up in the cloud.

Jonathan was startled by the sound of clinking glasses. He whirled around, jumping backwards from the visitor. Before Jonathan could speak, it spoke first.

"I assume you are in here because a little bird couldn't help but dig her nose into adult business," Hazth spoke casually, tending to his own needs. He gathered the materials Baal requested of him, or at least the items that could be found in Abbitt's lab. Jonathan stood, frozen. He was sure he was done for. His heart bottomed out when the adrenaline kicked in. *This is... is this the demon lord?!* Fetcher was almost positive—he had *that* look about him: unnatural regal demeanor and fearsome composure. Jonathan stood starkly still with a grim expression, trying and failing to maintain eye contact.

He couldn't believe it. Bright, sapphire eyes leered dangerously into Jonathan. They had a luminescent quality about them, inducing a gravity that made Jonathan's feet into lead. The stranger's pupils were slim and feral like a predator's, making Jonathan into his prey.

"You must be Jonathan Fetcher. I thought you'd be dead by now." Jonathan didn't know whether to be more afraid of the stranger knowing his identity or the assumed state of his livelihood.

"Who are you?" Jonathan tried to come off as confident as possible.

"I could be anyone," Hazth said, continuing to gather supplies, chemicals, and other lab equipment. "But for the sake of simplicity, Hazth."

Jonathan began to panic. Perhaps he really was a fool for trying to save Ian's life. By such, he robbed his own children of a father, rendering definite heartbreak onto his wife.

But Hazth continued to act as if Jonathan did not exist. He spoke to Jonathan calmly and casually, his deep voice reverberating within the great room. "What are you looking for? Perhaps I could assist."

"Did you kill Liam?" came from Jonathan before he realized what he was up against. He regretted sounding so direct.

Hazth closed the clasps of a wooden box used to pack. "Not directly."

Jonathan needed to confirm this. He pressed on, fighting himself in the process. "So Liam is dead?" Hazth nodded. "You are a, uh, a shapeshifter—Baal's shapeshifter."

"It's true. The little bird has dug her nose into this." He sighed. "Oh well. It can't be helped."

"What's going on? Why do you want Ian?!"

Hazth shrugged, "It's not my place to ask, it's not my place to tell. I just do what I'm told."

"Where is he?" Jonathan held onto Hazth's shoulders desperately. "Please, for the life of me, please tell me where he is."

"I cannot answer that."

"Yes you can!" Jonathan held tighter, at his wits end. He was knocked away by Hazth with such intensity that Jonathan slammed into the lab bench headfirst.

Fetcher was roused by the blinding sun shining through his eyelids. Upon opening his eyes, he was met with a searing pain atop his head. As disoriented as he was, he recognized the interior of the truck he currently sat in, along with the smell of old cigarettes embedded within. Lizzy looked over to him, a few takes between Jonathan and the road. "Good. You're awake," she said in a tone bordering between callous and relief. When his eyes finally adjusted to the light, he observed the surrounding environment. One of the street signs read RICHMOND 295 EXIT RIGHT ¼ MILE.

"Where... "

"You got knocked out. Banged your head pretty bad. There's ibuprofen in the glovebox."

He popped four, squinting from the sunlight, and wincing from the pain. "It was Hazth."

"I know," Lizzy replied, hands remaining tight around the wheel. "I'm following their scent as best as I can. It's almost faded." Her mouth was pressed in a hard line and her jaw clenched repeatedly. He stared down at his lap in silence. The creeping feeling of hopelessness was now introducing itself to Fetcher's psyche. All he could picture was Ian's face, tear-streaked at the orphanage. He recalled the pale, sunken shell left behind after the tragedy of the Montgomery's, leaving Ian as the sole survivor at the age of ten.

"Find anything on Abbitt?" Lizzy asked, breaking the silence.

He passed his phone over to her. She flipped through each of his pictures, disgusted. "Whatever the hell I found, it doesn't look good. Abbitt is dead." Jonathan was clearly still shaken. He tapped his palms on the dashboard anxiously, "What about you? Where are we going?"

"Heading north." She continued with the breeze of the open window keeping her on course, "Something big happened. Michael's dead." Fetcher stared inquisitively. She sighed, "He was Spencer's bully. It did not look good at all. Michael was literally ripped apart. I caught Spencer's scent and followed it there, to Vapor Lakes. Spencer and Ian met up at Stephanie's afterwards. Her place was ransacked." He knew that she was doing all she could to remain composed. "I don't think Baal did this. It was too sloppy. And Hazth, by the time I found you, he was gone. Scent led to a dead end." She exited right.

They merged from one highway to a busier one leading towards Richmond. "Did Ian do it?" Lizzy remained with her face barely out the window, confirming with a slight nod. Jonathan gripped his fists tighter and cursed aloud. She wanted to tell him to drop out while he still could. This would only make a good man mad. She failed to see what he could do to help without getting killed. Although she felt a tad bit at ease with his company, she'd never say it out loud.

Kenneth parked the vehicle before a large, multistoried log cabin—the estate was grand on the outside, and private by the way it sat far into the woods, perhaps a mile from the back road they traveled on. The lawn was pristinely kempt; climbing ivy all but covered the entryway. A trickling fountain bubbled into a stream that intertwined through a rock garden.

Kenneth was the first from the car, grabbing all the guests' items with an arm and closing the trunk with the other. The door to the estate opened revealing a petite woman, a housewife straight from a fifty's magazine in all her galore. She lovingly held the door open for Kenneth and greeted him with a kiss, leaving a fuchsia print on his cheek; she waved with a big smile at the kids in the car. When no one made a move, she gestured towards the inside courteously. The young ones took their time, refusing to speak to one another in the process. Ian made the first move, introducing himself and the others to the woman—she named herself as Trisha, Kenneth's fiancé. Much to his relief, she didn't pry and instead went to console the others, soon to ease them from the vehicle into the comforting cabin.

When everyone was settled, Trisha headed into the living room with plates steaming with food. The smell was terribly invigorating, yet Stephanie and Spencer felt as if they could not stomach it. Trisha set the dishes before them, adding, "I will not let you two move until you've eaten," she smiled, "I cannot let you starve yourselves."

Kenneth excused himself, asking Ian to come along—they left through the back door and went into—Stephanie eavesdropped through the window—a shed. *More secrets*, Stephanie assumed, seething silently with spite.

Trisha looked to Spencer kindly, then to Stephanie—Stephanie looked to her feet. "This must be frightening for you both. Kenneth told me what happened. Therapy," Trisha started, "worked for me when I didn't have anyone to talk to. Keeping things in isn't good for you—solutions come from discussing your problems. You two are young... it's sad to see you two on your own. Why did you leave home?"

She was comforting and Stephanie felt compelled to unwind. It was a while before she responded, remaining posed towards the ground. "I'm only here for Spencer. I want to go home with him."

"Would you be here if Ian hadn't pressured the two of you?" Stephanie shook her head with slight hesitance. "Spencer, I want you to know that whatever happened to you wasn't your fault. You can talk to us. Whatever is said stays here. It won't leave this room."

It took a long while for the two to open up to the stranger, but Trisha showed genuine sympathy—they were a sucker for any amount of kindness in that moment. Trisha listened carefully to the kids, responsive and offering advice and insights. Finally Spencer was talking, bringing more relief to wash over Stephanie. Laden with tears, expressing their woes for the next few hours, Trisha managed to bring even the slightest of smiles to their faces.

"You guys shouldn't be on your own yet. I didn't have anything figured out until I was twenty-four. The world is a scary place. I apologize about Kenneth—he can be a prude often; I'll make sure to stay around if it would make you two more comfortable. I'm trying to teach him how to display more empathy. As bad as he is at it, he still has a heart of gold." Trisha tidied the space, collecting their emptied dishes and dismissed herself for a few minutes, urging them outside to get some fresh air.

They stepped out into the night's tranquil lull of crickets. Stephanie opened the driver's side to the car, retrieving the key from her bosom that she managed to swipe from inside. She looked to Spencer who fidgeted, biting his nails raw to the nubs.

"This is it, Spencer," she whispered. "This is our window. Are you ready?" He shook his head. "What? Spencer, we don't know these people. I mean, Trisha seems trustworthy, but she still dates Kenneth which means there's a possibility that she could be just as fucked up as he is."

"I don't want to leave Ian. He saved my life. And Trisha is nice."

Stephanie was at a loss for words, bubbling with sadness, anger, and much anxiety. "But we have to get out of here. The money! I'll grab the bag with my money, we can get a motel—no, I can drive the entire time home. We can switch off. Please, Spencer. We can't stay here."

"Stephanie... " Spencer clutched at his heart, "I don't know what to do, but I don't think home is the best place for me. My parents—"

"You can stay with me!" She was begging at this point. "We can get jobs and find a place together. I know places that are hiring."

"Stephanie... "

She began to panic. "And we just have to wait until we're eighteen to move out. You won't have to go back and forth to your parents' houses. And then we can—"

"Stephanie. That's fantasy. It won't happen. I can tell you what *will* happen. Every day—in school, at home, every-where—we will never stop expecting Ian to be there. We will be questioned. Michael's family won't let up on the search. My parents won't even have the slightest idea that I'm a depressed queer and that I was raped. If I tell them, they'll do more to make it worse, I promise you. We'll still be on the run. Or jailed. It's better to stay here for... a few months," his voice trailed off.

Stephanie's eyes welled up with tears, pleading as she made her way to Spencer. "No, no it isn't. We *have* to go. You don't know these people."

"Stop telling me what to do! I'm not going back there and I'm not leaving Ian!"

"Ian *will* get you killed, Spencer. He's made it clear that he doesn't love you. He almost took advantage of me. Something is wrong with him."

"So just abandon him? I was violated and guess what? Ian saved me. As fucked up as he is, he saved me."

"He also killed someone! You're not in his debt! Don't rent yourself out to him just 'cus you're in a fragile place. He'll continue to use you and fuck Kenneth behind your back. Have you forgotten?"

"I made up my mind, Stephanie! You're the only one who wants to go back. You're the only one with a family that will tend to your every need. Not us. You have something to go back to. Not me, not Ian. You go."

"I'm not leaving you here."

"Yes you are. I'll be fine."

"Spencer, listen to me. You're not thinking. No, you will not be fine. This place... no one can hear us out here. There're no police, there are no stores, no one around—"

Their attention snapped to the tree line. The branches rustled and the two backed towards the door, eyes fixated towards the shadows. Sounds of crunching leaves pushed them together. A voice in the darkness called out, "Stephanie?"

She froze.

Lizzy ran up to her, embracing her tightly. "Thank Nyte you're okay." She cupped Stephanie's face in her hands, studying her grave expression. "Let's go." She pulled Stephanie along against her will.

"Lizzy, we still have to get Ian," Jonathan said as he finally caught up. "Oh, Spencer," he breathed a sigh of relief, kneeling to his level, "I'm taking you and Ian home. It's dangerous out here."

Spencer and Stephanie looked on in confusion, fear settling in once more when unpredictably around familiar faces.
Lizzy held onto her hand tightly—Stephanie didn't know how
to react although completely relieved by her presence.

"Back there. Ian's in that shed with Baal. Be careful,"
spoke Lizzy.

"Right. Spencer, go with Liz. I'm going to get Ian so we
can go home, okay?"

But Spencer didn't understand. "Mr. Fetcher, why are you
here? I thought... "

"I'll explain everything later, but you need to go."
Jonathan disappeared around the side of the house.

"C'mon, Spencer," Lizzy commanded.

He didn't respond.

"Spence... please?" begged Stephanie. Her heart was in-
credibly heavy with sorrow.

Jonathan sidled the house, buying himself enough time
to gain the confidence he'd need to face Baal. He had a plan, but
he wasn't sure how effective it'd be, and to make matters worse,
he only had one shot at it—failure wasn't an option, yet it had
the highest probable outcome. Sweat collected on his brow, and
the more he tried to calm his neuroticism, the worse it got. Every
failure he could conceive of played on an endless loop: Alejandra

choking on her own blood trying to squeeze out his name, his unborn's body in pieces, and Ramona's eyes made to capture all only to have her brain pulled from her skull by the master of alchemy; a house fire, a sacrificial pyre.

These thoughts didn't give way to an inkling of sanity, yet Jonathan tricked himself into stepping forward, instantly halting all breath and motion when the door of the shed squealed on its hinges, and the six-foot-two man trekked towards the home. *That's him, the demon lord!* Jonathan, tucked safely around the house, made a silent break to the shed. When the door closed behind the man, he crept inside. His eyes adjusted from the pitch-black night to the face illuminated by a desk lamp. The workbench Ian sat on shook as he jolted upright at the sight of Jonathan's entrance.

"Jon—!"

"Shhh!" Jonathan crossed the shed, pulling Ian up and over towards the exit.

Ian only followed, a torrent of thoughts rushing through his skull. *Did Kenneth plan this? Did he take me up here only to rat me out? I would have to go to Willard... Oh God! Jonathan must know about the murder!* "Jonathan," Ian whispered, "What are you doing here?"

"Shhhhhhh!" hissed Jonathan, looking to and from the cabin's back door to the line of the woods. He could see Kenneth in the window rummaging through the kitchen, settling his sights downward.

Jonathan could do it. Make a break from here through the woods for the truck. He glanced at a knife, serrated and slender stainless steel glinting the light towards his eyes, beholden by Kenneth. He pulled Ian's hand and started for the truck, "Run. Ian, run. Run!" Jonathan pressed send on the message titled to Patrice.

14

BAPTISM

Spencer stood stubbornly looking to his feet, his arms tightly packed across his chest. He had reached his limit of tears, rubbing at his puffy eyelids. Lizzy gritted her teeth, squeezing the feeling from Stephanie's hand. They had to go and Spencer was not budging.

Stephanie was sobbing now. "Please! Please Spencer! I love you. I can't leave you!" He stood still wanting more tears, truly torn, yet he remained composed.

"We're going." Liz had had enough, putting Stephanie over her shoulder.

"No! No! I can't! Spencer!" Stephanie protested, pounding and kicking Lizzy as if she and her never had anything in common. "Let me go! Let me go!" Lizzy held tightly. She cursed to herself when the front door opened to reveal the petite brunette, sneaking a snaky hand around Spencer's shoulder and coddling him as if he were her own son.

Trisha spoke with great concern. "Stephanie, you're leaving? Is this your friend?"

Lizzy went stiff. This was the other lord, a succubus.

"Stephanie, don't leave, hun. Weren't you comfortable? Was the food not good enough for you?" Trisha's voice was overly enthusiastic, her perfect smile bore into her. "Your friend Stephanie is trying to leave you, Spencer. How does that make you feel?"

Spencer looked up slowly from the ground and emotionlessly uttered, "It makes me feel sad."

Trisha slid her other hand lovingly up and down Spencer's arm, pulling him close to her bosom. "What does Spencer want?"

"I want to stay here with Trisha and Ian."

The silence filled the distance between the pairs illuminated by the flood light. No sound filled the void between, creating an atmosphere thick enough to cut.

Without a second thought, Lizzy broke into a sprint, disappearing into the woods. She was swift, rounding every tree with precision, never slowing.

Stephanie's hair whipped her face as she watched behind, eyes wide open. Trisha's smile bore into Stephanie, growing ever larger. It followed, closer and closer. Attached to her side was Spencer, keeping pace and locked onto both Lizzy and Stephanie.

The succubus was fast, running with both velocity and grace, bent and propelling forward. A dark energy tethered her possession of Spencer as he ran behind her. The chase seemed to amuse her—Lizzy had to get off the ground.

"Hold on." She commanded and soon her body rumbled, stretched, and burst into a beastly owl.

Stephanie barely held onto its wing for her life as Lizzy shot ninety degrees sharply from ground to sky. The owl softly shook Stephanie onto its back once leveled. Bellowing a deep hoot, Stephanie grabbed hold of the feathers of its massive head and was jolted forward, thousands of feet from the ground. The beastly owl engaged its wings in powerful thrusts, hoping to disrupt the pursuit of the demoness by breaking through the layer of clouds, but the full moon was sure to give away her presence.

"Jonathan, what are we doing?"

"Get in the truck!"

"But Spencer and Stephanie—"

"Get in the fucking truck!" Jonathan wasted no time pushing eighty miles-per-hour down the country back roads. Tires protested the curves, and Ian held onto the door handle in preparation for the next one of Jonathan's stunts.

For the next ten miles, Jonathan pushed the vehicle until he reached the outskirts of a hilly rustic town. Although the adrenaline flowed heavily, he slowed the truck just above the legal limit. Houses were illuminated in the young night, roads cleared free of traffic. People closed stores for the evening; families gathered indoors initiating their bedtime rituals. Normalcy continued around Jonathan despite his world inverting on its axis. His eyes scanned the landscape with keen attention, silence overtaking the car's cabin. Ian thought this to be a good time to inquire again. "Now can you tell me what we're doing? This is crazy."

"I'm sorry, Ian. I can't think right now. I need to focus."

"Focus on what? Kidnapping me?"

"Goddammit, Ian. Please, just shut up!" Jonathan suddenly slammed the brakes, pale head to toe, barely stopping the truck in time before hitting the boy. Ian raced out just as Jonathan yelled, "Stay in the truck!"

Ian approached with caution, "Spencer? What are you doing all the way out here?"

"Ian," Jonathan warned, "It's a trap. Get away from him!"

It was too late. Spencer clamped his teeth onto Ian's shoulder, ingesting the full length of Ian's arm as his form elongated. Ian staggered backwards, agony flushing through his screams, the blood pooling from Spencer's teeth, growing sharper. The clamp of teeth tightened as Ian tried to pull back. Jonathan watched horrified as the behemoth emerged from Spencer's form; it carried a wailing Ian in its mouth, towering above the truck and himself. He dropped to his knees, petrified to the core when the behemoth stared directly into his soul before bowing.

The slap of the truck jolted Jonathan into submission as Kenneth stood beside him.

"I said stall them, not rip his arm off, Hazth." Looking down onto Jonathan, Kenneth sighed, shaking his head, "Well, does not this sweeten the deal? You might want to try a stronger spell next time." Kenneth set the truck onto Jonathan's leg; his torment echoed throughout the hillside. "I hope that was not your friend. Did you know that a witch's soul is forever the slave of a demon? It is the price you pay for the sight. See?" Kenneth held a glowing, shapeless anima before Jonathan, laughing. "This so-called 'New Age witchcraft' is so weak, it is laughable. Let us see, to capture a demon lord is going to take a lot of blood. I will not bow to a call unless the payment is there. Sadly, one soul is not enough." The lights of the area flickered out consecutively until they were in complete darkness save for what the unforgiving moon gave.

Ian screamed himself ragged. Curious neighbors stepped outside of their homes to see the commotion. Per the lord's signal, the behemoth returned Ian into the hands of Baal who was the ringmaster, spreading his arms in a huge display before the town's perimeter was set ablaze.

"This was going to be a private affair, but since you brought us out here, I might as well make it a show." The Lord of Knowledge turned his back, spreading his massive wingspan from one side of the road to the other, shooting off with the boy with the red eyes.

Lizzy was throwing herself at the demoness. The sharp snaps of her beak could sever limbs clean. It was a dance of feathers and horns—Godimus' snaky tail caught a hold around Lizzy's leg, yanking her into Godimus's space. The shapeshifter's face was slashed by claws, and then a porcelain horn sprouted from the back of the demoness' arm, impaling only Lizzy's feather down. Lizzy used the close proximity to her advantage—she casted a gale strong enough to stagger the succubus and without pause, snatched the leathery wing within her talons.

The demoness was no stranger to the sky. The nightmare and the owl fought wildly in the inky expanse; the treacherous thrashing and thunderous bellowing echoed something ghoulish through the vacant Pennsylvania woodlands until absorbed by the hillside. In a singsong voice, the demoness taunted, "You are truly magnificent! I want you all to myself!" She giggled, then latched onto the owl's talon; Lizzy was now plummeting downwards hundreds of feet before regaining her balance. Stephanie dug her fingers into the owl's pelt. Suddenly, she was face to face with Godimus.

Within an instant, Lizzy came out of her owl guise and shifted into her innate form, alabaster hair whipping wildly in the wind as she slashed at the demoness with feathered arms and clawed fingers.

Stephanie was freefalling, nothing to hold onto, deciding whether to watch the ground grow closer below or the impossible conflict above between the creatures who had not existed before today. Stephanie could die, whether it was by meeting the earth or by the flying nightmare—a certain peace was found. At last, life wasn't as mediocre as she thought.

She let go before her body impacted the pine.

She soon became weightless. Lizzy caught Stephanie, pivoting her body to take the brunt of the impact. With the air knocked out of her, she lay on felled branches, using a considerable amount of strength to gather herself. She was severely injured beyond measure, bleeding from her midsection and her lacerated face, making audible breaths as the blood puddled by her bare feet. She swayed, yet kept her feet planted, refusing to look away from Godimus.

Lizzy growled, "Leave. Or die."

The demoness took a fair share of the damage, the vessel losing hold onto the demon inside. Before Godimus left from the body, she smiled ear to ear before rushing out as ectoplasm from the vessel. Once the lifeless body collapsed, so too did Lizzy from exhaustion and blood loss. Behind her, she heard a staggered trickling of liquid and a stifled struggle.

Spencer held Stephanie for Lizzy's display as he dug the car key from one side of her throat to the other, a shade of fuchsia overlaying his blue irises. The blood cascaded in perfect sheets, drenching Stephanie's chest. Spencer let her body fall as he faded through the ethereal aperture, vanishing entirely.

"No no no no no no no no no." Lizzy covered the gash with her hands to no avail. "Stay with me. You're not dying. Look at me," Stephanie's eyes began to lose focus. "Look at me, Stephanie!" As Stephanie's eyes fluttered, Lizzy's blood loss caught up. With her remaining strength, she pressed her will onto Stephanie, wrapping her arms around her and grasping her back. From her hand, Lizzy's skin began to merge into Stephanie's, rooting to her spine. Her veins protruded all over with a fluorescent azure glow. Stephanie convulsed as the change began spreading within her.

Lizzy couldn't stay conscious. She kept her eyes open long enough to watch Stephanie's body go still.

The town panicked. Townies woke their children and neighbors. The small, local fire station was overwhelmed by the blaze, calling for the citizens to evacuate and recruiting help from its neighboring towns. These flames were persistent—no amount of extinguishing snuffed the ring of chaos. The inferno grew towards the inside, taking houses, trees, and people in its path. Slowly the townies were being pushed together. Jonathan could not move as the trucks weight was too great. He watched as the fire spread towards him from all directions. The hillsides were the first to disappear. People in his vicinity stood by in shock, many packing their vehicles to journey to safer territory.

"Hey! This guy needs help! Push the side!" Three random strangers tilted the truck just enough, and a fourth dragged Jonathan into clearance.

His foot was broken. They helped him to a safer place, lending him a shovel to prop himself up with.

Jonathan was exceedingly grateful, but he stopped short of its expression, yelling, "You must get out of here! You all are in trouble! The flames are getting stronger!" Jonathan began to yell and wave like a madman. "Leave! Everyone leave!" People remained with great faith in their taxes, hoping that the firemen would handle it before they had to leave all they owned behind. He could not comprehend why they refused—only he understood what was truly happening. No one would believe him even if he tried to tell them the extent of the danger they faced.

A loud explosion rumbled through the hillside, followed by several others. Cars attempted to speed through the flames, but none saw the other side. The heat could be felt on Fetcher's skin even at this great of a distance. More people began to panic. Jonathan looked around desperately for Ian. Instantly, he caught the silhouette of wings through the smolders atop the city council building, hunched over Ian's body. Shapeless anima hovered over the top of residencies towards the demon—Fetcher was sure he was the only one who could see this happening.

Souls...

He hobbled over to the building against the flow of civilians, smashing the council building's window with the shovel and entered, hopping as best as he could up the stairs. He burst his way through offices until he could sight the demon lord. Now he was changed, no longer in the vessel of Kenneth and replaced by the gargantuan colossus Baal, who gazed across town whilst tunneling the souls into Ian's unconscious body. Jonathan smashed his way through another window, steadying himself onto the roof. Looking below was absolute hell on earth.

Sounds of movement brought Baal's attention backwards. Jonathan approached slowly, hands up in a submissive posture and head low. Jonathan stammered, "P-p-p-p-please hear me out, your highness." Baal looked onto the man who refused to look at him, reeking of fear. "Please. Don't hurt Ian. Please." Jonathan reached the altar where Ian lay lifelessly. He felt Ian's face, ran the back of his hand across Ian's cheek, still warm... barely warm enough. "C'mon, bud. Wake up. Ol' Jon has come to get you and take you home." His voice trembled and failed to keep the tears choked. "He's dead," Jon said in hardly a whisper.

Baal watched the man, intrigued by the theatrics; Jonathan struggled to sit Ian up, continuously begging Ian to get up, move, hang in there. Baal had achieved what he wanted. Why not play around for a bit?

"Ian was naive."

The strange tongue the demon lord spoke caught Jonathan off guard, unable to comprehend by listening alone—he understood from within as Baal spoke in a deep, guttural voice. "This boy had no respect for anyone but himself. Look what he did to his friends. I did not understand how one could be so obsessed with the past, even after all the harm it caused him. Why risk your life for such a thing?"

"How could you do this? He was a kid!"

"Pathetic. Look onto me if you want answers," sneered Baal. He admired his possession once more, the soul which would ensure Baal's personal victory and induce an age neither demon nor human was prepared for. "Do not you think it to look odd when your authorities find this place? The Frances family would be heartbroken to know the old caretaker was a deranged psychopath." Jonathan did not understand what the lord spoke of until Baal began to stalk around Ian. "Give up. Ian is dead. His soul lies dormant. Your medicine will not do him any justice."

"AAAAAARGH!" Jonathan swung the shovel at Baal in a blind rage. The demon was unmoving, letting the man unleash his fury until he wore himself ragged. He then looked the demon in its eyes—eight red orbs peered directly into him, and Jonathan staggered with fear.

Instead of making the man meet his ends, Baal raised his arms towards the sky as the stream of souls increased in quantity. In the sky they lit up the atmosphere, silent and luminescent, creating cascades of pure light in waves. They descended into Ian's body and within Baal's hands emerged a violet-orange fire. Before Jonathan could lift the shovel again, Baal had him by the shoulders. Rows of sharp teeth settled beside his ear and time stopped. The fear and the fire catalyzed him to a halt, and Baal's guttural voice was clear as the sky above.

Into Jonathan, Lord Baal gave him knowledge of Ian's being without using word or sound. Jonathan was transported through many millennia watching a montage of all the victims of Lord Baal. In each life, the demon lord appeared to the summoner in the disguise of their desires. His victims were surrounded by wealth and fame of all sorts, some cluttered in material gains, others rising to the top in presumed success. And after Lord

Baal removed himself from the picture, Jonathan could see their lives turn base and dull, see their possessions overtake their lives and become repossessed; their companies failed and soon went into bankruptcy; their essence became siphoned by the creature's arrival and the light in their eyes faded. Soon they were walking shells left to deal with the aftereffects of the promises Baal delivered.

Other instances included isolated men surrounded by reams of books, reaching for innumerable wisdom, yet failing to make an impact. Their lives of solitude were self-inflicted; they believed their information would take them further than any man, yet failed in exemplifying the actions their precious knowledge gave them. Each time the collateral was of their own life-force expended on fancies presumed to be their ticket to freedom, wealth, or success. Lord Baal had no direct hand in their undoing, and once their forms succumbed to lifelessness, he merely collected the souls for his personal use.

The breadth of their experiences weighed heavily on Jonathan, left in tears whilst feeling every emotion of the fallen. He felt all those years bear down on his being so much so that he could no longer remain propped upright by his crutch. He was back in his own experience, clutching his heart to lie down beside lifeless Ian. There was absolutely nothing Jonathan could say to Lord Baal to change his ways. Yet still he had to try.

He lifted Ian's arm and wrapped it around him as best as he could. Shifting his weight, he used his hip as a fulcrum pulling Ian onto his back.

His free arm reached for the shovel, but it was inches from where he lay. "Come... on... " Jonathan chipped to himself as he sidled inch by inch. Lord Baal placed his cloven foot before Jonathan's reach, lifted Ian from him, and then kicked Jonathan to the side resulting in his descent from the building's edge.

That was it for Jonathan. He cursed at himself over and over to move, yet the sharp pain from his broken leg forbade any further movement. He was too low to see above the building—all around him were the deaths of townies. The smell of charring cinder and smoke filled his lungs, choking on the harsh soot, eyes watering to brim. Soon enough he was unable to keep them open.

He succumbed to darkness.

Within the deep black, he saw a full panoramic view of the lights all around him flowing into a central point. Formed from the void were small imps, all servants of these pieces of light, assisting in the capture and delivery towards their lord's feet. They fluttered, scurried, and clawed their way up the building, affixing the stray lights into Ian's. Their lord now stood as a tower in a perfect black that resounded ad infinitum.

Lord Baal roared with victory into the hellish scape—his entire being vibrated and his horns directed his message. "An thou art not worthy of a world such as this. Dawn will come to bring ruin or justice, when worlds align as one, and a Ruler shall emerge. Eyes as embers, blood as oil. From the great veil of beyond, the Young Ruler will rise! Find your place and remain complacent for nature will no longer determine worth. Discard your vessels for there will be no need. The boundary shall be lifted by the Great Force and the Ruler shall lay claim to all!" The imps all whooped and hollered, stomping on corpses and tearing through the fires. Jonathan felt himself rise. He was granted a vantage point beside Baal although he knew his body lay far beneath him—feeling the magnetic pull towards the light affixed within Ian, he was met with resistance.

The Lord of Knowledge targeted his message into the caretaker's soul. "Look around you, Jonathan. No matter how much dominion man thinks he has over his world, he ends up consumed by it in the end. That is the fate of everyone. Your religions are founded on eternal life—all strive to achieve this great feat. But those who are successful wind up in an existence far lower than the one they once had. Ian is no different than any other human who wished for answers. Often the quest for answers leads many to their downfall. Those that have the solutions in their possession will never tell a soul to keep their place at the top. Imps seek power just as people do to become a lord of his own strength. But even lords answer to a master. Life is nothing more than a series of hierarchies, Jonathan. Even in the Uver this holds true. The only thing that sorts us beings is knowledge of self."

Lord Baal tumbled Jonathan's soul within his leathery palm, "Tell me, Jonathan... am I truly wrong for robbing this boy of his human life?" Fetcher felt nothing but arid cold surround him and the graven scent of earth. "For centuries people have sacrificed to me for the desire of influence. You humans have an innate thirst for change, yet you all reject the outcome. Although your trap failed, I will leave you with this, free of charge." Lord Baal cupped his clawed hands around Jonathan's consciousness.

Then there was nothing.

Jonathan woke in a cold sweat drenched head to toe in his bed. Alejandra lay peacefully asleep beside him in the tranquil house. He looked frantically left to right patting his body. Suddenly the sharp pain from his broken leg provoked a series of grunts from him, stirring Alejandra from her sleep. "You okay, honey? Ah ah, don't move! I'll get you some more pain killers, don't move."

Jonathan shook his head in defiance and yelled, "Where is he? Where is Ian?!" He propped himself to stand, suddenly collapsing onto the floor, immediately trying once more to lift himself onto one leg.

"Honey, honey! Get back in the bed," Alejandra held him firmly in place as he fought to escape from her grip. "Take it easy, Jonny!" she fussed.

"I have to get Ian. Move out of my way!"

Alejandra had a sympathetic look upon her brow and continued to hold him firm. With her nurse authority, she used her body to guide him back towards the bed. "What are you on about? You had a pretty good fall at work today. You need bed rest."

"What? No! No I didn't!" He struggled his way up once more—Alejandra practically sat on him. "You don't understand, honey. Please, move!"

"What is going on with you, Jonny? Ian is fine, he's with the Frances family, remember? You don't have to worry. Are your nightmares returning?"

"Nightmares? What? No! This is real! Ian was taken!"

Alejandra wore great concern, "Jonathan... do you re-member your fall? They found you at the bottom of the stairs at your office."

Jonathan violently shook his head. "No, no, no, no you don't understand!" Looking at the expression she bore, Jonathan took a moment to reconfigure his position. "It wasn't a dream..." He reached for his phone and upon flicking on the screen, he gawked as he read the date: five days after the day it was supposed to be. "How long have I been out?"

"You fell yesterday evening. I picked you up from the hospital about five hours ago."

The clock read 4:34 AM. Tuesday morning.

It slowly donned on Jonathan that the more he spoke, the more of a hole he and Lizzy's existence would be dug into. And when news of this event was to finally break air, Jonathan would be the first scouted.

He sunk deep into Alejandra's shoulder and wept. She guided him back into bed and placed two prescription meds in his palm and followed with a glass of water. "You were having a bad dream. Ian is fine, he's going to be alright, okay? You can't keep worrying about him. Please get some rest, honey, you are in no way fit to be moving around." Jonathan's despair did not let up by her words and she began to grow concerned. She had never seen her husband this broken.

And when the daytime news rolled around Wednesday morning, Alejandra was frozen before the television screen with a hand covering her mouth.

She clicked the television off and sat in silence.

The subsequent days she tended to Jonathan with a stoney look upon her face and raised eyebrows so taut it was clear she was holding her fear back. The medication Jonathan was on made it hard for him to be coherent enough to answer her questions, so she would hold it in. She took it upon herself to visit the Frances family on the following weekend bearing no gifts as sympathy—she found it may come off as distasteful. Before she lifted her arm to ring the doorbell, she caressed her stomach connecting with the life that formed within her and for the first time she felt dread wash over her family's livelihood. Nothing was making sense.

The door opened not long after she knocked with Greg there to answer. He did not look to be in much distress, but she nonetheless prepared her voice in the friendliest way she could manage. "Hello, Gregory. I am Alejandra, Jonathan's wife."

For a moment he did not recognize her, yet he accepted her handshake. "Ian's old caretaker, that Jonathan?"

"Yes, that's right."

She was searching for the next thing to say, nothing that didn't sound superficial came to mind, however Greg saved her the trouble by responding with, "I'm sure you heard the news. Come in, please."

He gestured towards the sofa in the living room, "You can sit wherever you'd like. Would you like anything to drink?" She shook her head pleasantly denying the offer. "I didn't want all of this to make news. To be honest with you, I wanted to hire a private investigator and keep this within the family. But Jennifer insisted that people know, says we'd be better off with word of mouth for now. I don't think Ian wandered far to be honest. It's just that the parents of his friends are looking to us for involvement. That dang boy... "

Alejandra waited for Greg to finish before speaking. "Where do you think they could have gone?"

"Beats me. I saw Ian off before he went to school earlier last Thursday with a classmate of his, Kenny or something like that. It was a normal day. He didn't come home for supper, I figured it was typical of him as of late, he'd be out late with friends and cover with some sort of project he was doing. I'm not stupid, I was a young man myself once. But then I see the report of one of his high school classmates declared dead right by the spot Spencer's father lives. Didn't think much of it, then the wife starts freaking out. When he didn't come home the next night, I knew something was wrong."

"Is there anything I can do to help? Ian is very dear to Jonathan. He recently got into an accident at work and I'd rather him rest than to get worked up about this."

"What happened?"

"He fell down a flight of stairs on the job. Broke his leg."

"Yikes. I'm sorry to hear."

"It's alright," she smiled, "Jonathan is tough as nails, I'm sure I won't be able to stop him from hobbling around very soon. I'm just concerned more about you and your family."

"No need, like I said I'm sure Ian is up to no good. Only Mr. and Mrs. Carter insist on answers. They are convinced Stephanie was last with Ian and Spencer. They're prepared to press charges, ain't that a bitch? And the Holland's aren't much of a help, they believe that Spencer is goofing off as well. The gravity of this whole thing somehow got placed on us."

Alejandra understood the hidden implications within Greg's tone. They were looking to the Frances' to shoulder the blame due to their status as adoptive parents, dubbed unfit compared to the experience of biological rearing. Jonathan used to rant to her about the unconscious bias people held over adoptees. She nodded with understanding. "I'm sure this is a stressful time for everyone, I would not take it personally. Is Jennifer okay?"

Greg shook his head, "She's a mess, not being logical. I told her getting the media involved would make things worse but after that report on Michael, she couldn't help herself. Talked to Mr. Carter to invest in a private investigator with me; any PI worth his weight is going to take a lot of money, something I can't afford alone."

Alejandra reached for her checkbook, "Please let me help. I'll do all I can to—"

"With all due respect, Mrs. Fetcher, I'd rather us handle this for the time being. Please do not involve yourself."

Instead, she wrote her name and number on a piece of paper. "Don't look at this as any kind of debt. I want to help you. I pray that this is what you say, that these kids are just being kids. However, if it isn't, I want to be of help. I am with you. If you need anything, please be sure to let me know."

Greg nodded. "I appreciate it. Thank you. I'll be sure to keep you updated. I hate to ask you to leave, but Jennifer and I need a bit more time to sort things through."

"O-oh of course, yes, I am sorry to come through unannounced. Please take care of yourselves." Greg accompanied her to the door as she searched for something else cordial to say. "Please give Jennifer my love for me."

"Will do," was his only response before the door shut and Alejandra was left outside on the overcast day.

Greg remained in the dark of the living room, hands pressed to his brow. He bit his tongue until it bled, wracking his mind of any memory that clued into his son's whereabouts, but all that surfaced was a haze of the previous few weeks.

Natalie clutched her handheld game to her chest watching the transfer take place between her mother and father. The harshest words were spoken and violence was already introduced into the mix. "He was your responsibility for the week and like always you never pay attention to him or any of your kids."

"He's just as much your responsibility as mine. I'm not going to let you keep blaming me for Spencer running off. How long are you going to keep playing this game, woman?"

"Game? Our son is missing! I'm glad you think I think this is just a game because clearly I'm searching for a win."

"And that's nothing new to you, now is it? All you play are games! I've only ever tried to have a family with you but you think you can do everything better by yourself. I had to find out that Spencer went to the emergency room for stitches by the bill in my mailbox. I can never count on you to hold yourself accountable."

"Don't start this, Timothy. It's only because you couldn't keep your fidelity that I did what I did, don't act like it's my fault."

"Instead of working on anything with you, you always, ALWAYS have to be the victim. You take the kids, divorce me, take half my money, now you want to blame this on me. But God forbid Laura's ever wrong." Before he could finish his statement, his ex-wife was already resorting to throwing whatever object she was closest to at his head. "What the hell is wrong with you?!"

"Get out!"

"See? Just like that you kick me out again because your female ego can never be wrong. Do you want to find our son or what?"

"Get out! Just get out!"

He breathed in, "Fine, I'll leave. Fine. You try to have Jake or one of the other tools you're fucking help you find a son that isn't theirs, see how willing they'll be to come out of their pockets to help you. Outside of your looks, you are nothing." He left without saying another word to Laura and Natalie.

Laura Georgian turned away, pressing the phone to her ear, rambling in tears to her current boyfriend. Natalie observed from her corner of the room, seeing the gymnastics her mother did to get her way. Laura took to relaying the moment back with as much pity as she could muster. "Yeah I'm alright, Jake... no, please don't come over. I don't want this to turn into a fight... no he didn't put his hands on me... Natalie? She's fine, she's never any trouble... "

Natalie's disgust for the world cemented into her heart. She needed Spencer here so they could have each other to count on when their parents acted this way. He was always the one to come between their arguing with the soundest of logic whenever emotions flared, when the adults acted like children. How could they fight each other at a time like this? The arguments were as loud as it had been when she was barely five. When dad lived with them, they were happy, she was happy. Things were alright. Spencer was alright. When dad left, her mom had a switch turn off and she no longer felt like mom. She always found a way to be busy. Natalie took a seat by Laura while she spoke on the phone, trying once again to get her mom's attention. All they had was each other. Laura frowned with, "I'm on the phone, Natalie. Can it wait?"

Natalie clenched her fist standing defiantly at her mother. She thought of all she might do in the moment, but knew it was a battle to be lost. Instead, she gathered her games and curled into Spencer's bed, sobbing wishes to her video game heroes to bring her brother back to her. She imagined running off with the mages and ninjas to embark on the mission that would bring him back. She wished she had a dragon to burn down Willard so that everyone could see how she needed help. They'd all pay attention once the dragon appeared, and she could fly away to find him on her own if they decided to remain heartless humans. It wasn't fair—she wanted to disappear with him.

As much as she convinced herself that her dragon would arrive at any moment, it never did. The heroes never approached her to offer the chance to embark upon a quest. Perhaps it was true what Spencer had once told her, that magic didn't exist after all. Her young heart quivered, feeling the remainder of fantastic imaginings disappear along with her big brother.

The rain never let up and began to leave lakes pooled around the grounds of Destiny Baptist; flocks of crows inhabited the surrounding tree line, their caws filling the dreary air. Mrs. Carter's head remained hung in prayer during the service's entirety as Mr. Carter preached with fire in his throat. The offering baskets were the fullest they'd ever been and the church held it's loyal followers eager to pray for the missing daughter of the preacher. Their days had been full of grief since Stephanie disappeared, yet the Carter's had their faith nonetheless and it wouldn't be broken. Mrs. Carter yelled out in reverence as her husband and messenger of God shouted with zeal.

"We ask you, Lord Jesus, to make sure you watch over these children, Lord Jesus. We ask for your blessing and your infinite wisdom to ensure their safety. Because it is You and only You that is the Savior. We know that all that happens is a part of your plan. You have given us all a place to rest our head and food to keep our stomachs full. We trust all that you do, Jesus. Shepherd your flock, use us as the instruments of your will. Bless each and every one of your children that walk with you. It is in the Lord's name that we pray, amen."

Pastor Carter raised his head from prayer and his congregation followed. "Open your bibles to John 10." He waited for the sound of pages to settle. With conviction to mask his anguish, he spoke aloud, "And the Lord said, 'Very truly I tell you Pharisees, anyone who does not enter the sheep pen by the gate, but climbs in by some other way, is a thief and a robber. The one who enters by the gate is the shepherd of the sheep. The gatekeeper opens the gate for him, and the sheep listen to his voice. He calls his own sheep by name and leads them out. When he has brought out all his own, he goes on ahead of them, and his sheep follow him because they know his voice. But they will never follow a stranger; in fact, they will run away from him because they do not recognize a stranger's voice.

"'Very truly I tell you, I am the gate for the sheep. All who have come before me are thieves and robbers, but the sheep have not listened to them. I am the gate; whoever enters through me will be saved. They will come in and go out, and find pasture. The thief comes only to steal and kill and destroy; I have come that they may have life, and have it to the full. I am the good shepherd. The good shepherd lays down his life for the sheep. The hired hand is not the shepherd and does not own the sheep. So when he sees the wolf coming, he abandons the sheep and runs away. Then the wolf attacks the flock and scatters it. The man runs away because he is a hired hand and cares nothing for the sheep. I am the good shepherd; I know my sheep and my sheep know me—just as the Father knows me and I know the Father—and I lay down my life for the sheep. I have other sheep that are not of this sheep pen. I must bring them also. They too will listen to my voice, and there shall be one flock and one shepherd. The reason my Father loves me is that I lay down my life—only to take it up again. No one takes it from me, but I lay it down of my own accord. I have authority to lay it down and authority to take it up again. This command I received from my Father.'

"The Jews who heard these words were again divided. Many of them said, 'He is demon-possessed and raving mad. Why listen to him?' But others said, 'These are not the sayings of a man possessed by a demon. Can a demon open the eyes of the blind?'"

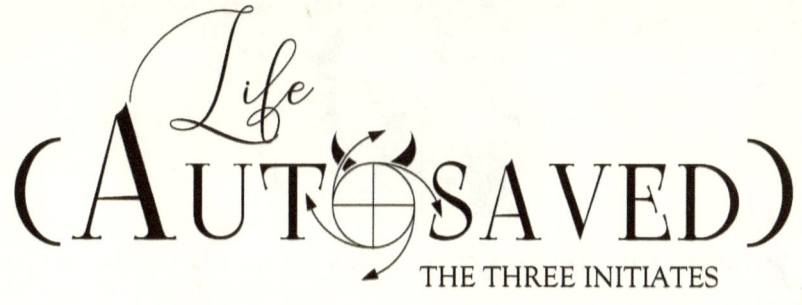

THE THREE INITIATES

W. E. BROWN

W.E. BROWN
AUTHOR

Y ou're either reading this because you finished the story or you were casually flipping by. Either way, I'm glad I have your attention! For those disembarking from this literary thrill ride, hold on tight because the series is far from over.

Life (**Autosaved**) (LAS for short) is my first published novel and has been a passion project since 2008. Nearly two decades later and here we are. My interests at the time were strictly reading manga, listening to screamo, writing stories, and watching anime, particularly yaoi (IYKYK). I wanted to portray all I've gathered in my pubescent, edgy, essential research, so I started writing about a few gay dudes who have demonic powers. It was a mess, a total cringe fest. At the time, we were reading Twilight and the House of Night series; vampires were so cliche, I wanted to entertain myself with something new. Little did I know it would come this far. As far as the title goes, one day I didn't save my .docx file, so it autosaved itself—the first word of the doc was 'Life', and I never renamed it. That's literally it, nothing special.

My aim is to warp reality and bring together like-minded individuals. Kinda sounds like a cult now that I think about it—but it's not, I swear! What I mean to say is, I think that humans are more capable than we truly think, and when uniting beneath a common vision, we begin to embody what we wish to create. Be it art imitating life or life imitating art, there is something to admit: *we create reality.*

Our perception determines how we categorize our environments, beliefs shape it, and our experiences test beliefs' foundation. The characters I write about are archetypes I encounter in myself and the world around; Ian, Spencer, and Stephanie are all fragments of how I wish to be perceived, how I perceive, and projections of how I think I am perceived. I believe that my writing will take root in someone's spirit, and so far experience has shown me that dreams are not only realized during sleep. I hope my writing truly makes you feel, and by all means, do not hesitate to reach out—I'm an open book.

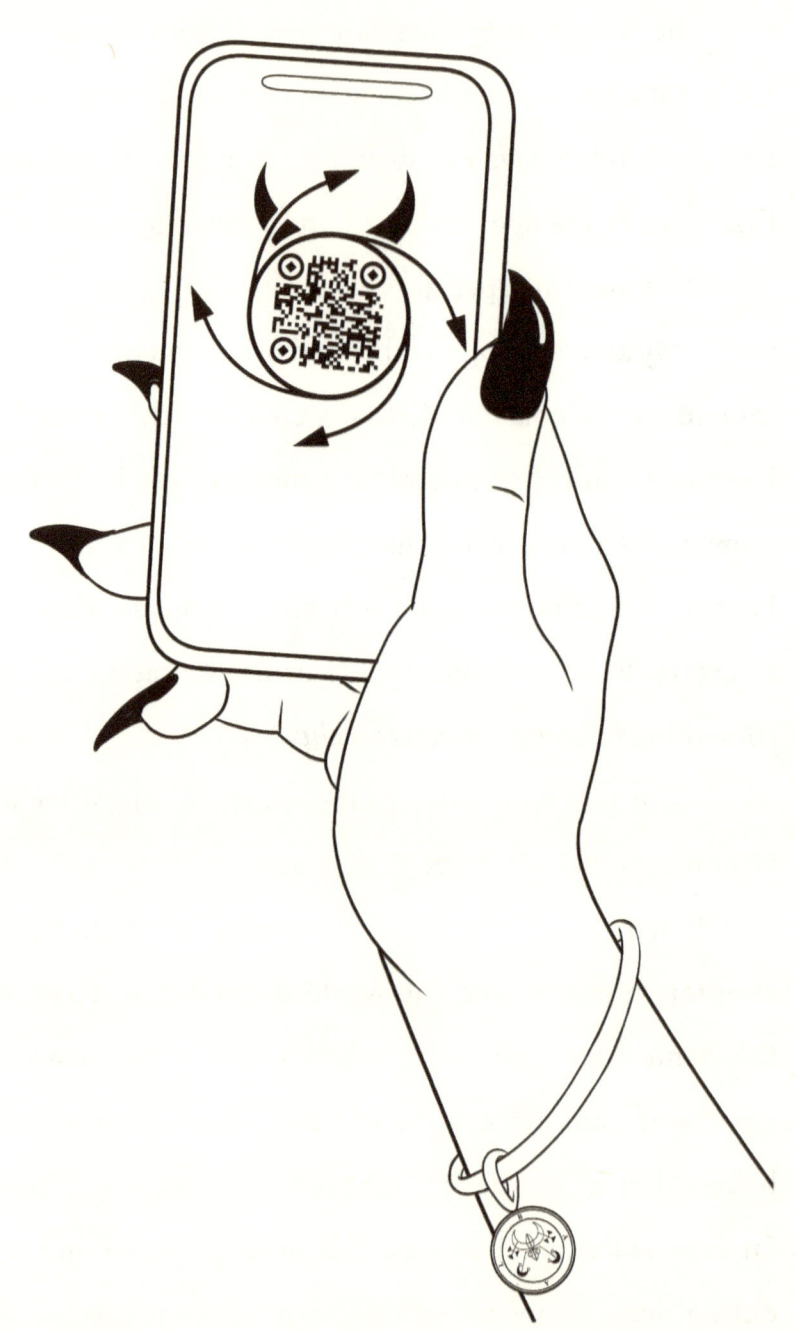

www.ingramcontent.com/pod-product-compliance
Lightning Source LLC
Chambersburg PA
CBHW031022030726
47497CB00004B/958